Camp Supernatural:
Mind over Matter

Jonathan Solis
1st Edition

Esperanza Publishing

Edinburg, TX 78542

Copyright © 2025 Jonathan Solis

Edited by: Naidelyn Ramos

ISBN: 979-8-218-10121-3

Acknowledgments

The work and heart that was put into this book would not have been possible without the love and support of those closest to me. To Mark Esperanza, for believing in me and giving me this incredible opportunity to share my vision for others to read. To my family: my mother, Teresa, father, Jesus, brothers, Nathan, Joseph, and sister, Megan, thank you for all your love and support in helping me to become the person I am today. A very special shout out and thank you to Naidelyn Ramos, who read my book and offered some wonderful creative responses to it. Lastly, I want to thank Rigoberto Solis, the first friend who read my book and my first fan.

Contents

Camp Cabins (Alphabetical Order/Words)

a) Atlas's Agony (Weight of the World)

b) Blunt Bear (Honest but Fearless)

c) Cathedral Cove (Come and See)

d) Daredevil Delinquents (Want to Bet?)

e) Elegant Eagle (Eager to Impress)

f) Forsaken Fox (Far Too Sharp)

g) Gloomy Gnomes (Gum Up the Works)

h) Hollow Hill (Hauntingly High)

i) The Imaginarium Illusion (Mind Over Matter)

j) The Jaded Jester (Jokes On You)

k) The Kruel Kingdom (Would You Kindly?)

l) The Lost Lord (Last Seen Nowhere)

m) The Majestic Meadow (New Horizons)

n) The Ninth Night (Not Too Late)

o) Obnoxious Offspring (Original Pranksters)

p) Pyro Prison (Light the Fire)

q) The Qualified Queen (Quite Acceptable)

r) Rasping Raven (Raging Messengers)

s) Swan Song (Final Curtains)

t) The Tears of Titan (Heavy Rain)

u) The Underrated Unicorn (United Especially)

v) The Violet Virtue (Viscerally Potent)

w) The Weeping Willow (Weather or Not)

x) Xiomara's Axe (Excellent Warriors)

y) Young and Yearning (Eager to Serve)

z) Ziggy Zion (Ground Control)

Chapter 1

Lucas Fargo

Lucas Fargo sat in his history classroom, bored out of his mind, on the last day of school. His teacher was showing a movie about the Civil War and appeared to be sleeping as it was playing.

I don't blame him. No one cares enough about the past to sit through someone talk about it, Lucas thought as he drilled a pencil through his desk.

Even though he knew that school would be ending in less than an hour, the uncomfortable silence in the near-empty classroom made it feel longer to him. If not for the movie playing, the only sound Lucas would have heard would be his own constant stream of thoughts.

What to eat when I get home, how best to enjoy my summer vacation, when will this day end already?

His middle school wasn't noteworthy, but it was the only school that catered to all children from misfits, to criminal misfits, and to future criminal misfits.

Not to mention school fights are more common than the common cold around here.

The school's slogan was, 'All children can achieve'. Lucas rearranged them once to say, 'Can all children achieve?' This prank caused many of his peers to ridicule and belittle him. Even so, this did little to change his frame of mind.

I just made it a question rather than an answer.

Lucas was drawing a crude stick figure of his teacher on his desk when one of the clerks from the front office walked into the classroom. He didn't try to act surprised when he was told to report to the principal's office.

1

It took them long enough.

He got up, swung his backpack across his right shoulder, and walked out of the classroom. Lucas had done this many times before. When he exited the room, the clerk led him toward the principal's office for what seemed like an inevitable showdown.

I wonder what I did this time, he pondered.

Since the beginning of his education, Lucas struggled to behave properly in class and was a noted at-risk student in the school district. His older sister, Shelly, often voiced her concern over his behavior.

I've heard the lecture hundreds of times: 'You need to graduate so you can go to a good college.' 'What will you do with your life without an education?' But what if I don't want any of that? What if I don't know what I want?

At the age of thirteen, he was in his second year at middle school. Due to his poor behavior, many of the schools who heard of him refused to give Lucas a chance.

During his first year in middle school, he stopped a group of bullies from hurting a fellow classmate by telling them to stop. To his and the classmate's surprise, the bullies did. No one could explain the phenomenon, but the bullies had to be carted out because they were as still as statues.

I remember hearing the next day that they were in some kind of coma. All I did was say one word to them.

Another instance happened at a school field trip to the zoo during his last year in elementary school. Walking past the caged animals made Lucas feel as they did; anxious, irritable, and confined. What followed was an outburst of which he could not recall with a clear memory.

His teacher called his parents to come pick him up, and when he tried to explain that he could feel and hear what the animals were thinking, they thought he was crazy.

I couldn't understand them. The sounds in their heads weren't words; they were feelings. Like feelings that people have but don't say out loud. After that, Lucas was

2

diagnosed with schizophrenia. He was prescribed aripiprazole and clozapine.

Following these unnatural incidents, his sister helped him enroll in another middle school and put in a good recommendation for him. Nevertheless, Lucas continued to struggle so much that he ended up not passing any of his core classes.

This was his final chance to make things right and to get a proper education. Unfortunately, that is not how things turned out.

He only managed to pass one class with a C and this was only because the class required just forty-five minutes of writing for each day.

I just wrote random stuff that I doubt the teacher even read. It wasn't until I started falling asleep in class that my grade began to drop.

Appearance-wise, Lucas had long dark brown shaggy hair that covers his ears and forehead like a wet mop. He was also noticeably thin, with a long skinny neck and dark green eyes. In addition to having schizophrenia, he was also diagnosed with anxiety, possibly on the autistic spectrum, and a severe form of bipolar disorder. The doctors he went to were unable to give him a conclusive diagnosis, and all said the same thing; it was likely unstable. He was required to be on medication in order to control the rate of his mood swings, as well as the voices in his head. Sadly, this did not always work, and Lucas found the side-effects were more apparent than the benefits. These included feeling agitated easily and experiencing compulsive tendencies.

Funny thing is I only hear voices when I am around people. I have to be around a lot of people. I tried explaining that to one of my doctors, and he upped my dosage.

After the clerk left him, Lucas walked into the principal's office and saw the small chubby figure sitting in his throne-like-chair that looked much bigger than the man sitting on it. The principal was a short man, with a shorter temper. His most notable feature being his shiny bald head.

It's as shiny as a bowling ball. I'll bet he polishes it too, Lucas would often joke to himself.

The principal also wore glasses with big lenses that made his squinty pig-like eyes look like peering into a magnifying glass. To Lucas, the glasses made the principal look like a toad. He often wondered if others thought the same thing. When he spoke, the principal possessed a very hoarse and loud voice as if he had a built in megaphone on full blast.

It sounds worse when he speaks on the intercom. Blech, word, blech. Rumble, rumble.

To his shock, Lucas spotted both his parents seated on opposite chairs. Both looked weary and tired, as they often appeared to him. His father's dark brown hair was disheveled and the suit he wore was the only nice one he owned.

I think that suit is even older than I am. My dad isn't known for his fashion sense.

Lucas's mother appeared similarly, with her hair all over her shoulders like spaghetti strands. Her face made her look older with eyes that seemed heavy with worry.

I've seen that look before many times, and it's never for my sister; only me.

He read the golden-inlaid name plate that was the principal's pride and joy:

'Principal Lowe.' What a fitting name, Lucas thought humorously. *He definitely set the bar 'low' for principals as far as they come.*

Lucas wanted to burst out laughing every time he saw that ridiculous name plate. In this occasion though, it would not be appropriate.

Three strikes and you're out.

The principal's office was nothing to write home about. It wasn't small but it wasn't a big room either. Lucas

4

saw awards and degrees from other schools on the walls that Principal Lowe went to before finding employment in this particular school. He often wondered how many of those awards and degrees were real or fake. Even some of the books, which had a neat and organized appearance, looked like they were bought in a store that sells plastic merchandise.

I've never heard of the Canterbury Tales or something called Ulysses. Those sound like books that smart people read, or in this case, someone trying to look that way.

Principal Lowe observed Lucas carefully and stayed silent for some time. His parents didn't say a word, but their body language told him that they were already aware of the reason he had been called here today.

About a minute past, Principal Lowe decided to speak up first.

"Do you know why you're here, Mr. Fargo?"

Lucas noticed how he was being addressed with courtesy and formality like an adult.

And in front of my parents no less. He's definitely acting nicer than usual. Let's see how he likes this.

"I know it's not because you enjoy my company. Even you wouldn't stoop that low, Mr. Lowe," Lucas replied sarcastically as he tore a new hole into his jeans.

Strike one. Oh, shoot.

Principal Lowe grimaced, as if something flew into his nose. Composing himself, he sighed and continued as Lucas's parents still remained quiet.

"You are here, young man, because you have failed every class offered to you since the beginning of the school year. Which means either you can take a series of remedial classes throughout your summer vacation or risk expulsion from this school."

Go ahead, expel me. It's not like I have a future beyond this school. That's what everyone says anyways.

5

"He will take those remedial classes," Lucas's mother suddenly said, to her son's shock. "When are they happening?"

"This summer, ma'am," the principal said in a quizzical voice now, as if he didn't understand the question. "Your son will be required to take classes all summer in order to make up for the credits he didn't receive from the classes he was supposed to take."

Lucas suddenly felt anxious about this idea.

Summer school? That's their solution? If they think that's going to make a difference, they got another thing coming.

Principal Lowe continued as Lucas left his mind.

"I understand your son has been struggling with his medical conditions, but I have done all that is possible to ensure that he has every advantage anyone else would. Isn't that right, young man?"

Lucas did not respond to this, knowing that an answer would only validate the excuse. As if a heavy object had just fallen, his father spoke.

Here comes the thunder.

"Will he be gone all summer?" Lucas's father asked, with a tone suggesting hope for a specific answer.

The principal nodded.

"This is the only way I know how to help him. You are his parents, so you must also do what you believe is best for him."

Lucas sighed and threw his head back, forgetting, once more, that his parents were around.

"That seems to be the lowdown then," he said, hoping the principal caught wind of his tone.

Strike two. Seriously, what is with me today?

The principal appeared visibly upset by this, but rather than show it, he tried to compose himself.

"Your sister, Shelly, is a bright high school student with a promising future ahead of her," Principal Lowe said.

"I'm sure your parents here are proud of the young lady she is becoming. I only wish I could say the same for her younger brother. I would like to show your parents something."

Lucas scoffed as Principal Lowe pulled out what looked like a quiz that he took earlier in the semester.

"This is from one of your elective classes, Mr. Fargo," Lowe explained. "What's worth noting about this quiz is that it tests a student's intellectual and critical thinking skills based on two answers per question. You got many of them wrong and like your teacher I believe that you did this purposefully."

Now, it seemed like Lucas's parents were wide awake. He could feel their suspicions regarding this idea.

Okay, yes, fine! I admit it. Is that what you want to hear? Lucas wanted to say these words out loud, hoping they would sound less factual if spoken with his usual sarcastic tone. Sadly, that isn't what happened entirely.

"The only thing purposeful about that quiz, is how low the score was vs. how high I thought I was while taking it."

Strike three. Okay, if I wasn't dead before, for sure I'll be buried alive now.

The look his parents gave him said more than any words they could.

Yeah I'm definitely looking at an early grave once I get home.

"I wish you would try to be more like your sister," he heard his mother say, exhaustively.

Lucas groaned hard and loud to show his annoyance at being compared to his sister. More than being misunderstood for his mood swings, he hated it when people compared him to his sister.

Anyone with eyes could see how different we are in every way.

Shelly is Lucas's elder sister by two years and a freshmen student in high school. Since elementary and middle school, she's been an honor-roll student. Next year, Shelly would be taking college preparatory classes. She especially loved to volunteer for activities and charities, earning her even more praise from those around her.

She also has more friends than I care to count.

Her brother, in contrast, found himself labeled as a black sheep and mocked by those who adored her. He had no friends and no one he could trust with his secrets beside Shelly.

I don't tell her everything. Like how bad the voices in my head get, or that I sometimes want to… no I can't talk about that, not even to myself.

One of the most common insults told to Lucas's face is: "'you're nothing like your sister'."

In his heart, Lucas knew Shelly was one of the few people who loves him, and cares deeply for his well-being. She also takes his conditions seriously, and is the only true friend he has.

It isn't that I don't want friends. I just don't know how to talk to people because they judge anyone who isn't considered 'normal'.

Lucas came back to reality with the rising sound of his principal's voice. "I expect to see you back here Monday morning," Principal Lowe said, his tone not sounding as snide as Lucas expected.

I don't get it. If he doesn't like me, why is he acting like this is harder on him than it is for me? Maybe he's trying to save face since my parents are here.

"He'll be here. Thank you for your time, Mr. Lowe," Lucas's father said as he got up to leave. His mother did the same almost simultaneously.

No I won't, Lucas heard himself think. *No I won't?*

He suddenly felt lightheaded, as if he was slipping out of himself. Before he could stop himself, his eyes began to flutter violently and everything turned dark…

...Lucas found himself inside his father's red Chevy truck. He was seated in the back right next to a girl whose face became familiar to him as it began to take shape. It wasn't until she spoke when he recognized his sister.

"What have you done, Lucas?" Shelly asked, to his confusion. Lucas wasn't sure what his sister meant, as he tried to recall the events leading to being driven home by his silent and enraged parents.

My head hurts, Lucas realized, as he lay a hand on his scalp. *I remember feeling light-headed. I didn't take my medicine today... Didn't I take my medicine today?*

Lucas began to recall images in his mind: the principal's office in disarray, like a tornado had torn through there. Principal Lowe's awards and books were scattered around the room. Lucas's body had been shaking violently, to the point that if he had been anywhere near an edge, he surely would have fallen off.

I've had blackouts before, but this was something else. It was like I couldn't stop whatever was happening around me.

It took Lucas a moment to adjust his vision and when he did he saw his sister as clear as day. The expression on her face, like his parents, showed the disappointment and fear in her eyes.

The only features the two siblings shared physically was their dark brown hair, although Shelly's was straight. She wore her hair long, and had it tied back today. Her attire was a light purple shirt with dark jeans. Her small curved lips often looked displeased with her brother's actions, and her sharp nose often inhaled the air she would later exhale through her sighs.

Much like how she looks right now.

Her eyes were light hazel eyes and Shelly wore mascara on her eyelashes, which Lucas always disliked.

She looks better without make-up on her face.

9

His sister repeated her question from earlier, which only caused even more confusion from her younger brother. Impulsively, he tried to listen to music, hoping the sounds would drown out the conflict he felt around him in that cramped trunk. To his dislike, Shelly was quick to remove his earphones.

"What happened, Lucas?" his sister whispered sharply. "Mom and dad are saying you yelled at Principal Lowe and destroyed the inside of his office?"

I did what? Did I what?

"What I did," Lucas heard himself say in a whisper. When he spoke, he avoided eye contact with his sister. "I don't remember what happened, Shell. I just remember something about summer school, and after that, I was… here."

Shelly looked as if Lucas had told her, 'I don't want to waste my time in summer school instead of being at home doing nothing all day.'

That's what she wanted me to say. Even that would have been better than, 'I think I had a psychotic breakdown and ruined my chances of finishing school.'

While the future seemed bleak, Lucas stared out the vehicle window, as they passed through the neighboring homes in Austin, Texas. Compared to his family's house, the rest looked like a row of columns that all had similar appearances.

Shelly and her brother could feel the cold expressions of their parent's backs from the front of the truck. They both knew well that silence from them was no better than the word's they'd hear once behind closed doors.

Let's see; dad is the strong silent type, but when he talks people tend to stop what they're doing to listen to him. He's also very persuasive which is why he's popular in advertising. Mom is more 'do this, do that', then, 'start all over because I didn't like it.' She has this weird thing about having to do something herself or she isn't happy with how it's done.

"Why did you do it, Lucas?" Shelly asked in concern. "This is the worst thing you've done yet. You promised me you would try and do better and I believed you."

I did tell her that I would stay out of trouble at least long enough to finish the school year, Lucas remembered telling his sister. *It's bad enough that she's getting closer to finishing high school and closer to leaving home. What am I going to do if she isn't around? Stay with mom and dad? I rather live in the wild than live with my parents alone.*

He knew his sister was already planning her life for the next couple years. She would finish high school and begin college immediately while working on a degree for architectural design. He wanted to believe Shelly would invite him to live with her when she moved out, but he also knew she valued her independence.

Something she will never get with me around.

Turning away again, Lucas said, impulsively, "I shouldn't have come today. Nobody was here. If you hadn't made me come, none of this would have happened."

Lucas didn't feel good about blaming his sister for his current predicament. At the same time, he was afraid to admit the whole story.

I'm pretty sure I didn't take my medicine today, or yesterday, or the day before that, Lucas thought to himself in fear. *I didn't forget. I just hate how they keep making me feel sleepy and tired all the time.*

"Don't you dare blame me, Lucas," Shelly told her brother in a sharp voice that sounded louder than she had intended. "You're not a child anymore. You can't blame others for every mistake you make. You know I'm always here for you and I love you, but don't ask me to choose, because I love mom and dad too."

Lucas knew this to be true. His parents, although they cared for him, were beyond frustrated with his unpredictability and only avoided more drastic measures because of Shelly's intervention.

By drastic measures meaning sending me away to a boot camp or an insane asylum. Where electroshocks are as common as desert weather in Texas. By comparison, summer school is starting to sound not so bad if that's still on the table.

They spent the rest of the drive in silence. Lucas put his earphones on and played his music so loud he was sure everyone in the vehicle could hear it. This was his way of telling the world he didn't want to be bothered further. Shelly, similarly, pulled from her backpack a book she had been reading for a while.

It's funny how that all started; I just hate confrontations in general and Shelly hates to be interrupted when reading a good book. She's been reading that one since the last time I pissed off mom and dad, which wasn't that long ago.

Lucas clenched his left hand tight, while using his right to scroll through his music playlist. His last therapist suggested he make a playlist based on his moods. For happy, he had pop and soft rock. For sad, he had grunge and folk. For angry, which is what he felt now, he had heavy metal and instrumental.

My therapist said that music can help to organize my thoughts and maybe lessen the severity of my mood swings. I also have sounds like ocean waves, wind blowing on blades of grass, birds singing, and jungle noises.

As the instrumental music played, he felt the glances from his sister, which were like lens flares in his eyes. He hoped that Shelly wouldn't have to be present when his parents punished him.

I guess summer school isn't punishment enough. What will it be this time? No TV for a month? No solid foods for a week?

Finally, Lucas and his family arrived home. Their house made the rest of the neighborhood look like cardboard cutouts in comparison. There were four windows, two on top, and two below. It always looked as if it hadn't aged a day. The red paint still looked fresh even when the weather threatened to chip at it like termites on wood.

Entering their two-story home, Lucas walked in calmly through the front door as Shelly followed close behind him. He kept his backpack on while Shelly threw hers down to the side like she always did. Their mother walked into the living room, while their father made his way into the kitchen. The inside of the house was plain. The walls were decorated with very few family photos. The one Lucas liked the most was the one they all took when he was six.

I kind of remember that day. We were at Hall Mart, this old store that used to do cheap family photo, and I wanted a new toy from a show I used to like at the time. My parents promised to buy it only if I behaved while taking the picture. I must have because I got the toy. Then I found out how durable it was when it broke apart against the staircase.

Since his parents didn't have guests over, the house often looked unclean and messy. Both of them worked full time jobs, with his father working in advertisement and his mother at a local hospital clinic. In their absence, Shelly would often clean up and prepare meals for everyone upon returning home.

She can cook an amazing casserole which would put restaurant food to shame. Also, a delicious pasta verde, or as I like to call it simply; green spaghetti.

When it didn't seem like anyone was going to speak, Shelly decided to say something.

"What's for dinner? I can make some chicken vindaloo. What do you think, Lucas?"

That usually works, but not today, Shell, Lucas thought in distress.

13

"Go upstairs to your room right now, Shelly," her mother ordered her sharply.

Shelly complied dutifully and gave Lucas a worried glance. Her brother nodded at her and said, "I'll see you in a bit. Don't worry."

After what will probably be a very loud screaming session.

When his parents heard Shelly's door close, his mother turned to one of the cupboards and pulled out Lucas's medication.

"You haven't been taking your medicine."

It wasn't a question.

Before Lucas could speak, his mother spoke instead.

"This is completely unacceptable, Lucas. It's bad enough that you don't want to take your education seriously. Now you're not taking this medicine that is supposed to help you. Do you know how much these cost? No, you don't."

His mother undid the pill container and took out two tablets.

"I want you to take these right now in front of your father and me. If you don't, I'll call Dr. Hoffman and tell him. Do you remember what he said last time?"

He said he'll commit me to a psychiatric facility for the criminally insane, Lucas embellished. *Okay not exactly like that.*

Lucas took the two tablets from one of his pill containers, put them in his mouth, swallowed, and put the rest in his pocket.

"There, I did it. I'm sorry, mom. It won't happen again."

"That's not good enough anymore, Lucas," his mother said, sadly. "We have no choice now. No choice."

After his mother repeated the last two words, Lucas's father walked back into the living room with an envelope in his right hand. It looked weathered and wrinkled, like it had been through a perilous journey before reaching their doorstep. The seal had been broken as well, leading Lucas to wonder what its contents could be.

"We've had this for... a while now. I didn't want to bring this up, but for some reason, I think I wanted to now. We've done all we can for you, Lucas, and even though we love you, we don't want to deal with you anymore," his father said in a cold emotionless yet frail voice.

Why did that sound forced? Like his tone wasn't exactly how he meant it to be.

Lucas reached out for the envelope while his father's hand shook. Holding the envelope, he turned it over and noticed there was no return address or postal stamps.

That's definitely strange.

After this, he opened it and read the letter.

Camp Supernatural, where children discover abilities related to their disabilities. Ages 10 to 18 are welcome to join as campers. Camp begins June 1st to August 7th.

Before Lucas could understand what he was reading, a message appeared at the bottom of the information section of the invitation. At first it was blurry, but after a moment, the words became clearer.

Dear fellow reader, my name is Henry James. I am the Camp Director of Camp Supernatural. Since the year 1963, this camp has stood as a training ground for children who exhibit abilities related to their disabilities. If you have received this invitation, it means you are one of many from all around the world with a unique ability that requires training and discipline to master. As such, it will be your obligation to hone your skills and partake in the activities we will be offering to help you achieve this goal. Admission is free and transportation will be provided. Upon reading this letter, a cab driver will appear at your residence to take you to the campgrounds. Then you will be assigned to a specific cabin of our choosing based on your specific

15

abilities. If you wish to change cabins for any reason, please inform me at your earliest convenience. 2013 is our 50th year anniversary of which myself and our fellow Camp Counselors are most proud of. I wish you luck on your journey and keep in mind our camp slogan; Control <u>It</u>, So It Doesn't Control <u>You</u>.

He read the letter once, then twice, as the truth began to dawn on Lucas. He heard it in his head like a whisper.

What is this place? A camp for crazy kids like me? All I need now is a matching straightjacket to go with it. Camp Supernatural? I've never even heard of this place.

"You should go now. We don't want you here anymore. You're a burden to us," his father said, stuttering and clenching his fists as he spoke. He turned his back on Lucas and hung his head low. His body began to shiver.

"I thought I was going to summer school?"

"That's not happening now. Your outburst caused you to be expelled from the school effective immediately. It's either you go to this camp for help or we'll let Dr. Hoffman deal with you."

Lucas's father shook hard as if he were about to burst at any moment. He looked to his mother who nodded stiffly, turned away and began to shake in a similar fashion.

I don't understand. I know I messed up with Principal Lowe, wrecked his office, and probably yelled his ears off. But that can't be the only reason they want me gone now. It just can't. Does Shelly know?

As the thought sank in, Lucas wanted to go upstairs and talk to his sister.

Either I go to a camp for crazy kids or I go to a hospital facility for crazy people. I should talk to her and see what she thinks.

"I want to say goodbye to Shelly," Lucas asked his parents. "Can I see her or can she come down here?"

His parents looked at each other simultaneously and nodded with hesitance.

"Hurry up," his father called out as Lucas started up the stairs. The climb felt longer than the time it took to get home. When he made his way to the top, he saw his room to the right and his sister's to the left. Both rooms were right across from each other. In the middle front was their shared bathroom.

I just have a toothbrush, while Shelly has more shampoos and conditioners than I care to count.

He knocked on his sister's door. To his surprise and dread, Shelly was near enough the door to have heard everything.

"Your leaving aren't you."

This wasn't a question. Lucas nodded reluctantly and his sister looked upset by this.

"I thought I was going to summer school, but whatever I did in Principal Lowe's office must have been bad. Now I'm going to a summer camp for crazy kids. Look at this."

Lucas showed her the invitation. When Shelly looked at it, her face went blank.

"There's nothing on this," his sister said, handing it back to him. "Are you sure you read this right?"

Lucas nodded and shook his head in disbelief.

It's either camp or a hospital very far away. Then again, how far is this camp exactly? It might be farther away. Maybe I'll be with others around my age in Camp Supernatural. I just remembered; I don't like people my age.

While Lucas tried to let the benefits of the idea sweep through him, his mind kept taking him to the moment that led to all of this.

I didn't take my medication so my mood swings acted like a whirlwind. Which would explain the way Principal Lowe's office looked after I was done with it. Why was my throat sore? Why were my hands clenched so tightly?

"I don't want you to go, Lucas," his sister said, tearfully.

Oh no. I didn't want to make my sister cry. Why did I come up here in the first place?

"Mom and dad don't want me here anymore. They said so themselves."

"But why a place you've never heard of? That no one has heard of? Is this what you really want? Do you feel like you'll get more help in this camp than you would from a medical professional like Dr. Hoffman?"

Lucas shrugged, looking at the letter again.

I don't know why, but it feels right to go. Like it's calling me from a distance. Either that or I'm definitely about to have another psychotic breakdown.

"What if I go with you?" Shelly suddenly said to his shock. "At least that way you won't be alone. Plus, I've never been to a summer camp before. I think it could be fun."

Lucas shook his head, though he half regretted this.

"Not this time. This is something I have to do on my own." *What am I saying?* "I'll be back by August." *How do I know that?* "It might be good for me." *Wait what? I don't know. Know I don't.*

Lucas started to feel anxious all of a sudden, his body swaying back and forth. His chest felt tight and his nails buried themselves in his palms. While this happened, Shelly wrapped her arms around him, just as she had many times before. He tried to recall his breathing exercises.

Breathe in...out....inhale...exhale... Looking up... looking left... sideways... forward... right.

"It's okay, you're okay," Shelly whispered to her brother. The sounds of these words felt familiar and calming to Lucas.

This is my lullaby; I'm okay.

Just as he was calming down, he heard the sound of his mother demanding for him to hurry up.

"I hate them," Lucas heard himself say aloud, still in his sister's arms. "I wish they would—"

He heard a shushing sound from his sister.

"Don't leave angry," Shelly told her brother. "Mom and dad love you so much, Luke. Please, tell them how you feel before it's too late."

After their hug, Lucas's sister got together some supplies for him, which included a change of clothes, bathroom essentials, road snacks, and his medication.

"You better take them," his sister commanded. "I'm going to be texting you constantly to check on you."

Lucas managed a small chuckle and promised to do so.

"I'll be back by the end of summer."

"You promise? The moment this camp ends?"

Her brother nodded. Shelly extended her pinky towards him.

Our pinky swear, Lucas thought as they shook pinkies. *Breaking this kind of promise would be the literal point of no return.*

He was about to walk downstairs when his sister gave him one last parting gift.

"Do you remember when you got this for me?"

I saved up my allowance to buy it for Shell on her twelfth birthday. It's the first letter of her name in cursive.

Lucas nodded as his sister undid the necklace and handed it to him.

"I can't take this, Shell. What if I lose it? You know how often I lose things."

"You better not, because I want that back when you return from camp. When you look at it, think of home, and think of me."

Shelly put the necklace on her brother's palm and hugged him one last time.

Lucas began the walk downstairs with his mind growing louder and harsher.

Camp Supernatural? Henry James? Control it, so it doesn't control you? What is that supposed to mean? Am I crazy? I am crazy.

19

When he reached the bottom floor of his house, Lucas's parents continued to glare at him. He tried to remember the words his sister said.

Don't let anger be your last thought. Don't let anger be my last thought. Alright, I know what I want to say.

"Mom, dad," Lucas started. "I'm sor—"

Before he could finish, he felt a sharp stinging pain on his cheek. His head was turned and when he moved his hand to his face, the sensation was like an opened wound.

"Get out now!" his mother yelled, her body shaking violently. "We don't love you anymore. Nothing good ever came from you being here." Her teeth were grinding and she looked to be on the verge of tears.

Just then, a honking sound came from outside the house. The repetition of this, in synchronous with Lucas's heartbeat, made him feel similarly to before. He couldn't help the feeling he had, even as he thought of his sisters words.

It's okay... You're okay... It's not okay... You're not okay... Not you okay... Not it okay... Please stop... Stop please...

Lucas began to shake like his parents. His eyes began to flutter like butterfly wings as his fists began to clench. The last thing he saw was his father coming up to him, his arms reaching out for him.

Feeling his vision returning, Lucas saw his father lying face down on the ground, his face obscured by the floor. His mother looked horrified as she attempted to resuscitate him.

What? What just happened? Dad? Mom? I'm sorry.

With great haste, Lucas darted out of the door without looking back at his parents, with his backpack slung over his shoulders. He ran outside to find the source of the honking; an old beat-up taxi which looked like it had been teleported to the present from the past.

A taxi? Why is there a taxi in front of my house?!

The clouds in the sky began to drizzle rain as a voice called out from inside the taxi.

"Are you Lucas Fargo?"

When Lucas didn't reply, the voice repeated itself with more irritation.

After a moment, Lucas nodded.

"Get in. You're expected in Camp Supernatural. Do you have the letter?"

Lucas pulled out the letter, only to shield it from the incoming rainwater. To his disbelief, even as water hit it, the paper remained dry.

That's not possible. There's no way this paper is waterproof. That's definitely not normal.

"What are you doing? Playing in the rain?" the voice from the taxi called out. "Get in here before you catch a cold."

Just as he was about to, Lucas heard his sister calling out to him.

"Lucas! Don't go! Wait!"

He wanted to believe it was his sister calling out to him, but he couldn't be sure.

Not taking my medicine, the meltdown in Principal Lowe's office, and now my parents... my dad. I don't know what's real anymore. I can't stay here right now and I'm not going to a crazy hospital. I'm go to a crazy camp. These are my thoughts. Are these my thoughts?

The last words lingered in his mind as he made his way into the taxi and was seated in the back across from the taxi driver.

"Alright, kid. Next stop; Camp Supernatural!"

Chapter 2

Camp

Supernatural

The taxi drove so fast that Lucas's heart nearly burst through his chest. He panted and desperately tried to speak but each bump on the road felt like a punch to his voice box.

SLOW DOWN! ARE YOU TRYING TO KILL US!?
The words never reached his mouth. Lucas had a hard time making out the drivers overall appearance from the back. All he could see was the driver's demeanor, as he hummed what sounded like a marching hymn.

He looked around the shabby cab which had seen better days. The seats were discolored and the insides stuck out like open circuits. There was a wad of gum on the floor but luckily Lucas had missed stepping on it on his way inside.

Despite the ugly appearance of the taxi, Lucas couldn't smell anything resembling what he saw.

That's strange. Either I'm seeing things or this taxi looks like a used car that was put back together badly.

The front looked typical for an older-looking taxi, except for the pale cab driver.

"Who are you?" Lucas finally croaked.
When the driver stopped humming, his head began to turn around like an owl in Lucas's direction. He saw the shape of the driver's skull.

"The name's Francis," the taxi driver said with an accent Lucas never heard before. "At your service, kid."

Lucas's eyes widened as his gaze met the hollow sockets of the skeletal cab driver.

He's a skeleton. A talking skeleton! With no skin, no eyes. He just has bones.

Lucas suddenly had the urge to scream out loud, but he restrained himself. It was all he could do to avoid puking all over the backseat. The cab driver heard his gagging sound and turned back to the front with a groan.

"Please don't vomit inside my taxi," Francis asked in annoyance. "I may not have a nose, but I can still smell."

Lucas couldn't stop staring at Francis even with his skull turned away from him. He was amazed by the cab driver's skinless face, and his unnatural ability to talk without a tongue. His only form of clothing was an old blue grey uniform that looked like it belonged in a museum.

He looks like someone stole him from an anatomy class and dressed him up to look like a soldier.

Francis turned back to look at Lucas, his hands remaining on the wheel and yet somehow he still drove straight.

"You seem different from the other campers I've picked up in the past. Don't tell me this is the first time you've seen a talking skeleton, kid."

Lucas calmed himself down enough to muster an audible response.

"This is the first time I've seen a skeleton talk. How are you able to live without skin?"

Francis bobbed his head to the side.

"At least I don't have to worry about sunburn," Francis quipped. "Anyways, you have the prestigious honor of being escorted to Camp Supernatural by yours truly. As we speak, more taxi cabs are picking up campers for the summer. I happen to be running a little late since you took your sweet time accepting the invitation. It looks like you'll be my last fare for today and the last kid to enter camp."

Lucas gasped and heard himself impulsively say, "So there are more of you?" without giving much thought as to how the cab driver may take it.

Francis's bony face twisted into a mess like an Etch-A-Sketch. "That's not very nice. I find that both racist and offensive," he responded with a hurtful tone.

Racist? He has no skin!

"I'm sorry. I just feel weird talking to a skeleton or is that offensive too?" Lucas asked, with a small hint of curiosity and sincerity.

Francis chuckled, with his bony jaw clanking like a tambourine.

"How do you think I feel, kid? I fought in the Civil War and it wasn't anything like them wars that are fought now. This war had guns, sure, blood, definitely, sweat, lots of it, and holes for, well, you don't need to know that part. I even did time serving as a prisoner of war. The last thing I wanted was to be reanimated more times than I can remember and take kids like you to some camp for the summer. At least I get holidays off, like Day of the Dead. Get it?"

Lucas worked up a false smile and chuckle as Francis cackled at his own expense.

I don't get it? No, I don't.

"Yeah, I get it. Again, I'm sorry," Lucas replied, meekly.

Francis bobbed his head, which the young camper took as him nodding.

"All good. Now, tell me about yourself. In this here camp, you got to have an ability that is in some way related to your disability. If I may ask, what's yours?"

Lucas shrugged truthfully.

"I honestly don't know. I read something about it in the invitation. What's that all about?"

Francis went on to explain how certain children from every part of the world discovered an ability that was connected to whatever disability they have whether it be physical or mental. He also explained how the camp is a training ground and safe haven for all who attend.

"It's okay if you don't know your ability yet," Francis continued, "Camp Director James is a man of honor. He will help you figure it out. If you got an invitation, you're meant to be in this camp."

Lucas tried to be hopeful, but despite his best judgment, he was beginning to have doubts.

I'm sure some of the kids are going because they want to. Not me. What if this Camp Director finds out about my past? That I'm an at-risk teen. Either way, coming late like this doesn't look good on me.

"We're nearly there. Don't be discouraged by what looks like fog outside. I mean, it is fog, but it's more like the curtain for the big reveal," Francis assured him.

Lucas peered outside to see where they were. As Francis had said, the fog was too thick to see through.

How can he see through this fog? How can he see at all?

"Can you see anything past this fog?" Lucas asked the skeletal cab driver with concern.

Francis snickered at the question.

"Kid, I may not have eyes, but I ain't blind. I happen to have a great sense of direction," the skeletal cab driver boasted, pridefully. "That's what helped me get away from my capturers...well, at least until they found me and used me for target practice."

Lucas shuddered as he said that, and Francis turned to look at him with that still-blank skull of his.

"Yeah, I admit it wasn't a nice way to go. It was quick though. Trust me there were worse ways to die back in the day than getting shot. Ever heard of dysentery? A friend of mine died that way and it wasn't quick either. It took him a week before his body finally said, 'Out of Service,' if you catch my drift."

Lucas knew what that word meant.

It means having a really bad headache right? That isn't a pleasant way to go.

Suddenly, Francis hit the brakes so hard that Lucas found his face planted in the skeletal cab driver's backseat.

"We're here, kid."

After wrenching himself free, Lucas looked outside, but didn't see anything. Just the thickness of the fog that covered everything as far as the young boy's eyes could see.

"Where is the camp?" Lucas asked, baffled.

The desolation only added to his anxiety.

I hope it's not one of those things that will just pop up out of nowhere. I don't think my sanity could take another surprise today.

Francis started clanking his teeth together as if he were chewing gum.

"It's there."

He pointed his boney finger towards the fog. Lucas still saw nothing.

"Is this some sort of joke?" he asked the skeletal cab driver hesitantly.

Francis shrugged.

"I dump every camper here. Don't like it, too bad. I got a long rest ahead of me after this so get going."

Lucas didn't have much time to protest as the door opened to his side. He forced himself to climb out and heard Francis's last words.

"The Camp Guardian will come along and escort you the rest of the way. If you thought I was something to look at, just wait till you see him. Maybe next time you won't think I'm the scariest thing you've ever seen. I'll see you around, Lucas."

After that, the door slammed shut, silencing Francis's last laugh. In a millisecond, the taxi was gone.

Lucas was left there with only his backpack and himself in the deep thick fog.

This is officially the weirdest day of my life. At least it will be something I can tell Shelly, Lucas told himself, humorously. *Speaking of...*

He pulled out his phone and was disappointed to see that he had no bars at all.

So much for texting Shell. Maybe they'll have reception in this camp.

To conserve his battery, he turned his phone off.

Lucas suddenly felt very cold, wrapping his arms against his chest to keep warm. He went through his backpack and found his red jacket.

The one time packing my jacket actually came in handy.

However, even with the jacket on, it was so cold that he saw his own breath in a puff. He usually did not get cold easily during the winter season, but right now, he was both nervous and anxious to reach his destination.

Before pressing on, he made sure that his medicine was inside his backpack and was happy to find his pills for Aripiprazole, which specifically treated his severe bipolar, and Lithobid. These medicines, along with other pills he was required to take, helped to control his mood swings and irritability.

Of all the medicines I take, these are the only ones that actually do something beyond putting me to sleep.

After taking one pill from each, he made his way forward, sliding the pills back inside his backpack.

Lucas began to wonder what a place like Camp Supernatural was like.

What if the people there have powers that make them look different? Like someone who is invisible and has to wear bandages around them? I only know that because Shell like's classic horror movies. Also why supernatural? It's catchy, but I would have named it something else. Like Camp Fog?

Rather than walking too far into the fog, Lucas decided it would be best to remain where he was just in case the Camp Guardian was closer than he thought. While he waited, he decided to rummage through his backpack and found fiber bars his sister packed for him.

My sister is a health freak and she wouldn't have given me anything she herself wouldn't eat, Lucas thought with a groan. He ate two of the bars he had and decided to save the rest for when he was in camp.

I wonder why a camp that is supposedly a 'safe haven' has to have a guardian. Unless it's to make sure we don't go crazy with our powers. Even then, how big can this guy be?

Out of the fog, his answer came in a giant form. Despite the thickness of the fog, Lucas immediately noticed the obscured figure's towering height. The immense figure stood at about eight feet tall, the tallest person he had ever seen. As it came closer, the face it bore was physically grotesque, with pale translucent yellowish skin, making Lucas believe it wasn't human.

It looks like a walking corpse. Like Francis, only with skin, and very big. Emphasis on <u>VERY BIG</u>.

The figure's eyes glowed sharply as if it were seeing through the fog. Facially, the tall monster had a beaten face with long features, its eyelids looked like they were drooping, and it had strange symbols on the sides of its temporal ridges like tattoos. The monster had a small hunch and walked steadily towards him. It finally stopped and called out to Lucas.

"Come, boy, let's go!" The monster's voice rumbled and seemed to rock the earth.

He looks like Frankenstein's Monster, Lucas noted, anxiously.

The young camper held onto his backpack and ran towards the figure. He stopped when the immense figure stood over him and was so scared that he didn't dare utter a word.

If I say the wrong thing, he might get angry and kill me right here.

The monster looked down at him impatiently and sighed.

"You are here for Camp Supernatural, yes?" the monster asked him plainly.

Lucas was silent.

"Don't be afraid of me. I won't hurt you," the monster rasped gently. The monster tried to sound amiable, but its voice sounded too sharp to be anything except friendly. "I am the Camp Guardian. The campgrounds are not far from here."

The monster's lips were a dark shade like it was wearing lipstick and it wore an oversized shirt that read 'Camp Supernatural 1963-2013.'

After he gulped, Lucas finally mustered the courage to speak.

"You're the Camp Guardian?" He heard himself ask in a squeak as if he were more mouse than boy.

'You're the Camp Guardian?' What kind of question is that? Of course he is. Otherwise, I am so dead.

The monster nodded and put on what looked like a crooked smile, with similar teeth to match it.

"Tasked to bring children like yourself to the place where you will receive your training from the wise Camp Director Henry James," the monster explained, solemnly, as if he said this line to every camper before taking them to camp. As he brushed some of his blackened hair from his face, Lucas saw his hands. His fingernails were either gone, cracked, or blackened.

"Do not fret, young one. My job is to ensure the safety of everyone in this camp. No harm will come to you."

Lucas nodded and followed him through the fog in silence. The walk to camp seemed like hours to him and in that time the two had not said a word to each other. Glances were not exchanged either.

However, after feeling his anxiety rising heavily, Lucas broke his silence.

"What's your name or do you just go by Camp Guardian?" Lucas asked with curiosity. The monster did not reply.

Is he just ignoring me or is this a trick? First a talking skeleton and now a giant undead monster? I wish Shelly was here. She'd know what all this stuff means.

Lucas kept a good pace with the monster's footing and thought about running if he had to.

Where would I go? Francis is gone and I don't even know where this is. I'm here so I may as well see this through.

"We are here," the Camp Guardian suddenly said.

Lucas saw the weathered sign on the top saying, 'Camp Supernatural,' and he saw another sign below it that said, 'Control <u>it</u>, so it doesn't control <u>you</u>.'

I wonder why those words are underlined. They must mean something important.

The scenery began to suddenly change. It was no longer foggy or humid. Now, everything appeared a warm sunny day. Lucas saw cabins, tents, and small buildings. Some children were running around laughing and wearing camp T-shirts. The words 'Camp Supernatural' were stylized differently to be either italicized, or, in some cases, side-ways. Other shirts were in different colors with different words to go with them. Straight ahead from him was a pole sign with arrows pointing in different directions.

Those shirts look cool. I wonder where I can get one.

When Lucas got a good look at the cabins, he thought to himself, *I hope I get a decent cabin. The invitation didn't have a list but I'm sure there's one somewhere around here.*

As he walked through the entrance, Lucas removed his jacket and tucked it inside his backpack, turning sideways to admire the structures and environment.

The camp looked as alive as the children and teens Lucas saw walking amongst the grounds. There were trees that cast shadows from the forest ahead, and cabins that encircled the camp. The giant upside down U was like a cluster of cars parked in unison with each other. Peering to the middle, there was a building that he assumed was the cafeteria, with some tents that were pitched to the sides of both the left, middle, and right parts of the camp. To a right, closer to the end of the cabins, was a building that appeared more notable than the rest due to its medium height and structure.

That looks important. Probably the Camp Director's home.

The way the sun shone and the wind blew calmly through the campgrounds made Lucas want to go exploring.

"Please make your way to the main pavilion area straight ahead," the Camp Guardian instructed Lucas. "Announcements will begin shortly."

"Can I look around first please, sir?" Lucas asked, hoping it wouldn't be met with a rude response. Instead, the Camp Guardian nodded.

"You will get the chance to look around more after being assigned a cabin. Don't take long, young camper."

The Camp Guardian made his way towards a crowd that was beginning to form around the main pavilion.

As he walked around the camp, Lucas saw what looked like a forge with a giant anvil sitting on the left side close to the entrance of the camp. The forge itself appeared untouched at the moment and was going through some kind of renovation for the summer.

'Will be open in July: Camp Supernatural Forge Ahead', Lucas read to himself from the sign posted near the forge.

That tagline isn't as clever as it sounds.

Lucas spotted a gift shop nearby that read, 'Camp Supernatural Merchandise', and looked to be as small as a convenience store at a gas station. There was also a sign that looked newly added with the words: 'Fifty-percent off select items all summer.' He wanted to go inside and look around but decided to wait until after orientation.

Behind the cabins, he noticed a handful that were smaller in comparison to the main ones. He thought these were used to separate the elder kids from the younger ones.

I'm guessing the big cabins, which is where I will be, are for my age and up, and the smaller ones are for anyone younger than ten.

Lucas had been so focused on looking around that he did not notice a girl who got in his way. They bumped into each other abruptly, both falling in opposite directions. Before he could apologize or say anything to her, the girl spoke up first.

"Hey, watch where you're going. Are you blind and stupid?!" the girl shouted out. He was about to respond when the girl shook her finger.

"Too slow. Talk fast or else you won't talk at all," she threatened. Her group of three female friends began to laugh. Lucas began to shake, his hands flapping, but he tried to hide it by speaking up.

"Sorry, I wasn't looking."

"Yeah obviously. Is this your first time here?"

Lucas nodded and let his eyes adjust to the girl in front of him. She was towering in height, though not quite as tall as the Camp Guardian. Her dark brown eyes began to look especially muddy, while her curly long light brunette hair began to stand up as if it were sentient. She wore a simple attire that consisted of a red camp tank top and short pants with combat boots.

Her shirt has words on it: 'Excellent Warriors.' That's creative. Also, are they the welcoming committee or maybe they are like the bullies who stalk the hallways on the first day of school?

It didn't take him long to realize they were the latter. He hoped that an adult would come to his rescue before anything happened.

I doubt I could win in a fair fight against this girl, even with powers.

"Are you all first year campers like me?" Lucas nervously asked the strong-looking girl.

Wait, why did I ask that? Now I'm a target for sure.

"Not really. What's your name, Twig?"

"Lucas Fargo."

"Well, Lucas Fargo the Twig, tell me something, have you ever tasted dirt?"

He looked at her with a confused expression and shook his head.

"Well then, let me and my friends help you try it."

She was closing in on him when he involuntarily lurched forward and bumped into her shoulder. The big girl fell and landed hard on the ground. Her friends looked at her with faces that looked ready to burst into laughter, but stopped short of this after she rose up swiftly. The Camp Bully glared at Lucas and was about to charge at him when someone appeared from behind her as if they had been there all along.

"The announcements are about to begin, Alexia," said the adult with a cold tone.

The girl named Alexia scoffed and gave Lucas a scowl.

"This isn't over. I'll deal with you later, Twig," the Camp Bully threatened Lucas. "Welcome to Camp Supernatural."

Alexia and her friends walked away to join everyone else at the main pavilion.

Great. I just got here and already I made my first enemy, he thought, drearily.

The adult who stopped Alexia turned to look at Lucas and frowned at him.

"What are you waiting for, camper? Get over to the main pavilion with the rest of the children."

He pointed towards the fully formed crowd of campers who were settled in by their ages.

Lucas nodded and began walking forward.

As he entered the crowd of campers, Lucas noticed some of them were staring at him with baffled expressions and muttering silently amongst each other.

Why are they all staring at me? Does it have to do with that crazy girl I just met?

He looked around to see how many campers were in attendance. Despite being unsure of the number, Lucas only counted about less than a hundred, but he couldn't be sure.

If these kids are from around the world, it can be any number imaginable.

Lucas tried to calm himself, his anxiety making it so that even a slight bump against someone made him shiver like diving into cold water. When he found a spot with not that many campers, Lucas spotted the Camp Guardian below the platform. The Camp Guardian looked attentively at both the surrounding campers and the camp itself.

Is that all he does? Watching and staring? Now that I'm seeing him more clearly, he looks more like a gargoyle statue than a person.

Lucas saw eight individuals sitting on the medium sized platform, four to each side. He assumed the ones sitting on both the left and right sides of the platform were part of the camp faculty. There were four men and four women, with one of the men looking particularly younger compared to the others. He spotted the adult who helped him with a tag that read, 'Camp Activities Director.'

The man with this tag was skinny, with very hairy sideburns, a thick black goatee and he looked to be in his early twenties. In the middle of the Camp Counselors was an old man who Lucas assumed had to be Camp Director Henry James.

He looks old. Like maybe between sixty or seventy. He's still got his hair so he must have good genes.

The Camp Director had long grey hair that was almost shoulder length and a medium-sized grey beard that covered the lower part of his face like a mask. He also wore a blue robe with the sleeves hanging like a turkey's chin.

When Lucas noted the Camp Director's wrinkleless face, he rethought his age theory. His skin was chalk-white, as if his blood was completely sucked out. The Camp Director's most notable quality was his ocean blue eyes which looked calming.

Those eyes have more to them than what is being shown.

The Camp Director's smile was the only enlightening feature he had, as it immediately made Lucas feel welcomed among strangers. When the old man's eyes turned to him from the platform, he smiled warmly and waved at him.

"Hello Lucas, we have been expecting you."

Lucas's eyes widened when Henry said his name. He felt every eye in the camp on him now.

How does he know my name?

"How do you know my name?" Lucas asked with astonishment.

The Camp Director waved his hand backward and pointed towards Lucas's shirt.

"Why, it says so on your name tag."

Lucas looked down at his shirt and found a name tag glued there that read, 'Hi, my name is Lucas Fargo.' He tried to get it off, but it wouldn't come off.

What the … how did this get here?

Henry chuckled and threw his hand forward, with the name tag disappearing. Some of the other campers were giggling as well while the counselors regarded Lucas with impartiality. The Camp Guardian didn't laugh or smile.

Lucas blushed embarrassingly and nervously covered his face with his hands like a paper fan.

Great, first I make a new enemy and now I am the new joke of camp. Way to make a positive first impression, Lucas.

After the laughter subsided, the young camper rubbed his hands against the spot where the name tag was but felt nothing.

That had to have been some kind of magic trick. The way he waved his hands around and the way that name tag appeared, only to disappear.

"Before we get started, I would like to acknowledge a very special individual in this camp who has helped me for fifty years now," Henry announced proudly. "Campers, please give our Camp Guardian here a most deserving hand."

Some of the older-looking campers began clapping for him while many of the younger campers looked frightened at his appearance. The monster blushed embarrassingly and nodded stiffly.

The clapping subsided when Henry stretched his hands out.

"For those of you who have been here before, welcome back to another summer here in Camp Supernatural. If this is your first year, let me welcome you with the opportunity to be a part of something that is unlike anything you've known until now."

Lucas looked around at the assortment of campers surrounding him and counted children who ranged from being as young as ten to others being older than him. Many of the campers looked as if they were fully entranced with everything the Camp Director was saying, while some, notably the older campers, looked uninterested.

They've probably heard all this before already. If I am here long enough, that'll be me too.

"We may have a few more campers joining us shortly. I will do my best to address you all first before meeting with the rest accordingly. Now then, this camp was founded many years ago with the express goal of maintaining and helping various specific children to control an ability associated with a disability. Allow me to explain further: each of you has an ability that is related to your disability, whether it be physical or mental. Many before you have been trained to better themselves. The trainings provided in this camp will help to minimize the possibility of failure, but they will only be successful if you embrace every lesson given no matter the demands. Do not be discouraged if your power is unknown at the moment. In the coming days, you will have a chance to discover each of your abilities, including during our yearly game called Relic."

Lucas observed that some of the campers looked especially excited about this, notably the group near the Camp Bully.

Relic? As in something old and boring? Hard pass.

"This game is mandatory for every first year camper, no matter what your abilities are."

Darn.

"Introductions are in order; my name is Henry James and I have been the Camp Director of Camp Supernatural for fifty years now. To my left and right are our current Camp Counselor staff. This summer, we regret not having our veteran counselors, Naomi and Zane, but they will return next year for certain. Here to the left we have Jane, Lucinda, Marcus, and my son Daniel. To the right is our Camp Activities Director Richardson, Alexander, Betty, and Margot. Please give them a hand as well. After the games, you will all be assigned in groups based on your abilities and be trained by one of these Camp Counselors."

While the campers were clapping, Lucas fixed his eyes on Daniel, who was sitting closer to Henry on the left. He appeared handsome and the way he stood made him seem like he tried to emulate the Camp Director. Daniel had a clean shaven face with long black hair brushed behind his ears. His eyes were a mismatched green and blue. Lucas tried to see if there was a resemblance between Daniel and Henry but saw little.

Maybe he looks more like his mom?

"To complete orientation week here in Camp Supernatural, all campers will be required to do three things; be assigned a cabin, of which the selection will be made after introductions, acquaint yourselves with your cabin mates, and finally, each first year camper will take part in our Relics game. Younger campers will play Tag. Our events will be held on the outskirts of the Infinite Forest. At the end of every year you are here, you will receive a certain number of beads. Each one will be personalized to you, so you cannot barter with them amongst yourselves. The goal is to earn forty-two in order to become a Camp Counselor. Are there any questions or concerns at the moment?"

Lucas wanted to raise his hand, but when he saw no one else doing so, he came up with questions to possibly ask later on.

Can I skip playing Relic and play Tag instead? I don't know my power yet, so is it okay if I watch everyone else fight each other instead? Why forty-two beads? Why not four or two?

"Very well then. I wish you all a wonderful summer here in camp. Remember our camp slogan; learn to control your abilities, so they do not control you. Have fun summer everyone!"

I guess the slogan is interchanging, meaning either the one outside is old, or it's just rephrased to sound new.

The Camp Director looked about ready to leave when he turned back to the audience and made one final speech.

"On a last note: Any form of electronic devices that are used for recreational purposes will be obsolete in this camp. I want you all to be prepared and focused, not texting friends or family."

Some of the teen campers groaned and even Lucas found himself frustrated.

Great, now no one will know when I want to be left alone. Plus, how will I be able to reach out to Shell and let her know that I'm alright?

When he exited the stage, Henry made his way towards Lucas. Once he reached him, the Camp Director leaned in towards his right ear and whispered, "We must talk." The old man motioned for him to follow. The young camper did so reluctantly.

As they walked away, Lucas could hear the Camp Activities Director instructing the campers on the rules and expectations of the camp. He spoke with an authoritative tone that was unflattering and lacked the Camp Director's enthusiasm.

"Ground rules to follow at all times; Rule number one: no using your powers beyond the training grounds and during the camp games, unless your life is in danger. Otherwise, expulsion from camp. Rule number two: do not be tardy to your training sessions and make sure to eat your three square meals a day. You won't be able to get any food once the cafeteria closes so be mindful of the times that they're open and closed. Rule number three: any and all payments made must be in cash. Credit cards will not be accepted in the camp gift shop. If you need currency, you may consult with a Camp Counselor about doing some work around the camp when you are not training or participating in activities. Rule number four: Once you are assigned a cabin, all campers will receive a colored camp shirt with the words of their cabin embroiled on them. Be sure to wear a camp shirt at all times like school uniforms. Rule number five: boys and girls are not allowed to mingle inside their cabins unsupervised. That means you teenagers. Cabins are for those assigned only. Rule number six: all campers are to be in their bunks by 9:00pm unless otherwise noted. The Camp Guardian will ensure this rule is followed. Now for the last rule; Rule number seven: all cabins will be inspected every two weeks beginning next week, for cleanliness, organization, and overall care. Failure to follow these rules will result in demerits. Earn three and you will be denied beads at the end of the summer. Now onto cabin placement…"

He could be a drill sergeant outside of camp, Lucas thought humorously. Henry had been humming to a tune when he started to chuckle softly.

I wonder what he finds so funny.

Just then, a young girl about Lucas's age appeared in front of Henry as if she had been there this whole time. Her long blonde hair extended down her back, while her face was sprinkled with small freckles that were barely noticeable across her nose and rosy cheeks. She also wore a cap on her head that read 'Camp Supernatural', and a purple camp T-shirt that read, 'Weather or Not'. Her large green eyes looked as radiant and playful as her smile.

She looks very pretty. I wonder if she will notice me standing next to the Camp Director and think I'm a cool guy for that.

"Hello, Camp Director James," said the blonde-haired girl with courtesy, "I wanted to ask about the cabin arrangements?"

It was evident to Lucas that she was nervous based on the way she was standing and slightly shaking.

Like me right now. That's one thing we have in common.

"Please, Ashley, call me Henry," the Camp Director said with a warm smile. "I believe the placement is starting right now. Unless you have an immediate concern you wish to address."

The girl named Ashley nodded and despite being anxious still mustered a small smile.

"I was wondering if Hailey and I could have a different cabin instead of the ones being assigned to us."

Lucas had only now just noticed how distinct she was compared to the girls he knew from school.

She's not wearing any make-up. Girls always wore make-up in my school. If not they'd be made fun of by both guys and girls. I never agreed with that, but then again I was in no position to voice my opinion when my sister was one of those girls who wore her fair share of make-up.

As the Camp Director thought for a moment about Ashley's request, her eyes briefly glanced at Lucas, then back to Henry.

"Which cabin do you wish to have?" Henry asked with great interest. His eyes never left Ashley's.

"If I may be bold, Henry, The Weeping Willow cabin is the one I want. I even have the shirt for it already." Ashley gestured to the words embroiled on her grey shirt. Lucas could tell that the stich-work wasn't professionally done.

They look cheaply made. Like the person who made it doesn't know how to stich properly.

"May I ask why you would like this cabin instead of the one assigned to you?"

"I was told from a reliable source that I will be assigned to the Majestic Meadow cabin and Hailey will be in Xiomara's Axe."

Who is Xiomara? Also, why does she have an axe?

Although Henry's attention seemed to be on Ashley, Lucas believed he felt the Camp Director's indifference on the matter.

I think Ashley is too busy trying to say it all right instead of wondering if Henry even cares.

"I know it's not fair to grant favors for one camper and give everyone else their assigned cabins. If it's possible, I would really appreciate it, Henry."

The Camp Director suddenly appeared intrigued by the request, Lucas noticed immediately.

She's bold, definitely a lot braver than I would be in her shoes.

"As I understand it, the Weeping Willow is one of the most popular cabins among the females in camp and already has occupants. Tell me, what is wrong with Majestic Meadow?"

Ashley frowned as she turned to face the cabin, which to Lucas looked like every other cabin in camp. She then turned back to look at Henry.

"With all due respect, Henry, I didn't know about the camp's assigning policy. Daniel told me that every cabin would be assigned to the campers whose abilities matched with it. From what I've read, I don't see how what I can do suits Majestic Meadow," Ashley insisted. "I feel I would be better fitted to be in a cabin that represents not only what I can do but who I am as a person. The same applies to Hailey too."

Wow, she really is bold. I wouldn't be surprised if Henry let her down easy. She's actually asking him to bend the rules for her.

To Lucas's surprise, Henry only chuckled and gave her a concentrated but warm look.

"It may come off as sudden and even unfair to the current campers in that cabin," Henry pointed out, to Ashley's disappointment. "However, in light of tomorrow's game, I believe we can reach a compromise. Are you familiar with the term?"

Ashley nodded, but then looked unsure.

"Does it mean that what I want ruins things for others?"

Henry shook his head and turned to Lucas.

"Lucas, can you tell me what a compromise is?"

The young camper suddenly felt like he was thrust into the spotlight, as Ashley's attention was fully on him now. His eyes began to look in every other direction except at the pretty girl staring at him with interest.

43

Why couldn't he use a smaller word?

Lucas shook his head shamefully.

"It is an agreement between two mutual parties, in this case you and me, for a fair deal," Henry explained. She was still confused until he continued.

"At the moment, there are three campers scheduled to receive that cabin, but they may be willing to admit you two as last additions should your team win in tomorrow's Relic game. If you can do this, I'll see to it that you and Hailey move in by the end of the first week," Henry proposed, as Ashley began to look hopeful. "Is this an acceptable arrangement?"

She smiled brightly in response and nodded enthusiastically. "Thank you so much, sir, I mean, Henry. I promise to do my best to help my team win," Ashley vowed with a playful smile that matched her eyes.

Ashley said her goodbyes to Henry and went off so fast in another direction that Lucas hadn't seen where she went.

She barely even noticed me except for when Henry asked me what a compromise was, Lucas thought in embarrassment. *She must think I'm dumb now for not knowing what that means.*

While Lucas's attention was still on Ashley, Henry tugged on his shoulder until he turned to look at the Camp Director.

"Shall we?"

As they approached the Camp Director's house, Lucas began to feel nervous. This moment reminded him of going to the principal's office back at school. In contrast, he felt fearful and unsure of Henry's intentions.

Why does he want to talk too just me? Is it because I arrived late or does he know that I ran away from home?

He saw the sign outside of Henry's house that read, 'Open twenty-four hours except on Wednesdays.' Henry noticed Lucas looking at the sign.

"I added that when the house was built. Do you like it?"

Lucas nodded admirably but was baffled by the exception of Wednesdays.

Why Wednesdays?

"How come you're not open twenty-four hours on Wednesdays?" Lucas asked the Camp Director with curiosity.

Henry tilted his head to Lucas's ear.

"Wednesdays is Pizza Day at the cafeteria," the Camp Director whispered. "I always take two hours for lunch to catch up on some old soaps that play specifically on that day."

Lucas smiled and felt more comfortable and at ease than a few seconds ago.

Henry seems like a cool guy, down to earth, and definitely a lot nicer than any adult I knew back at home, Lucas assessed. *It's strange because even though I barely met him, I already I feel like I can tell him anything and he won't judge me for it.*

"It looks cozy," Lucas noted, after scanning the house up and down. "I bet it's nicer on the inside."

So dumb. Stop talking, Lucas. Let him do all the talking instead.

Henry nodded and beckoned for Lucas to follow him inside the house.

The Camp Director's house looked like a regular single-bedroom home and was almost as wide as the entrance to the camp itself. There were no windows, which Lucas found odd. The front door was plain with a red doorknob and a welcome mat that read, 'Welcome campers one and all'. Henry wiped his shoes on it and opened the front door.

The room in front of them was just one long hallway that stretched about maybe twenty feet long with nothing but walls in-between.

"This way. Mind your step," Henry cautioned him.

Lucas felt a small little bump on the floor and narrowly avoided it.

I can't see anything in here. Maybe he has the lights off here to save on electrical bills, Lucas thought.

When Lucas went through the door leading into the office of Henry James, he saw, to his amazement, the immense room which outweighed the structure of the house by a hundred fold.

The contents inside the Camp Director's office could give a packrat a run for their money. Lucas saw stacks of books that lined one side of the wall, record's that were arranged in alphabetical order on a small row next to his desk, a small old television that looked to be from the earlier days of cable network, and an old record player playing a song that Lucas vaguely recognized. Henry smiled in delight as the music played.

"Top of the World by the Carpenters. They are my favorite musical group. Karen Carpenter had a divine voice," Henry admired.

Lucas nodded slowly.

Who's Karen Carpenter?

Henry gestured for him to sit in the chair across from his desk. His desk was meager compared to everything else in his room. No nameplate, only one drawer, and a candy bowl with no candy at the moment. It wasn't until Karen sang the song's chorus when Lucas recalled where he heard the song from.

That's the song that was playing on the radio when we went to Colorado for the summer years ago, Lucas remembered. *I think I was six, and Shelly had to have been eight. We actually had a good time that year vs. other summer vacations.*

For a moment, he was calm until Henry asked him the big question.

"Why are you here, Lucas?"

46

He tried to come up with an answer, but ultimately could not think of one.

I want to tell him about everything; I'm here because I need help. I need to get better so I can go home and apologize to my mom and dad. I promised Shelly I would go back when the summer was over.

He was in deep thought when Henry interrupted him.

"You seem particularly unsettled by the question. Please take your time in answering. What is spoken in this office remains here."

The young camper nodded and thought before speaking.

Maybe I can just lie a bit and let him think I don't have a choice to be here. That might make me seem more like I should be here.

"Anywhere is better than home," he heard himself say with his most pitiful tone. Henry leaned over and studied Lucas's facial expression.

"Why do you say that?"

The young camper shrugged, suddenly feeling the real emotions he tried to bury away.

"My parents hate me and all I ever do is cause them trouble. They couldn't help me so they sent me here to get help. I just don't know if this place would be good for me on top of whatever my ability might be."

That last part is true.

Henry gave Lucas a sympathetic smile.

"In this camp, we give up all outside burdens for the duration of our time here. We are no longer plagued with the past. Instead, we focus on making a brighter future regardless of the difficulties that may follow."

Lucas looked at the Camp Director with hope in his eyes and realized that Henry was genuine in his effort to reach out to him.

"I wish I was like my sister. She has everything figured out and doesn't have to struggle with herself the way I do. Her life is perfect and so is she."

Henry chuckled at this, which made Lucas bewildered.

"No one is perfect, my child. I'm sure your sister struggles with more than you realize. Just because you can't see the pain in someone's face doesn't mean there isn't any. You have to keep an open mind about the feelings of others along with your own."

Lucas tried to understand what Henry meant by this, but at the moment drew a blank.

Keep an open mind? Like be open to new experiences? That's why I'm here.

"Do you have any medically documented physical or mental disorders?" the Camp Director asked, changing the subject.

Lucas nodded.

"I have a bipolar, anxiety, and schizophrenia. I take medication for all three."

"May I see the medication you are prescribed?"

Lucas took out the pills he brought, and showed them to Henry. The Camp Director read the labels and handed them back to him after examining each of them.

"Because of your schizophrenia, I assume you hear voices. Can you differentiate between your own thoughts and the other voices you hear?"

Lucas thought for a moment.

I could tell him about the incident with the animals, but he might think I'm crazy. So, maybe I'll leave that part out for now.

"I've never noticed the difference to be honest, sir. Sometimes I feel like they could be voices I've heard before, or my voice that just sounds a little differently than how I hear myself."

That part's true too.

Henry nodded, but did not appear as satisfied as Lucas had hoped.

"I mean, do you think my powers are like my mental issues? In my head? I feel like I'm crazy enough without having some kind of superpower to go with it."

Also why can't I choose what powers I get? Who made this rule that people are born the way they are? That's lame.

Henry shrugged and let out a soft chuckle.

"Perhaps you have only begun to discover what your power can be. You are not alone; here in camp, everyone is coming to terms with mastering both their abilities and disabilities. As you should know, you will be among the first contestants, but fear not. Your teammates will be campers who are familiar enough with their abilities to provide a fair chance. I look forward to your demonstration during tomorrow's game."

Lucas wanted to protest this idea entirely.

So I'm going to be the only one on my team who doesn't have their power figured out? How is that doing them any favors, let alone me? As long as that psycho Camp Bully isn't on the opposite team, then I'll be fine.

After a minute of silence, the Camp Director asked Lucas a different kind of question.

"What do you fear, my child?" Henry asked him.

"What do you mean, sir?"

"It is a simple enough inquiry; what do you feel will hold you back from realizing your full potential here?"

Lucas shrugged, not knowing how to answer that.

A fear? Like being alone? Being misunderstood? Unwanted? Wait.

"I fear being trapped in myself," the young camper revealed. "Of not being able to express my thoughts aloud, and being unwanted. Like a broken thing. I never want to be a burden to anyone."

This answer seemed to disturb the Camp Director, who did not press it further.

Without warning, another man entered the room. It was Daniel, the Camp Director's son.

He looks like something is bothering him.

He wore a purple camp shirt that was tucked in along with regular blue jeans. Lucas observed that he had a wristwatch that didn't look like it was just for telling time.

If I had to guess, it's one of those watches people who run use to measure their heart rate. Shelly plans to get one for herself once she starts working since she loves to jog.

The Camp Director's son looked at his father and approached him, ignoring Lucas's presence.

"Father, we completed the cabin arrangements for the current campers," the counselor informed Henry. "More children have been brought to the campgrounds, but we're still missing a few more that were scheduled to arrive. I don't understand why this keeps happening when I've shared with you their recent locations. Those cab drivers of yours may not have eyes, but they can follow instructions just as well."

Lucas paid particular attention to the words Daniel used, including 'missing campers' and 'keeps happening'.

Is he suggesting that kids go missing here all the time? That isn't exactly a strong reason to stay here. What have I gotten myself into?

Henry nodded in compliance. "Yes, I will address this matter when I am able. Have you met Lucas, Daniel?"

The Camp Director's son noticed the young camper and extended a friendly hand in his direction. The two shook hands but something about the way Daniel shook it was like he was trying to pull Lucas's arm clean off.

"Good to meet you, Lucas," he noted with a smirk. "It's not every day a camper gets invited into the Camp Director's office on the first day. You should feel honored. My father's time is rarely spent on individuals."

The tone Daniel said the last part made Lucas feel anxious, until Daniel let out a small laugh.

"Forgive me. If you're here, that means you are meant to be. My name is Daniel Harrison. However, when addressing me in front of other campers, I am to be referred to as Counselor Harrison, for professional courtesy. Do you understand?"

Lucas immediately noticed that he did not share the same last name as Henry.

Maybe he's adopted.

Before he could ask about that, Henry rose from his desk, walked over to Lucas and whispered in his ear, "Follow me." Daniel noticed the two leaving and was perplexed.

"Father, wait! What about the new campers? You said you'd welcome them as well."

Henry lifted his hand and turned back with a smile.

"You will handle that in my stead. Richardson will assist you with that and the remaining cabin placements," the Camp Director commanded. "One day, you will stand where I am, and this will serve as good practice."

Despite Daniel seemingly compiling with the request, Lucas could tell it bothered him more than he showed.

When a person's emotions are strong enough, I can feel them. His emotions right now are like me when I want to stop talking to people.

After leaving the Camp Director's house, Daniel made his way back to the pavilion while Henry and Lucas moved in the opposite direction.

Lucas observed the new group of campers who were gathering for the second round of announcements. He tried to count how many more had come but lost track after the first few ones. While he was distracted, Henry spoke.

"In this camp, we have twenty-six main cabins, with each of them housing up to five children per cabin. This year,

51

we are estimated to have as many as one hundred and fifty campers. Some are younger so they will be in different cabins instead of the main ones. You might not meet all of your cabin mates initially, but over the summer you will," Henry explained as they walked around the cabin's area.

That's a lot of people in one place, the young camper thought to himself with anxiousness. *I don't like the idea of sharing a living space with someone, let alone four other people. Why can't I have the option to cabin on my own? On my own, why can't I have the option to cabin?*

Lucas looked around to see which cabin he would get. He wondered what the differences were, because on the outside they all looked the same.

"How do you decide who belongs where," Lucas asked Henry as the Camp Director stopped walking for a moment. "I noticed you were fine with bending the rules a bit for that girl who wanted a specific cabin. Would you do the same for others, or is it all mostly fixed?"

Henry smiled as if the question flattered him. "Rest assured that all necessary preparations are made prior to a camper attending the summer here, in addition to their respective cabins," the Camp Director emphasized. "There have been cases where campers do not get along with their cabin mates. In those instances, we try our best to accommodate them. Our main goal in this camp is to help everyone here hone their abilities so that when they return to the outside world after the summer ends, they can better conceal and utilize their abilities for their own safety and those around them. Abilities, much like disabilities, can range from mild to severe. No one is treated any lesser for it here."

As they continued to walk, Henry went on to explain how each cabin had its own unique quality.

"Each cabin has a unique name and words that goes with it. For instance, one of our more popular cabins is called Atlas's Agony, with the words being 'Weight of the World'.

Campers assigned here may possess disabilities that make physical tasks difficult in the outside world. However, in this camp, they can perform numerous useful tasks such as helping to build the cabins, setting up the tents we use, working at the forge to make weapons and armor, and they are often favored candidates for positions as Camp Counselors. Every cabin has an assortment of different kinds of campers categorized as 'mentals' and 'physicals'. Once training commences, you will likely be paired with another who has similar abilities to yourself within these two categories."

So that's how it works here, Lucas thought with curiosity. *I must have a mental ability since what I have is in my head. Is it possible to have a bit of both?*

"Can I be assigned to Atlas's Agony, or a cabin that is similar to it?" Lucas asked, hoping to be as bold as Ashley had been in her statement.

Unfortunately for him, Henry shook his head.

"That cabin is already occupied. But do not fret, your cabin is not too far off from here."

So much for that. I was looking forward to being in a popular for once, he thought with a frown. *For the first time. The only time. Only for the first time.*

From where he and the Camp Director stood, Lucas could see the rest of the cabins up close. The giant upside down U looked to be like a horseshoe that surrounded and possibly protected the camps interior.

Or painted a large target on it like a bright Christmas tree.

Lucas was so focused on his thoughts that he didn't notice the cabin they stopped in. It would neither have been his first choice, or last choice.

The Imaginarium Illusion? What does that mean? Why here? Why not further down the line, like closer to Henry's home?

"I shall leave you to it," Henry said with a pat on Lucas's shoulder. "Give this place a chance and it may yet surprise you."

"Wait a second," Lucas heard himself say aloud. The Camp Director stopped walking away suddenly, but his back remained turned to the young camper. "Why here? I don't even know my power yet. Does it have something to do with imagining? Like I'm making up everything I say?"

Henry was silent. Lucas couldn't see his expression. He only felt something he could not describe. Not with words, but what it was could best be categorized as the way cold water feels when it's breezy in the day.

"Be sure to get plenty of rest," Henry said, cheerfully. "After today, there is no turning back. I look forward to seeing your ability manifest itself."

The Camp Director was gone before Lucas could even ask about the part of no turning back.

Lucas gave the cabin a quick scan, seeing that it appeared it could house no more than one or two kids at a time. There was nothing distinguishable about it except for wood that appeared to be as old as the tall trees in the forest.

Making this observation, the young camper climbed the small steps towards the cabin's front door and opened it cautiously.

I'm sure he assigned me here with the best of intentions, Lucas thought, encouragingly.

When he opened the door and began to survey the inside of the cabin, he was disappointed to find how plain it looked compared to the other cabin that Henry described.

Well, at least I can't say it looks anything out of the ordinary in here.

To the right was the kitchen, which was small, consisting of only a sink and a not-so-big refrigerator. To the left was the bathroom and to the very front was the television set that looked old, with a wide yellow old couch that could seat up to three people. To the far left and right of that part of the cabin were the individual bunks for five cabin mates. Because of the dimness in the main part of the cabin (and the lack of windows), the only light that came from within was from the television screen.

Lucas spotted a person slouching on the couch with an opened bag of potato chips on his chest. When he noticed a visitor, the boy got up and dropped them on to the floor.

Lucas's cabin mate was a tall boy, slightly taller than him, with medium sized dark brown hair, dark hazel eyes, and light medium skin. He wore a dirty old maroon shirt that said, 'Mind over Matter', and purple shorts. He also wore sandals, had a soda can in one hand, and the TV remote in the other.

He looks like he's been here for a while now. I didn't see him out there with everyone else.

"Hi there, you must be my new cabin mate," the older camper said. "My name is Bill Cooper. We'll be spending a lot of time in each other's company, so remember my name." He said the last part with smugness in his tone.

Bill put down the soda and extended his hand for Lucas to shake but the young camper didn't.

After a few seconds, Bill withdrew his hand awkwardly and wiped his fingertips on his shirt.

"Can you talk at least?" Bill asked with a confused expression. "Don't tell me you're mute. Well, if you were you couldn't tell me anyways because you wouldn't be able to talk. Duh."

He talks too much. Why did I have to get a cabin mate that talks too much?

"My name is Lucas Fargo," the young camper responded irritably. Bill nodded approvingly and smirked.

"Oh good you can speak and in English," Bill noted. "Well, Lucas Fargo, do you know more or less what you're expected to do here in camp?"

Lucas shook his head and the older camper looked annoyed.

"Okay then, here's how it works, pay attention because I am only going to say this once; you are what Henry calls an Alter Child. Alter like alternate. You have to be one in order to enter the campgrounds. You will be assigned a Camp Counselor, who will help in training you to control your abilities, whatever they are, and...how old are you?" Lucas had been paying attention up until the point where Bill mentioned the word 'alter' a second time.

I knew the part about being trained by a Camp Counselor, but what's this about being an Alter Child?

Lucas stood there in silence until Bill repeated his question.

"How old are you?"

"I'm thirteen."

Bill scoffed and threw his arms up as if in exhaustion.

"This is rich. You sure don't look it in any case. You're small for someone your age," Bill said bluntly. "I'm sixteen years old. This is my fourth and last year of training here as a camper. By next year, I'll be a Camp Counselor like Daniel."

Lucas nodded and tried to keep to himself as much as possible.

I hate talking to people who love to talk. I wish I could hear music right now.

After about a minute of silence between the two, Bill sat back on the couch and resumed what he had been doing before Lucas entered the cabin.

"Do you know your power? I'm guessing you don't since you looked lost during the whole conversation we just had."

Lucas shook his head while Bill flipped through the TV channels.

"My disability is I'm color blind. I've been told that grass is red and that stop signs are green. Also that oranges yellow. Is that normal?"

Lucas looked shocked by the last one, until Bill stifled a chuckle.

"I'm messing with you, dude. I know oranges are not yellow, but I've seen apples that look red and green. I could be wrong about those though."

There are apples that are green and red, Lucas wanted to say. Before he could think to, Bill continued.

"You're probably wondering what my power is. It's related to colors and it's really cool. Let me show you what I can do."

He rose from the couch and stared at it long enough that it turned from yellow to green.

Whoa! What was that? He just changed that couches color. That green isn't solid though. It has bits of red in it like polka dots.

Lucas looked amazed and Bill grinned with pride as he switched it back to its original color.

"I can change anything into the shades of color that I see. And if you think that's impressive, get me a bag of popcorn so I can show you my latest ability from last summer."

Lucas went to the cabinets and found them empty. As he was about to tell Bill, a bag of popcorn appeared out of nowhere.

"That happens a lot here," Bill noted when he noticed Lucas's surprised expression. "It's one of the many reasons this cabin is my favorite. That and the bunks, which you'll see soon if you stick around here long enough. Each cabin has their own unique trait based on their name. Ours has the word 'imaginary' so you can imagine anything you want. Don't try to imagine a person though. I tried imagining an actress I like once, and it was weird."

Lucas grabbed the bag of popcorn and handed it to Bill. Bill held it up and stared at it the same way as he had the couch. Only this time a small concentrated beam came out of his eyes towards the popcorn and it started popping inside as if there were firecrackers dancing within. After a few more seconds, the popcorn was ready. He handed it to Lucas, who found out the hard way how hot it was.

"OUCH!" Lucas yelped and dropped the popcorn as Bill laughed. "That was a mean trick!" the young camper bellowed out as he clasped his burnt fingers.

Bill shrugged and picked up the popcorn from the coolest side.

"You fell for it. Also it's not a trick. This isn't magic camp. Rule number one: expect the unexpected."

Lucas frowned and, after setting his backpack to the side, sat next to his older cabin mate on the couch. He brushed aside pieces of potato chips as Bill continued to flip through the channels mindlessly.

"What are you going to watch?" Lucas asked with interest.

"Whatever looks good. There's not a lot of channels here and no adult programs which is a real bummer for me. Just a bunch of re-runs and some music channels. It's all old music from the 90's downwards."

Lucas didn't mind since he never saw much television.

The only television I ever saw was whatever Shelly watched. She liked old movies, sometimes teen dramas, and this one show that never ended about doctors in a hospital. I couldn't understand the appeal of it. She's seen every season it has so far, and I couldn't even sit through one episode before falling asleep.

"What kind of movies do you like?" Bill asked his younger cabin mate.

Lucas shrugged and clasped his hands together.

"I don't really watch anything."

It's not that I don't like to watch movies; I just can't see a movie that is longer than maybe an hour before I start getting bored with it. I can only see long movies with someone and the only times I saw anything long was with Shelly.

"I like all kinds of movies," Bill said, ignoring his comment. "Mainstream movies are cool, but low-budget films are where it's at for me. I'm into the classics like Evil Dead, Texas Chainsaw Massacre, and Poltergeist. Do you know those movies?"

He talks more than the voices I used to hear in my head.

"You know, I'm a good judge of character, and you, my new friend, seem like a chill kind of guy. As long as you don't walk in your sleep we'll get along just fine."

Bill's manner of speaking began to cast doubt in Lucas's mind.

I don't know if to take him seriously or think he's a joke for thinking he's as important as he probably feels. I can't imagine being friends with someone like him.

As Bill flipped through channels, Lucas was preparing to make his exit from the conversation.

"Can I call you, Luke?"

Lucas shook his head.

"No."

Bill frowned and looked disappointed.

"Shame, well do you want me to make up a nickname for you?"

When Lucas didn't respond, he was unceremoniously given his nickname.

"Then Luke it is," Bill decided.

Lucas nodded irritably.

"Sure, whatever."

The older camper laughed to himself.

Bill was changing the channels again when Lucas looked at the remote in his hand and noticed how they had small little words etched on each side of the device.

Circle for Off. Triangle for On. Rectangle for Mute. Square for Menu. Arrows up and down Channel's left side. Arrows up and down Volume right side.

The remote itself was a medium sized rectangle device with tape over the bottom where the batteries were.

It looks old and worn out, Lucas noted. *Like someone dropped it a couple of times.*

He wondered how Bill saw the remote, because to him the colors were red, green, yellow, orange, blue, and purple for each button.

When the commercials came on, Bill rose from the couch.

"I'm going to get myself a soda. Do you want one, Luke?" Bill asked him.

Lucas nodded while Bill walked into the kitchen.

"What's this Relic game?" Lucas asked, curiously. "How does it work?"

Bill grinned as he walked back with the sodas in hand. When he threw one to Lucas, the young camper caught it like a baseball. Before answering, Bill took a long sip from his soda.

"How do I put this... you ever play video games like multiplayer shooter games?" Bill asked, smacking his lips after another sip.

Lucas nodded while Bill snickered and shook his head.

"Well, they are not the same thing," Bill chuckled.

So why even ask or mention it?

"But the idea is there, let me explain." Finishing his drink, the older camper let out a burp and continued. "You're going to be split into two teams: Yellow vs. Orange. Your placement is based on your cabin. For example, Atlas's Agony will be yellow, Blunt Bear orange and so on down the row of cabins. Now, both teams are comprised of first year campers like yourself and most of the time yellow team has had the bad luck of losing. You following me? Each team will receive the relic which will be two orbs, one for each team. Both teams are going to try and charge up their orb, with one camper being what we call the orb wielder. Their job will be to hold the orb and only they can hold it. If it falls or if someone else touches it before it finishes charging, automatic fail. How the orb will get charged will be within the Infinite Forest. There's a light that makes it the brightest part of the forest. The orb guides the wielder to it. Charging takes about five to ten minutes depending on how protected the orb was and the strength of the person wielding it. Meanwhile, everyone else will have different jobs. Besides the orb wielder, there needs to be a runner to carry the charged orb. There's offensive and defensive. Offensive's job is to act as tanks and distract the enemy while defense will head up the center of the field. Like offensive, they'll protect the orb wielder and the runner. The runner's job will be to retrieve their respective orb once it's been charged and bring it to the center of the training field, which is where the game will start and end. Whoever does it first and with a fully charged orb, wins. Simple? Questions?"

Lucas heard the majority of the instructions, but was beginning to feel sleepy.

I should have asked Henry. He seems better at explaining things in short sentences. I got the point of it after he mentioned the first charge. The whole charging ahead thing.

"In short, you better figure out your power and fast. Otherwise, you'll be spending the whole summer in the hospital ward or be sent home in a body bag."

Lucas gulped hard at that last part.

Hospital Ward? Body Bag? Is this place like a minefield; one wrong step and I'm dead?

He was beginning to think the couch he sat on felt like the safest part of the camp.

"Wait a minute, we can actually *die* from this game?" Lucas asked in horror. "I thought it was just to figure out what each of our powers are?"

Bill laughed as if his new cabin mate had said the funniest joke in the world.

"What's so funny?" Lucas asked, irritably.

"Nothing. It's just that you first years get dumber every year. Of course you can die in a game where kids have supernatural abilities. It doesn't happen often though, so relax," Bill assured him.

That still doesn't mean it can't happen. Knowing my luck, I'll either die in agony, or die slowly. The point is, in this story, I die!

"Okay then, how do I discover my power so I can at least have a fighting chance?"

Bill shrugged.

"Usually you develop it before you come to camp. The whole point of the game is for you to show off your abilities to the counselors, not figure it out as you go. I don't know if you saw them. They were on the platform next to Henry. There's ten of them, but two are absent this summer for some reason," Bill mentioned as Lucas struggled to stay focused.

Bill's rapid changing of the channels made Lucas feel woozy.

I should probably take my pills after I get out of this. That'll calm me down a bit.

"How does it work to become a Camp Counselor?" Lucas asked since he wanted to know more about it.

"The way it works is like this: let's say you come here at the age of ten. Most of the younger kids you'll see here still have what is called latent abilities, meaning they won't be trained yet until they reach a certain age. Abilities don't usually fully manifest themselves until at least the age of twelve to thirteen. Imagine in this scenario you're ten and you begin training when you're twelve. Then, you'll have the choice to either become a counselor or there are other roles Henry can offer if you decide to stay on to help new campers. There isn't much else except the hospital ward, activities director, which right now only has the one position, and Camp Guardian. The Camp Guardian has been here since the beginning though so I don't see that position opening up anytime soon," Bill explained with a matter-of-factly tone. "He keeps the peace and makes sure that we don't' receive any surprise visits from outsiders. It also helps that the Camp Guardian is big and scary because there's a lot of kids here who would misuse their abilities if he wasn't here to keep an eye on them."

Lucas didn't find that last fact as surprising as Bill would think.

I believe that. It's just like in school except here everyone has some kind of power that, if used for the wrong reasons, would be really bad. I wonder how many kids here end up misusing their abilities both in camp and outside of it.

"Why do I want to be a counselor? Thank you for asking, Luke. Because I want to help others to manage their own abilities. It's a dangerous world out there for ordinary people, but for us even more so. Imagine a person who cannot handle sunlight and their power is to absorb its energy to become like a bomb."

The young camper's eyes widened, until Bill chuckled.

"That's just an example though. I don't know if that's really a thing. The point is this place is supposed to help us be well adjusted enough to function in the outside world. Think of Camp Supernatural as both a training ground and social skill builder."

Lucas considered that, but decided not to pursue that topic further. The next question that came to the young camper's mind was regarding Daniel and Henry's relation.

"Why does Daniel, I mean Counselor Harrison, have a different last name than Henry and yet they are father and son?"

Bill shrugged.

"Honestly... I don't know," Bill's tone sounded ashamed for not knowing the answer to that question.

Finally I asked him a question he didn't have an answer to.

"Daniel doesn't talk about personal stuff. As for Camp Director James, he's very old, very wise, and he built this place. Everything you see here, the cabins, the training field, his nice house, everything was from him. This place has stood the test of time for fifty years now and as long as Henry is around, it always will."

Lucas was impressed by this bit of knowledge despite wanting to know more.

I mean, fifty years is a long time to have a place running. He's definitely old. Now my questions are: What does he do outside of camp? Does he have any other kids besides Daniel? Does he give every camper a personal tour the way he did for me?

Lucas wanted to know more about the Camp Director, but could sense that Bill didn't know much aside from what he already told him.

Maybe it's best to save those questions for later.

"Tell me about yourself, Luke," Bill questioned.

Lucas felt perplexed by this. Not so much by the question as much as why that question.

No one has ever asked me to tell them about myself.

"What do you want to know?" Lucas asked hesitantly.

"Where are you from? Do you have siblings? What do your parents do? Where do you go to school? What's your favorite food? Do you like pineapple on pizza? Let's start from there for now."

Lucas thought about this for a moment, considering the questions, but found that he did not want to answer all of them.

If I don't answer anything he might ask again later and I don't like to be asked the same question.

"I'm from Austin, Texas," Lucas began, "I have a sister. My dad is into advertisements and my mom works at a local clinic. I like spaghetti. I've never tried pineapple on pizza but I also don't care to. That's it."

Bill nodded but noted something Lucas had hoped he wouldn't catch.

"You didn't mention where you go to school. Is it because you got kicked out or what?"

Lucas wasn't sure if he was that obvious, or if Bill was taking a wild guess.

"Something like that," was all Lucas dared say.

Bill luckily, did not press for more.

"Alright, my turn. I'm from New Mexico. I have a sister also who happens to be here in camp. You might run into her soon. Her name is Vanessa. My dad sells cars and my mom sells jewelry online. My favorite food is chicken nuggets. Pineapple on pizza is alright but not something I'd eat every time. Some more information; I've been in this cabin since I started coming here at the tender age of twelve. I've had other cabin mates here before but they're not around anymore. It's a bit of a sore subject so maybe some other time I'll tell you about it."

Lucas nodded, understanding.

He thought about asking more questions, despite wanting to initially leave, until Bill looked at his watch, then back to Lucas.

"It's been nice chatting with you, but I think it's about time you get some rest," Bill noted as he made a bed out of the couch. Lucas looked at his phone and was perplexed by the time.

"It's only five in the afternoon?" he noted with puzzlement.

"Trust me, you're going to need the rest. The game alone take up most of the day, starting at eight in the morning and running into later in the day. Other times, it can last all day. Plus I need to discuss the battle strategy with yellow team, which is where you'll be."

Lucas heard himself yawn and decided to take Bill's word for it.

"Fine, so which one is my bunk?"

Bill pointed towards the one on the far left side of the TV room.

"They are imaginary bunks. Just think of any kind of room you want: a five star hotel room, one of those ship cruise rooms, first class, even a nice little beach house with the sun, water, and sand to go with it. Of course it's all fake, don't forget that part. With that in mind, try not making something too close to home because the last thing you want is to be homesick. Ultimately, it's your choice."

Lucas was hesitant to believe him, but after seeing what he could do and everything he saw in camp that day, he strangely believed every word he said.

On my first day of camp I met a talking skeleton, the Camp Guardian who looks too much like Frankenstein's Monster, the camp bully, an old but interesting Camp Director, and my cabin mate who can melt and change the color of things... I'd be an idiot not to believe it after I've seen it.

Before he could finally take his leave, Bill called out to the young camper.

"I get the feeling this is the first time in your life you've been on your own like this. The best thing I can say about this place is you're amongst likeminded people. We've all been where you are, so don't be embarrassed about anything because we're all in this together. Whatever you need, just let me know," Bill assured him. "For what it's worth, I really hope that we can continue to get to know each other, because I got a good feeling about you too."

Lucas nodded and entered his bunk.

Without giving it much thought, Lucas imagined his own room from home, despite Bill's warning. To his amazement, it was an exact replica of his room. He saw every small little detail starting with his unsteadied wooden floor, which he had ruined when he dropped his father's bowling ball at the age of nine.

I mistook it for a golf ball until I found out the huge difference between their sizes.

He saw a hole in his room's wall from when he used a hammer on it after seeing someone do that in a cartoon when he was six

I was seven actually. I got grounded for five months because of that. I never got the chance to get it fixed, or ask my parents to fix it. Not that they would have.

His favorite part of the room though was the ceiling fan, which was missing a blade he had removed when he was eight.

That's what I told everyone. What I never told anyone, even Shelly, was that I wanted to see if it would keep spinning without one of its blades. When I took off the one blade, I tried making it into a surf board. The surf board idea didn't work, but at least the fan still did.

The rest of his room was pretty small. His walls did not have posters covering them. He only had a lamp with no light bulb in it and shelves for things like his toys which were still in their boxes. When he tried to grab his superhero action figures, they went through his hand like water.

I can look but I can't touch. Hopefully the bed isn't that way.

To his joy, Lucas was happy when he threw himself on his small bed and did not go through it. Recalling Bill's warning, he did begin to feel homesick and missed Shelly dearly.

Oh great, I am starting to miss home, but I can't help it. I don't want a fancy place to be my room; I want my room. I wish Shell was here with me. I wonder how she would have handled half the stuff I went through today. This might sound crazy aloud, but I feel like I belong here. I may as well see what my abilities are and how I can control them. Hopefully they're something cool like super-strength or turning invisible. Invisibility would be cool since I like that one movie Shelly likes about the invisible guy.

In the silence of his bunk, Lucas's eyes went to his backpack on the floor and he quickly took out his pills. However, instead of taking them, he decided to put them back inside his backpack and try to sleep on his own.

I'll need to keep my head straight tomorrow and, if what Bill says is true, attached to my neck.

With that last thought, Lucas looked at the necklace his sister gave him and thought of both his home and Shelly in that instant. He could almost picture them while holding onto that image for the rest of the night...

Chapter 3

Relic

Early that fateful morning at around 8am, Lucas awoke to the sound of a trumpet playing. His head flew from his pillow as sweat poured down his disgruntled hair. He tried his best to comb it and make it straight, but it did no good.

I hate my hair. No matter how long or short it is, it will always be like, as Shelly once put it, a dog's wet fur after a bath.

Lucas put on a cap in an attempt to hide his messy bedhead. Bill discouraged him from wearing one and claimed it was unceremonious to have headwear during the game.

"Whoever said caps hurt anyone?" Lucas protested. "Golden rule on the battlefield and rule number two: Don't wear anything that can mess with your concentration. All you need is a shirt, shoes, and pants. Anything else is a liability. You have the option of using armor if you want, but odds are that will slow you down. It's up to you if you want to die slow or fast."

Lucas frowned despite understanding. He slipped on his most comfortable pair of clothing and his blue running sneakers. He didn't bother to take a shower, knowing he would be drenched in sweat and dirt by the time the game ended.

Hopefully just that and not blood. Not just that, and hopefully blood. Wait, what?

Hastily, Lucas followed Bill outside of the cabin and took in the early morning scenery. Even this early in the morning, the camp was very lively and the sun's rays made the campgrounds appear illuminated as if a thousand fireflies were frolicking like the campers.

It's so beautiful. I've never seen a morning that made me forget about sleep.

"What are you going to do while I go out there and get myself killed?" Lucas suddenly asked his older cabin mate.

Bill chuckled and patted him on the shoulder. "Since this is my last summer as a camper, I get to sit by the counselors and Camp Director James. Daniel is the coolest out of all the counselors, and not just because he's Henry's son."

Lucas still wondered about Daniel's last name, but decided not to bring up the question right now.

I'll ask Henry. Hopefully, he will give me a shorter answer.

Before the game could start, Bill showed Lucas around the camp, starting with the cabins.

"In this whole camp alone, the cabins encircle the center like an upside down U. The front is the entrance with the big sign, the center is where the pavilion is, and where everyone gathers when Henry makes announcements. Over there to the left of Atlas's Agony is the hospital ward. It's always full and busy, especially after the games. Hopefully you won't have to know what that's like in your time here."

Lucas gulped at the thought. Bill then pointed towards another nearby cabin.

"Next to the Majestic Meadow cabin is the cafeteria. Its small and the food isn't the best, but the ladies there are pleasant if you don't mind most being divorced middle-aged women." Lucas grinned at that before realizing something vital.

He's not kidding.

"Not sure if you've seen the forge over there. It has a sort of medieval rustic charm to it," Bill noted. "The campers in Atlas's Agony and Xiomara's Axe are usually the only ones who go there. Even though it's open for anyone to use, it's just that mainly the campers in those cabins are known to be weapon specialists and enthusiasts."

Why do those two words sound bad together like that? Specialist and enthusiast. I don't even know if Bill caught that or cares to.

The last building Bill directed him to was the camp gift shop.

"Maybe if you survive today's game, you can go there and get yourself a free shirt. It's part of the promotions going on right now for the fiftieth anniversary of Camp Supernatural," Bill noted, though his tone suggested he didn't expect Lucas to come out of the game unscathed.

When they neared the training field, his older cabin mate pointed towards it. To Lucas's surprise, it was bigger than a football field, complete with a running track and training equipment laid out on the center of the field for anyone to use. This included blunt swords, wooden shields, and padding gear that looked like used hockey pads. There were bleachers that looked weathered but still durable. The campers who weren't participating in the game were already seated there along with some of the Camp Counselors. Lucas couldn't see Henry anywhere amongst them.

"This is where campers can practice their abilities. It's mostly full during the day and, unlike the rest of the things in camp, there is no curfew for training. The swords have no edges so you won't get cut by them, but they'll still hurt if you slap someone with them. The weapons are more for show than brute force. Depending on your ability, you might not need to worry about knowing how to use a weapon."

Bill pointed his finger above the field, where Lucas spotted the forest.

"That's where the competition will take place. You'll only be in the outskirts of the Infinite Forest. Beyond that is forbidden, even for counselors. Going there guarantees you won't be allowed back into camp, or worse. Also very important: you are never, and I mean ever, supposed to use your abilities on anyone, a camper, a counselor, no one, even if it's for fun, unless it's part of training or the Relic game. I'm sure it was mentioned in the announcements. Even so, I want to emphasis softly; DON'T DO IT!"

The warnings were plain enough, Lucas did not need to hear it twice. Nonetheless, Bill repeated it before changing the subject.

"Finally, those small house-like-tents right behind the cabins are where you will meet with your counselor to begin training. The way training works is you'll start to use your abilities which in turn will help you with learning how to master them. Suppressed abilities are like disabilities that are not treated properly; they can lead to bad things happening. Now, do you have questions for me?"

That was a sudden shift in tone, Lucas noted. *I've got only a few questions: Is everyone in this place insane? Do you ever get tired of hearing your own voice? And, is it too late for me to get out of this crazy place?*

Abruptly, Bill did not wait for an answer. He started to walk off while Lucas had to swallow his questions and catch up with him. They made their way to the where the game was going to begin near the forest. The girl who spoke to Henry the other day spotted the two campers approaching and waved at them. Lucas blinked and before he knew it, she was standing in front of them.

"Hey Bill, are you leading the yellow team this year?"

Bill shook his head. "No, this year I'll be observing you all, but you're in good hands with Josh," he said with a confident grin. "Have you met Lucas yet? He's my first unofficial cabin mate in the Imaginarium Illusion. If he survives the game, he'll be official."

Unofficial? Why wouldn't I survive this game? I wouldn't survive this game why?

Ashley turned to Lucas and nodded in recognition. "I saw you yesterday with Camp Director James," she recalled with a smile. "It's nice to meet you, Lucas. I'm Ashley." She extended her hand and he shook it meekly.

Bill frowned and looked offended by the handshake. "Was that so hard? How come you didn't shake my hand?"

Lucas shrugged feebly. "You had crumbs all over your hand from the potato chips," he reminded Bill plainly.

Why did I say that? Do I want more people to hate me?

In response, Ashley giggled and Bill grimaced, but ultimately agreed.

"I'm guessing this is your first summer here like me?" Ashley asked Lucas.

Lucas nodded bashfully, as he clasped his hands and turned away from Ashley.

"Yeah, is it that obvious?" he muttered.

Bill dismissed himself, giving the two campers a knowing look.

"I will let you two get acquainted. Luke doesn't know his abilities yet so help him out, Ashley. Just make sure he doesn't get killed out there. I'd hate to have the cabin to myself, at least until Henry puts in the next few campers coming up," Bill said, with a hint of sarcasm. Lucas frowned at the last part.

Yeah, I can't say I'd miss you either if I had the choice. Maybe depending on how I do today, I can move to a different cabin.

Ashley nodded as the older camper walked off to meet up with the yellow team.

From what Lucas could tell, the team consisted of kids his own age and three that were a few years younger.

Just as I feared; we are the rejects. I'm starting to see why this team often loses, Lucas thought irritably.

When they were alone, he asked Ashley about Bill.

73

"Do you and Bill know each other outside of camp? Also, is he always so chatty?"

Ashley nodded and let out a small laugh.

"Yes, and yeah, you could say that." He waited for her to continue, until she abruptly changed the subject. "Come on, let's go show you off to the rest of the team." Lucas nodded and followed her.

She looks even prettier than yesterday for some reason.

Ashley had her blonde hair tied back in a pony-tail and wore a yellow camp T-shirt with the words 'Weeping Willow' embroiled on it. She also wore purple shorts, and orange sneakers that looked worn out.

She looks like a jogger. I wonder if I'll see how fast she can run.

"So, what's your super power?" he asked almost too impulsively.

Ashley shook her head, appearing to disapprove of the question.

"They're not super-powers and you'll see during the game."

Lucas shrugged it off.

"If you say so."

He began fidgeting. His hands moved sideways and he had the urge to run in the opposite direction. To distract himself, Lucas looked around for yellow team.

"Where is the orange team?" Lucas asked Ashley.

"They're already on the other side of the forest preparing their defenses. You'll hear them soon. Trust me on that."

Defenses? What kind of game is Relic?

After a moment of silence between them, she asked Lucas, "By any chance have you met Bill's sister Vanessa?"

He shook his head while Ashley sighed with relief.

"That's good. She's something else, I swear."

He laughed and blurted out loud as if he meant for Bill himself to listen.

"If she's anything like Bill, she can't be that bad."

I hope she catches the sarcasm.

Ashley did not laugh or smile.

"Don't say I didn't warn you."

She pointed towards a black-haired girl, whose figure was slender with a straightened posture. Her olive skin was a darker shade than her brother's slightly lighter one. She wore a yellow shirt with the words 'Kruel Kingdom' in bold lettering and tied the bottom of her shirt into a knot. Lucas had to keep from looking there too much.

Looking at her, Lucas thought Vanessa looked even more beautiful than Ashley as she cracked her bones in many different positions.

My eyes are playing tricks on me, right? I am not really looking at someone that beautiful, am I?

After rubbing his eyes twice, he realized she was real.

He began to feel slightly annoyed by the sounds Vanessa's bones were making while each of her joints popped like bubble wrap. Ashley noticed his discomfort and nodded irritably.

"She does that often. Vanessa has scoliosis, but you wouldn't know that looking at her now. Since discovering her powers, she makes it known to everyone else."

Lucas rubbed his ears in irritation.

So I've heard.

"That must be exhausting."

Ashley nodded.

"For her ability, she can bend her bones to any form she wants and never break them. If you stay close to her for too long, you'll probably lose your hearing if you don't lose your mind first."

As Ashley spoke, Lucas's eyes remained fixated on Vanessa. He watched as she stretched her legs as if she meant to do the split. Her hair was so long that it covered her whole back down to her waist. When it blew to her face it fell in strands and made Bill's sister look even more exotic.

If this is a dream, I don't want to wake up yet. I've never wanted to talk to a girl more than I want to talk to her right now.

He stared at her dreamingly until Ashley waved her hand in front of his eyes.

"Hey listen, I need to check up on the rest of the team. By any chance do you have anything to snack on? Chips, sandwiches, anything like that?"

"Sure, yeah. They're in my bunk, right by—"

Ashley sped away faster than he could finish the sentence.

The side of my bed.

She reappeared with all the fiber bars Lucas had along with his chips and sodas. Ashley fumbled with some of them and ended up dropping some of the chips and one soda.

"Is it okay that I have these? I'm sorry, but I really need them for the game," Ashley spoke while trying to scoop up the chips and soda that fell.

Lucas nodded reluctantly and felt awkward about a girl being in his bunk without him there.

It's the same as her being in my room since technically it is my imaginary room.

When picking up the chips and soda didn't work, Ashley asked Lucas to pick them up for her and put them in her backpack. She then did the same with the fiber bars.

"Go ahead and meet the rest of the team. I'll check up on you in a bit after I get prepped. You may as well meet Bill's sister while you're at it. Good luck."

After she left him, Lucas walked over to Vanessa, who noticed him immediately.

"Hi. I'm Lucas, and I'm your brother's new cabin mate."

76

He tried not to sound so timid or obvious, but found himself sounding like a child trying to say his first words without stammering.

Why does she make me so nervous? Because she's a girl and I suck at talking to girls. What about Ashley? She's a girl and I just talked to her.

Vanessa smiled amiably at him and nodded.

"I heard about you. Bill told me he had a new cabin mate."

She scanned him from head to toe and smiled.

"He didn't mention that you're cute though."

Lucas couldn't stop himself from blushing at the compliment. He thought she was too pretty to even acknowledge his existence.

Girls like her would fit in perfectly at my school. Then again, if she did she'd never talk to me or acknowledge my existence.

"I'm single, by the way, in case, you know, you wanted to ask me out anytime," Vanessa added forwardly.

While the prospect intrigued him, Lucas ultimately shook his head.

"Tempting, but let's get to know each other first," Lucas said while avoiding eye contact with Bill's sister.

What am I saying? Is she messing with me or is she for real? I hope she doesn't get the wrong idea about me not looking her in the eyes.

Vanessa sighed, disappointingly.

"That's a shame. Is it because of my brother?"

That was the crack on the wall. As attractive as Vanessa appeared to Lucas, he knew she was not worth risking Bill's possible wrath.

Especially since her brother can melt my face off.

Falling for hard-to-get girls was a complication Lucas wanted to avoid during his first summer in camp.

To quote Shelly on how it works: 'Boys like it when girls play hard to get, girls hate it when guys try to play hard to get. It's an endless circle of stupidity that is older than men's inflated ego'. Why do only men have an ego? This feels one-sided.

He changed the subject abruptly and hid his displeasure.

"That's a neat trick. The whole breaking your bones. I wish I could do that."

No I don't!

Vanessa nodded and cracked her knuckles.

"I know. People seem to be annoyed by it, but it's actually really neat. It beats having to wear a stupid back brace."

"No, really, no," Lucas heard himself stammer, to Vanessa's amusement.

After a few seconds of silence, Lucas decided he desperately wanted to end the conversation he got himself into. His teeth clenched and his hands clasped themselves.

"Well, it was nice meeting you," he finally croaked.

Vanessa nodded with a friendly smile.

"Likewise. See you on the battlefield. I'd hate for you to die just as we were getting to know each other." She winked at him and he felt himself shudder as if a cold breeze blew itself against him.

Why did that sound similar to what her brother said? Either way, she's what I call an off-limits girl. I'm starting to see why Ashley tried to warn me about her, Lucas thought, drearily.

Since his eyes were still glued on Vanessa, he nearly bumped into the Camp Director. The elderly man saw him coming and managed to catch the young camper by the shoulders.

"Lucas, you seem to have been startled by something," Henry said calmly as the young camper tried not to seem nervous. "We are about ready to start the games. Are you prepared?"

Lucas leaned towards the Camp Director's ear.

"That girl over there scares me," Lucas whispered nervously.

Henry looked towards where he was pointing and saw Vanessa.

Don't look! So embarrassing!

The Camp Director smiled warmly and chuckled.

"Ah yes, young love is a blissful thing," Henry said, encouragingly.

Lucas sighed and rolled his eyes.

Why do old people have to say things like that?

"It's annoying. That's what it is," Lucas said drearily.

Henry patted his shoulder softly.

"Someday you may not mind it so much, Lucas. Learn to give new things a chance and smile even when there is no cause too. You may find that others will appreciate you for the effort," Henry advised him.

Before Lucas could think about the Camp Director's words long enough, Henry walked over to the where the attending Camp Counselors were standing in preparation for the game. Lucas eventually came across a boy who had the other team members huddled by him. What caught his attention was how the boy spoke with a monotone quality and used hand signals.

I can tell he's even more of a talker and show off than Bill.

In an instant, the boy noticed Lucas walking by them and approached him.

"Hey, you lost or something?" the boy asked with a concentrated pitch. He sounded like he was measuring each syllable carefully.

Lucas stared at the boy in confusion.

He sounds like he's reading off of a script or something.

Lucas noted his appearance as well. The obnoxious boy had long curly light auburn hair that appeared like flames in the early morning sunlight. He wore a green camp T-shirt that read in big bold letters, 'Camp Supernatural', along with plain shorts and black sneakers. His skin tone was peach colored with green eyes that seemed to match his temperamental hair.

Where do these guys keep coming from? Is everyone here weird and anti-social? The only normal one seems to be the Camp Director.

It took Lucas a minute to realize that he had been standing there in silence as the boy waited for an answer.

"I'm on this team," the young camper heard himself murmur.

After a moment, the boy threw his hand to his ear.

"What was that? My good ear is a little stuffy today. Mind repeating that a little louder," the boy teased while making mocking hand gestures.

The other team members nearby were giggling amongst each other while Lucas felt anger building up in him.

He's trying to piss me off. I know what this is; it's the same stupid stuff that people do to the new kids in school. Well, if he wants to play that game, before the actual game, then it's on.

"Are you deaf or something? I said I'm on this team!" Lucas shouted inside the boy's ear while enunciating each word.

The boy seemed unaffected by the sound being projected directly into his ear.

Okay, now that's weird, Lucas observed.

After a few seconds, the obnoxious boy nodded approvingly.

"Excellent, you've got spunk. I can tell," the boy said and with a grin. "Maybe we'll be friends."

Lucas doubted this very much.

The obnoxious boy handed him yellow wristbands, pointing to his own. Lucas noticed how everyone in front of him, including Ashley and Vanessa, had yellow wristbands as well. He also gave Lucas a yellow shirt that read 'Camp Supernatural'.

"My name is Josh in case you asked. Not sure if you did. Now you won't have to," Josh exclaimed like someone rehearsing for a play and moved his hands around as if secretly giving commands to someone.

He's a strange one. I shouted into his ear and he didn't flinch.

Lucas couldn't figure it out, but decided to shrug it off and slipped on the team t-shirt. He tossed aside his old shirt and didn't bother to pick it up after putting the new one on.

Anyways, I'll need to start wearing shirts for my cabin as per the camp fashion sense.

Suddenly, Ashley appeared out of nowhere. She tapped on Josh's shoulder until he turned to face her.

"Hey Josh, have you met Lucas yet?" Ashley asked him, using similar motions with her hands that Josh used previously.

Josh nodded.

"Yeah, he just yelled at my ear. Can you imagine how much it hurt? Well, I'm trying to since, you know, I'm deaf," Josh said with a rapid gesture and grin.

Lucas suddenly felt dumb.

I'm officially an idiot. That explains everything.

Ashley laughed and looked at Lucas with surprise.

"He didn't tell you? Of course not. Don't take it personally. Josh does that to everyone he meets the first time."

"What's with the yellow wristbands?" Lucas asked Ashley.

"It's in case they need to identify us. Orange team has something similar."

Before Lucas could ask further about that, Ashley turned her attention back to Josh.

"Are you guys ready? The game is about to begin in a few minutes. Bill already finished explaining the battle strategy to the others. I hope you can explain it just as well, Josh."

Josh nodded when he understood the last part.

"Sure, no problem. You can count on me to say Bill's strategy word for word," Josh responded sarcastically and tapped on both his ears with his index finger.

Lucas did not seem as amused by Josh's joke as Ashley.

She's probably familiar with his sense of humor, Lucas deduced. *I don't see anything funny about being deaf.*

"Do you know how the game Relic works, Lucas?" Ashley asked the young camper.

I know Bill explained it last night, but it was such a long explanation that I don't want to hear it all again, so I'll just say—

"Yes," Lucas said, with a not-so-convincing confirmation.

Leaving his group, Daniel made his way towards yellow team. Lucas noticed that the Camp Director's son was beginning to grow out faint stubbles after his fresh cut the previous day. He wore a purple camp shirt that read 'Camp Counselor' and he wore black jeans that looked new.

I once heard someone in middle school say when a person grows out their facial hair after a day, it means they can grow a beard in a week. I wonder if that's true. I still haven't hit that growth spurt yet, Lucas thought as he touched his hairless cheeks.

"We meet again, Lucas," Daniel said with a warm smile, though it was not as warm as his fathers. "Good luck in today's game. If you all prove yourselves, Henry might let me train you all for the summer."

Ashley looked at Lucas as if she found something he said fascinating.

Does it matter who trains us? Even if he is the Camp Director's son, that doesn't make him better than anyone else here.

Daniel turned to Ashley and looked at her knowingly.

"Watch yourself out there, Ash, and keep an eye on this one for me. My father seems particularly interested in him." Lucas noted the way Daniel said the last part.

Interested in me? Is that why he talked to me privately?

It didn't take long for Daniel to rejoin the other counselors on the benches near the field. He sat next to his father, with Lucas noting their demeanor.

They don't look comfortable being that close to each other.

Bill was among what looked like a group of older campers. Meanwhile, the Camp Guardian watched with complete attention towards Lucas and his team. Henry briefly whispered something in his ear, but the monster seemed indifferent about it. This made it hard for Lucas to know what had been said. After hearing Ashley tell the yellow team about what Daniel had said, Lucas realized that the campers held the Camp Director's son in high esteem.

Bill did say he's the coolest of the counselors. I wonder why though.

In a way, this made Lucas envy Daniel. It particularly nagged at him how everyone seemed to revere him.

I may be new, but I'm sure at some point, so was Daniel, Lucas thought in annoyance.

Just then, Henry rose from the benches and made his way towards a medium sized platform with a microphone in front of him. He began to tap on it with a finger and cleared his throat.

"Testing…Testing… can everyone hear me?" the Camp Director asked as he tapped on the microphone.

His voice boomed like the sounds of broken glass. Daniel rose to assist him and configured the microphone so that it gave his father a clearer sound.

"Thank you, Daniel." Henry's son resumed his spot with everyone else.

"Good morning, everyone. I trust you are all prepared for the game?"

A cry went up with all the campers screaming, "*YEAAAAAAAAAH*", like a battle cry. The same sound came from the other-side of the forest.

Ashley wasn't kidding when she said I was going to hear orange team. They must be close by for right now.

Henry glanced around the playing field at the yellow team.

"Excellent. It is time to begin with the instructional portion of the event. Orange team, if you can hear me, please give another shout."

Another cry went up as if the forest itself had just exploded.

Yes, they can hear you, and so can the rest of the world.

Henry pulled out a small set of flash cards and studied them as if he were preparing for a test.

I don't think he really needs those. Then again maybe he does?

"First rule: you will be divided into two teams: yellow vs. orange. I trust this has been done already?"

The campers nodded with the yellow team showing off their wristbands. Lucas was the only one who didn't do this, but quickly followed suite before anyone could tell him anything.

I wonder if orange team has orange wristbands or if it's just us?

Henry read the next set of rules.

"Second rule: you will have thirty minutes to ready your positions and to go over your battle strategies as a team.

Runners, you will flank the left, defensive will cover the center, and the offensive will accompany the right with three campers acting as defense for the one orb wielder. Once the orb is fully charged, the runners will take charge of their respective orbs and one camper, either defense or offense, will help to protect the runner."

Lucas tried to do that logic in his head.

At least I know I won't be a runner. I think I know who has that position in mind.

"In total, each team consists of ten campers. Remember your roles. If you are protecting the orb, you cannot let the orb fall, or allow anyone else to touch it until it is fully charged by the light. The orb will guide the wielder to this light."

Lucas looked amongst his teammates and began to wonder who could be the orb wielder.

Do they already know, or are they selected before the game starts?

"Third rule: you are allowed to use any form of weaponry and your abilities but only to incapacitate the opposing foe. You may not aim solely for killing. If I see that it is getting to dangerous, the Camp Guardian will intervene. I trust that will not be necessary."

The Camp Guardian looked bigger suddenly, like an inflatable man.

Either that or I am having an anxiety attack, because, I swear, he's at least a couple of inches bigger than he was before.

Despite his gruff and towering appearance, there was something almost sad about the Camp Guardian. Like he was hiding some tragic backstory that Lucas could only speculate.

I'm sure Henry has a good reason for wanting him here. I wonder what the Camp Guardian is exactly, Lucas pondered to himself. *I feel like he's either a zombie, like a mummy, or maybe he just hates bathing? Good thing he can't hear my thoughts.*

After flipping through the cards, Henry finally reached the last one.

"Final Rule: the goal in this game is to demonstrate everyone's abilities, both known and unknown. You will all be judged based on individual use of your powers, teamwork, and ultimately who emerges victorious. Pick your positions carefully and may the best team win."

The orange team howled like a pack of wolves, while the yellow team seemed less inclined to shout as loud. Lucas found himself standing alone as the rest of the team huddled together.

Just like in school; no one waits for anyone, Lucas thought in annoyance. Wanting to know the game plan, he joined his teammates as Josh contemplated something openly.

"I wonder if we can super glue or wrap the orb in duct tape," Josh muttered aloud. "Either way, I'm sure the other team is thinking the same thing."

Lucas looked around at his team carefully. They consisted of Josh, Ashley, Vanessa, and six others that he didn't know. One of them looked to be about thirteen with medium sized brown hair and a yellow 'Camp Supernatural' shirt. The other team member was a little girl with black hair, purple eyes, and a yellow shirt with the words 'Cathedral Cove' in bold lettering. Her most distinguishable physical feature was having bare feet.

Bear feet… those are some hairy feet for a girl, Lucas thought with a look of discomfort.

The third team member was a younger tall boy with short hair, a yellow camp shirt tank top that read 'Gloomy Gnome' on it, and was missing a finger on his left hand. Lucas thought he looked big for a kid his age.

And they say I look small for my age.

Another boy was dark-skinned with a yellow 'Camp

Supernatural' shirt and look of reservation. The fifth person's blonde hair was similar to Ashley's, but she was much younger in comparison and looked shy from the way she turned so fast from Lucas's glance. She wore a similar yellow shirt as Vanessa which read 'Kruel Kingdom.' The sixth and final person looked fairly muscular. His physique made the young camper feel intimidated, though he noted a feminine quality to this person.

He has long hair like a girl, and a body like a guy. He has a chest like a girl, and a face like a guy. Also I can't tell what cabin he's in because he just has a yellow shirt also that reads 'Camp Supernatural.'

Before Lucas could think more on it, Josh came up to him with a weapon and armor in hand. It was a small sword that looked more blunt than sharp.

I can whack someone unconsciously with this, but against a real sword, forget it, Lucas thought, irritably.

Lucas looked at the blunt sword in confusion until Josh pointed out, "Do you want to go in there with just your hands? Sorry, you don't look like you can fight."

Lucas looked at his deaf teammate in confusion until he explained further.

"You don't know your power. Ashley told me. So what you want to do is whack someone. Not hard, just knock out. Got it?" Josh signed and sounded aloud.

When Lucas grabbed the blunt sword, it fell off his hands despite not being nearly as heavy as a real blade. He tried to pick it up and was barely able to swing it without straining. Josh looked at him with a suppressed laugh.

"I guess we can forget about armor then," Josh emphasized, pointing to a crude excuse for an armor piece. It had bits of string holding up what looked like a breastplate.

That looks like it will come off when it's supposed to protect me.

"Do I get a shield to protect myself at least?" Lucas asked after setting the blunt sword down.

Ashley shook her head as she joined their conversation.

"Shield's slow you down. We're allowed one protector once the orb is charged. I'll need you with me for when that happens."

Lucas suddenly felt anxious, not understanding how he could help without knowing his power.

"You won't need to do much if the plan works," Ashley continued, seeming to sense Lucas's discomfort. "It's just in case there's trouble."

He began to imagine himself as being like a knight in shining armor and Ashley the damsel in distress. She seemed to sense this and shook her head.

"Just don't slow me down, alright?" The way she said this came off as a bit harsher than she had intended.

I get it; she wants to make a good impression for Henry and probably Daniel too. Compared to them, I'm nobody to her.

"Is anyone else getting weapons?" Lucas asked, as he looked around his team and noticed he was the only member being told to have one.

"No, don't worry about it. You'll be fine. Whatever she said," Josh absently said, as Ashley sighed.

"You don't need a weapon. Just follow whatever Josh tells you to do and you'll be fine. He has the battle strategy. He'll be protecting the orb wielder and you'll be with them until the last part of the game. Then you'll help me with the orb."

Alright, that doesn't sound so bad as defense and runner. Maybe Vanessa will be with me too.

As if reading his mind, those hopes were quickly dashed away by the next thing Ashley said.

"Vanessa will be with defense, along with Gary, Mike, Caroline, and Bruce."

Which one is Bruce? The big one or the other big one?

Since the games were unable to accommodate every camper at once, this meant that the rest of the campers not competing today would have to wait until the following days to participate on their own teams. However, this gave them an advantage to watch how the games were played, something Lucas had hoped for given his powerless status.

This will be what I like to call a trial and error run. Hopefully more one than the other.

As he saw the others preparing themselves through their abilities, all of which were physical ones, Lucas began to feel like the black sheep of the group. He seemed to be the only one who didn't know what his ability was.

Is it too late to head back home? Most likely. Maybe this is the worst part; the calm before the game. It could be the game isn't so bad.

Before he could help himself, his hands began to shake, from both anxiousness and, to his surprise, excitement?

That's not it. I didn't take my pills and now I'm going to feel the withdrawal that comes with it.

Lucas stuffed his hands into his pockets, clasping the insides of his jeans.

He watched as Henry handed the orb to the bear-footed girl. It looked like a plasma ball, with bits of what looked like streams of flickering lights coming on as soon as the girl touched it.

What does that thing do? Ask us what we had for breakfast?

He was so distracted by this thought that when turned left, he saw Ashley there in an instant and gasped.

"Please don't do that!" Lucas shouted louder than he had intended. As if barely realizing where she was herself, Ashley began to stumble, until he caught her by the shoulders.

"Thank you and sorry about that," she said, as Lucas helped her steady. "The downside to being so fast is that I have poor motor functions. I've fallen more times than I can count, but at least I have one less time now thanks to you."

Lucas looked away from her and tried to hide his small smile.

She complimented me. I think.

"You can let go of me now," Ashley said, bashfully. When Lucas realized his hands were still on her shoulders, he quickly retreated them and started to shake again.

"Are you nervous because of the game? It's okay if you are. We're all scared."

He wanted to tell her about his medication, but feared that would make him a liability to the game.

"It's just nerves," he said, trying to calm himself. "Who ended up being the orb wielder?"

"Her name is Sasha. She's the girl with bare feet. I don't know much about her personally, only that she keeps to herself and isn't quite as fast as me. There's a reason Henry chose her to be the orb wielder though."

"What's the reason?"

"The orb wielder has to be someone who has a strong constitution. From what Daniel told me, the orb wielder doesn't have to worry about fighting or anything. Their job is just to hold the orb while everyone in their team defends them."

Wait, so it's the laziest job basically? Just hold a stupid light ball thing and let everyone else do the work for you? Is it too late for me to trade jobs?

"In Sasha's case, she can make a run for it if she has to. The only thing is she can't fight so she wouldn't be able to fend off orange team and Alexia. Do you know her?"

Lucas nodded and shuddered at the sound of her name.

"I had the unpleasant honor of meeting her yesterday."

Ashley chuckled and apologized.

"I'm sorry, it's just that Alexia has a reputation here. The kind that tends to scare people who first come here, but she's mostly bark and no bite in front of her friends. She won't try anything with the Camp Guardian around."

"Don't tell me she's in the orange team?"

Lucas waited for an answer. After about a minute, Ashley shrugged.

"You said not to tell you," Ashley pointed out.

"Yeah, she's on orange team."

Beep, because, you know, I don't like to curse. Alright, fine, I'll say it; fudge.

"We've got a good team. Josh knows what to do and Hailey too."

Who is Hailey?

Before he could ask, Josh moved in front of them, as if possessed. He went to the front of the forest while Lucas turned to see that Henry was speaking to Sasha in regards to her role as the orb wielder.

Does anyone else notice what Josh is doing?

Suddenly, Josh let out a small concentrated burst of sonic waves that hit a nearby bush.

Whoa, that is insane! How did he do that? Also why did he do that?

To Lucas's surprise, two kids, a boy and a girl, jumped out of the bush and staggered in pain as they walked out of their hiding spot. Lucas observed that both wore Camp Supernatural orange shirts. Josh chuckled softly.

"I don't need to hear to see where cheaters are," he boasted and opened his mouth as if he meant to use his ability again. "Go tell the others what you heard. Scram!" The last words he said were emphasized heavily in both his now hoarse tone and aggressive signing.

The two children whimpered in pain and ran off sobbing. They rubbed their ears in pain.

Now I'm scared of angering four people; The Camp Guardian, Alexia, Bill and Josh...

His thoughts were interrupted when Josh turned to him and his face suddenly reverted back to its regular carefree expression. He softly clasped his throat as if he were scratching an itch.

"Wasn't that cool?" he signed to Lucas enthusiastically. Josh's voice had become noticeably softer. "My ability annoys people, but not me. I am sound proof."

Josh tapped on his ears again with a finger and laughed. Lucas put on a fake grin, but continued to flap his hands behind his back. He knew if his hands weren't attached to his wrists, they would have flown away like birds a long time ago.

My hands are like a dog's tail; they show the world how anxious and nervous I am.

Josh scouted ahead to make sure no one else was around, while the defense team got together.

For a guy who's deaf, Josh sure gives hearing people a run for their money.

Lost in his thoughts, Lucas didn't notice Vanessa walk over to him.

"It's too bad we're not in the same group. I was hoping we could talk and get to know each other more."

Lucas began to blush and leaned in towards her ear. "If you were by my side, I would be more courageous than I feel," he whispered back, playfully. Vanessa giggled quietly at that. Ashley seemed to notice and gave the two of them a displeased look.

Did we just flirt? Was I flirting? I think she liked it.

"Come here, Lucas. I need to speak to you," Ashley told him, sharply.

He shook his head but she remained firm about it.

"I wasn't asking."

"Jeez, Ashley, you're such a buzzkill," Vanessa said with a frown.

Ashley pulled Lucas by the hand and ignored her comment.

When they were earshot away, she turned toward him with a firm authoritative look.

"You need to stay focused, Lucas. We need you to be here for this," she asserted.

Lucas nodded and tried to compose himself.

"I'm sorry, your right, Ashley. It's just that I don't know anything about this game. I'm not here because I want to be. I shouldn't even be here and I'm only here because..."

He stopped himself short of saying too much. Despite his fears, Ashley didn't push the issue further.

"Well, you're not with Vanessa so let her focus on her group. If she comes and talks to you again, just tell her to go away."

Is she seriously telling me that? Lucas questioned. *What is she jealous?*

"Why would I want to do that? She wants to talk to me and I could use the distraction. It's not like we have a chance of winning with Alexia in the orange team anyway. If I had known that..."

If I had known that I would have bailed out of here without a second thought, is what Lucas wanted to say.

Despite this, he didn't mean for what he said to come off as uncaring. Unfortunately, that's how Ashley took it and her response was like a raging wave.

"If you had known that, what? You would have bailed on us? Do you really think we're going to lose? Is that what you really think? Well, if it seems so hopeless then why don't you go on and get out of here. Better yet, join the orange team to keep yourself alive? After all, they have a more fighting chance than us. Are you really that scared of Alexia that you rather hide behind her than trust the campers on this team? I'm not just in this to win a spot in a cabin, Lucas; I'm here because I believe in this team and this camp. I was starting to think you might be a nice guy, but you're just like most guys; a coward!"

This freaked Lucas out to the point where he was shaking in embarrassment. He had only known Ashley for a short while and though they talked well before, it was like speaking to someone completely different based on her reaction.

I deserved that. I should have kept my doubts to myself, Lucas thought, regretfully.

Josh had just finished surveying the area when he noticed Ashley's angered expression. Lucas tried to avoid looking her in the eyes as she waited for his response. He finally relented and owned up to it.

"I'm sorry," said Lucas, sincerely. "I didn't mean to sound like a total jerk just now. Honestly, the only thing that's keeping me from losing my head is the thought that maybe, big maybe, I can get out of this without being killed or injured."

Ashley sighed and calmed herself down.

"I'm sorry too, Lucas. I didn't mean to get so upset just now. We're a team and we'll help each other through this," Ashley assured him. "Don't think of this game as the first and only time you'll be in a situation like this; that's what this camp is preparing us for. Our powers can either work for us or they can break us. Remember our camp motto: control it, so it doesn't control you."

Lucas nodded, suddenly feeling better than he expected.

She's right. This isn't just a game; it's preparing me for what's to come. I've never been alone because I've always had Shelly there to help me. She got me through all those times I was kicked out of schools and all the times mom and dad were mean to me. But she's not here and all I have to rely on is myself and this team who could become the allies I need to get through this summer. If I can avoid Alexia and her goons first.

"I'll believe in us," Lucas said with affirmation. Ashley seemed very pleased with this response and looked like she wanted to hug him. This was cut short by Josh signaling their time was almost up.

"You'll get through this, Lucas. Do your best out there, stick closely to Josh, Sasha and Hailey. Most of all though; have fun," said Ashley with a smile. "And don't stress about Alexia; she doesn't kill people. At best, she just maims them."

She then sprinted towards the left side of the Infinite Forest. Lucas fixated on one thing she had said.

Alexia maims people but doesn't kill them? How is that better?!

He walked over to his group and saw their positions. Josh was in front of Sasha, the muscular guy was behind her, so Lucas decided to take a vacant side.

She's holding the orb to the left, so maybe I should to go the right since I wouldn't want to get in her way, Lucas noted.

After taking position to the orb wielders right, Lucas tried to greet Sasha. The girl looked calm, though her eyes betrayed her demeanor.

"Hello, I'm Lucas. I'll be protecting you," he stammered.

Why did I sound like that?

Sasha regarded him with a blank expression, nodded softly, then looked forward.

Strong silent type, got it.

When he didn't feel he'd get anything out of her, Lucas tried to get Josh's attention.

Josh wasn't looking in Lucas's direction, which made Lucas poke Josh's shoulder until he looked at him.

"I was thinking, I can run offense as well as any guy can, but maybe I can hold the orb for a little bit?"

Unfortunately, he did not get the response he wanted. "Stop thinking about Ashley, Lover Boy. She can take care of herself," Josh murmured, turning his attention back to the front.

That's not even close to what I asked.

"You can't hold the orb," Sasha said suddenly, her voice was like a soft wave that barely made a sound when it hit landfall. "Once someone has been assigned orb wielder, only that person can hold it until it charges. Right now, I can feel its hunger. It's… almost alive."

Lucas started wanting to back away from the orb wielder.

I liked her better when she was the strong silent type.

As the countdown commenced, Lucas caught sight of a cliff that overlooked the camp. He noticed how it stood directly above the training field. It gave him a cold and eerie feeling as he stared from point A: the top, to point B: the bottom. He didn't know if it was a trick of the eye, but Lucas thought he saw someone on the cliff.

Lucas cupped his hands to his eyes, but the rays of the morning sun rising blurred his vision.

That's odd. I could have sworn that was a person...

He was forced to brush off the brief distraction as the countdown reached its end.

"3...2...1 ... GO!"

Lucas expected a stampede; the rustling sounds of many footsteps. In contrast, it was quiet and that made it somehow worse.

Did the game start? Did I miss the part where everyone was about to kill each other?

He was so deep in his thoughts, he didn't notice Josh, Sasha, and the muscular person walking ahead of him.

"Hey, New Guy, over here!" Josh shouted softly in annoyance.

When Lucas leveled with his team, Josh pointed to the side where he had previously been. "You be my ears, only you'll have to be both because I can't hear nothing!" Josh exclaimed.

Lucas nodded and decided not to argue against him.

It's just odd to me how he makes what he has seem like a joke instead of taking it seriously.

Lucas looked around to see if anyone else was around them. The forest was dark, with a lot of shades obscuring the trees around them. Any signs of light were scarce, but it was still bright enough to see his teammates nearby. The trees heavy leaves covered the skies and sun like umbrellas. He looked at the orb wielder, who looked almost like she was in a trance as she held the orb in her hands.

"So you said that thing is alive?" Lucas asked Sasha. "Do you mean it's alive like an animal, or like some kind of egg with a chicken in it?"

Josh noticed the young camper talking and beckoned for him to stop.

"Don't distract the orb wielder. She needs to focus on where it is leading her. If we're lucky, orange team will be too busy dealing with everyone else and ignore us," Josh said breathlessly and steadied each word. He spoke like someone who had to carefully measure their tone and each word that went with it.

This suddenly made Lucas think of another question.

"What about the other team? Shouldn't we try to, I don't know, stop their orb wielder from finding the light before we do?"

"Our defense team will take care of that," the muscular guy spoke. His voice was feminine, which caught Lucas off guard. "We just need to worry about protecting Sasha from any enemy that comes our way."

If she's a girl, she's not very pretty. If she's a guy, he's not very handsome. I am very confused right now.

They walked in the left direction for a while, before Sasha indicated for them to go straight ahead. All of a sudden, Josh stopped and motioned for everyone to do the same. Lucas noticed how he observed everything around them, taking glances in every direction more than once, as if he were memorizing the playing field.

Since he's deaf, he's got to make the best out of his other senses; his sight being his main one. I think he knows what he's doing, Lucas observed. *Scratch that, I hope he knows what he's doing.*

"Okay, everyone, huddle up, so that I can discuss Bill's strategy, word for word," Josh signed and enunciated with a hint of sarcasm in a low voice. "While the other teammates keep the majority of orange team busy, our job is to secure a good spot of light for the orb. Once that's done, Ashley will meet up and take the orb along with Luke here. What I lack in hearing I make up for in a good sense of direction. Something important Bill emphasized is the idea isn't just to use the light source that the orb wielder's light will show; it's to find other sources since orange team will be tracking their own light too."

Lucas was confused by some of the things Josh said, both because some of his words were hard to hear in his low voice and because he did not understand sign language.

A lot of what I just heard I put together as best I could, Lucas told himself.

"Bill said not to trust every light source because the forest will play tricks. The orb wants the light, so it will lead us to a source. We just need the right one."

Lucas began to understand more than just the purpose of the game.

Following the orb completely isn't the way to win? It's by using deduction, our senses, and even abilities? I'm starting to understand not just what this game is about, but maybe even the camp itself.

"Going forward, my voice will be low to preserve it. My abilities rely on the vibrations I can emit using my voice, so if I step on something sharp, there's the warning. Just keep your ears open and you'll hear instructions. For now, let's head in the opposite direction the orb is advising. That happens to be where Luke is."

Bill probably told him to call me that, Lucas thought in annoyance.

As the group began to walk in his direction, everyone remained silent. The silence was beginning to drive him crazy, so Lucas tried to think of numerous things to make his head sound loud.

This orb. It's a ball. It's got light inside. I wonder if it comes with batteries. Is there a secret to how else it works? Why an orb? Who else thinks it's weird that it feels alive?

Lucas didn't remember being shoved to the ground. When he came to, he saw Josh in a similar position. Sasha was lying on her back, with the orb nesting on her chest.

"Glad you could join us," Josh signed with a whisper.

That was a different kind of blackout then before.

Josh did his best to sound as quiet as possible and relied mainly on his hands for both signals and certain word choices. "There's a patrol here. At least two of them. Probably the weak ones who don't know their powers yet."

Like me basically.

Josh made hand signals, which the others seemed to understand except Lucas.

It looks like he's playing charades instead of leading a battle plan.

"We need to take them out. Quietly."

"I'll do it, Josh," the muscular team member enthusiastically volunteered. "I'll make them regret being on the opposite team."

Lucas suddenly felt like an idiot.

I don't think I was paying attention before because now I realize that this must be Hailey, Ashley's friend.

In height, Hailey towered over the others. She physically appeared similar to Alexia but with more muscle.

She could probably give Alexia a run for her money in terms of strength, Lucas surmised.

"Give them a black eye for me, one on each eye, Hailey." Josh signed quietly. She nodded back in confidence.

All of a sudden, Hailey's skin changed from her peach toned skin into a metallic form.

WHAT! Metal skin! Seriously? Here I thought I was almost done seeing weird stuff.

"Hailey has the ability to transform her body into a metal form. It's a condition with a weird name." Josh struggled to sound it out and sign it. "It's called Vil...Viltango?"

"It's Vitiligo. I've got pigmentations on both my wrists, shoulders, and knuckles up to my fingertips," added Hailey, bashfully.

It became evident to Lucas that Hailey was more than fond of Josh based on the quick glances she shot his way.

She likes him, he realized, pitifully. *Either he recognizes this or chooses not to, because to me it's very obvious.*

Hailey tiptoed towards the two unsuspecting boys, with her heavy metal skin not making a sound as she crept closer to them.

Josh grabbed a rock and threw it close to the two orange team members. They turned to where the rock fell. Suddenly, Hailey took hold of both their heads and slammed them together with neither of them catching a glimpse of her. Their bodies crashed to the ground hard with their weapons clanking against each other.

After this, Josh clapped his hands in pride.

"I guess the old saying is true: The bigger they are the closer they fall!" Josh enthusiastically signed and remarked aloud.

In an instant, Hailey returned to her regular skin. When Lucas saw the unconscious children, he panicked.

"You didn't kill them, did you?" Lucas asked, fearfully.

Hailey shook her head.

"I only knocked them out. They will wake up soon with a massive headache," said Hailey, confidently.

He felt reassured.

It's just a game, or at least that is what I keep telling myself. It's just a game. Calm down, Lucas.

They changed directions again, this time on Hailey's side. As they continued onwards, the darkness around them made it hard to see if they were going the right way.

Shouldn't we be reaching the light by now?

Almost to his relief, he spotted two other campers from his team; Vanessa and the young boy with plain features. They ran to his group and explained what was happening to the defense team.

"Gary, Bruce and Caroline are holding off three members of the defense team, but we lost two of them," Vanessa told Josh. "Have you seen them?"

Josh pointed towards Hailey and explained how she dealt with them.

"Their heads are out of the game, much like Luke over there," he joked, to Lucas's annoyance.

"That's great, two less enemies to worry about then. Can I switch places with Iron Woman now?" Hailey looked annoyed by this comment and turned to look at Josh for confirmation.

"Whatever, fine. Hailey go help out with the defense and make sure those three orange team members stay right where they are. Mike, keep an eye on the enemy orb wielder and tell Ashley what you see when you find her."

Mike nodded and went off with Hailey. She shot an angry glare at Vanessa but kept to herself.

I'm betting she's thinking some serious angry thoughts right now.

"Together again," Vanessa suddenly said, causing Lucas anxiety. "How did you all manage without me?"

Say something clever. She liked that before.

"It was getting quiet with just the sounds of Josh barking orders."

Unlike his previous attempt, this one was met with more of an indifferent reaction from Vanessa.

Why am I so bad at talking to girls?

"Lead the way, Sasha," Vanessa said, walking ahead of Lucas.

Sasha was beginning to appear weaker, something that worried the Lucas.

"Is she supposed to look like that?" he asked Josh.

"The orb takes energy to use. Holding it takes energy to use."

"So why don't we help her? I know we can't touch it, but maybe we can share the load somehow?"

"Worry about making sure our sides are clear, alright?" Josh barked in annoyance.

He's definitely got a power trip going there.

They walked in the opposite direction of where the orb was leading until, without warning, Sasha turned forward.

"This isn't good," Josh noted, to Lucas's confusion. "Usually the orb points left or right, but never in front. We might be heading straight for the opposite team. Be on guard, both of you!"

Lucas nodded and looked at Vanessa, who seemed uninterested at the moment.

What happened to her flirty behavior before? Was it something I said?

It didn't take long for Josh's prediction to come true, though something was off about this patrol they encountered. It comprised of the two kids he spooked earlier and an additional camper. This camper wore an orange camp shirt which read 'Daredevil Delinquents.'

"They ARE cheating," he grumbled in a low whisper. "They have two more players. I knew something was off when I spotted them before the game started. If they're here, that means the orb wielder has a small group."

That sounds good. I mean, not the cheating part but the less people part.

The two kids were holding blunt swords much like the one Lucas previously had and wore bandages around their ears.

That's a bit much. It isn't like Josh used his full power on them. It was just enough to scare them away.

"Fine, they want to play dirty. I don't mind getting a little dirty myself," Josh angrily declared. He drew out a small little marble-sized ball from his left pocket.

It looks like some kind of grenade. Maybe a smoke bomb.

To his surprise, he was half right.

"Sticky situation guys. Stand clear," Josh cautioned his teammates.

He threw it in the middle of the three kids. Within a few seconds, it exploded and engulfed the orange team members in some form of rubber glue. It wrapped around their whole bodies like duct tape, head to toe, and left them immobilized. When they saw the yellow team members coming out of cover, they tried to scream for help, but the glue wrapped itself tightly on their mouths. Josh smiled triumphantly as he walked over to them.

"That was originally meant for their orb wielder, but I like this better," Josh boasted in a leveled tone rich with pride as he made funny faces to the cheaters. "Sticky grenades, courtesy of Mike."

Someone made that thing? At this point, I shouldn't piss anyone off in this camp.

As both Josh and Vanessa taunted the cheaters, Lucas decided to seize the moment himself.

"That's what you get for cheating you bunch of losers!" Lucas shouted triumphantly.

Josh noticed him having fun and grinned proudly.

"Very good, you're finally loosening up. Good to know you can have fun, Luke," Josh exclaimed, patting Lucas on the shoulder.

Lucas found himself smiling. He was beginning to get into the mood of the game.

I wonder if Henry can see me from here. He'd be proud since I am smiling, just like he said.

Even Sasha joined in, though she had to conserve her strength without yelling like the other three.

"Don't mess with the best," she exclaimed softly, before coughing. She managed to steady herself after staggering and cautioned the others from helping her. "No, don't touch me. We're almost there, I can feel it."

Her feet dug themselves into the ground, and Lucas could tell she was preparing to run.

Oh boy, here we go.

Vanessa quickly tied back her long hair, making the young camper blush even more.

She looks nicer that way.

In an instant, all four of them were running forward, passing through trees that were as tall as skyscrapers. The Infinite Forest went on for what felt like hours to Lucas. He tried his best to keep up, but began to stagger a bit himself.

I couldn't cut it as the orb wielder and I can barely cut it as an orb protector/runner.

Josh noticed Lucas wasn't keeping up, and threatened to use his power to motivate him.

"No thanks, I can go faster."

As they neared the edge of the forest, the orb began to vibrate. Sasha stopped suddenly and cautioned the other three to take cover. Not only did they spot the enemy orb wielder, they also spotted the other two campers that were there. One of them caught the attention of Lucas, as he felt himself shiver.

Alexia. Just when I hoped we wouldn't see her.

Her weapon of choice was a war hammer that looked more suited to the Camp Guardian than Alexia herself. Its solid blunt edge promised to be excruciatingly painful to the unfortunate soul who got hit by it.

It's a hammer... a big giant hammer! And I know it's not for hitting nails.

She was also covered in war paint, which Lucas thought was over the top.

What is it with the orange team and doing weird stuff like wrapping Band-Aids on their ears and now war paint?

Her curly brunette hair was tied back to show her broad face and stiff frown that made her look even more barbaric.

I don't see any way of doing this without her coming after one of us, or all of us. Even if their orb wielder can't do much of anything, there's still their runner to worry about.

Lucas tried to hear what they were talking about, but the runner was talking faster than a radio show host. Her lips moved rapidly and her body seemed to be doing an almost synchronous dance.

All I can get from her is, 'The orb's light isn't bright enough,' and 'This game is taking too long.'

Lucas looked at their orb wielder, who was a frail boy in comparison to Sasha, but something was off about him.

He looks like he's about to fall over. Maybe he's been holding that thing for longer than Sasha.

Sasha, despite putting on a strong front, was feeling weak as well. Because Lucas's could sense it, he began to feel even more anxious.

As if on the same wave length, Josh saw the three members they were up against, and went chalk white.

"Whoa. That over there is Alexia. The meanest fifteen year-old girl in camp," acknowledged Josh. "She's big, she's mean, and anything else you can think of, except nice and good, she is."

Lucas nodded and explained briefly how she would have beaten him at the camp entrance had it not been for Richardson's intervention.

"No such luck here. In Relic, it's fair game."

Fair game? As in, if I or anyone of us go up against her, we won't be coming back with all our pieces attached to us?

Josh took a few minutes to come up with a plan, but ultimately came up with nothing.

"It's only her, their orb wielder, and their runner. We have the upper hand. Between your loud scream and Vanessa's bone cracking, we can take them down." Lucas tried to sound encouraging, but once Josh understood everything he said, he made a *Tsk* sound.

"Alexia alone could be counted as all of orange team combined. She will wipe the floor with us before the big Camp guy can make his way here," Josh stressed, his hands doing a fearful signing. "I wish Ashley was here with us. She always knows what to do in stressful situations."

Just then, Ashley appeared out of nowhere. She almost lost her footing when she stopped running but Lucas caught her once more.

"Thanks again for that, Lucas," said Ashley gratefully. She looked towards Josh after composing herself. "You called me, Josh?"

He smiled and threw his hands upwards as if to thank an unseen deity. "Well I'll be deaf. If I had known you'd be here so fast I would have called you sooner. Perfect timing," Josh said gratefully in a faint whisper. "Now, not to put you on the spot, Luke. Do you have a
hidden ability that can make Alexia disappear or float away like a balloon?"

Lucas shrugged, causing Josh to sigh.

"Okay, so then Plan O, for only. Ashley, you surveyed the best path to take back the orb through and I know Mike filled you in on where to avoid the main action. So you're good to go. Here's what I will do: I'll distract Alexia while Sasha charges the orb. How close are we to the light?"

Sasha was about to speak, but found she couldn't. Instead, she pointed to the left of where Alexia and her group were. Even though Lucas couldn't see the light, she assured them that it was there.

Maybe it's something only the orb wielder can see.

"Vanessa, use your bone crunches to annoy everyone once Sasha finishes charging the orb. We don't want to accidentally cause her to faint, so wait until I give the signal. You'll know."

Vanessa nodded and softly cracked her knuckles.

Josh then turned to Lucas.

Great. I wonder what my suicide mission will be.

"Lucas, you're with Ashley once the orb is charged. I hope whatever your ability is it involves running very fast because if Alexia gets her hands on you, it won't matter if you can fly," Josh signed with a shrug at the end.

Lucas worked up a hopeful smile. He tried his best to be warm and reassuring like Henry, but he felt his hands shake and his body began to tighten at the thought of Alexia pummeling him like dough.

This isn't going to work.

Ashley patted Lucas's shoulder and smiled at him reassuringly.

"Stick with me and you'll be fine," she promised.

Lucas nodded, trying to calm himself while Josh spoke as if it would be his last words before dying.

"If this all works out, we'll live to tell the moment. I mean story. To tell a story. Good luck, Sasha. Thank you for being our orb wielder. I hope we can get to know each other more, Luke. You seem a good guy. Vanessa, if I die, I want you to be the last face I see, not Alexia."

Vanessa let out a soft chuckle, which made the young camper slightly irritated.

Is he flirting with her? After she flirted with me? Why do I care? I should be more concerned about getting out of this thing alive than who flirts with who. Who cares? Not me. Me who not cares.

"Don't worry, Josh, you'll have enough time to stare at my pretty face once you're out of here."

And great, she's flirting back with him.

Josh nodded and looked pleased with himself.

"They say everyone dies, it's inevitable, isn't it? But, anyways, let's just make this the day I don't die, because inevitable can wait," Josh softly proclaimed and signed with a heart on his chest.

I don't know if that's from a movie, but it sounds rehearsed.

Before leaving, Josh pulled something from his pocket and slipped it into Sasha's right pocket.

What did he give her?

After that, he threw his hands behind his head and began walking towards the orange team members. The runner pulled a dagger from her back and Alexia readied her weapon in his direction.

They look serious. Be careful, Josh.

Up close and personal, Alexia's war hammer was very real, right down to the steel. It had a heavy metal head of pure iron. If swung correctly, it could send the person flying backwards or possibly kill them upon impact.

I'm guessing the last thing on Alexia's mind is to play baseball with her teammates. More like golf, maybe.

Alexia growled at Josh like a lion when she noticed him approaching.

"What is this? Is the deaf one lost or something?" Alexia asked, angrily.

She gnashed her teeth at the sight of him as if she meant to chew him up.

She probably could. All he needs to do is distract her, not piss her off.

Lucas began to look around to see if the Camp Guardian was watching nearby in case it was necessary.

Josh went into this knowing he might have to sacrifice himself. What is he trying to do? He's not the main character of this story.

Josh put on a bold smile and waved a hand towards the hostile foe.

"Nice to see you too, Alexia. Tell me, how's that bruise?"

Alexia's eyebrow went up as she walked towards him.

"What bruise?" the camp bully asked, hoarsely.

To everyone's shock, he walked up to Alexia and, with his right hand, sucker punched her cheek so hard that she staggered about an inch away from him. Lucas and the others gaped in horror as the Camp Bully's right cheek turned bright red. Josh was sweating anxiously with his heart beating fast.

He is so dead, Lucas thought, drearily.

The runner quickly grabbed Josh by the arms. Despite grunting, he did not put up a struggle.

Why doesn't he use his power? Lucas wondered. *Do they know what he can do? Maybe he's waiting for the right moment.*

The moment didn't last. Once Alexia regained herself, fresh tears glistened in her eyes, as she began to glare menacingly at Josh. The side of her cheek looked like it was going to swell up.

Josh is not as weak as he looks, Lucas admired.

After wiping the tears from her eyes, she angrily swung hard with her right knee and struck Josh hard on the stomach. He coughed out in pain and fell to his knees. She took a firm hold of her war hammer and leveled it towards Josh.

"I will kill you for that, Deaf Boy," Alexia snarled loathingly

Josh wasn't looking at her face, so he couldn't see what she was saying. His face almost kissed the ground. Meanwhile, Sasha began to walk forward on her own, as if possessed, with Ashley and Lucas preparing to follow her.

I don't like this plan, not if it means Josh has to die just for us to win some stupid game. Come on, do something already!

The spot where Sasha claimed the light was in was closer than Lucas thought. It was far enough away that, somehow, ended up becoming the most convenient spot. The bare-foot girl pulled from her right pocket two little ear plugs and jammed them into her ears.

That's what Josh gave her? Are they to help her concentrate?

After this, Sasha lifted the orb up and it began to glow as yellow as egg yolk. Ashley looked like she was preparing herself mentally for a jog, while Lucas looked at Josh with concern.

"How long is this going to take?" Lucas asked Ashley.

"It can take as long as five minutes, ten minutes, less if Sasha has complete and total concentration."

Something tells me that isn't going to happen the way we hope.

"How would you like to die, as whole or smashed to bits?" Lucas heard Alexia ask Josh.

Josh did not understand what she said, but closed his eyes and stiffened backwards.

"Not the face," was the only plea he could come up with without knowing the threat.

Alexia smiled triumphantly and raised the weapon upwards.

"Smashed to bits it is. Starting with that face of yours!"

Before she could deliver the killing blow, Josh took a deep breath. Lucas could hear his own heart beating almost in synchronous with Josh's. The way both their hearts beat was like the way Ashley's feet were tapping the ground and the emission the orb was giving off as it continued to absorb the invisible light.

Bump bump...bump bump...bump bump... Can it be? It can be.

When it was dead silence, Ashley quickly pulled out two pairs of ear plugs and instructed Lucas to put them on. He did so fast and would soon be glad he did.

Suddenly, as if a gust of wind had blown in from the Caribbean, Josh let out a loud scream and the sonic shriek made his first one seem like a burp in comparison. The sonic wave he emitted sent Alexia flying away, along with the orange team's orb wielder, who was still holding the orb. The only one remaining was the orange team's runner, who prepared to run after them when another sound invaded her ears. Lucas couldn't hear it, but he felt it through the ground.

It feels like the rumbling from my game controller. Whatever it is, it's definitely distracting.

Lucas saw Vanessa rushing to Josh's aid, cracking her arms like they bubble wrap. The orange team runner staggered and fell unconscious, while Josh tried to stop himself from screaming. The sonic vibrations he emitted didn't blow down any trees. Lucas couldn't tell how far Alexia and the orange team's orb wielder had been blown away.

This was his plan all along; he wanted Alexia to hit him, and he wanted her to be distracted enough by him so that he could do this. Vanessa's role was always to take out whoever remained. Josh, I will never say this out loud, or figure out how to sign it, but you are a genius.

Josh narrowly clenched his teeth, but the vibrations continued to emit and escape through the thin gaps of each tooth. He gave Vanessa a knowing look and she nodded in recognition.

What is she doing? She can't use her power on him since he can't hear.

Instantly, Vanessa elbowed Josh in the back of the head and sent him down to the point where he was out cold.

That works too.

Vanessa fell to her knees and was breathing heavily. It didn't take long before she, like Josh, was out cold.

We're down two team members. That's not great.

It took a few minutes for the orb to be fully charged. The whole orb had a yellow color to it, and began to float on its own. Sasha collapsed too, joining the beaten down Josh and Vanessa. All who remained were Lucas and Ashley now. The orb continued to float like a bubble, while Ashley girl reached out for it.

"Wait, what if it explodes?" Lucas asked Ashley. The look she gave him suddenly made him feel stupid for asking.

Only a girl can look at a guy like that.

Just as she was about to pick up the orb, a giant roar burst through the woods similarly to Josh's sonic scream. Instead of immobilizing anyone, this sound foreshadowed the arrival of a massive force to go with it.

All I need is one guess to know who that is.

The roar was followed by thunderous steps that sounded like that one dinosaur movie everyone loved in the 90's.

"That doesn't sound human," Lucas noted with panic in his tone. Ashley was holding the orb now and grimaced in pain. "Are you okay?"

"Yeah… it's very warm and it feels alive."

Sasha said the same thing and that was before it glowed.

"We got the orb. Now, we run!" Ashley shouted. She planted both hands on the orb, which caused her to wince in pain.

"Do you want me to hold it for a bit?" Lucas asked with concern.

"No you can't!" Ashley shouted, but then calmed herself. "It's being imprinted onto me, and only I can hold it now. I'm going to give you a bit of my speed. It won't last for long, but you'll be able to match me when running. I hope you don't get sick easily. Are you ready?"

Lucas hesitated, but before he could question the bad stomach comment, he felt a soft thud as Ashley kicked his right leg with her own. He felt vibrations going through his legs and before he knew what he was doing, he was running alongside her.

Am I crazier, or am I actually running fast? This feels insane. I have so much energy running through me that I don't know what to do with it.

After about a minute, Lucas began to stagger similarly to Ashley when she stopped running. She continued ahead of him, but it was becoming clear that the orb was making it harder for her to use her full ability.

"Lucas, come on!" she shouted. She kicked his leg again and winced in pain, nearly dropping the orb.

Lucas picked up the speed again. It lasted less time than the previous kick. As if intervened by a divine presence, Lucas and Ashley encountered their yellow team defense group. They were still fighting off the rest of the orange team members, who, unlike yellow team, wore orange armbands. Gary was fighting against one camper who looked twice his size, Mike was dodging the hits from one camper who was fast with a dagger, and both Hailey, along with Bruce, were trying to fight off a shark boy.

A shark boy?! Seriously, where do these people come from? Atlantis?

Lucas couldn't focus too much on how the boy looked when he caught sight of another camper who was sitting next to a tree. She was weeping and barricaded herself using metal pipes.

Where did she get those from? She looks too small to have done that herself.

"Lucas," Mike called out to him. "Where's Josh, Vanessa, and Sasha?" Right when he asked this, the orange team member with a dagger nearly cut him. Luckily, Gary was able to finish off his opponent and help him with the dagger-wielding one.

"Pick up the slack, Mike," Gary barked. "I can't do all the leg work today. I'm going to help out the big girl and Bruce."

Mike nodded and went over to where the pipe girl was.

"She's in shock," he explained to Lucas. "Caroline's freaking out because she thinks she hit that kid over there with one of her pipes too hard."

Lucas turned to look at an unconscious camper whose head was wide open.

Yikes, that doesn't look good.

"We got to help him. Even if he's the enemy, it's not right to leave him like that," Lucas insisted. Mike shook his head, cautioned him from approaching the unconscious boy.

"He's playing possum," Mike explained. "If we go near him, he'll spring up from that spot and attack us. Caroline doesn't believe me and I can't convince her otherwise."

Lucas wanted to help, but he didn't know how to. His attention was suddenly redirected when the thunderous roar returned. Ashley came to check on them.

"What are you still doing here?" she shouted in exhaustion. "Come on already. She's gaining on us!"

What if...?

Lucas nodded and instinctively grabbed one of Caroline's smaller pipes and threw it at the unconscious camper. He winced in pain and the wound on his head suddenly disappeared.

I don't know what made me do that, but it made sense at the time.

Caroline noticed this, began to calm down. As she did, the bigger metal pipes around her began to fall down with heavy thuds.

Okay she definitely did not lift those herself.

"Thank you, Lucas," Mike said with a soft smile.

Lucas nodded and with every ounce of energy he had in him, he ran in the direction of Ashley. It didn't take him long to catch up to her, which was something that troubled him.

I should not be able to match her speed without the kicks she gave me.

When they were far enough away, she tried to give Lucas some of her speed again, but he shook his head.

"We can't keep doing this, Ashley. I know why you wanted me around." *And it wasn't for my company or dashing good looks.* "You wanted me to help you in carrying the orb, but if this keeps up neither one of us is going to make it past this forest."

"What do you think we should do then? I can't give you any more of my speed or I won't be able to make it back. If you take it, you won't get much further from here without my speed energy."

Lucas considered that and came to the same conclusion. He gulped hard and prepared himself to say the stupidest thing he's ever said before.

"You need to go on without me and conserve the rest of the speed energy you have. I will deal with Alexia," Lucas heard himself say aloud as if some madness overtook him.

This shocked Ashley, who objected stubbornly.

"I'm not leaving you with her. Forget what I said earlier about her maiming people; she will KILL you. Let's just... how about we do this: I'll try and take the orb most of the way through, and you take it after that. I'll give you the last of my speed and you just go from there which won't be far."

Wait, I can do that? That was an option?

Lucas wanted to question it, but he did his best to keep from showing the fear he was beginning to feel creep on him.

"Even if that worked, I don't want the orb to hurt you the way it did Sasha." Those words made Ashley stare at Lucas as if he had just professed his undying love for her. "I know how badly you want that cabin, the Weeping Willow. If I can help you and this team win, then let me do this."

No one else will get hurt now. It's my turn to be useful on my own.

Ashley carefully contemplated this and finally nodded.

"Fine, but take this. If you're set on having some macho showdown with Alexia, use this last boast of speed to run in the opposite direction. It will only last less than a minute so make every second count."

That's a good idea. It's better than just running around like an idiot waiting for Alexia to find and attack me.

Lucas nodded and felt the soft vibrations from the kick she gave him.

"Alright, now get out of here and win this for me," he said encouragingly.

Ashley nodded and corrected him by saying, "For us," as she darting off with the orb in hand.

Shockingly, this action took Lucas by surprise.

Wait what? I didn't think she'd actually do that and leave me behind to die pretty much a hero's death. I'm going to end up in one of those body bags that Bill mentioned,

116

Lucas realized anxiously. *No time to complain. I have to run in the opposite direction. Side direction. Whatever.*

With the last of the speed given to him, Lucas darted to the left, hoping that the worst he would encounter would be tall trees. Instead, the stomping footsteps from before approached and Alexia's eyes were locked on him like torpedoes. He dared not look back, doing his best to use the seconds he had of speed to get him to lead Alexia away from Ashley. The trees nearby were falling and bumping against each other like stacks of dominos. Lucas knew Alexia wasn't far now.

What have I gotten myself into?!

As he felt the last of the speed energy leaving him, Lucas kept running, but found himself quickly becoming tired. In another instant, Alexia appeared in front of him and kicked his stomach with her left leg. He flew back fast and rolled violently on the ground before finally stopping abruptly. Despite scrapping his arms and legs, Lucas still had the strength to get up.

Argh. That really hurt!

As he rose to his feet, Alexia used the butt of her weapon to slam against his stomach. He staggered backwards and fell to his knees.

GAAAAAAAAAAAH!

Lucas felt the breath fly out of him, his eyes widened and it felt like the war hammer's butt had gone through his entire stomach and come out of his back.

He screamed in agony and was barely standing up. This soon changed when Alexia used the opposite end of the war hammer, the blunter side, to knock him down to the ground face first.

I'm dead. Most definitely dead.

He coughed out hoarsely and was drenched in dirt, blood, and sweat. Despite being face down, he was able to look upwards and glimpsed an orange glowing orb in one of

Alexia's hands. The hand itself looked charred, like burnt meat.

"Looks like we meet again, Twig," she rasped. Lucas could feel the pain she felt. "That deaf friend of yours helped us after all. Because of him, Martin found the source of the light and was able to charge it enough so I could take it."

I thought only the runner could take the orb after it was charged. Unless she was the runner all along.

"I can't touch you because of the orb, but I can pummel you with my war hammer until your insides are out.

I'll only break a few bones if you tell me which direction your orb wielder went? The little-miss-perfect blonde girl."

Lucas shook his head stubbornly, even when he knew it meant certain death.

Where is the Camp Guardian? Why hasn't Henry sent him out here yet? She's going to kill me. Going to kill me she is.

"I won't tell you," the young camper coughed out. "You'll have to kill me because I'm not scared of you."

How can she even lift that thing with one arm? She must be crazy strong. Stop talking, you idiot. Stop it.

Alexia smiled sinisterly and nodded.

"I was hoping you would say something stupid like that," Alexia proclaimed, snidely. "Any last words before I squash you like the twig you are?"

This can't be how it ends. I'm going to be smashed to bits by some crazy super-powered bully. Come on super power, ability, whatever you are, reveal yourself and save me, Lucas pleaded feebly. *No, this isn't how I die. No, I won't. Not like this. I need to see Shelly again. I need to be with my family again. I need to get better from all this. This has to... She has to..."*

"Nothing? Alright then, time for you to meet your maker!"

Before she could bring the war hammer down on him, Lucas finished his thought and shouted it aloud:

"STOOOOOOOOOOP!"
STOOOOOOOOOOOOOOOOOOP!

After a few seconds of panting, Lucas opened his eyes slowly. The taste of dirt and blood still lingered in his mouth, while sweat dripped from his hair like raindrops. The pain was enough to assure him that he was still alive. What he didn't expect was seeing Alexia standing still with the war hammer behind her.

She's frozen! Did I do that to her?

Her face was struggling as she tried to move. The other hand still held the orb up, although its glow was beginning to flicker. Lucas slowly rose from the ground, noticing his clothes were torn and tattered. He looked at Alexia and tried to see just how frozen she was. He snapped his fingers in front of her face and waved his hand back and forth. Her pupils did not move, she did not flinch either.

This can't be happening. I should be dead, but I'm not. The orb she's holding is still glowing. I wonder if...?

Lucas was tempted to see what would happen if he touched the orb. Rather than do this, he decided to try and wrestle the war hammer from Alexia's grip first. It was as firmly in her hands as the orb was embedded on her open damaged palm. After he finally managed to get it loose, the weight of it was too much for him to bear and it fell to the ground. The war hammer narrowly missed taking off Lucas's left foot.

What was that?! Talk about being lucky, or just being stupid lucky.

As he was sighing in relief, the orb suddenly began to move on its own and fell to the ground. Lucas had the sudden urge to try and catch the orb, but feared what would happen. He imagined himself doing it and the action that would follow.

I catch the orb and it explodes! That thing is charged up with something that is more than light. Whatever it is, it's enough to leave what looks like burn marks all over Alexia's palm.

Instead, he let the orb fall. To his shock, it did explode, but not like a grenade. More like how a vase breaks, with many tiny pieces scattering around the area. Lucas shielded his face from the debris.

Well, that's broken. No amount of super glue is fixing that.

He decided to leave Alexia behind, hoping that whatever trance she was in would last long enough for him to get away. One thought kept plaguing Lucas even more than how the orb broke after falling and how saying one word caused the camp bully to freeze in place.

Why didn't the Camp Guardian come? Was this a test of some kind? I could have died and I almost did. If it wasn't for my power, I'm sure Alexia would have either killed me or hurt me badly.

It took Lucas awhile to find his footing, with each step being more painful than the last. He clasped his stomach and the back of his head, both of which were inflamed from the pain of Alexia's blows. He staggered a couple of times, but luckily there were enough trees around him to act as support for him to grab onto when he felt he was going to fall over.

After what felt like many minutes, he finally made his way towards the playing field where the game had originally started. The sunny day was obscured by clouds which masked the time of day. Ashley still had the orb and was preparing to set it in the center of the field, when both she and everyone else in attendance noticed Lucas's arrival. There was a group of what looked like medical personnel who were all in white already attending to members from orange team.

As the cheers began, Ashley dropped the orb into the center of the field. Rather than shattering as the previous one did, this time it burrowed itself into the ground and looked like it was sinking into the center of the earth.

That is really insane. Why is it doing that?

Before he could think on it further, Ashley staggered towards him and exclaimed, "Lucas! You're alright. I'm so happy." She threw herself on him as he groaned in pain. Ashley suddenly blushed as she stepped back and patted his shoulder softly.

"Sorry, I didn't know how badly you were hurt, but we won!" she exclaimed happily.

Lucas nodded stiffly, gasping from the pain around his body.

"Yeah, we won, thanks to you," he said, breathing hoarsely between each word.

"We all won this together." Ashley's demeanor suddenly became concerned. "How did you survive Alexia? Didn't the Camp Guardian go and help you?"

Lucas shrugged and looked to where he last saw the Camp Guardian. He was still standing in the same spot, just as he had before and looked like he had been that way for the duration of the game.

That would explain what he was doing while I almost got killed.

"No, he didn't help, but I think I discovered my power. Alexia was getting ready to bring her war hammer down on me, when the next thing I know, she's frozen and I'm alive. It was like something I said or did stopped her."

"Stopped her how?"

As he was about to continue, Bill came towards him and gave him a satisfied grin.

"Looks like Alexia didn't kill you after all. That means you're still my cabin mate. Also, yellow team just scored their first victory in years. Color me impressed, Luke."

The young camper tried to smile, but winced in pain from moving any part of his face.

What's that old saying? 'It takes something something something muscles to frown, and something something more muscles to smile?' I can never remember the numbers. I only know one is definitely more than the other. Either way, those muscles all hurt!

When Lucas turned towards what sounded like many footsteps approaching, he spotted the yellow team emerging from the forest, as well as the remaining orange team members. They appeared bruised and defeated. Hailey had Josh's arm slung over her shoulder, while Mike, Gary, and Bruce helped out Vanessa, Sasha, and Caroline. The one who appeared to be in worse shape was Sasha, the orb wielder. Her skin was grey and her eyes sunken.

Was that because of how long she held the orb, or because of something else?

"Hey, Lucas. Hey, Ashley!" Josh signed and spoke aloud with a hoarse voice. "I missed what happened. Did we win? If not it's okay, because we did our best."

"We won, Josh," Ashley signed, to which Josh's spirits improved.

"That's awesome! We won! I knew we would. The whole time. I was just testing to see if I was right."

Sure yeah. He definitely had no idea.

Gary took Sasha towards the white dressed medical staff who strapped her to a gurney.

I hope she's okay. What kind of game was this? What kind of camp is this?

Bruce set Vanessa down, allowing Lucas to get a good look at him now. He was a semi-big child with a jaw that looked like it was used to sharpen swords. His hair was cut short with the top falling down like flakes. He looked like a miniature Camp Guardian, though not as intimidating.

Bill came over to his sister, frowned upon seeing her condition.

"You overdid it with the bone crunching thing again," Bill groaned, irritably. Vanessa was barely awake, but managed a sly wink in response.

"That was really stupid what you did. Brave, but mostly stupid," Ashley told Lucas with admiration. "Please, don't ever do anything like that again."

Lucas nodded and winced in pain, feeling his legs begin to give out on him.

I'm running on fumes here.

"I won't be running again for a while," Ashley said with a small chuckle. "How long did the last speed energy I give you last?"

"Only about a ten seconds," Lucas admitted, trying to recall the actual time.

It may as well have been with how fast Alexia was able to catch up to me.

Josh got in-between the two of them, causing Ashley to go over to where Hailey and Caroline were.

"Where's Alexia? That is a story I would like to see you explain, not hear sadly," Josh asked, enthusiastically.

Lucas was not in the mood to be answering the same questions repeatedly.

Telling him wouldn't do any good. I can only hope for a distraction of some kind.

As if someone overheard his thoughts, Henry made his way towards him and congratulated him along with yellow team. Daniel walked closely behind him like a shadow.

"Excellent job, everyone. You all performed admirably. I am especially impressed by you, Lucas," Henry exclaimed, proudly.

Lucas nodded with a weak smile and looked at Daniel who nodded with a similar expression of his own.

"That was quite the show you put out there, Lucas. Sacrificing yourself to help your team win and keeping

Ashley out of harm's way. You're a true gentlemen, young sir."

Ashley blushed at this, which slightly annoyed Lucas.

Yeah, it's nice when you're not the one staring at deaths door about to bite the dust. I'm a true gentlemen? That's a first. He definitely doesn't know me well enough yet. And what's with Ashley making googly eyes over him? He's like twice her age!

"So, how did you do it? Did you discover your ability?" Daniel asked Lucas.

"I just said 'stop' and that's what she did."

Daniel and Henry looked at each other in astonishment, like they knew what he had done. Lucas also noticed the other campers murmuring to each other when they heard this.

It's like everyone is in on some kind of big secret and I'm not. I mean, I came here to get better from what I had. Not to be some guinea pig to be tested on their strongest warrior.

"However your power works, you've only just begun on your journey to understanding it better," Daniel noted.

Lucas staggered forward and did his best to avoid falling.

"The yellow team wins!" Henry announced suddenly. A cry went up as the remaining team members cheered and began patting Lucas's shoulders softly. "You will all receive free time to yourselves for recreational activities. After which, you will be appointed to my son's training sessions starting next week." This made the team even more excited, although Lucas would have been happier with a comfortable bed and some sleep at that moment.

Also my pills. I should have taken my pills when I had the chance.

When the excitement finally died down, Henry turned to the remaining orange team and spoke with the same courtesy, but not the same enthusiasm.

"Be prepared for training tomorrow morning with counselors Richardson and Alexander. We will begin the next games tomorrow as well. Those of you who did not participate today will do so during the rest of this week."

The orange team groaned as the two counselors snickered together and gave them maniacal looks. Lucas could tell, just by looking at them standing side-by-side, that they were more menacing as a duo than separate.

The Camp Activities Director is the one who helped me out, so he can't be that bad. The other one I'm not so sure about.

Everyone who wasn't on the yellow team returned to their cabins as Ashley assembled the remaining campers and gathered them around towards the announcements pavilion.

"Alright everyone, so in a few hours, we're going to check up on Sasha, Vanessa, and Caroline to make sure they're okay. After that, we're celebrating yellow team's victory all night long! Lucas, you can be our guest of honor since you ended up saving this game for all of us."

Lucas was unsure if he deserved that honor, but he accepted it regardless. He remembered the Camp Director's words.

'Smile even when there is no cause too. You may find others will appreciate you for it.' Is this what he meant? Did he know this would happen? Is that why the Camp Guardian didn't help me or anyone else today? Yes, I'm still upset about that.

Just as he was beginning to feel proud of himself, he spotted Alexia finally freed from her frozen state and glaring loathingly at him as she was being taken to the hospital ward to treat her injured hand. He noticed Ashley did not have the same damage. This was possibly due to her using both hands and speeding to the field's center faster.

Lucas gulped hard and thought drearily, *one thing's for sure about today; this is just the beginning...*

Chapter 4

Great Minds Think Alike

The camp hospital ward was full of campers who had injuries from the Relic game. The orange team members still suffered from Mike's glue bomb that Josh had used on them. Surprisingly, only two of them had it so bad that they could be mistaken for conjoined twins. The glue ended up so tightly on their hairs that the nurses and doctors had to shave their heads altogether. By the end of the ordeal, they had shiny heads like Lucas's middle school principal.

I think it suits them and serves them right for cheating, he thought approvingly.

Yellow team, similarly, had members of their own who needed medical attention. Vanessa was exhausted from the bone breaking she did. Caroline was given medicine to calm her down from the game and iron supplements. Sasha, the orb wielder, was in the worst shape, and had been immediately taken to a more private room as opposed to where all the other campers were being treated. Josh was being given painkillers and bandages for his injuries. Lucas received similar remedies and was advised to avoid lifting anything heavy for at least a week. The only team members who didn't need immediate attention were Hailey, Gary, Mike, Bruce, and Ashley. Despite losing much of her speed, she assured Lucas that she would be back to herself by the time training started.

I wish my powers were to heal fast. Alexia really hurt me.

In private, Lucas was given a particular prescription, since he mentioned that the medicine they gave him didn't work for him.

That's always been my problem; some medicines don't work on me and so I need stronger dosages.

Alexia, who was being treated with her fellow teammates, rebuffed any medical attention aside from the bruise Josh gave her, which was beginning to swell like a grape. Her eyes were on Lucas and Josh, so much so that he began to feel what she felt.

She's angry, very angry, but anyone with eyes can see that plainly. No, she feels something more. Like shame? A shame that can only be from being humiliated by someone considered inferior to the other person.

Josh was very proud of his 'warrior marks' and he decided not to accept the painkillers. It was his way of trying to be cool for surviving his encounter with Alexia. He quickly regretted it after being unable to walk out of bed without groaning in pain.

More like he tried to limp out of bed.

Josh spent a good portion of his time in the ward flirting with one of the nurses working there. According to an older nurse, the young nurse was fourteen years old. It surprised Lucas to learn that campers could also become doctors or nurses, even psychiatrists. A big reason many didn't choose to practice medicine is due to Henry not paying them; their services were truly from the kindness of their hearts.

How does that work? That's not work at all. Like my dad always said 'A job is when they pay you. If they don't, then its charity'. I don't remember if he said the last part though.

Lucas could not fathom why Henry wouldn't pay his nurses and doctors.

They do a much better job than any doctor I've ever been to. Even the nurses in my schools only prescribe a bandage for bruises that were not water resistant.

When he asked the main doctor in charge of him and Josh the answer surprised him.

"Even though Henry doesn't pay us, he helps by paying for our mortgages, taxes, healthcare, and helps us with life insurance policies," the main doctor explained to Lucas. "We spend the nine months outside of camp with our families and continuing our studies at universities. Camp Director James takes care of all the expenses."

He's kidding right. He has to be. There is no way it's possible for Henry to pay for everyone to have it made for nine months. He can't be that rich, otherwise why have a camp at all?

The young camper began to think of crazy scenarios which might have sounded worse aloud.

Is he a drug dealer with millions of dollars' worth of blood money? Maybe he owns islands that have gold in them? That's a thing; I'm sure of it, Lucas thought, doubtfully. *Or maybe he has a distant relative who left him a lot of money. That also happens.*

It quickly dawned on Lucas that he knew nothing of the illusive Camp Director. All he knew about Henry is that he has a son who is very young compared to him, that he built Camp Supernatural, and has been its director for fifty years now.

But how old was he when he started the camp? Also, why did he start the camp to begin with?

Josh told the pretty young nurse, who smiled and blushed at him, that she reminds him of an actress named Anne Hathaway. He also told her that she would look pretty with shorter hair. What followed was a mixture of clichés and uncanny pickup lines that ultimately made him the center of her attention.

He's been hogging her attention so much that she didn't even bring me dinner, Lucas thought with annoyance. *She gave Josh enough food to feed everyone in this ward and he didn't share any of it with me.*

His own meal was delivered by a less attractive nurse. As he ate, Lucas heard the young nurse giggle as Josh kept flirting with her and quoting from movies that sounded familiar. Some of the things he said didn't quite add up with his tone, but it looked like his hand gestures were as effective for her as juggling.

How can Josh talk like a person who can hear when he is completely deaf? He's even better at talking to girls than guys who can hear. Not to mention those pick-up lines. They sound rehearsed, like he memorized them from somewhere.

In the evening, after Lucas got his new medicine and was discharged from the hospital ward, he departed along with his new friend Josh. Before leaving, Josh got the nurses phone number and she told him to call her. When they were a good distance away, he crumbled the paper up and threw it.

"I can't hear the phone ringing. How am I supposed to hear her on the other end?" he pointed out with a grin.

There's such a thing as texting, but I'm sure he doesn't care about that. She's too pretty for him anyways. I'd call her even if I was deaf.

Lucas decided to mention this, to which he received the response he expected from Josh.

"I text, but I can say more with words and sign language than I can with writing. Besides, I wouldn't date her. Why lead her on like that?"

You kind of did by flirting with her, Lucas wanted to say. Instead, he kept the thought to himself.

They were just in time for the celebration that was taking place in honor of the yellow team's victory. There was a small campfire near where the announcements were made. Many of the campers huddled in together and wore jackets or long sleeves. The days were often hot or humid, while the nights were cold, Lucas discovered quickly.

Good thing I packed a jacket just for any cold occasion.

Lucas tried to weasel out of the celebration, reminding Josh of his social anxiety, but his deaf friend shook his head.

"Get out of that shell for a bit and maybe you'll like what you see," Josh signed and said aloud, with his voice sounding hopeful.

I highly doubt it.

Before joining the celebration, Lucas went to his cabin, showered, changed clothes, put on his red sweater and tugged at Shelly's necklace under his shirt. He was grateful nothing happened to it after his near-death experience with Alexia. As he was leaving, he thought about how, for the first time in his life, he didn't have Shelly with him to help him through social settings.

I wish she was here. Stuff like this is more something she'd be better at handling. .

Lucas brushed the thoughts aside, took a deep concentrated breath, and made his way to the camps center.

When he joined Josh and the rest of the campers in attendance, they began to cheer for him.

"Let's hear it for Luke everyone!" Josh shouted.

While the campers in attendance cheered for him, he pushed his mind to the outside of his body so he wouldn't feel as uncomfortable as situations like this tended to make him feel. He buried his hands in his pockets so no one could see them shaking, and gritted his teeth so his head wouldn't shake. The only thing he couldn't hide was his eyes, which still darted left and right, avoiding all eye contacts. While Lucas tried to mingle with his new friends, he overheard Ashley recounting how they won this year's game.

"...Lucas and I were running back with the orb after it was charged. I had to give him some of my speed power so he could keep up," Ashley pointed out to Lucas's annoyance. "It was my first time trying that out and it worked. Anyways, then Lucas had the amazing idea to split up and he decides to distract Alexia while I took the orb and put it in the center of the field. Daniel told me that yellow team never got that close to winning a game since Alexia has been in camp. She helped orange team win for two years in a roll before now."

I wouldn't say it was an amazing idea so much as me being very lucky that my ability happened to be something that saved my life when I needed it most.

Lucas had questions regarding his ability, including how else it worked beyond making people stop what they were doing. When he mentioned this to Ashley, she assured him that he'd learn more about it and how to control it in the coming days.

"You're a mental," she noted. "I don't mean crazy. I mean to say your ability is mental. There are a few mental ability campers here, but physical abilities are a lot more common. You're the only one with telepathic powers though."

Sounds like I drew the worst half of something, Lucas thought, with disappointment. *I was hoping for a power like Josh's, less loud, or Bill's, less colorful.*

As the festivities commenced, Lucas's anxiety forced him to take to the shadows and away from his new friends. He wanted to enjoy being amongst others, but found that he could not in his present state.

Back when Shelly would go to parties with friends, she would invite him in an attempt to make him more sociable. Much to her annoyance, Lucas would constantly leave her and retreat towards a deserted spot and remain there until she ultimately got the hint and took him home.

In camp, surrounded by adolescents like himself, he wanted nothing more than for the celebration to end. Lucas was suddenly at war with himself. One side wanted to be social and forget about home. The other side fought the instinct to run and hide until the noise and people went away.

I wish I wasn't like this. I don't know how to talk to people, much less make friends. These people seem to like me now, but what if I don't come back? Then what is the point of having friends at all?

Suddenly, his eyes began to tear up. Lucas wasn't sure if it was because he missed Shelly, or because of something else.

This isn't the time or place to think about it. I wish Shell was here. If she was, I wouldn't feel so alone.

Lucas wiped the tears from his eyes as Josh came and sat next to him on one of the benches that was put up for the gathering. His new friend handed him a soda and got another for himself from a cooler that was a few feet from them. He casually took a long sip from it, savoring the taste as if he wanted it to last the whole night. Then, he congratulated Lucas with a grin.

"You did great out there, Luke. I am impressed. Next time, make Alexia hit herself. I'm sure you'll eventually learn how to do that," Josh signed and spoke aloud.

Lucas nodded, but deep down felt unsettled by what he could do. He remembered doing something similar years ago and wondered what made this time different.

I don't know if my power only works when I'm in danger, or if it's connected to how I feel about something. Or someone.

Not wanting to appear uninterested, Lucas tried to be cheerful as Bill came to sit with them.

"Maybe next time, I'll get Alexia to break that war hammer of hers against her big forehead," Lucas said, in an attempt to be humorous. Josh did not understand the joke until Bill explained it to him in sign language.

Josh finally got it and laughed, he seemed to only understand the 'big forehead' part of the conversation.

"She does have a big forehead, that's true. You could hang a billboard on there and still have space left over," Josh jested.

Bill chuckled and complimented Lucas on the attempt.

"You're becoming a real surprise, Luke," Bill remarked admirably. "Mind-based powers, specifically the kind you might have, are hard to come by. Mostly because they are the worst ability an Alter Child can have. Not because of the power itself, but because it is very unstable. Even the strongest minds can never master it 100% like most abilities. Having mind powers also makes you crazy, so give me a heads up if you become homicidal or rabid."

Lucas grimaced, most notably at the last comment.

"I'll keep that in mind, no pun intended. So, what's the deal with your sister Vanessa?"

Bill looked at Lucas with one eyebrow raised and a curious face.

"Are you looking to date my sister? After I was just starting to warm up to you."

Lucas shook his head and Bill, after a few seconds of looking at him intensely, burst into laughter. Josh also began laughing without really knowing what was going on. When he finished, Bill shook his head.

"She's out of your league, my young friend. Anyways, her bone popping is a constant habit and will give you tinnitus eventually. Even more than Josh's screams."

Josh snickered when he understood the word 'bone'.

"I can't hear so her power wouldn't bother me."

Bill gave Josh an intimidating look.

"You are especially off limits from my sister, Joshua."

Bill specifically made sure that he saw his lips when he said the name. Josh gulped and nodded. He winced in pain as he put his hands on his stomach.

"Alexia hits like a girl; a really strong girl."

Lucas nodded.

"That took guts to hit her in the face the way you did. At least your face is still intact." Lucas made sure that Josh understood the words 'guts' and 'face'.

"Ha ha, very funny. Want me to scream out in pain?"

Lucas shook his head and turned his attention to Bill.

"So my powers are mind-based?" the young camper asked his cabin mate.

"That's correct. Don't worry, there's little chance you'll end up like the last guy who had mind powers like yours."

This story piqued Lucas's interest.

"There's another camper with the same powers as me? Who is he? Is he still here? I thought I was the only one."

Bill shook his head and gave him a look that suggested he couldn't believe the last question.

"They say there is no such thing as a stupid question, but that last one you asked is really stupid. Why would a maniac like that be allowed to stay in camp? Don't get me wrong, all abilities are welcomed. Unstable powers, however, that's a big no-no."

Lucas wasn't dissuaded. He wanted to know more.

"Tell me who this guy is. Is he still alive?"

Bill shrugged.

"Hard to say. He left before my time and the chances of him returning are about as slim as my chances of growing a beard by the end of the summer."

While it was apparent that Bill had small bits of facial hair, it was not nearly enough to be called a moustache or even the shadow of a beard.

I wonder what age most guys get beards.

Just then, Ashley and Hailey came over with another soda for Lucas, which he took out of courtesy.

"If I keep drinking these things, I won't get any sleep tonight," Lucas joked.

The two girls giggled.

"I know that feeling. I might end up sleeping in tomorrow," Hailey admitted amiably. "Thank you for helping us win, Lucas. Ashley and I really wanted to be in the Weeping Willow cabin and now, thanks to you, we are."

Lucas smiled and tried to make it as sincere as he could. Ashley seemed to be the only one who noticed the difference. Regardless, she decided not to call attention to it and was instead drinking more than one soda at a time.

Speaking of being up all night, with those sodas, Ashley is going to end up having a sugar rush at this rate.

She let out a loud burp and promptly apologized for it.

"Sorry, I'm really craving sugar right now," Ashley explained in embarrassment. "So, what were you guys talking about just now?"

"I'm telling Lucas about Jacob, the previous mind-based ability camper," Bill said, casually.

Ashley looked at him as if he said something inappropriate.

"That's not exactly a story Lucas needs to hear right now."

"But I want to hear about it," Lucas insisted, to Ashley's hesitation. "What about Jacob? What happened to him?"

Before telling the story, Bill decided to take Lucas, Josh, Hailey, and Ashley to an unoccupied campfire. From a distance, Lucas could see Vanessa with two other campers dancing to some music playing on a CD player.

She looks so pretty dancing. I can't tell who the other two campers are, but they better not be guys.

As the celebration continued in the background, Bill began the story.

"Jacob was a camper, like you. He had mind powers, like you. Those powers made him crazy, not like you, so far." Lucas frowned in annoyance, but decided not to say anything and let Bill continue. "Anyways, the story goes that Jacob was born with the most powerful telepathic abilities ever seen. As it is, telepaths are hard to come by compared to most of the abilities here in camp. It's also said that he discovered his ability at a very young age. Typically, most Alter Children discover their abilities as early as five or six. Even so, they are still considered latent, until they turn between ten to thirteen years old. There are cases where powers take longer than that, but that's very uncommon. I think the youngest camper we've ever had here discovered their power at age seven. According to my source, Jacob was only two years old when his ability manifested itself. So the story goes that he was in an insane asylum until Camp Director James rescued him and brought him to live in camp. He quickly became the star pupil of Camp Supernatural and was even said to have been close to Henry."

This shocked Lucas, who felt a bit envious at that moment.

Is that why he has a weird interest in me? Here I was thinking it was because maybe he saw something in me beyond whatever my ability might have been.

"Jacob's power was so great that, after a while, his mind slipped into madness. He ended up running away from camp only a few days shy from what would have been his third year in camp. He's been gone for ten years now. However, some think that he still lingers here, like a shadow, waiting for the right moment to STRIKE!" He thrust his hand forward and some of the younger campers who began listening shrieked in terror as Bill chuckled. Even Ashley and Hailey appeared fearful of the last part.

"Relax, everyone. It's just a story. A lot of it isn't true anyways. In any case, we are well protected. For as long as I've been here we've been safe and I'm sure we will be for years to come."

On that, Lucas found himself agreeing.

I doubt Jacob would mess with the Camp Guardian, even if he could get into his head. Something tells me in a fair fight he'd lose.

When the story ended, Lucas's eyes went back to Vanessa. She was no longer dancing. Now, she was talking to some other female campers and drinking a carton of milk. When she saw that he looked at her, her friends started giggling and whispering to each other as Vanessa smiled. Lucas blushed and he tried not to look at her, but he couldn't resist.

She's too pretty to be single, let alone interested in me. Either she's messing with me, or worst case scenario; she really does like me.

To his dismay, she dismissed herself from her group to join him. He tried to avoid eye contact, but found it hard when she came closer to him. Lucas pretended to acknowledge her just as she had made her way to him and his group.

"I'm glad to see you made it out of the games with all your pieces intact," Vanessa said in a flirtatious tone. "You impressed a lot of people today. Daniel has been bragging to the other Camp Counselor's that he'll be training you and your team during the summer."

Lucas regarded the news with a fake enthusiastic nod. But deep down, he still felt reserved about it.

It's not that I'm making the wrong kind of assumptions. I just don't know Daniel well enough to imagine how he'd be as a trainer of superpower abilities. I'm sure he knows what he's doing though. I don't think Henry would have him around otherwise. Then again, they are father and son so there is nepotism.

138

Brushing the thoughts aside, Lucas began to feel happy. Even the fear of Alexia or her team retaliating did little to frighten him if she decided to get revenge, because he was already building his allies to back him up should he need it. Against his better judgment, he began to wonder which of his new 'friends' would ultimately help him beyond this point.

I think I can count on Ashley and Hailey, maybe Josh, but I'm not sure about Bill and Vanessa. As for the rest of yellow team, there's Mike, don't know about him, Bruce, too quiet, Caroline, also too quiet, Gary, he seems okay, and Sasha...

Just as Ashley was preparing to leave with Vanessa's arrival, Lucas decided to bring up an important question.

"I'm glad we're having this celebration, but what about Sasha?" Lucas asked Ashley. She gave him a conflicted look, which was shared amongst the other campers.

"She's not in good shape, Lucas," Ashley said with sorrow in her tone. "She held onto the orb for too long and the doctors had to transfer her to a different part of the ward. One that takes care of severe cases. She's there along with the orange teams orb wielder."

Lucas wanted to press for more, only to realize quickly that it was a touchy subject in an otherwise cheerful event.

"He deserves to know more than that," Bill insisted. "Okay so look, the Relic game isn't just a risk for the players in it; it's a risk for the orb wielders themselves. Henry chooses who gets selected and because of this, the camper knows the risks going in. I was never chosen, but one of my old cabin mates was. His name was Isaac and I never saw him again after the game. Another year, a cabin mate named Jordan had to be sent home from an injury he got during the game. To put it simply; I've lost a decent amount of my friends because of that game. It's still an important part of the camp and I know Henry has his reasons for it beyond the risks."

Lucas began to show discomfort at that knowledge, but Bill quickly tried to ease those fears.

"That was awhile back though. Henry's been better at helping to avoid stuff like that from happening again. For instance, last year there was another kid who was about the same age as Sasha is now and he turned out alright. The point of Relic is that the orb is something important to this camp. Whatever it is, we just have to trust that Henry has our best interests at heart as I'm sure he does."

Lucas nodded and began to rapidly finish his soda.

The celebration alone lasted until close to nine since most of the younger campers fell asleep an hour earlier. The breaking point that killed the whole event was when someone brought a karaoke machine and Josh decided to try singing. Unfortunately, he was extremely hyper after drinking almost five sodas mixed in with Pop Rocks. The end result: his powers manifesting itself loudly through the microphone and speakers. The sound waves disintegrated the speakers into static silence and the microphone collapsed underneath the vibrations, becoming nothing more than a gooey residue.

Despite this, Josh laughed off the whole situation, until the Camp Guardian marched towards him with complete irritation at all the commotion and forced the remaining campers to return to their cabins.

As much fun as I had tonight, I almost wish that could have happened sooner.

As Lucas and Bill headed towards their cabin, Josh tagged along as well.

"Hey, so I think I'm with you guys now," Josh revealed, to Lucas and Bill's surprise. "Is that cool, Bill?"

Bill nodded in approval.

"Yeah, just be careful not to yawn when you wake up. Do you have that thing you use for when you sleep?"

Josh nodded and pulled out what looked like a mouth guard.

It looks unpleasant to sleep with. But if it keeps him from blowing up the roof, I guess that isn't so bad either.

As they entered the cabin, Josh ran inside and took his spot on the couch, declaring it his. Bill shook his head and leaned in towards Lucas's ear.

"He has no idea that he can just imagine himself another bunk," Bill said loudly.

Lucas let out a small chuckle while Josh never once looked in their direction. A knock came at the door. Lucas opened it to reveal two other campers standing side to side, backpacks slung behind both. They were both members of yellow team.

Gary and Mike, Lucas thought uncertainty to himself.

"Bruce and Gary," Lucas ended up saying. He quickly regretted the confusion when they confirmed their names.

"I'm Mike, and that's Gary," the young boy named Mike pointed out, politely. He had been grateful to Lucas for his help in calming down Caroline. The other boy named Gary extended his hand for Lucas to shake.

"Looks like we'll be roomies, Louie," Gary boasted.

Who is Louie? Does he think that's my name?

"It's Lucas," he said, but before he shook the young boy's hand, he noticed a buzzer in his palm and quickly gave Mike a glance. He softly shook his head.

Something tells me he knows about that.

Lucas calmly withdrew his hand and licked the palm.

"Sure, put it there."

Gary immediately withdrew his hand, with Mike chuckling to himself.

"Who's in charge of assigning bunks?"

"That would be me," Bill said, as he appeared swiftly besides Lucas. "Mike, yours will be to the far right, and Gary, you'll be in-between Lucas and Josh. You guys can imagine your own bunks to be whatever you want it to be."

Gary looked more excited about this as opposed to Mike, who took a little longer to enter the cabin. Lucas thought about offering to shake his hand, but waited for the younger boy to offer his first. He did not.

The new cabin mates made themselves at home with Gary taking a spot opposite of Josh on the couch.

"Don't ask me to change the channel, I know this movie," Josh insisted in annoyance, as he set the subtitles.

"How can you see something when you can't hear it?" Gary pointed out.

I've actually been curious about that myself.

Bill shook his head, while Josh's attention was on the screen.

"What he doesn't have in hearing he makes up for in what he sees. He can remember lip movement probably better than you can remember the last thing you heard."

Gary's eyebrow went up, while Mike made his way into the kitchen. He was carefully touching the refrigerator like it was going to explode upon contact.

"You can help yourself to anything in there, Mikey," Bill offered, but the meek youth seemed to just be examining the contents inside.

"All I see in here is junk food," Mike pointed out with a hint of dissatisfaction. "Isn't there anything else in here?"

"Only what your imagination can think of."

To Mike's surprise, a small section of the refrigerator changed, as did his perception of it. Lucas saw this as well. There was a heavy emphasis on dairy products including milk, cheese, and something white that he wasn't familiar with.

"That's tofu, for tofu burgers," Mike revealed, smacking his lips at the thought of it.

Lucas heard Bill sigh and mutter under his breath, "God's help us".

As the night began to end, Lucas made a quick snack for himself consisting of a peanut butter and jelly sandwich with some of the milk Mike imagined up. Taking his food to go, he retired to his bunk for the evening.

He imagined his old room again without a second thought.

I wonder how this training will help me improve both my disorders and abilities. What should I do for this week to kill time?

He pulled out his phone and saw the date as being June 4th. Before going to sleep, he turned his phone off and lay on his bed, wondering what the next day would bring...

Chapter 5

Ashley

The next day, Lucas found himself looking through the camp activities log to find something exciting to do. It was a big board that was near the main pavilion. It had many activities ranging from archery, canoeing, pottery, and something with plants, Lucas observed. He kept rubbing his eyes and mused to himself how all the soda he drank the previous night kept him from sleeping.

That and anticipation for my first off day in camp.

"Points are awarded to each team that participates in as many activities as they can," Bill explained. "The team with the highest score by the end of the summer will be awarded five beads. These beads are awarded at the end of every summer, with forty-two beads needed to become a counselor. Because this is the camp's fiftieth anniversary, Henry is doubling that amount so you can earn as much as ten beads in your first year here alone. You still lose points if you break any rules. Break enough and you'll be denied beads."

Bill showed Lucas his beads which were decorated on his wrist. They all had different colors and even shapes to them, making them appear uneven. Lucas noticed one bead that had an amber color to it, with a fiery red beam seemingly emanating from it. Another bead had an asphalt thickness that looked murky yet similar to the anvil Lucas saw earlier at the camp forge. Another bead had a yellowish hue that was prone to changing green before turning back to its original color.

"Each bead represents not only a camper's abilities, but their personalities as well. The Camp Director decides this by observing us during our stay here. The choices we make, how involved we are, and how our abilities reveal themselves. When I get my last beads in August, I'll be able to start training to become a counselor like Daniel. If you play your cards right, you'll be able to be a counselor by the time you're my age."

As Bill went on, Lucas felt himself dozing between consciousness and fatigue, until his cabin mate slapped him on the arm.

"Listen up! This next part is about missions. Missions are given to campers who have had at least one years' worth of training. Counselors are in charge of leading these missions. Before you ask, they're like the Relic game; meant to test your abilities and involve something that helps the camp. The ones who have been most active on missions have been Zane and Naomi which is why they're not here this year. I've been on a couple of missions. It's nothing big, mostly just finding new locations for the camp to set grounds, making sure the camp is safe from outside forces, and sometimes even checking in on fellow Alter Children who are out there and have moved on from camp. The reason for that is a long one so I'll explain another time. Since you have some down time before training begins, I'd focus on doing as much as you can with the activities, getting a good grip on your abilities, and making more friends instead of just Ashley and Deaf Boy."

When Bill asked Lucas if he had any questions, Lucas had several, including about the different points mentioned for the missions. Instead of asking about those immediately, he decided to start simple.

"What is the nature of Alter Children? How many of us are there? How does Henry decide who to invite?"

"I'm not sure what you mean by the nature. If you mean where we come from, I don't have a definite answer sadly. How many of us are there is still kind of a mystery. Since Henry began this camp, the number of known Alter Children has grown dramatically. That's not to say there never were children like us. Just that with the camps creation, it's made it easier to find and identify potential Alter Children. As far as how Henry chooses who to invite, you'd need to ask someone else because I don't know. If I had to guess, I'd say it's more about the abilities themselves. It's not every day we get telepaths you know. Jacob was the last known one and look how he turned out."

Just because I have a similar power to Jacob means I'll end up like him? Lucas thought irritably. *Why disabilities? What makes us this way that we have to be a certain way in order to have a chance at abilities?*

"Two more questions then," Lucas asked, to Bill's slight irritation. "First, you said a telepath can never have 100% control of their abilities. Does control decide the strength of an ability? My last question also goes with that. What if a person can overcome their disability? Would that mean I wouldn't have mind powers anymore? That I'd be cured of whatever it is I have?"

Bill contemplated these questions before responding, with Lucas beginning to dread the answers. Finally Bill spoke.

"I'll answer your second question first; no, you won't lose your ability because of how much you can control and master your disability. Think of the two as being in the same playing field. You have your ability, which goes with your disability. In most cases, one influences the other. Even in instances when the disability is controlled and diminishes, your ability can either become stronger or weaker for it. It also has a lot to do with the person who has these abilities. Mind-based is going to reflect largely on who you are as a person: your morals, your vigor, and the usage of your abilities. As for your first question, your strength isn't determined by how much you can control your abilities; it's by how much you nurture the part of yourself that will help your abilities become stronger. Your mind, for instance, means a healthy physical body and in my case my eyes, sight is my strength. Other examples include the fact that Ashley needs to consume a good amount of sugar and calories, while my sister needs to drink milk to keep her bones healthy. Without that, we wouldn't be able to use our abilities, at least not in their current form."

In this current form, Lucas zeroed in on. Before he could ask further, Bill promptly dismissed himself.

"Anyways, I think that's enough questions for now. If you have anything else, just let me know at a later time. Don't worry about the upcoming inspection; I'll take care of the cabin and if you can just keep your bunk tidy that would be great. Imagination, like everything else, has its limits."

Lucas nodded and was about to leave when Bill called out to him. He handed him a pocket sized version list of the camp activities and information related to the camp itself.

"Here's a pamphlet filled with information about the camp, including the cabin names, their words, and symbols. Memorize them, because you might make friends in those cabins and knowing their names will help you identify their abilities. These were all taken the first day, but I managed to get a few spare. Your welcome."

Lucas scanned the pamphlet over and found the section having to do with the cabin names. They began with the first letter in the alphabet and ended with the last alphabet word.

"What are these symbols for each cabin?"

"It's used as a way of identifying them," Bill revealed. "When you get all your beads together, they form something that all Camp Counselors have and will use on occasion; a Sanctuary Stone. They can transport counselors from wherever they are back to the campgrounds. Also, in case you're wondering, those stones are fixed on their counselors, so not just anyone can use them. It's as much a way to get back here as it is a sort of badge to show others that they are Camp Counselors, since those stones can only be made using the beads earned through attending camp."

Bill rummaged through his pockets and pulled out a wrinkly five-dollar bill. "Here's some money, go buy something at the camp gift shop. Maybe a new shirt since the one you wore for the game was trashed. Consider it a house warming gift."

Wow, five whole bucks. At least he didn't give me change. I always lose change.

After that, Lucas left his cabin and saw the Camp Guardian standing vigilant at the front of the camp. It was almost nine in the morning and the guardian looked neither weary nor famished. Even when Lucas tried to smile and give him a friendly wave, the monster seemed to ignore him.

His attention was on a small patch of flowers near the entrance of the camp. In that moment, Lucas felt sorry for the monster.

It must be hard to live that kind of life where people fear and dislike someone just because of their looks, he thought, pitifully. *It makes me wonder how Josh deals with being deaf and how he can make a joke about it like it's not a big deal when it is.*

Most of the time he saw the Camp Guardian, the monster roamed around the campgrounds making sure everything was in check and kept to himself. Even at night, Lucas saw him still standing solemnly as if he were a scarecrow meant to ward off evil from the camp.

That's probably why he's the Camp Guardian; the job is made for him.

Lucas walked around the camp, taking in the morning air and watching some of the younger children playing around near their cabins. He noted the sheer size of the field which served as the training ground for Alter Children.

At the moment, the next Relic game was being prepared for the next batch of campers to take part in. Lucas noticed more campers huddled around than the previous day. He thought about watching to see how it went, but decided to seize his free time for recreational activities instead. He spotted the losing orange team from the previous game being scolded by Alexander near one of the counselor's tents. Alexander made one of the children drop and give him fifty push-ups while mocking his bald head.

"It's so shiny that I can see the empty spot where your brain is supposed to be!"

Lucas also saw Richardson lecturing his group and while he did not seem as harsh as his friend, he got especially prickly when he noticed two campers muttering to each other as he spoke.

Even though the camp looks big, everything is actually close together to the point where I feel like everything is accessible. Since this camp has been around for fifty years, I wonder what's been added or removed during that time.

He was so immersed in his own thoughts that he forgot about home. The thought of Shelly worrying about his well-being made him want to hit something. His parents were also in his thoughts, but when he remembered seeing his unconscious father, he pushed the memory away.

I can't think about that, not now… I have to focus on learning to control this new ability before I can even think about going home with it. Not to mention the other stuff I have…

Lucas felt his hands shaking and did his best to hide them. Instinctively, he worried about someone telling him something about it. To his surprise, nobody seemed to be looking in his direction. He cautiously took his hands out of his pockets and let them be natural.

Maybe everyone is too busy with themselves to care about what I do.

As Lucas walked through the camp bathrooms, which were near the cabins for young children, he heard gagging sounds coming from inside one of the girl stalls. He stopped walking and made his way towards the noise. He heard what sounded like someone having something caught in their throat followed by the sounds of flushing.

Before he could move backwards fast enough, the female camper emerged, revealing herself to be Alexia. She wiped her mouth and spotted Lucas. Her glare met his eyes like a strung up bow about to let loose an arrow.

"What are you doing here, Twig?" the Camp Bully bellowed out angrily. Lucas saw her bandaged hand and noticed it was still looking bad.

"Are you alright?" Lucas asked with concern. "It sounded like you were in a lot of pain in there."

Why am I asking that? It's not like I care. I'm just being polite.

Alexia's face flushed red, as if the very question gave the wrong insinuation.

"Mind your own business, you stalker! If I see you again, you won't have a jaw to talk with. This will be your first and only warning."

The Camp Bully clutched her stomach and walked away towards Richardson's group.

I wasn't stalking her. What was that all about?

Following that unpleasant experience, Lucas decided to visit the camp gift shop and see what they had for sale. The outside of the store looked plain, with a big sign that read 'Camp Gift Shop' and a smaller sign on the door with the words, 'Three free items for first year campers, while supplies last.' The exterior was painted in white, with blurry windows that made it hard to see what was inside, but Lucas knew whoever was in the store could see outside clearly. Walking inside the cabin-like building gave him a different perspective on the campgrounds itself. The inside had items scattered around with no price tags on them. The walls were covered in camp merchandise ranging from bedroom accessories, to clothing, water bottles, and various other items.

If I didn't know any better, I'd say this was the first normal thing I've seen in this camp so far. It is a bit weird that nothing has price tags on them though. I guess we ask how much something is.

In one part of the store, there was an assortment of different colored camp shirts that made Lucas wonder who chose each of them. There was red, orange, blue, purple, green, yellow, white, black, rainbow, tie-dye, and much more. He noticed more items near the shirts such as towels, backpacks, candy, and toiletry items.

Giving the store a thorough examination, Lucas turned towards the cashier, who greeted him amiably. He was a big muscular boy with short cropped hair that made him look like he was in JROTC. The muscular boy looked to be about Bill's age, but Lucas couldn't be sure. He wore a maroon camp shirt that read, 'Weight of the World' and shorts that showed his hairless legs.

He looks like a jock. Maybe he waxes his legs. I heard that's a thing they do.

"Hello and welcome to the camp gift shop," the muscular cashier said, with a tone that suggested he said that often. "Are you new here? If so, we have a special promotion for first year campers."

Lucas nodded and asked about this.

"All first year campers can receive three free items from the gift shop, along with a complimentary camp t-shirt. We also have fifty percent off almost everything for the whole summer as part of the fiftieth anniversary for the camp."

Lucas contemplated this and scanned the price tags with his eyes.

Everything is already priced pretty cheaply. It's a wonder they make any money back, unless there's some secret to it beyond this.

He saw the cashier's nametag and read it: 'Jeremy.'

"You're Jeremy?" Lucas heard himself ask aloud. The cashier nodded and pointed to his shirt.

"My cabin is Atlas's Agony. I usually handle the forge, but it's going through some renovations for the summer. In the meantime, Henry has me working here for now. It isn't so bad. The only thing is I had some kids who tried to steal some of those camp mugs for some reason. The Camp Guardian took care of them easily."

Camp mugs? Take care of them? What did he do? Send them to a mall jail? Smash them to bits? Not the mugs I hope.

"What can I interest you in? We've got a new shipment of toiletries. You'd be surprised how fast those go around here. There's also some clothes, all of it is camp-based. The mugs I mentioned, keychains, coloring books, and caps. The caps are accessorized too. You can even make a special order if you want, but they take up to two weeks to come in. If you want one, now is the best time to put in a request."

Lucas was confused by the amount of information Jeremy gave him, similarly to Bill. Unlike his older cabin mate, Jeremy spoke in a quieter and subtler tone.

For a guy who looks like he can bench a lot, he seems really nice and chill. I'm not getting any bully or superiority vibes off him either like from Alexia.

Lucas decided to give the store another look around and began to admire the backpacks with great interest. One looked grey with blue straps that felt flimsy to the touch, but Lucas could tell it wouldn't break as easily as it felt.

It's stretchy like elastic, he noted when he held one and patted the bottom. *I would never have been able to afford this type kind of backpack no matter how many lawns I mowed.*

Lucas decided to make the backpack his first free item. Jeremy seemed a bit perplexed by this but obliged him regardless. He also decided to take a mug which read, 'It's only natural to be supernatural.'

I wonder why that wasn't the camp slogan.

Lastly, he chose a red cap with the words, 'Mind over Matter', embroiled on it. Lucas wasn't sure if he'd wear it often.

Jeremy was putting the free items together when Lucas pulled out the crumbled five dollar bill and asked what he could get for it.

"A five dollar bill won't get you much here," Jeremy said, frankly. "Maybe a toothbrush, some cough medicine, or a towel. Did Bill give you that?"

When Lucas nodded, Jeremy smirked and told him to hold onto it.

"If he asks, just tell him all of this cost you five dollars. He's not very good with numbers, but don't tell him I told you that."

Lucas chuckled and wanted to say something else but kept it to himself.

If Bill turned this money from green to red, it would be like giving me blood money.

The thought made him laugh and wiggle his hands. Walking out the store, he heard Jeremy call out to him.

"You forgot your complimentary t-shirt."

Lucas turned back in and looked at the pile of colored shirts. He chose a yellow medium sized shirt that read 'Camp Supernatural. Founded in 1963,' with the back saying, 'Control it, so it doesn't control you.'

Maybe Henry was in his twenties or thirties when he founded this place. If he was older than that, he'd be dead.

Outside the gift shop Lucas examined the things he got, including the mug, which looked less appealing outside the store. The cap looked decorative but not wearable and the backpack appeared to be the only thing usable. To his dismay, Lucas noticed that it only had one big pocket and one small one.

Maybe this is why Jeremy looked at me in confusion; this thing is cheaper than what they sell at a thrift store.

Lucas sighed as he stuffed the shirt, mug, and cap inside the big pocket. Not long after that, he found a board with the daily activities being held over the summer. They had an X on it for finished and an O for current events. Since it was still the beginning of camp, the majority of the events had O on it. On the right hand side of the board was also a mini-map of the campgrounds. Going through the list he made a mental note of each activity.

Let's see, there's archery. I'm not sure that's a good fit for me. There's something about pottery. I'm not much for meditative stuff either. I like the musical activity for learning a new instrument, but it's booked for the week. Arts and crafts is mostly a kid's thing. Other than that, all that's available today is some kind of a scavenger hunt and pop culture trivia, which would be fun if I knew what that was, Lucas thought in annoyance.

He also glanced at the catalog and back to the board, still finding nothing of interest from what was available.

Canoeing isn't a bad idea later on, maybe if I can talk Josh or Bill into it, Lucas mused. *There's an activity that maybe Ashley or Vanessa might be interested in. If I invited Ashley, it might make Vanessa jealous. On the other hand, if I invite Vanessa, Bill might not like that.*

Lucas was so fixated on the board that he didn't notice Daniel appearing from behind him. When he turned around, the Camp Director's son stood behind Lucas with his hands behind his back.

If it weren't for the fact that he sometimes dresses professionally, I would mistake him for a camper like me. He's too young-looking.

"Hello there, Lucas. I see you are looking for something fun to do?" Daniel acknowledged as his hair blew in the wind. "You also visited the camp gift shop. What did you get? I hope Jeremy gave you the complimentary shirt as well."

The Camp Director's son did not have the same level of warmness that his father had, but something about him made his appearance more than accidental.

I don't know what it is about him, but Daniel doesn't feel as genuine as his father. Maybe it's the way he smiles like it's expected of him, or the way he talks to the campers like he comes off as superior to everyone else. Maybe I'm just overthinking it.

Lucas nodded and showed him the list of suggestions.

"Because yellow team has some down time before training starts, I figured I could do something productive, you know? Bill said if we get enough points that we'll earn as much as ten beads by the end of summer and we only need forty-five to become Camp Counselors."

Daniel laughed as if Lucas told him a joke.

"It's actually forty-two beads, but forty-five was close. You're looking forward to becoming a Camp Counselor already? That's a great goal, even though you just discovered your ability since yesterday. To my knowledge, there hasn't been a lot of mental Camp Counselors, mostly physical ones. You'll need to have a good grasp on your ability by the time you become one. Do you feel you can achieve that within the time your here?"

Lucas shrugged and tried not to give the impression that he didn't care.

"I'm not sure. I would like to try figuring it out as I go," answered Lucas back uncertainly. "I guess I wish I had another ability, but it's like the life a person is born into. Even though I didn't choose it, I can choose how I use it."

Daniel nodded with Lucas thinking about the words he said.

I don't know why I said that last part. I don't disagree with myself, or the thought. I just wonder why it sounded so perfect right now.

Wanting to test Daniel's knowledge, Lucas began to think of questions that he knew Bill wouldn't know the answer too.

Maybe he can get Henry to help me get better faster so I can go home sooner.

"Is there any way that my training can be faster than everyone else's?" Lucas asked Daniel impulsively. It didn't take long for him to regret his choice of words based on the look Daniel gave him. "I don't mean to say I want special treatment or anything. I just have a promise I need to keep by going home as soon as possible."

"Unfortunately, that's not up to me," Daniel admitted, though he did not sound disappointed. "Something to keep in mind is telepaths are hard to come by and even harder to train in proper power usage. You have a long road ahead of you and my father has already determined he wants to help you. So, leaving any earlier isn't an option for you right now."

This wasn't the answer Lucas hoped for, though the last part of what Daniel said caught his interest.

Henry wants to help me? But why me? Is it because of my powers? Are telepaths really that uncommon?

Daniel looked at Lucas and cleared his throat.

"You know…I was like you at one point," said Daniel, softly. "I came here not knowing what it would be like and not understanding what it meant to be an Alter Child. I met Henry and wouldn't find out until years later that he's my father. He never gave me any special treatment; the way he was with me is the way he is with everyone else here. I never saw him do that with anyone, until you arrived. Even when I became a Camp Counselor, I offered the Camp Activities Director position. No, that went to Richardson, who isn't exactly a people person any more than Alexander is."

This got Lucas's attention, enough that he looked Daniel straight in the face.

Until I arrived? How am I the exception Compared to Daniel who is his actual son, I'm nobody, Lucas pondered in confusion.

Daniel's tone sounded annoyed, which Lucas could not understand.

The way he mentioned not being treated differently and not being given special attention. Is he making fun of the fact that I just tried to ask for something like that?

Daniel distracted Lucas's train of thought as he continued.

"Since you've been here, my father has talked about nothing else except your progress and potential," explained Daniel, with slight annoyance. "My father believed in your abilities so much that he stopped the Camp Guardian from helping you yesterday. He believed you already knew what your abilities were and just needed to be reminded of them in a moment like that."

Lucas was both shocked and slightly upset by this revelation.

Wait, he intentionally stopped the Camp Guardian from helping me?! What if Alexia had killed me, or hurt me badly? What kind of gamble is that? I guess it's nice to know he believed in my capabilities that much. That's what I want to believe. How could I know what my abilities are if I don't know how to use them?

"I didn't know what my abilities were and that's why I wish the Camp Guardian would have helped me. If I'm the only telepath here, why would Henry gamble with my life like that? Even if he knew what he was doing, I sure didn't."

To Lucas's surprise, Daniel laughed. He half-expected the Camp Director's son to be sympathetic, but Daniel seemed to find Lucas's uncertainty amusing.

I don't see what's so funny. A joke should make both people laugh and I'm not laughing.

"You're not too far off the truth I'll tell you that, Lucas," Daniel chuckled.

Daniel's mismatched eyes stared intently at Lucas, whose own eyes were ricocheting around in his sockets.

"Tell me something and I promise this is not a test; knowing now what your abilities are, would you have still used them to win the way you did?"

Lucas shrugged and had no real answer for him.

I don't know.

"I don't know," Lucas said aloud. "I honestly can't say for sure since I have no way of knowing whether doing nothing would have resulted in anything different."

Daniel nodded and understood Lucas's situation more than he showed.

"My ability is something similar to what you're talking about," Daniel revealed to Lucas's surprise. "I can see possible outcomes of different choices. Just glimpses and they're not always accurate. For instance, before the game started, I saw different variations of what could have happened to you based on your choices. To put your mind at ease, the end result you got was the best one."

Lucas was curious about these different possibilities, since he himself pondered what could have been.

I wonder if he can see more than that. If I never came to this camp, if I had been a better son and brother, maybe things would be different. If I knew what could have been, even glimpses, I could have made better choices.

"I shared these outcomes with my father and that's why, despite my insistence that I didn't know for sure, he chose to risk letting you discover the power for yourself. Another perk my ability gives me is finding other Alter Children based on how pronounced their abilities are. The only downside is I can't track latent abilities as accurately and often those are the ones that have more unstable powers."

Lucas suddenly felt as if he was hearing more than he was meant to, notably with the last part.

Why is he telling me this? Maybe he doesn't have anyone else to vent to. I'm not going to be that person though. No way.

"I'm sure Henry has his reasons for what he does. All I want now is to not be this way and to be better so I can go home as my best self," Lucas admitted to Daniel's silent approval.

After a moment of silence, Daniel finally pointed to one activity Lucas had briefly overlooked.

"If you want something interactive, I recommend the nature walk later on this afternoon. You get five points for each item you can identify from the forest, plus its good exercise for your legs. Get yourself some fresh air and a nice case of Vitamin D. You need a hundred points to win and that is as a team. Just so you know, Ashley is also interested in that one."

Why would he think I care if Ashley was going to be in it? Still, it's a good distraction, and that's what I need right now more than anything else. I need to see who from my cabin I can talk into taking part in the activity. I doubt Mike and Gary would care for it.

His thoughts diverted to Henry and the strange recognition he was receiving from the Camp Director.

What exactly does Henry see in me? Why doesn't he say that about his own son instead, were some of the thoughts Lucas contemplated rapidly.

"I think I will give that one a try. What about the canoe rides?" Lucas asked as he scanned the lists down once more.

"That's a nice one, but it's not until tomorrow," explained Daniel. "Richardson will be supervising that activity as per his job title. There's pottery too with Jane if you're interested in something soothing. She always plays Enya and Dido during the activities. At least she doesn't reference that one ghost movie."

When Lucas looked confused by the last part, Daniel suppressed a chuckle.

"Forget pop culture trivia then. It's alright, I enjoy certain movies and it's nice that I get to share that with my girlfriend even though she doesn't like a lot of the same movies as me."

Lucas looked surprised at the revelation of Daniel having a girlfriend.

Is she one of the Camp Counselors here? He didn't seem to mingle with anyone in particular from the ones I saw.

When he returned to reality, Lucas heard Daniel say, "I'll be taking part in the nature walk activity and be in charge of campers from yellow team. Boris is in charge of bringing in activity items, so we'll see what he has for this activity in particular."

Who's Boris?

Lucas nodded and began to feel himself relax, even more than he expected from talking with Daniel. He didn't notice until just now that his hands weren't shaking anymore.

Maybe he is like Henry in that both are warm and welcoming, Lucas thought, pleasantly. *He seemed a bit off before, but after mentioning his abilities, I'm starting to see what exactly he contributes to this camp. Beyond the fact that everyone here seems to worship him as much as his father.*

Daniel looked at his watch and clapped his hands together as if applauding.

"Well, I must be off," Daniel said, casually. "The next game will be starting any moment. Betty and I will be assisting in it since Alexander and Richardson are with the first game's orange team. You should go get some breakfast while it's early. The cafeteria starts serving at eight and ends at ten. Look over the schedule or if you want I have a spare copy with me. Highlighted for your convenience."

He pulled one out from his back pocket and unfolded it.

When Lucas grabbed hold of it, Daniel's hand did not let go.

What's he doing? Lucas thought, his anxiety beginning to build up like a shaken soda can ready to burst.

As the two stared into each other's eyes, Daniel gave Lucas a very intimidating look.

"My father is many things, but you know what he isn't? A trusting man. He keeps everything to himself. So much so that no one knows anything about him. Not even me, his own son. Yet here you are and you're all he talks about now. Why is that, Lucas? What are you to him?" Daniel asked, tensely.

Lucas suddenly felt fearful, as his eyes darted in every direction to see if anyone was around to come to his aid.

What is this? Is he trying to scare me, because it's working! I can't use my power on him to make him stop or I'll get kicked out of camp. I could try calling for help, but he might not like that.

Daniel suddenly became very frightening at this moment and Lucas did not dare answer him back. He felt like the Camp Director's son was holding a deadly weapon against his neck and would slit his throat if he said the wrong thing.

What did I do to deserve this? I knew something was off about him. What am I to Henry? I'm nothing.

To Lucas's relief, Vanessa's voice called out to him and Daniel released his hold on the camp schedule. He shifted back to normal and smiled friendly, as if he had been that way the whole time.

"We are very lucky to have you here, Lucas," said Daniel, with a fixed grin. "I look forward to training you this summer and seeing the potential you have."

He patted Lucas's shoulder and began to walk off like nothing happened.

What was that…? What the heck was that?!

The Camp Guardian was watering the plants when Daniel walked by to greet him. The monster smiled warmly at him and the two began talking like old friends.

That's the first time I've ever seen anyone besides Henry talk to the Camp Guardian, Lucas thought in astonishment. *So if he's on Henry and Daniel's side… I'm doomed.*

Lucas was still in shock at Daniels sudden change from attitudes when he was brought back to reality by Vanessa. She tapped his shoulder and smiled at him when he turned to look at her.

"Hey, my brother is looking for you," said Vanessa cheerfully. "He said for you to get your butt to the cafeteria for breakfast and that you're a rotten egg."

Lucas frowned, knowing full well what that meant.

At least she saved me from what could have been a nasty encounter with the Camp Director's crazy son.

He walked with Vanessa to the cafeteria and decided to get to know her better.

She looks very beautiful today, he thought as his eyes looked at her from bottom to top.

She wore sandals, with her painted red toenails showing. Vanessa wore a purple camp T-shirt that read, 'Would You Kindly.' Lucas's eyes went to her chest often, noticing the outline of her bra, but he tried not to look too much and instead diverted his eyes up to her hair. This morning she had it tied in a ponytail which went down her spine. The most eye-catching thing was her lips. They were thin, petite, and looked glittery.

Vanessa's eyes gave Lucas a prideful feeling while the way she walked made every step more pronounced than the last.

I think she's used to getting what she wants based on how she carries herself, Lucas concluded. *She's also not afraid to show her stomach. Her very flat stomach.*

The young camper gulped at the thoughts he was having.

Now I know she's doing this to me on purpose.

"I've been wondering when did you discover your power?" Lucas decided to ask Vanessa, in an attempt to push away his intense thoughts.

Vanessa took a moment to answer. Then spoke.

"I've had scoliosis since I was nine," she revealed, plainly. "I used to wear a back brace to school, and it was terrible. Everyone made fun of me and called me ugly names. Which I won't say out loud so don't ask. I know I don't look it now, but I was unpopular before. Half the boys in my school wouldn't look in my direction without snickering. Even all of Bill's friends would be mean to me when he wasn't around. Then, at the age of twelve, I came home from school and decided I couldn't stand wearing the brace anymore. When I took it off, I suddenly felt my back fix itself. I thought I was dreaming. I couldn't believe that my back brace had just become useless. I felt so happy that I started dancing and running around the house even though the floor had just been moped. I didn't notice until I slipped and fell on my back so hard that any other person probably would've had to go to the hospital. Not me though. I felt my back break and it instantly fixed itself. I also dislocated my shoulder in the fall. The point is all my bones fixed themselves. I was laughing with joy when Bill got home from school. He looked so shocked to see me laughing and without a back brace that he thought I lost my mind. I remember when he asked me if I was crazy, I laughed and said, 'No Bill, I just broke my back, not my brain'."

Lucas chuckled as Vanessa continued.

"My parents pretty much freaked out too. I don't know how else to explain what happened to me except that one day I needed a back brace, the next day I didn't. After all that, they took me a doctor who confirmed that my back was naturally straightened. More than that, it was like my back brace was what kept me the way I was rather than helping me. Without meaning to, I discovered my abilities on my own. I don't know if it's a hereditary thing because Bill has powers, although I'm not sure about my parents. The only thing that sucks is I need to drink milk regularly, or else my bones will be in pain."

When she finished, Lucas found himself smiling at her and laughing.

"Did Bill discover his power at around that time too?"

Vanessa nodded.

"Yeah, my brother was diagnosed with color blindness when he was six and turned my hair green by accident when he was twelve. My mom thought I was wearing a wig at first, until she tried to pull it off and realized it was my real hair. She wasn't convinced when I told her that Bill had done it to me. I'm pretty sure she thought I was trying to be rebellious by changing my hair color. Luckily, he figured out how to change it back on his own. It didn't take long for him to receive an invitation to camp. His came in faster than mine, which was about a month ago."

Lucas thought about how ironic it was for both siblings to be Alter Children.

If there's a genetic factor to it that could mean Shelly can be one also.

"How about you?" Vanessa asked Lucas, suddenly. "I know you only discovered your ability yesterday, but if you're a latent Alter Child, that means you've had it for longer than you realize."

Lucas didn't quite understand what she meant until she explained further.

"Henry says that sometimes Alter Children can use their abilities before the age when they become old enough to learn how to control them. The only thing is that when they're latent they go away for a while, so that's probably what happened to you. Bill was like that too. Before changing my hair color, he changed the fur color of our dog from light brown to charcoal. He wouldn't be able to do that again until later on."

Lucas began to realize how much sense that made in his own life.

I was diagnosed with schizophrenia because I heard voices that weren't my own. The medicine I took made that go away for a short time. Here it all feels so natural. Like the medicine didn't help me as much as it held me back from knowing what I had.

While he pondered this, they neared the cafeteria, which made Lucas feel a sense of sorrow.

Why do all the best things have to end so fast? He thought with sadness. *I wish this moment could last just a little longer. I still want to tell her about myself. About Shelly.*

She touched his hand and gave him a long look.

"You can hold my hand if you want," said Vanessa playfully as she took his hand in hers.

Lucas shook his head and in a panic pulled his hand away from hers.

"Not in front of Bill. He'll melt my face off."

"Do you honestly believe he will?" Vanessa asked almost as if it were a trick question.

When Lucas nodded nervously, Vanessa scoffed.

"You have the ability to make someone stop in place with just a thought. All he can do is turn your hair green."

Lucas touched his long shaggy hair as he thought about that.

I've never much liked my hair, but I don't want to see it look like broccoli either.

He reached for the door to the entrance of the cafeteria until Vanessa blocked it with her hand.

"Are we going to talk more later?" she asked him, firmly. Lucas nodded reluctantly and felt uneasy.

The problem is not so much that I like her, because I think I do. It's how Bill will take it. Brothers and their sister's boyfriends don't usually get along. It will make things even more awkward since we share a cabin together. With three other guys who can be witnesses to my murder.

A moment passed before she let go of the door and turned her head to the side.

"I already ate breakfast. You should join Bill before he wonders where you're at. I'll see you later, handsome."

She gave him a quick kiss on the cheek and hurried off.

After regaining himself, Lucas walked calmly through the door and saw a majority of the campers eating, laughing, and talking amongst each other. This had been the first time he entered the cafeteria. The eyes of the surrounding campers glanced at him briefly, before returning to their individual breakfast. The cafeteria itself was wide enough to be mistaken for a school auditorium. It became apparent to Lucas that each table was specifically for cabin-assigned campers. He scanned the surrounding area nearest him and spotted the menu. It was pinned to the wall nearest the left side of the entrance. On it he saw eggs, hash browns, cereal, and bacon, along with a variety of other choices including waffles, pancakes, yogurt, and toast.

Looks like a lot of choices, Lucas thought with difficulty. *I think I'll just order something simple for now.*

When he got in line, he was given a choice of how he wanted his eggs and he chose scrambled.

That's the way Shelly always made them.

Unfortunately, the young lady he got did a poor job of scrambling them.

"I'm new at this job," claimed the young cafeteria lady, bashfully. "You're my first camper. The rest of them went the other way for their breakfast."

I can see why based on the way your murdering my eggs.

Nonetheless, Lucas took what little remained of the meal without complaint and added bacon with pancakes to go with it.

The bacon looks alright, but I'm pretty sure those pancakes were burned and redone. I'm sure she means well.

Lucas chose orange juice as his beverage while the young cafeteria lady added in a carton of milk for him.

"You need to keep those bones of yours healthy," she said, trying to sound encouraging. Lucas gave her a meek smile and gathered the food together in one tray. He made his way towards the tables which had multiple campers seated in different sets.

She sounds like a mother even though she looks too young for that.

There were a total of forty circular tables with each holding up to about five campers per table. Twenty were at the bottom rows and the other twenty on the upper floor near the line for meals. The last tables in that row were reserved for the camp staff.

Like the gift shop, this place seems pretty normal too. The food is even badly made like in an actual school.

He also spotted a salad bar on the other side of where the bottom tables were. To his surprise, it was closed and had a sign that read, 'Open from 11:30-7:00.'

Shelly would love that. I think she's still a vegan.

Lucas peered around the room and noticed campers were wearing different colored shirts, all with their cabin words embroiled on them and sitting together.

I didn't know I was supposed to wear mine right now!

Feeling the onsets of a mini-panic attack creep towards him, Bill surprised Lucas and led him to their table which was not far from where he had been standing originally.

"To avoid future embarrassments, Luke, you might want to get here a little earlier next time," Bill advised. "This is the seating arrangement for the cabins and faculty of the camp. You can always figure out the table that belongs to which cabin based on the first letter in each cabin."

The Imaginarium Illusion started with an 'I'. The letter Lucas saw on the table was not an 'I'.

What is the point of sitting like this? We already live together. Why make us eat together?

Lucas wanted to ask, but Bill's voice distracted his train of thought.

"At least our table isn't near the bathroom. Swinging doors and smells that will ruin your appetite for the day," Lucas heard Bill say with a humorous tone.

That's true. I rather be here, which is a bit farther away from everyone else's tables.

Josh had just come back from talking to one of the lunch ladies after getting his plate of breakfast and noticed Lucas had finally arrived.

"Hey, about time. Did you happen to get the name of that new lunch lady? She looks single."

Lucas didn't pay much attention to her beyond how she cooked his breakfast poorly. He did think she looked a little out of place. While the other lunch ladies had a distinctive look (clearly dyed hair, wrinkles, and too much perfume) the one that served him his breakfast looked fairly young. She had short brown hair underneath her hair net, some light make-up applied mostly on her eyes, and a burn mark on her left hand.

I think she was blushing at me, either from embarrassment because of how she made my breakfast, or

169

maybe because she finds me cute. She's got to be older than me though. Probably in her early twenties like Daniel.

Bill seemed to know the lady Josh was referring to and shook his head.

"Leave her alone, Josh. She has a kid with Richardson."

Josh didn't understand everything Bill said, but picked up on the word 'kid' and the name 'Richardson'.

"She has a kid with that guy? That's just gross?" exclaimed Josh in disgust.

Lucas laughed softly to himself. He wondered under what circumstances a camp counselor...*Camp Activities Director,* could have a child with someone working in camp.

I thought there's a rule that says people who work together can't date. Maybe they dated before coming to camp.

While Lucas dug through the remnants of his eggs, Bill noticed something on the young camper's cheek. He licked his thumb and rubbed it against Lucas's cheek. He did not find this amusing and swatted Bill's hand away.

"Hey, what's your problem?" asked Lucas angrily. Bill gave him a surprised look.

"My sister just marked you. Either that or it was the lunch lady that Josh was crushing on."

Lucas didn't understand until Josh explained it in sign language. His way of saying it was pointing to the cheek and smacking his lips to look like a kiss. Lucas touched his cheek and looked at his finger to see the glitter from it.

You got to be kidding me. She did this on purpose to piss off Bill. That would explain why the lunch lady with a kid was blushing. It's one of those girl things that I could never understand even when Shelly tried explaining it to me.

Either way, he couldn't tell if Vanessa was genuinely infatuated with him, or purposefully messing with him.

I wonder if that story about her back brace was true. The way she looks now, she's too pretty to think about a guy like me as anything more than a friend.

Meanwhile, Bill was impressed by his sister's subtle, yet obvious attempt to annoy him.

"She really is serious. Vanessa has never shown this kind of interest in anyone. I've always known her to flirtcasually, but with you she's doing more than that apparently."

Lucas shook his head and tried to think of a way out of this mess.

Who else can I say kissed me instead of Vanessa? I haven't talked to any other girls around camp except Ashley.

"It wasn't Vanessa. No way. She didn't kiss me. I haven't even seen her since yesterday," Lucas insisted defensively.

Bill's eyebrow raised high.

He doesn't believe me.

"Oh yeah, well who did it then?"

Lucas looked to his so-called friend for help, but Josh was taking a long sip on his orange juice and played with his cereal like he was digging for buried treasure.

He's making himself look unaware of the situation. That's smart. Which is more than I can say for myself right now.

Lucas then looked around and saw Ashley. She was laughing with Hailey and eating with another girl camper he didn't recognize.

"Ashley kissed me," Lucas impulsively insisted. "That's right, yeah. She said it was for being so brave in the battle against Alexia. In all the excitement yesterday, she forgot to thank me for taking one for the team. I know it came late, but at least it shows she cares," he lied, terribly.

Of all the lies I've ever told, this is probably the worst one.

Bill stared at Ashley observantly. His eyes were fixated mostly on her lips, which had no signs of lip gloss.

"She's not wearing any lip gloss," Bill observed. Lucas shrugged and attempted to defend himself.

"She was this morning. Earlier this morning."

This time his lie sounded even worse. Only a real idiot would have believed it now.

If Bill is as smart as he likes to think he is, he should have no problem seeing through the lie.

Unfortunately for him, Bill noticed the weak lie immediately. Josh still played with his food and tried to stay away from the conversation. Lucas noted how Bill forcibly got Josh's attention by waving a hand to his face.

"Look at me, Josh."

When Josh looked up at Bill, he was asked, "Has Ashley ever worn lipstick or make-up?"

It took a few seconds, but once Josh understood, he shook his head. Bill smiled triumphantly and scoffed at Lucas.

"You obviously don't know Ashley that well, my young naïve cabin mate," Bill remarked as he chuckled to himself.

Lucas could feel his face burning with humiliation.

I was always a bad liar. Shelly used to tell me I have the worst poker face she ever saw on anyone. Maybe I am on the autistic spectrum like that one doctor thinks.

"Just do me a favor; next time you tell a lie, try to at least make it more believable," Bill said, as he took a big bite out of his blueberry pancake.

The one thing that comforted Lucas at that moment was only Bill knew of the embarrassment and not Josh.

One is enough, but that could change if Bill tells Josh about it… Who am I kidding? He will eventually. Probably when I'm not around.

After Ashley and Hailey finished eating, they came over to the three boys, with Bill suddenly excusing himself.

"I just remembered, I need to make sure our two latest cabin mates haven't messed with anything in the cabin. I don't know if you can see it, Ashley, but Lucas tells me that you're so grateful to him for his noble sacrifice during yesterday's Relic game."

Bill took off before he could explain further to a confused Ashley.

He doesn't even try to hide it, Lucas thought, glaring at him.

Ashley sat close to Lucas while Hailey positioned herself next to Josh. She greeted him, but he pretended not to notice her. Lucas couldn't tell if it was intentional or not.

"Why am I so grateful to you exactly, Lucas?" Ashley asked in regards to Bill's comment.

He shook his head and dismissed it as he chewed his bacon slowly.

I'll try lying again. Two times the charm is what they say. I think.

"He's probably having something called morning sickness," Lucas lied once more. "I hear it comes from lack of sleep and I know for a fact that he stays up all night watching the same shows on TV."

Lucas didn't realize it at the time, but he had no idea what morning sickness meant.

It's when you're sick in the morning, right?

Ashley looked at Lucas with a suppressed smile as she struggled not to laugh.

"That only happens to girls when they're pregnant, Lucas," said Ashley with a small giggle.

Lucas felt humiliated, again, as she finally broke the restraint and laughed out loud. Hailey did as well when Ashley told her what he said, but Josh was again not aware of the situation. Lucas's face turned bright red as he remembered the saying.

Fool me once, shame on you; fool me twice, shame on me twice.

In this case, it was his fault for falling into his own hole. He remembered Shelly telling him that guys get morning sickness when they get moody.

I actually believed her. I take things so literal sometimes it's not even funny. I remember thinking the days when I woke up in a bad mood were the signs of morning sickness. Now I know that it was just my bipolar side, or my side in general.

When Ashley finished laughing she wiped a small tear from her eye and apologized.

"I'm sorry, Lucas. Who told you about that?"

"My sister Shelly," he said, stopping himself from saying anymore.

"I didn't know you have a sister," Ashley noted with interest. "Why didn't she come to camp with you? I would have liked to have met her."

Ashley wanted to know more, but backed off when Lucas gave her an uneasy look.

"Can we please change the subject? I'm sorry I just can't talk about it right now," said Lucas, uncomfortably.

Ashley nodded and apologized. This made him feel bad when he saw how sincere her curiosity was.

She seems like a nice person, but the more I talk about Shell or think about her, the more I miss her. I know if she were here, Shell would become fast friends with Ashley and Hailey. Maybe Vanessa too.

"Do you have any plans for today?" Ashley asked Lucas.

Lucas looked at Josh who was pretending to sleep, with little success, while Hailey tried to make conversation with him. He sensed that Josh found Hailey more of a nuisance than pleasant company.

How can she annoy him when he's deaf?

Lucas shook his head and Ashley smiled brightly.

"Want to join me for an activity? It's a nice way to pass the time around camp. Plus we get points for our group. I don't know if Bill has told you about that."

Lucas nodded and thought about something Daniel mentioned.

"What about the nature walk one?" Lucas suggested.

He thought about that activity and was almost close to deciding against it until Ashley offered a positive response.

"Alright yeah, that's one I was actually thinking about going to also. Do you have a schedule for the other activities?"

Lucas pulled it out from his pocket and handed it to her. Ashley noticed how it was circled on the specific time, along with a name written on the top left corner in red ink.

"This says 'Daniel and Lucas time' in the middle. Do you see?"

She pointed the circled time out to him when he hadn't noticed it before.

After the way he was this morning, I wouldn't trust him as far as I could recite the alphabet backwards. Also, I don't know how to do that.

He shrugged the thoughts aside.

"I don't know why he put that."

Ashley smirked and handed it back to him.

"Daniel and I talked about you after the games. Not anything bad, just that he's looking forward to seeing your progress during training." Ashley stopped herself short, as if she meant to say more, before composing herself again. "Do you know what his powers are?"

Lucas nodded.

"He can see visions of a possible future, right?"

Ashley nodded and explained further.

"That's one of his abilities. Daniel has a condition called narcolepsy, which causes him to fall asleep at random during the day. It's not as bad as it used to be, but he had to give himself a strict schedule for being active and controlling his sleep patterns. When he sleeps, he dreams of the future. Then, when he wakes up, Daniel writes it down to make sure that it doesn't fade away. He told me it fades completely after about five minutes or less depending on how long he slept while it happened. The only downside is needs to be monitored so he doesn't stay asleep for too long. His girlfriend, Keira, usually helps him with that. Last time we talked she told me about wanting to come back to camp as a psychiatrist, but I don't think Daniel likes the idea. When I mentioned it to him once, he didn't offer an opinion on it."

Lucas suddenly had questions about Daniel's ability.

If he can see into the future, even just a glimpse, how accurate is his predictions? Can he change the outcome? How does he use that ability?

"How often are Daniel's predictions correct?" Lucas decided to ask among the other questions lingering in his mind.

"That's tough to say. He once told me that it's like rolling dice and hoping you don't get snake eyes. As far as how often his predictions are correct, I'd say Daniel's made a lot of good predictions based on not just his abilities, but his own perception on things."

Lucas was about to ask when Ashley volunteered the information.

"Another ability Daniel has in relation to his perception is finding other Alter Children like us. He's able to sense Alter Children the way people pick up on certain smells or sounds. It's connected to his visions also since what he sees are possible futures, meaning he can determine who would be successful in camp vs. kids who wouldn't be a good fit amongst others."

Doesn't sound like it's a fool proof ability if he missed Alexia and her goons, Lucas mused bitterly.

"Why doesn't Daniel have a good relationship with Henry? His father built this place to help kids like us. Why wouldn't they be closer?"

"I honestly don't know anything about that. Daniel doesn't like to talk about his past. I only know what Keira has told me about his mother. They were very close and she passed away when he was young. To tell you the truth, Daniel is the reason I'm here. He told me about this place and I'll always be grateful to him for that," Ashley revealed with a smile at the thought.

I wanted to talk about Henry, but sure, I guess she would prefer to talk about Daniel.

Despite wanting to know more, Lucas sensed that Ashley didn't know anything else about Daniel or Henry. As he was about to leave the cafeteria, she asked about the white lie Bill mentioned.

"What was that about me being so grateful to you for our victory yesterday?" Ashley asked inquisitively.

"I told Bill that you kissed me because we beat orange team yesterday. He saw glitter on my cheek and thought Vanessa had kissed me."

Ashley looked both puzzled and concerned by this.

"Did she? Kiss you I mean?" Ashley asked cautiously.

Lucas looked troubled by this and thought about coming up with another lie.

I don't think I can take being embarrassed again for a third time if I lie about something that I'm wrong about.

"Yes," Lucas heard himself say, shamefully.

Ashley sighed and let out a small chuckle.

"We better get going. I've eaten enough to be full for the whole week," Ashley proclaimed, as she got up to leave with Hailey. "I'll see you at the activity, Lucas."

He nodded in response.

Before leaving, Ashley gave Lucas a brief warning.

"Watch out for Bill's sister," she said, her eyes looking like they were hiding something more. "She likes to flirt a lot. I'm just saying, don't think too much of it. I don't want her to hurt you."

Lucas felt uneasy about that.

I already knew that part, but to hear it from Ashley sounds like she knows more about it than she's saying.

When they were alone, Lucas turned to look at Josh, who suddenly appeared attentive.

"Best part about being deaf: I never have to hear when girls talk. I don't know what they talk about, but from how her mouth kept moving, I know I'm not missing out," Josh signed and said aloud in a concentrated tone.

Lucas nodded, not paying much attention to the comment.

She likes to flirt? What does that mean? Why does Ashley care whether or not she flirts with me? It's not her problem if I get hurt or not.

Finishing his breakfast, Lucas returned to the cabin along with Josh. Bill was already there with Vanessa watching a movie that Lucas had seen before and didn't like because of its length.

When he saw them come in, Bill turned his attention to Josh and Lucas.

"How did it go with you and Ashley, Lover Boy?"

Bill's voice projected itself from the couch towards Lucas.

He shrugged it off, trying not to mention it in front of Vanessa.

"We are going to an activity later on today," Lucas replied, plainly.

Vanessa got up from the couch and walked over to Lucas. Abruptly, Josh got in the way.

"How about you and I grab a spot on the couch and talk? Only you'll have to do all the talking, and I'll pretend to listen," said Josh with a wink.

Vanessa rolled her eyes and Bill looked at Josh with a threatening look.

"Are you looking to get hurt, Joshua? Because it will be very painful."

Bill's tone sounded as sharp as a knife and just as deadly. Even though Josh couldn't hear the manner in which Bill spoke, the look he gave him was enough for Josh to know full well not to mess with him.

I'm guessing that's not the first time he's pissed Bill off, Lucas assessed.

Lucas grabbed a soda for himself and Vanessa. She thanked him as he handed it to her. After she opened it, some of the fizz soaked her hand. When Lucas got a paper towel to clean her hand with, Vanessa asked him about the activity.

"What activity are you going to that has Ashley in it?"

"The nature walk one," Lucas said, taking a sip from his soda after saying this.

"Oh, that one seems boring to me," Vanessa said, flatly. "I rather go to the pottery one. I've always wanted to learn how to do that."

Now that I think about it, the archery one does sound fun. Then again...

"The nature walk one must be fun if Daniel is in charge of it," Lucas said aloud.

Bill bolted from the couch at the sound of the Camp Counselor's name like a dog with a squeaky toy.

"What's this about Daniel? What's he doing?" Bill's tone was excitable.

That's the first time I've seen him get excited about anything since I've known him, which hasn't been long. He's acting like the very ground Daniel walks on is holy. That seems to be what everyone around here thinks.

Lucas told Bill about how Daniel said he's going to supervise and participate in the activity. If he wasn't interested before, Bill was now.

"It's not often Daniel hangs out with us campers. You're so lucky that you'll be trained by him soon," said Bill with envy.

So you've mentioned, but what exactly makes him cool? Being the Camp Director's son? That seems too easy. Is it his power? It's not bad, not impressive either.

"In that case, I'm totally game for the activity. Just let me know when it's happening and I'm there," Bill proclaimed before retaking his spot on the couch.

That was too easy to talk him into it. I didn't even need to ask.

Lucas didn't notice Vanessa was leaving as he entered his imaginary bunk. In the solitude, he decided to look over the pamphlet to see the cabins names and the current campers in each.

Let me see... Atlas's Agony has Jeremy, the guy from the gift shop, and four other kids. Then there's Blunt Bear... so many names, so many people. I don't know everyone yet. Do I care to know them all?

Lucas tried unsuccessfully to read the rest, but groaned in frustration.

Argh! I don't know why I do this to myself. Even when I know it will set me off, I keep making myself think something I don't want to think about. This really sucks!

He tried to swallow some of his medicine, hoping it would calm him down. Lucas still felt the anxiety building up and threaten to make itself known.

I hate this feeling of trying to keep myself from feeling like everything around me is so unknown and scary. How do other people make this seem so natural? Nobody in camp seems like they don't want to be here. Am I the only one? Am I the only one with a home to go back to?

Lucas remembered when his parents tried to help him with his anxiety by putting him in after school activities such as UIL and band. Sadly, he wouldn't last very long in these programs and not for lack of trying. Rather it was because of the way his fellow students treated him.

They would corner me outside of class and say mean things to me like I was dumb, a freak, and they'd hit me in my arm or head if I tried to say anything back... I hated them so much. If I had my powers back then, I could have done something about it. I know Shell would have helped if she knew what was going on. The thing is, some of them are close friends of hers. I worried that if she knew, she wouldn't like friends like me. I wonder what Shell would think if she knew what I can do now? No one would mess with me anymore, I'd make sure of that.

As the pills he took were beginning to take effect, Lucas felt sleep grasp him like an invisible hand.

It's funny; before coming here to Camp Supernatural, I never met anyone who liked me long enough to get to know me. That's why I worry about saying the wrong thing and don't know how to be...

Falling headfirst onto his bed, Lucas closed his eyes to a dreamless sleep.

After what felt like a few minutes, he felt a hand on his shoulder shaking him erratically.

"It's lunchtime. Come on. I'm hungry," Josh shouted, to Lucas's annoyance.

Lunchtime?! How long was I out?

When Lucas tried to get up, he felt very fatigued and almost lost his footing as his feet touched the floor.

The only downside of a good rest is I never want to wake up from it.

Lucas spotted Mike and asked if he would like to join them in the cafeteria, but he politely declined.

Maybe he already ate? I'm sure that has to be it and not because he doesn't like us.

Lucas felt bad about the invitation denial. When he offered to bring him something from the cafeteria, Mike still said no.

I think he's like my dad; the strong silent type.

The walk to the cafeteria was in silence. Lucas could tell Josh wanted to talk, but he wasn't sure what to say. He wondered what people did in situations like this.

I remember Shell said one time that during awkward silences, jokes are a good way of breaking the ice. I don't see how breaking ice helps, but I can try. I'll say 'What do a bee and bird have in common', then punch line.

Lucas tapped on Josh's shoulder and made sure he was looking at him as he spoke.

"What do a bee and bird have in common?"

Josh shrugged, although he looked uninterested in the joke.

"One sings and the other stings."

The way his cabin mate reacted to the joke suggested it didn't land the way he hoped it would.

I thought it was funny, because one sings, the bird, and one stings, the bee. Sing and sting are almost the same word, except one has a T in it. I guess the joke isn't funny if I have to explain it.

"Even though I can't hear the joke, it doesn't sound funny," Josh admitted to Lucas's annoyance.

When they both entered the cafeteria, Lucas was taken aback by how lively it was compared to the morning. It was a little past twelve and the lines went on like rush hour in a big city.

I feel like the whole camp is here right now. So many people, Lucas thought anxiously.

The two campers went to the back of the line and spotted Alexia sitting with three other girls. She gave both Lucas and Josh the stink eye, but otherwise did not bother them. Even though Lucas did his best to not look at her, he felt her glare through the back of his head.

It's as if she's seeing right through me, like someone with X-ray vision, Lucas thought nervously. *I wonder if anyone in this camp has that kind of power. That would be so cool. If I had that kind of ability, I would use it for… well… hmmm. Cheating on math tests?*

Josh didn't help much in avoiding the camp bully's attention when he spoke with a voice that somehow could be heard even in all the commotion going on.

"Did you know that Alexia means 'Defender of Men'? I read that somewhere. She doesn't do a very good job of defending 'deaf men'."

He laughed so loudly at his own joke, that if Alexia heard him she hid it well.

Forget it. If this camp doesn't get me first, Josh's bad jokes will.

It took almost fifteen minutes to get in front of the line with the amount of campers in the cafeteria. When Lucas finally got his plate, he saw the young lunch lady once again. She wasn't alone this time. She had a small little toddler with her. He looked to be about two years old with whisks of light brown hair on his head, a very puffy face, and squinty eyes.

He looks like those fake dolls in health class.

"His name is Teddy. He's named after Richardson's favorite president," the young lunch lady explained to Lucas and Josh. Only Lucas gave his attention to the young lunch lady. Josh appeared to be more interested in getting his food.

"Are you and the Camp Activities Director married?" Lucas asked impulsively.

I should not have asked that. Then again, I never thought a guy like that would end up with a lady like her.

She shook her head and began to fill his plate with food.

"We're not married, but he got me a job here so I could be closer to our son."

She didn't sound enthusiastic about the idea, so Lucas dropped the subject. The toddler was drooling and looked at them as if they were from another planet.

I wonder if that is how I looked at that age; so innocent and full of life. Ignorant of the hardships that would follow. What happened to that part of me? Oh that's right. I grew up.

Their meals consisted of chicken tenders with a fruit cup side and mashed potatoes covered in brown gravy. The young lunch lady slipped in a few extra tenders for both campers. Only Lucas thanked her, while Josh hadn't noticed the extra food.

I'm getting hangry vibes from him.

When they finished getting their lunch, Lucas spied Richardson and Alexander sitting where the other camp counselors were. This included Margot, Jane, Lucinda, and Marcus. The way Richardson and Alexander bantered reminded Lucas of Shelly for some reason.

"Do you know how old Richardson is compared to that lunch lady?" Lucas asked Josh, who was busy biting into his cheeseburger.

When Josh didn't reply, Lucas got his attention and repeated himself.

Josh shrugged.

"No idea, sorry. Probably as old as Daniel?"

I don't think he's much in a talking mood, something that surprised Lucas as he thought about it.

The rest of their meal was in silence, as they sat there quietly while the other tables were lively. Lucas looked around to see if he could find Ashley and Hailey. They were nowhere to be seen.

They probably already ate and are getting ready for the activity later on today.

Lucas overheard Lucinda, Margot, and Jane talking about various topics that both related to camp and involved their social lives.

Lucinda wants to stay in camp for another year before going abroad with her boyfriend of four years. She's also, according to Jane, waiting for him to pop the question to her. What question? Margot is studying to become a physician and is getting ready to leave camp after the summer so she can go through the program at her local clinic. Jane is talking about how she has a crush on Daniel, even knowing he has a girlfriend. The other girls don't sound like they approve of it, but they're not doing anything to stop her from being interested in him. Marcus looks like he's just keeping to himself, like me any other day.

Lucas stopped listening to their conversation, feeling that he was hearing information not meant for his ears. He didn't like knowing that someone else had a crush on Daniel on top of how much he was revered in camp.

Once the food lines died down, the beautiful lunch lady left her post with her son to join the Camp Activities Director. Richardson lifted the toddler up from her and gave him a hug. Alexander greeted the young lunch lady and the two shared a brief embrace. From the way they talked, Lucas swore Alexander seemed nicer.

He doesn't look like he's that way with everyone here.

Lucas was so fixated on all his thoughts and the surrounding people that he didn't notice his plate was empty, much to Josh's astonishment.

"You ate it all like a hungry dog," Josh exclaimed. Lucas noted that both he and his cabin mate had cleaned out their plates.

I just realized I've never been this hungry before. When I used to take medicines regularly, I wouldn't get hungry. Now that I'm not taking them, all I want to do is eat. As long as it doesn't turn into stress eating.

"Where are you from, Luke?" Josh suddenly asked conversationally.

Lucas took a moment to answer back. His eyes were suddenly glued on a cheeseburger that another camper had in the table next to them.

Why didn't I get a cheeseburger? I want a cheeseburger.

Josh snapped his fingers and got in front of Lucas's face.

"I'm right here, Luke. Where's your home?"

Lucas sighed and answered. "Austin, Texas."

"Austin, Texas? I'm from Denver, closer to the bottom of it. My family move back and forth between the places they own. One year I stayed in New Mexico. That's where I met Ashley, Hailey, Bill and Vanessa, before camp," Josh signed and spoke aloud. Some of what he said was hard for Lucas to understand due to the way he signed with his hands.

I'm not too familiar with sign language, but I feel the way Josh does it is considered unconventional.

Lucas made no attempt to keep the conversation going. The two discarded their trays and hurried to their cabin to prepare for the afternoon activity. To his surprise, Josh revealed his involvement in the nature walk.

"All we need is eyes for this activity. Luckily, I have two," Josh noted humorously. He pointed to himself and his eyes with his two index fingers.

That's stating the obvious.

Lucas took a shower, and tried to pick out the best clothes he could find. He didn't want to wear any of the shirts he brought with him because he knew all campers are supposed to wear camp-based shirts. The only one he had was the free one he got from the gift shop, but he decided he didn't want to wear that one.

It can be more of a momentum of this summer, since it has the year the camp was founded in.

Bill saw his dilemma and handed him a spare blue shirt he had with the words, 'Mind over Matter' embroiled in the middle with yellow indents.

"That shirt is a good fit for you," Bill admired. "Keep it on when doing activities. It helps to identify what cabin you belong to and it glows in the dark."

When Bill turned off the lights, the words glowed in the dark with a yellow-blue hue. Josh noticed the shirt and began to gloat about how it was his idea to make it that way, even though most of the other campers thought it was a stupid idea.

"I put in a special order at the gift shop last year for shirts like that. Josh had the idea before coming to camp, so I promised him I'd get a couple of these for him and everyone else here in the cabin," Bill explained proudly.

I got to admit; it's not a bad idea, Lucas thought to himself. *I'll keep that to myself. No need to boost Josh's ego further.*

Among the things Lucas got from the gift shop earlier, he decided to use the backpack despite its limited pockets. He did note that it could hold more in its larger pocket than the backpack he brought from home. He also wore the cap he got despite how it made his hair feel.

At least it'll keep me from sweating too much. I seriously need a haircut when I get back home.

Bill noticed Lucas's cap and complimented the headwear.

"I didn't figure you for a cap person, but it looks good on you," Bill noted to Lucas's bashfulness.

And it has our cabin words on it.

Before Josh and Lucas could leave, Bill slapped on a backpack behind him and walked to their side.

"I've decided to join you guys," announced Bill. "If this will be my last summer as a camper, I may as well act like one. Also, I need to lay off the sodas and chips because I feel fat."

Lucas didn't think Bill was getting fat.

If anything those chips and sodas are just giving him a bit of acne. That's about it. Shell once said that guys lose weight faster than girls anyways, so he should be fine.

As the three campers left the cabin, Bill handed Lucas his identification book from the last time he participated in the activity.

"This has most of the main flowers, rocks, birds and basic environmental things to keep an eye out for," Bill explained as he turned the pages. "The Camp Guardian is pretty good about getting stuff that's in here. He will usually put in old ones along with new ones. It's always a good combination of the two."

Lucas nodded and took a peak at Bill's identification book. The cover was plain and had a hand-drawn flower that looked like someone added it at the last minute.

This books a bit thick, Lucas observed. *Fifty pages? At least the pictures make it look like a coloring book. A colored book.*

When Lucas scrolled through the booklet, he found the pages contents were of many plant's he'd never seen before. This included a flower that had a purple center, with the pedals resembling a rainbow. While looking at this particular flower, Bill described it for Lucas.

"They call that one the 'Prismatic Glow'. It's an old plant that is said to not be from our world supposedly."

Not from our world? Now there's more than our world? Besides the planets we know of? I wish I could tell if he was messing with me or not.

Lucas hated how social norms were like a foreign language for him.

When to laugh, when to smile, and when to tell someone you don't want to talk. For instance, I hate talking on the phone. Hate it. Unlike me, Shelly hates texting. She still uses a phone like a phone. If we had reception here, I know she'd be calling me like crazy.

"Keep your head in the game, Luke," Bill suddenly said. "The sun isn't bright enough to get to you yet."

Lucas tried to keep himself focused, but found this more difficult than trying to make idle conversation with someone.

To be fair, I'm used to not saying anything and a person getting tired of me for that. The times I've talked in camp so far as a whole is the most I've ever talked to anyone in my life besides with Shell.

Thinking of his older sister made Lucas tug on the necklace around his neck impulsively. Bill noticed and asked about it.

"Are you wearing jewelry?" Bill asked in a joking manner. Lucas shook his head and tried to dismiss the subject.

"It's nothing important."

"Then why are you wearing it around your neck?"

Josh noticed it as well.

"What is that? Something worth a lot of money?"

Lucas shrugged it off and buried it underneath his shirt collar.

I don't want to talk about Shelly right now.

When he didn't offer a response, Josh and Bill eventually left him alone.

Ashley and Hailey came over, each carrying a backpack, and waved for the three boys to join them.

I hate groups, Lucas thought, uncomfortably. *I guess around here being solo isn't an option.*

It occurred to Lucas that amongst the five of them, he was the only one wearing a cap. He was nearly grateful when Ashley and Hailey didn't point that out the way Bill had done.

Maybe I should take it off. I hate being the only one who thought to wear one.

Lucas took his cap off and tucked it into his backpack. Bill noticed and got his attention.

"You alright, Luke? I thought the cap looked good on you."

Lucas just shook his head and did not offer a response. Bill nodded, understood.

"Are you excited for your first activity here at camp, Luke?" Even though Bill tried to be encouraging, his tone sounded insincere.

I know the real reason he's here and it's not because he wants to be my best friend.

In response, Lucas shrugged.

"I've never done activities with anyone before," Lucas admitted. "My summer's always consisted of soda's and playing video games."

Bill laughed and threw his hands behind his head.

"Sounds like good times," Bill replied breathlessly. "By any chance do you like RPG's? Games that require a lot of strategy and grinding?"

Lucas shook his head.

"I just play the games that are easiest to get through."

This answer seemed to satisfy Bill's curiosity.

As the others talked amongst each other, Lucas began to think of the things he couldn't have at the moment. Some of these things included being lectured by Shelly.

I'd take Shelly lecturing me any day of the week over being here and pretending that I like everything about this place. I'll put it this way; Bill isn't the kind of person I'd be friends with outside of camp. Josh isn't someone that I would talk to either. Ashley would never notice me, much less Vanessa. Alexia would probably be the only one, because bullies somehow always seem to target me or people like me.

Lucas tried to push the thoughts behind him, but found them poking at his shoulders with ill intent.

If I'm going to spend so much time thinking about home and Shelly, I should have just stayed in my bunk and wallowed in misery. Now I wish I had the power to run fast like Ashley so I can sleep off these feelings instead of living with them.

Lucas continued to be plagued by his thoughts and emotions as Bill talked about his first years in Camp Supernatural.

"The first year I came here, I remember not wanting to do anything either. Just talk to girls, hang out with Daniel, and watch television. I only got into activities like this one because Daniel encouraged it and I met people this way. You'd be surprised how many campers don't take an active role here despite the number of things to do. Henry tries to tell us that it's rewarding and fun, but Daniel is the one who sells the idea. He takes a more approachable way of asking vs. the way Henry kind of just stays on the sidelines and says..." Bill's voice trailed off as Lucas's own thoughts drowned it out.

I hope Shelly is okay. I remember she called out to me as I was leaving. At least I think she did. Maybe she was in shock at what I did to dad. I wish I could have turned back, just to know for sure.

He tried to convince himself what happened was an accident, but he started to wonder if it was.

Deep down, I think I always wanted to hurt my parents the way they hurt me. Not physically of course. I just wanted them to know what it felt like to not get up, to not speak up, to feel powerless. I'm not powerless anymore and I can handle anyone who messes with me now.

The last thought made him very uneasy, even more than the other thoughts he pushed aside. When it came to those thoughts, they felt more natural to him. The whole notion of using his powers to get what he wanted seemed to go against what he believed was right.

When they reached the rest of the campers gathered around, Lucas saw them all wearing different shirts ranging from ones that read: 'Gum Up the Works', to 'Original Pranksters', to 'New Horizons', and 'Final Curtains'.

If this camp turns out to be some kind of cult, I swear, I'll be on the first taxi cab out of here. Even if it's with another skeleton like Francis.

Ashley briefly explained the reason for all the words on the shirts when she noticed Lucas's uncomfortable demeanor.

"Each cabin possesses not just their own attributes, but names like royal houses. Your own, 'Mind over Matter', symbolizes what abilities you have and what cabin you belong to since that is what we go by here."

Despite the explanation, Lucas knew this already. He was still unsure of their significance though.

Some sound like wordplay, others like someone made them up at the last minute. At least I got a cool cabin. I can see how it relates to me. I don't see that for Josh, Bill, Gary, and Mike.

"What else is real here? Next thing you'll tell me unicorns are real," Lucas asked, hoping his tone would give off that he was joking. To his dismay, Ashley took his question literally.

"They were real once. In fact, there's a rainbow cabin with a Unicorn sticking out on the top called Underrated Unicorn. It's a popular cabin for girls under the age of thirteen. It's mostly used for housing younger children. The same goes for Obnoxious Offspring. Even though it's part of the main cabins, not the back ones, it always has at least one younger camper."

Lucas began to fixate on the idea of unicorns, beginning to accept that they might have been real at one point.

Shelly used to love Unicorns when she was little, he reminisced. *She had a Unicorn named Alex, after her first crush in elementary school. She stopped liking him after he ate her crayons. From what I've heard, his behavior hasn't improved since.*

When Shelly came home one day, she found that her brother had destroyed the Unicorn named Alex. His horn and legs were yanked off, with the bits of cotton scattered around the floor like confetti.

Shelly cried for days because of this, even after their parents got her a new unicorn toy.

What she didn't see was my dad slapping me and my mom calling me a spoiled brat, Lucas recalled bitterly. *The words somehow hurt more than the slaps since I remember them more.*

Despite still carrying the guilt with him, Shelly had long forgiven him for it.

Returning to the present day, Lucas noticed that the other children were carrying canteens with them and he began to panic.

I didn't know we were supposed to bring our own water, he anxiously admitted. *Why did I think there would be water provided out here? Oh wait, I didn't think that at all!*

Ashley offered to share the water she brought for herself with Lucas.

"Here, I got enough for both of us," said Ashley as she held it out to him.

Lucas hesitated when he noticed how much was actually in it.

"I can't take yours. You might need it," Lucas insisted, sincerely.

"That's why we're sharing it. In the meantime, you can hold onto it and I'll let you know when I need some."

Lucas accepted the idea and put the canteen in the left side of his backpack. As Ashley began to close her pack, he noticed a number of small meals and snacks that were bundled up inside.

It looks like Ashley raided the food pantry in the cafeteria. It's any wonder she hasn't gained any weight. Maybe she's into Zumba or whatever that's called.

As he thought to himself, Daniel came towards the group, wearing shorts, walking shoes, and a boonie hat with a thin strap at the bottom hanging by his lower chin. He also wore sunscreen on both his cheeks which went with how light his skin tone was.

He looks more like a camper than a counselor dressed like that, Lucas admitted to himself.

When Daniel approached the group, he pointed out the obvious overuse of sunscreen.

"This activity usually tends to last all afternoon," Daniel explained. "Betty is going to supervise the next game taking place in the afternoon so they'll be on the other side of the forest while we are here."

"Is Henry coming?" Lucas asked, half-hoping that he would join them.

To his disappointment, Daniel shook his head.

"My father doesn't partake in these sorts of activities," the Camp Director's son noted with a soft yawn. "He's supervising the remaining games for the first year campers. Besides, being the Camp Director of this place doesn't give him a lot of free time for much else." Daniel said the last part with a hint of dissatisfaction in his tone.

Lucas understood that not only was Henry responsible for everyone while they attended camp, but also in making sure that no one's powers went haywire in the process.

I wonder if super heroes and super villains are real. I've never heard of anyone who had powers do anything in the real world. Anyways, the sooner this summer ends, the sooner I can get back home and away from this nonsense, Lucas thought the last part anxiously.

What worried him most though was how his parents would feel about his newfound abilities, which as it turns out, are part of the reason he had a difficult time in everything he went through.

Maybe Henry can talk to them for me. Explain that I'm not crazy and that after this summer, I'll do my best to take things like my education more seriously. I can even say I made friends here. Friends I don't plan to see again after August comes. Yeah, this idea isn't far-fetched at all. It definitely is.

Back in reality, Daniel began talking with Ashley about the activity. Lucas could tell that the two had familiarity outside of camp.

I remember she mentioned something about Daniel being the reason she's here. Maybe she could help me get an audience with the Camp Director through his son. I don't want Ashley to think I'm using her, but I think she'll do it for me if I ask.

Abruptly, Josh distracted Lucas's train of thought.

"Are you good at finding things, Luke, because I have good eyesight, but a terrible sense of hearing?" quipped Josh in his usual tone.

In response to the question, Lucas shook his head, much to his friend's disappointment.

"I can't stand looking at anything too long," Lucas pointed out, curtly. "I don't know how to sign language that, so I won't bother trying."

The last words he said were muffled by his closed lips, but Josh caught most of what he said.

"I'm guessing you're not into this, are you?" Josh asked Lucas intuitively.

"If it gets my mind off of things then, yeah sure, I'm all for it," Lucas replied, sarcastically. This time he made sure Josh couldn't have known what he said.

While Lucas's mind was nowhere near his head, the only person in the group who noticed was Josh.

Even though he can't hear a word I'm saying, his eyes see the truth. He's a lot more aware of things than I think people give him credit for.

To his slight relief, Bill came over to get Lucas's attention.

"Just a heads up, Vanessa decided to join us." Bill's tone suggested his reluctance with the idea.

Lucas nodded hesitantly and suddenly had a bad taste in his mouth.

It's nice to know that an adult is nearby, even though that adult scared the bejesus out of me this morning.

It didn't take long for Vanessa to make her way to Lucas, who was less than happy to see her at the moment.

"Is Josh giving you a hard time, Lucas?" Vanessa asked, as she noticed him mumbling sounds to break the awkwardness between them.

"It's nothing I can't handle. In this case, I just turn the other cheek like that old saying goes."

Vanessa giggled and nodded.

I made her laugh. That felt mildly good.

Richardson and Marcus made their way towards the opposite group of campers. When Marcus noticed Daniel, he got his attention and the two suddenly turned into bitter rivals. Incidentally, Daniel looked like he anticipated it. Lucas could almost see the lightning beam in-between them, and it unsettled him.

This reminds me of when Shelly used to get competitive with Beatrice, this girl from when she was in middle school. She always knew how to get under my sister's skin in ways that made her do stupid stuff, like this one time they competed in the spelling bee. Shell got so riled up by the end that she misspelled one word because she forgot that the letter was silent. It was pseudonym.

"May the best team win today, Daniel," Marcus said amiably. He looked to be about the same age as the Camp Director's son, but with more stubble on his face to make a light beard. "I'm sure you'll all give it your best."

Daniel huffed at this as if he meant to swallow the air around him whole.

"If anything you should be more worried about your own team, because this team includes members who won the first Relic game of the summer," Daniel snapped back, adjusting his boonie hat.

They're like us; teenagers. And here I thought these guys were supposed to be role models for us. Instead they're exactly like us.

"Anyone can win a game, but life isn't a game," Marcus noted, leaving before Daniel could have the last word. The Camp Director's son persisted.

"Oh yeah, if life isn't a game, you're not playing it right."

Lucas waited to see if anyone else would slap their foreheads. When it didn't happen, he did so in his mind.

Was that a good comeback? No, it wasn't.

"Alright, break it up you two," Richardson commanded. "As Camp Activities Director, it's my job to instruct you all on the rules of this game. Pay attention because I don't like to repeat myself."

The instructions were as followed: Both teams had four hours to identify as much as they could in the forest, with everything they would need to find in the areas they were in. Once they identified something, their job was to mark it with a small flag featuring two different colors; yellow for Daniel, and orange for Marcus. The team with the most flags would be the winner. Lucas saw a lot of new faces amongst the opposite team and even a few from his own.

I only know Ashley, Bill, Josh, Hailey, and Vanessa. From the cabins I mentioned earlier, those kids stand out to me as much as a black dot on a white shirt.

"Each item is worth one point and will be tallied after the end of the third hour. After that, both teams will have one more hour to find anymore unidentified items. Amongst the identifiable objects are rare items which, if found, will result in an instant victory for the respective team. I'll be supervising both teams to ensure a fair contest and collecting your tallies in this here notepad. May the best team win indeed."

After Richardson explained the rules, the nature walk began with the two teams splitting up to identify as many items in the forest as possible. Lucas found himself stuck with Josh who, not long after the activity started, ended up drinking his own canteen empty. He then stole Ashley's canteen from Lucas as he tried unsuccessfully to identify a plant that he could not pronounce the name of. When Lucas discovered the missing canteen, he angrily confronted his guilty cabin mate.

"That was Ashley's water! She was letting me hold onto it. Now what are we going to drink?"

Josh shrugged and looked helpless against his sharp, but true accusations.

I'm really getting sick of this guy and his relaxed attitude.

Before a scuffle could happen, Daniel defused the situation by revealing he packed extra canteens for this very emergency.

"I made sure to bring enough for everyone. Try to only drink what you need and not the whole thing in one shot."

Lucas nodded and made sure Josh knew he wasn't going to share with him.

"This is for me and Ashley. You can share with Hailey," Lucas instructed Josh. When he deciphered what Lucas said, Josh frowned and resigned to his self-proclaimed punishment.

After the water was distributed amongst each team member, the real business began.

Marcus's team were surveying the left side of the forest. They ended up finding unique rocks, birds and some of the insects that inhabited the trees. He awarded some points to a child on his team for discovering a small group of blue ants.

Where did the Camp Guardian find those? They look more like spiders than ants.

To add to the strangeness of the ants, they also had only four legs instead of six and looked to be a few more inches bigger than a regular ant should be. Marcus told the child who discovered the ants not to feed or touch them.

I wonder why? Maybe they don't like handouts. Ha ha. I hate being the only one who gets my jokes.

While Marcus's team studied the actions of the ants, Daniel's team went on to identifying the specific plants and minerals of the environment on the right hand side. Both teams were due to switch sides within an hour apart. Ashley went with Daniel to identify plants, while Lucas and Josh focused on rocks. Thinking it would be easier than plants, Lucas soon realized all the rocks looked the same.

The only difference if any would be the shape or size, but in the end they all look rock solid.

Lucas tried to use the book Bill gave him, but it didn't have a lot of information about different rocks. Vanessa and her brother were looking for any birds in the area, with little luck, while Hailey and another girl were looking for ants similar to the ones Marcus's team found.

Looks like everyone is doing their own thing. Josh and I are the only ones on rock duty, and that doesn't rock. If I make one more pun I'm sharing it, I swear.

The way the nature walk activity worked was basically first come, first serve. Each person had to give whoever found an object a fair chance to identify it. If they failed, the next person waiting would be next. Daniel was racing against time with Marcus and the two would occasionally butt heads with each other while trying to hog the other's identification object.

They are like kids fighting over lunch money in the playground, Lucas thought, amusingly. *Marcus is at least trying not to make a scene, while Daniel is taking every chance he can to insult him. I feel like there's more beef between them than a jumbo-mega burger. Alright that's it, I'm sharing my puns with someone.*

Lucas decided to share his puns with Josh as he fruitlessly continued to sort through the rocks they had gathered together.

"Hey Josh, what do you call a burger that steals?" He didn't wait for an answer or acknowledgement. "A burglar."

Lucas began to laugh at his own joke, something which caught the attention of Ashley, who took a quick pause from her identification of plants to hear his joke. When she did, she chuckled, but didn't laugh out loud as he had hoped.

"I think I've heard that one before. It's cheesy, but funny."

"Cheesy and good enough to eat," Lucas quipped, as he found himself laughing more than he had intended. This positive energy did much to rejuvenate him of his anxiety and seemed to ignite a passion in those around him as well. Ironically, even Josh was beginning to be more active in his viewing of rocks as if circling through vinyl's in a record store.

I can feel the way everyone around me feels now; Ashley is happy for me having fun, Josh is less absent-minded than usual, while Bill and Vanessa are treating bird watching like looking at shooting stars. Why am I suddenly feeling this way? Is it one of my mood swings?

"If you two are done laughing at each other," Bill noted to both Ashley and Lucas, "we're having trouble over here with finding any birds. I think they migrated south earlier than planned."

Lucas looked around and to his amazement spotted a purple bird called a Stellar's Jay. It was perched atop a tree that had been overlooking the site where Josh had spent several minutes examining rocks fruitlessly. It was big enough that Bill was shocked he hadn't noticed it before.

Maybe it came from another dimension, because, you know, everything here seems to do that.

After Bill was able to successfully identify the bird, Vanessa ended up finding another bird that was similar to the Stellar's Jay. When Bill tried to claim the credit for the second though, neither he nor Vanessa could agree on the color of the bird.

"That's a blue bird, isn't it?" Bill asked Lucas with certainty in this tone.

"That bird is clearly grey. Your color blind so of course you wouldn't be able to tell the difference," Vanessa affirmed with a similar tone as her brother.

Lucas looked at the bird above them and saw that it was indeed the color Vanessa claimed. He tried to be oblivious the way Josh would be but, unlike his cabin mate, both his ears were in working order.

It helps that Josh is deaf and can't hear anything. Meanwhile my own head is loud enough to make it hard to hear anything else. Speaking of, I've been thinking about how else my power might make itself known. Maybe I can put thoughts into people's heads, make them think they're a fish out of water. Or maybe get them to speak in another language just to hear how different their voice would sound like.

Lucas was so immersed in his thoughts that both Bill and Vanessa got frustrated with his inaction.

"We'll ask someone else to decide what color it is for us since you can't tell the difference," Vanessa insisted to her brother. Ashley enlisted Lucas's help with her side of the forest while Josh continued to examine the rocks. Daniel had finished surveying his area and decided to see how many items Marcus had taken up on his side.

"Can anyone in camp talk to fish?" Lucas asked, almost as if his thoughts were being projected aloud.

"I have no idea. Now come on, help me find some more objects to identify before it's too late," Ashley insisted, as she shoved her identification book into his open palm. She pulled from her pack a candy bar and began to munch on it as she sprinted back and forth between the objects she was looking at.

Lucas sighed and read to her the names of various plants as she identified them.

She has a real sweet tooth and just when I was beginning to get into the mood too. Now I feel it coming down like the end of a sugar rush. Who cares if we win? Is there a medal for 'best effort' here?

By the end, Josh had found less than handful of different rocks, but was unable to carry the rest due to being the only one on rock duty. After the two siblings agreed to share half the credit for the second bird, Vanessa found three different kinds of birds, while Bill found a hummingbird, along with a yellow American Goldfinch. Hailey and the person she was with found an arrowhead, which looked more like a souvenir than the real thing.

It's probably from the camp gift shop. Still, I shouldn't ruin that for Hailey.

At three hours in, both teams halted and observed their flags. Daniel's team's flags amounted to twenty unique rocks, fifteen birds, one possibly fake arrowhead, and thirty-nine plants. In contrast, Marcus's team showed off more orange flags, with twenty-one unique rocks, twenty-five birds, and thirty-four plants.

"Daniel's yellow team leads with seventy-five points, while Marcus's orange team leads with eighty points," Richardson noted in his notepad. "The last hour will commence. Good luck."

"Winner takes all," Marcus proclaimed.

I feel so out of it from thinking about all these weird names these plants have, thought Lucas, exhaustingly. *Ashley has a better tolerance for this stuff than I do. Not to mention all the stuff I've been mauling in my head. Now I can't stop thinking about what's better: sandwiches with crusts or no crust? Because to me, the crust tastes kind of harder than the actual bread itself. It's why I personally prefer bread without the crust. On the other hand, it's like biting into an apple's skin before eating the apple itself... okay that's enough drowning in my own thoughts now.*

By the end of the hour, yellow team ended up with ninety-two points and orange team ninety-four points. Unfortunately, all areas were picked clean of identifiable objects without flags.

I noticed Ashley didn't use her speeding ability to just go through the whole area faster than everyone else. I think she's trying to be fair. That and Richardson will probably dock points.

Richardson allowed both teams an opportunity to find the rare winning item he mentioned earlier. When ten minutes elapsed, he prepared to call Marcus's team victor by default. Before he could, Josh poked Lucas's shoulder and pointed to a small flower with a peculiar appearance. It was behind a pile of rocks that had been moved to reveal the flower's location.

"Is it poisonous?" Josh asked as Lucas gazed at the unknown plant.

What kind of flower is that? I've never seen one look like that.

The inside ovary was a light red color and the pedals were a bright yellow. The flower looked like it was the sun in plant form. Lucas immediately called Daniel, who scurried to where the two campers were.

"Does this look familiar to you?"

Daniel, who appeared ready to fall asleep at any moment, looked even more shocked by the strange looking flower. After examining it, he shook his head and looked at it in admiration.

"This looks unique. Sometimes Boris puts these up. It looks like the last identifiable object here."

Ashley came fast as soon as she saw what was going

on, almost tripping on herself in the process. Once she collected herself, she carefully titled her head to level with the position the flower was in.

"How did we miss this one?"

Bill did not look convinced of the flowers validity.

"That's a pretty odd flower to just not see until this very moment," said Bill with reluctance. "How do we know it's the real deal and not some cheap knock-off like that arrowhead Hailey found?"

Hailey looked offended by this, until Richardson joined the group and noticed the rare flower.

"All the items here are legit, or at least close enough to count for the activity. With that being said, the arrowhead will still count, Hailey."

She looked satisfied and examined the arrowhead as if discovering it for the first time.

After Ashley gave the flower a final inspection, she glanced at both Josh and Lucas as if they were mad geniuses.

"Which one of you found it?"

Josh raised his hand since he saw her finger point towards the flower with an intrigued look and concluded what she had asked. She gave him a puzzled look, but nonetheless accepted the answer.

"I guess you get the honor of naming it as part of camp tradition. Unless you would prefer to hand the honor over to another camper?" signed Ashley. She turned to look at Richardson, who solemnly confirmed this.

Lucas half-expected Josh to pick Ashley, as she would have wanted. To everyone's surprise, he chose Lucas.

"I'm not so good with names. As it is I can't hear any cool ones. I give that honor to my good friend, Luke."

Josh laid a soft hand on his friends' shoulder as all eyes diverted to Lucas like a spotlight.

They are all treating this like someone just had a baby, thought Lucas, uncomfortably. *If I give it a dumb name, they'll never let me forget it.*

He could feel a variety of emotions coursing through him that were both his own and from the others surrounding him; excitement, anxiousness, anger, and he swore one person felt confused, but thought that could be him misunderstanding the feeling.

Lucas knelt down to examine the flower closer. It gave off a strange aura that was warm, but when he moved his hand to touch it, it was watery like melting ice. He turned his head upwards and saw Vanessa looking at him expectantly.

She looks like she wants me to name it after her. But I know this means more to Ashley than anyone else here.

Lucas didn't even need to look at Ashley to know. All it took was a quick thought, and his decision was made.

"The flowers name will be Ashley's Willow." He assumed a kneeling position and gestured for someone to dig it up delicately. "It's yours if you will have it, Ashley of the Weeping Willow."

I thought it would be a cool nod to her name and the cabin she's in, Lucas decided, proudly.

Ashley appeared stunned by this, as if someone had proposed marriage to her.

It probably looks that way because that I'm still on my knees.

Unsurprisingly, Vanessa found herself speechless.

"Yellow team wins by default for discovering the rare flower, Ashley's Willow," Richardson proclaimed, putting away his notepad. He gave Lucas an unsmiling nod.

The surrounding campers began clapping and congratulating Lucas's team on finding a rare new flower to name and claiming victory once more for yellow team.

Ashley mouthed a 'Thank You' to Lucas as she flushed cherry red at him.

Hailey smiled and patted him on the shoulder happily.

"That was really nice of you, Lucas. Thank you for that."

He nodded and smiled back. Lucas felt good for another accomplishment, feeling like his place in camp was becoming more solidified with each victory he helped his team achieve. Despite Josh being the one who actually discovered the flower, Lucas appreciated that he gave him the honor of naming it. Bill offered his congratulations as well.

"Impressive work, my friend. That's quite a streak you got going here," Bill remarked, admirably. "For a second there I thought you were going to name it after Vanessa. Maybe 'Vanessa's Kingdom'."

Lucas's joy was cut short when he thought about how this would make Bill's sister feel. When he looked at her, Vanessa gave him a reassuring smile, which betrayed what she was really feeling deep down.

I understand where she is coming from. But I wanted Ashley to be happy also.

Despite their loss, Marcus and his team took it in stride, and they were still honored with the points they earned, which could still count for them in more activities. He shook hands with Daniel, who still tried to play it off like he knew they'd emerge victorious all along.

He's not being humble about it either.

Once the activity ended, Lucas went back to his cabin with Bill and Josh. Mike asked the trio how the activity went, but only two of the three campers decided to talk to him. Lucas felt out of social pleasantries.

It's not that I'm having a bad time or anything. Today was the best day yet, besides the morning part. I have to admit that to myself. I am having fun. I have to remind myself this is only temporary. I don't want to get attached to the idea of being here any longer than I need to be. Even if I'm beginning to wish I could just stay here. No, stop thinking that right now.

Gary tried to join in on the conversation, but by the time he made his presence known, Bill had flipped the television on and turned his attention to Lucas.

"In only two days, I've seen something I never thought I'd see here in camp. Yellow team has won two events in a row this summer," said Bill, proudly. "It looks like all this time we were waiting for you to pull out the wins for us. You're becoming quite the lucky charm."

Lucas felt a smile creep on his lips. He wanted to hide it, but decided to let it show.

I don't know how I look smiling right now. If I had a mirror I could tell better, but based on how it feels, it's the most I've smiled since being here.

Josh threw himself on the couch face down just a few short inches away from Bill.

"Pizza day tomorrow. I'm so hungry I could eat a cow right now," Josh blurted out.

Bill rolled his eyes and shook his head.

"Don't ruin this moment please. This is your victory too. It was a really solid thing you did for Lucas out there."

Bill glanced at Josh while his attention was on Lucas.

"He's thinks of you as his best friend now," Bill noted humorously while Josh's face was still planted on the couch. "I'm glad we're cabin mates, and not just because you're helping us win stuff. It's because you're a good guy. Josh thinks so and he hasn't been wrong before."

Lucas nodded and decided to make a peanut butter and jelly sandwich. He debated between eating it with the crust or no crust, and decided to eat the bread the way it was.

Instead of sleeping in early as he originally intended, Lucas decided to enjoy some television time with his new friends. By this point, Josh had adjusted himself so he was now sitting next to Lucas. Surprisingly, Gary and Mike joined them as well. It wasn't long before the five of them were seeing a movie, all with sodas in hand.

For the first time since he arrived and against his earlier thought, Lucas felt awesome joy at being surrounded by his first real friends. At that moment, he didn't think of home, Shelly, or other distracting thoughts; only the moment itself...

Chapter 6

Mind Over Matter

The days leading up to training began to fly after the nature walk activity, as Lucas began to participate in more activities. He did this both for the points and to socialize with his new group of friends. The canoeing activity took place the following day.

Lucas's team passed with flying colors, mostly due to Hailey having very strong arms when rowing the team across the narrow waves of the camp's river canal. He also surprised himself with his natural ability to follow the tide and lead his fellow campers from the waters to safety, proving to be an excellent navigator. Richardson didn't have to take an active role since the campers in the activity were able to handle their tasks while working well together.

I never thought I had it in me to do that, Lucas thought with a smile. *I can't tell if Richardson is impressed by me or just thinks I'm lucky. His thoughts are about as lively as his facial expressions.*

Lucas and his friends were about to do a second row around the river to earn extra points when it began to rain, causing the waves to become tumultuous. Richardson assured everyone that stormy weather was a common occurrence in the camp.

What's that old saying? Summer rains are like people; both can't make up their minds. At least, that's what Shelly used to say.

The following day, Lucas decided to try archery with Betty hosting it, but failed to hit the target after a number of tries. He and Josh then tried Pottery, but the music that played for the activity made Lucas fall asleep. He woke up with bits of clay on the right side of his face.

It's not my fault that kind of music bores me to tears, Lucas thought in annoyance. *Also Josh just saw me fall asleep and didn't try to wake me. Some friend he is.*

The next activity they both did proved to be a bit more challenging. It involved surviving in the forest with only one canteen of water, a loaf of bread, two flint rocks, and leaves from morning to night. The goal was to use each as needed. Richardson escorted the campers to different parts of the forest and told them he would check on their progress within the morrow.

Morrow? What's a morrow? Like more row? What we just did in the canoeing activity, Lucas mused to himself.

He managed to survive all the way through the afternoon, until he ate a berry that caused him indigestion. Josh ended up getting a nasty case of poison ivy after losing the leaves he had. They failed to last the night and had to be treated at the medical ward. Both Lucas and Josh shared the same room, with two beds separating them a couple of inches from each other.

We weren't even out there that long. It's just been so humid since the rain from earlier and Josh ate that whole bread the moment I left him alone with it, Lucas thought with a groan.

Ashley and Hailey ended up participating in the activity as well and won their team points for the activity.

Vanessa made a surprise visit to the hospital ward and brought Lucas food and magazines about cars.

"They belong to Bill, but he doesn't read them. He just has them because he thinks it's a guy thing or whatever," said Vanessa with a sly grin.

Lucas chuckled and took the magazines without mentioning that he doesn't care about cars.

I know some stuff about cars. Like this car looks fast and that one looks slow. That's all I need to know.

As she was walking to leave, Bill's sister was greeted by both Ashley and Hailey.

"Hi Vanessa, what brings you here?" Ashley asked, trying not to sound annoyed by her presence.

Bill's sister smiled conceitedly at the two girls. She snickered when she saw their get-well gifts that were intended for Lucas and Josh respectively. Ashley brought chocolate-chip cookies while Hailey had bagels. Both were from the cafeteria.

"I was just visiting my future boyfriend," Vanessa said snidely. "Don't worry, I'll be a good girlfriend to him. And by the way, Speedy, those cookies look half-baked. I'm surprised you're not munching on them yourself considering your sweet tooth. And plain bagels, really, Mount Everest? Hasn't Josh suffered enough?"

Hailey scoffed at her, causing Vanessa to stop dead in her tracks.

"Your idea of being a 'good girlfriend' is being with Lucas for a day, then breaking his heart the next day."

Vanessa slowly turned her head and glared at Hailey for a while.

"At least I've had boys like me, unlike you. You're too ugly for guys to look at you. Well, unless they're looking over you for a girl like me," snarled Vanessa loathingly, as if threatening to bite Hailey's head off.

This really offended Ashley's friend. Lucas noticed clear tension between the two, something which made him think that they fought in the past.

Even if this is familiar to them, Hailey still gets hurt every time Vanessa makes fun of her like that. Why is she so mean to her?

Instead of hitting Vanessa or countering her remark, Hailey decided to let it go and begrudgingly kept her thoughts to herself. Ashley angrily took a stand for her friend.

"To think we invited you to join our cabin earlier. You're nothing but an egotistical spoiled brat!" Ashley barked back ferociously. "Bill has been nothing but nice towards Lucas and made him feel welcomed here. I'm sure he could do without your unwanted flirtations."

I wouldn't say Bill's nice, but he's not the meanest person I know. He is like my friend. Not like; he is my friend. I still won't say that out loud. Also, unwanted flirtations? I don't know about that.

Vanessa just scoffed and shot another insult towards Hailey.

"Yeah, well, Grand Canyon here is in love with Josh, who by the way will never like you back, because he's deaf, not blind."

This was the final crack to Hailey's shield as her eyes began to fill with tears. Lucas worried that others in the ward could hear the commotion they were making since the size of the hospital was not that big.

Their screaming reminds me of the times I had to listen to my parents fight, Lucas thought drearily.

He looked towards Josh who was busy scratching at the poison ivy all over his uncomfortable area.

I wonder if Josh would like Hailey back. I mean she's not ugly, and she could probably beat up anyone who'd mess with him. But something tells me he wouldn't see it that way.

After Vanessa left, it was quiet in the room, except for the television, which only displayed subtitles and had a low volume level.

This room is clearly set up for Josh. I wonder if it would be too much trouble to ask the nurse to heighten the volume so I could focus on the movie that's playing, thought Lucas desperately.

Then something unexpected happened to Lucas; something that he couldn't possibly comprehend at that moment. He began hearing voices in his head, and they weren't his own. It was like the times before, like in the zoo and amongst a large group of people.

What, who's there? Who are you...?!

Wonder...sure...her...feel...like...desperate...not...or...deaf...when...sound...into...strong...intimate...lacking ...

It didn't take Lucas long to realize that it was Josh's voice he was hearing based on how he spoke audibly.

It's like when I used to hear animal voices. These aren't thoughts in the traditional sense, like the way I hear my own internal voice. This is like if Josh's noise volume on the outside is at 100%, then this is more a projection of what I am hearing him think. He isn't saying these things in a complete way though.

He looked at Josh and suddenly began to feel as he did, while the room became as silent as a soundproof room.

There's so much silence, so much emptiness on the sides of my head... like all I can do to keep myself sane is drown myself in the idea of what sound is. How I feel it rather than hear it.

When Lucas tried to get his friend's attention, nothing he did worked. He crumbled up a piece of paper that was near his bedside and tossed it towards him. It landed on Josh's stomach and he turned to look at Lucas in confusion. His thoughts suddenly formed a cohesive sentence.

Wh...at...waaaaas that all about, Luke? Lucas heard Josh think, with the last part tuning itself to a clearer thought for him to hear.

Josh then proceeded to repeat the same thing aloud.

"What was that all about, Luke? Do I have something on my face?" Josh signed and asked in a hurtful tone.

I can't believe this. I think I just discovered a new ability, Lucas thought in disbelief.

Josh looked at his friend with a concerned expression.

213

"Why did you throw that paper at me?" Josh asked Lucas.

Lucas tried to figure out how to say 'I can hear your thoughts in my head' in sign language.

Josh groaned at Lucas's poor attempt at hand gestures.

"I can read lips, Luke. Just mouth the easy stuff. I'll catch the rest. Not unlike the paper ball you threw."

Lucas tried to move his head upwards so that Josh could clearly see his lip's movement.

"I can hear your voice in my mind!" he mouthed and said loudly.

Why am I shouting? Is this how he feels?

Josh only got the word 'mind' which made him even more perplexed.

"What about minds? I already know you can control them. Did you have something on your mind?" Josh asked him, half-wanting to laugh at his unintended pun.

Lucas sighed and repeated himself. This time Josh understood him.

But he doesn't believe me.

"Hold on, let me process this. You're telling me that you can read minds and that you're hearing my voice inside your head right now?"

Lucas nodded plainly. After a moment, Josh looked willing to listen.

"What am I thinking now? Also, how do I sound?"

Hmmm he's thinking about the movie that's on the TV. He's seen it once but didn't think much of it. He's also picturing some girl in camp I haven't seen yet. She's really pretty, and...

Lucas concentrated for a few seconds and picked a thought.

"You're thinking about fried chicken," Lucas confirmed, making a hand gesture he knew to represent a chicken.

Wait what? I didn't know that. I don't know sign language at all. But then how did I...?

Lucas put his hand over the back of his palm as if he were trying to cage something invisible. He wriggled his fingers like the tentacles of an octopus, but stopped when Josh looked confused.

"Are you asking if I want grapes, because I'll take some if you have any?"

What? Grapes? How does what I did look like grapes? First chicken now grapes? He's getting me hungry now and I'm not supposed to eat until tomorrow.

Lucas was sorting through his new ability when Ashley made her presence known.

"I'm sorry about that. Vanessa is a real handful a lot of times," Ashley said, with a sigh.

"What happened out there?" Lucas asked, both in curiosity and confusion.

Ashley explained how after she started bickering with Vanessa, Hailey ended up returning to their cabin in tears. Josh noticed her absence and seemed concerned by this.

"Where's Hailey? You two are always together like mac and cheese."

Again with the food.

Ashley turned her head towards Josh.

"Hailey needed to go to the bathroom," Ashley lied.

Josh laughed and jerked his head to the side.

"Oh, well thanks for letting me know," he responded sarcastically.

Ashley smiled but in her mind was thinking, *Should I just tell him already? He probably already knows how Hailey feels about him. The problem is how does he feel about her?*

Lucas, without thinking about it, blurted out, "I think you should tell Josh about Hailey being in love with him."

Ashley's eyes widened and gave Lucas a look of both disbelief and awe.

"What in the name of Antonius's beard... did you just read my mind?" shrieked Ashley in shock.

Who is Antonius, and what about his beard?

As the young telepath explained his new power, Ashley looked taken aback.

"You figured it out after having a bad case of indigestion... that sounds unpleasant."

Lucas groaned and nodded in agreement.

"I had this ability before camp though. I don't remember to what extent, but I don't think it was like this. Does everyone here discover a new ability the same way as me?"

Ashley nodded.

"It's called a latent ability," she explained. "On a subconscious level, you already discovered and even used this ability before camp, but you must have repressed it until now. That's not uncommon, although the way you've been discovering your abilities from nearly being killed by Alexia, to getting sick from poisonous berries. It's like your trigger is near death experiences."

The young telepath beckoned his head towards Josh as if to ask Ashley when or how his cabin mate discovered his ability.

"I can't say for sure. He probably discovered his before coming to camp. I don't really know Josh as well as I know Bill. You should know that you're discovering more abilities than most campers have during their first year," Ashley admitted knowingly.

Lucas carelessly mentioned Vanessa briefly, forgetting entirely that the two girls just had a heated argument.

"I'm sure she's told you the tale of how she figured out a way to become even more annoying than she already was before she could pop her bones. Too bad she hasn't popped her head open yet," Ashley joked, but her tone sounded too blunt to be taken as something to laugh at.

Nonetheless, Lucas understood and feigned laughter.

"You would love that wouldn't you?"

She would love that and probably Hailey too.

He half-expected for her to agree, but to his surprise, Ashley shook her head.

"I don't hate Vanessa. I don't hate anyone really, or at least I try not to. Hate is an ugly feeling and it's not who I want to be. You haven't known her as long as I have, so take it from me when I say she isn't as nice as she pretends to be. On the first day of camp, a little bit before I met you, I asked Vanessa if she would like to join me and Hailey once we joined the Weeping Willow. I didn't know yet if we were going to get the cabin or not, but I figured she's Bill's sister and he's my friend. Then she started talking about how she couldn't be seen with me, Speedy, and Hailey, the Tall Mountain or that green comic book superhero name she tends to call her. I don't know if she means to be that way or if she doesn't know how to make friends beyond a certain group, you know?"

Lucas didn't really listen to a word Ashley said. Instead, he ended up feigning interest.

I was always good at fooling teachers into thinking I was paying attention in class. It's a skill that got me out of trouble and in trouble more times than the other.

The young telepath felt bad about ignoring her, not because he wanted to, but rather he always had trouble sitting still or paying attention for too long before he lost patience and wanted to do something else.

I try to pay attention. I really do. My mind's always moving at a faster speed than my body. One minute I'm talking to someone, the next they already left because they realized I wasn't listening. Either that or they finished talking, so I missed out on everything they said. Kind of like now actually.

While Ashley continued to speak, Lucas's mind continued to drift away as if his thoughts were like birds taking flight.

"I want to tell you about my other cabin mates in the Weeping Willow," Ashley continued. "There's this one young girl named Tess, she can hold her breath and exhale it for long periods of time, a girl close to our age named Lila, she eats a lot of sugar to gain a temporary rush of speed similar to mine. The only difference is she's not as fast as I am. The last girl is the one Hailey was talking with during the nature walk activity, Giselle. She can light her finger tips like E.T., I don't know how familiar you are with movies. They're all so wonderful and made us feel so welcomed."

Before she could say anything else, Josh, who had taken a short reprieve from his thoughts, turned his attention to her.

"Did Luke tell you about his new mind thing?" Josh asked. He pointed at his forehead as if to paint a bulls-eye on it.

Ashley nodded while Lucas's stomach rumbled, then subsided.

"Do you know anything about Henry, Ashley?"

Maybe she knows something. I want to know his age, his birthday, where he was born, if he has siblings, and if he's married.

Unfortunately, like everyone in camp, she knew nothing.

"I haven't spoken to the Camp Director since the first day when you were with him," Ashley admitted. "I've known Daniel since before camp though. He works at my school as a substitute teacher and a guidance counselor. All the students like him, mostly because it's an all-girls school and, well, you've seen how he looks. He has a girlfriend though. Her name is Keira and they've been dating since they attended camp together. I like her a lot. She's really sweet and caring. A good person for him to be with."

Okay, so not about Henry anymore. Now about Daniel.

"I thought you had a crush on him for a second there," Lucas said aloud, a thought he meant to keep to himself. Ashley looked embarrassed by this comment and shook her head.

"He's like an older brother to me," she said in a firm tone. Lucas apologized and kept silent after that.

"Anyways, Daniels the one who invited me to camp in the first place," Ashley went on. "He offered me an invitation here, but when I told my parents, they were against the idea at first. I'm an only child, so that's probably why they were unsure of it. As far as they know though, this camp is for cheerleaders, so no boys like at my school. Daniels the expectation."

Lucas did not pay much attention to the last part. His focus was on getting Ashley to ask Daniel about talking to Henry for him.

I really want her to get Daniel to help me with Henry. I better not push it or she might think I don't care about her feelings. I'll ask about something else instead.

"I didn't know you attended a school for girls?" Lucas said, before he could reconsider asking about Daniel and Henry.

Ashley nodded and looked happy that her conversation topic was getting the Lucas's feigned interest.

"My parents moved me out of school after I got bullied for my Dyspraxia. I have a hard time controlling the muscle movements of my body and because of that I trip often and bump into things. It used to be worse and now it's mostly when I use my ability too many times, as you've noticed."

Lucas recalled catching her to keep her from falling. Even though the way Ashley spoke about it made it seem less than what it was, he could feel it bothered her more deep down.

She's better at hiding that than I am. Looks like we have something in common; we were both bullied.

"Why do you eat a lot of foods and snacks?" he suddenly asked. "Don't you worry about your health and..." *And gaining weight,* Lucas he wanted to say. He immediately regretted his choice of words when he saw how embarrassed Ashley appeared by the question.

Abruptly, she changed the subject.

"Training is already coming up in a few days. Do you feel ready for that?"

Lucas shook his head and suddenly a sick sort of feeling took him like madness. Before he could stop himself his mouth opened with the words pouring out in a full pious-like confession.

I can't take it anymore...

"I feel homesick. I miss my mom. I miss my dad. I miss my sister..." Lucas surprised himself, as Ashley stared at him intently while Josh read aloud the subtitles on the television screen. "I just want them to forgive me, to take me back, for all of this to be a bad dream."

Why did I do that? A full on confession? When I said I wouldn't tell anyone but Henry about it? Now she's going to think I'm a whiny person.

Despite Ashley giving him a sympathetic look, Lucas was grateful that Josh was deaf and hadn't heard a word at that moment.

"I'm sorry, Lucas. Why wouldn't your parents accept you back home? What happened to make you feel this way? Because, and I've only known you for a short time, you seem so kind, understanding, and attentive. I don't understand what could have happened to make you feel like your parents wouldn't forgive for any reason."

She gave him a hopeful smile but it was all Lucas could do to keep himself composed from both his tears and his stomach pains.

I should just tell her. I already said too much. No sense in hiding it now. Besides, I need to talk to someone about it.

He nodded stiffly while his mouth opened again with the words coming out as swift as a thunderous clap.

"I'm the reason for all the problems my family had. I won't blame my disabilities for it, because it was all me."

Ashley said nothing as Lucas continued.

"I didn't make my parent's lives easy, even though they weren't exactly 'Mom and Dad of the Year' either. Don't get me wrong, I love both my parents even when they made me feel bad about something I didn't choose. I've always felt like a burden to my family, like they only kept me around until they had a chance to finally get rid of me. It was my parent's idea for me to come here because they said it would help me. So far, I think it has."

He fell silent but resumed after taking a deep breath.

"Recently, I've done some serious thinking and I realized even after everything I've done, they've always been there and taken me back every time. Sure they would scold me or make me feel bad about it, but they never once said for me to pack up and leave. They always gave me so many chances and now I feel like the bad guy because I never appreciated them until now. It took hurting my parents in a way that I should never done in order to realize something needs to change in me. As much as I didn't want to leave my home, I believed that coming here was the right thing to do. Because without me, my family has a chance to heal and maybe even forget about the troubles I used to cause them. I still want to go home at the end of the summer. I just don't know if they want me around."

Ashley gazed at Lucas as he spoke and heard every single word he said as he struggled towards the end to keep himself from breaking down. To his surprise, her attention had been on him this whole time, causing the young telepath to feel guilt.

I'm such a jerk. She's here listening to me and putting up with my whining while I ignored her before, Lucas thought, regretfully. *At least I didn't tell her the whole truth. She'll think I'm a psycho if I tell her I blacked out and saw my dad on the floor before I left home.*

She touched Lucas's hand and smiled.

"I wasn't perfect either, Lucas," Ashley admitted, suddenly. "Because my parents were always busy with their jobs and trying to make a steady income, I played alone and never had anyone to call friends. It wasn't until I met Hailey that I made my first true friend. She got bullied too because of her condition, so we both helped each other out when we could. My parents worried about me even when they weren't around a lot. My dad would either insist on taking me to school, or ask Hailey's dad to take us instead. One day, when I was walking home from school with Hailey, I didn't look down and my foot tripped over a rock on the sidewalk. I fell and hurt my left leg to the point where I couldn't stand up and walk properly. Hailey had to carry me home after that while bystanders looked at me uncaringly. Some even snickered at me as if I was the funniest thing they ever saw. I heard someone call me a 'klutz'. That word hurts more than any nickname Vanessa chooses to call me."

The word seemed to have a negative effect on Ashley as she sniffled and covered her eyes before the tears could fall.

"After that, my parents didn't allow me to walk home anymore. My dad started taking me to school, which caused him to be late for work often. My point, Lucas, is that you were not a burden on your family. They obviously loved you and had your best interests at heart by sending you here to camp. I honestly believe you're a good person and being here is helping you to appreciate the best of what your parents did for you. When you go back home, I know your family will welcome you back with open arms and you'll have nothing but great stories to tell them about this place.

You should tell them everything when that day comes. Don't let the last memory of them be of sadness and anger."

Lucas looked at Ashley as she said every word and for the first time in his whole life, he was listening to somebody speak.

I listened to everything she said. No one, not even Shelly could ever make me do that.

She became the first person he ever listened to and also the first individual he was open towards. Even as he shared his feelings with Shelly, it always came from a place of obligation. This feeling with Ashley was something new Lucas never felt before.

She said the same thing as Shelly. They're more alike than I realized. I hope she's right about all that because she doesn't know the whole truth...

Part of Lucas wanted to tell Ashley everything. Maybe that would change what she said and how she felt, but he knew that her words meant more now than they would with the truth.

When I go back, I'll see my parents and how much they really care about me. I'll apologize for what I did and swear to do my best in school. I probably won't make the same kind of grades as Shelly because I'm not as smart as her. I'm still going to give it my all and get at least a high school degree.

"You asked me earlier why I eat a lot of foods," Ashley reminded him. Lucas nodded and waited for her to continue. "It's part of my abilities; I have to maintain a certain level of calories in order to use my speed the way I do. If I have enough, I can distribute it to others the way I did for you, but not everyone can handle it. For instance, if someone has a weak stomach or motion sickness, that wouldn't translate well with my ability."

The young telepath acknowledged that difficulty.

I do have problems with my stomach but nothing like that. When I had her speed power, it wasn't a lot for me to handle.

"At least I never have to worry about gaining weight because my body burns away fat faster than a train engine burns coal," Ashley mentioned with a soft grin.

"Aren't you worried that someone will think you have an eating disorder?"

"Everyone here has a disorder, physical or mental, of some kind," Ashley pointed out. "I don't know if you know this but Alexia has bulimia."

Lucas knew this. He wanted to tell her about how he heard her in the girl's restroom, but kept that knowledge to himself.

Maybe she'll think I'm a stalker too.

"Can you stay a bit longer? I want to hear more about yourself," Lucas asked his female friend.

Ashley nodded happily and began to tell her more about her childhood. He learned about her favorite holiday, *Halloween,* her favorite movie, *Corpse Bride,* and her favorite book, *something about little women.*

The next morning, Lucas and Josh were discharged and sent back to their cabin.

The young telepath didn't have long to sleep before the Camp Guardian arrived and told him that Henry wanted to speak to him. He felt excited to finally talk to the Camp Director, but to his disappointment, Daniel was in the room with his father.

I was really hoping to talk to Henry alone. So much for that.

The Camp Director's son smiled thinly as Lucas entered Henry's office and closed the door behind him.

"Hello, Lucas, I'm sure you're wondering why my father asked for you and why I'm here as well."

I hope he doesn't expect me to answer, Lucas thought, bitterly.

He looked at Henry who appeared frighteningly impassive.

He's showing no emotion at all. Maybe he's just so happy to see me that, for Daniel's sake, he's trying to keep it at a professional level.

"I saw a glimpse about you the other night, Lucas," Daniel explained. He felt his anxiety suddenly take hold of his body like paralysis. "You were falling. I don't know from where but there was someone watching you. I couldn't see who it was. The shrouded figure had golden hair as bright as the sun."

That doesn't sound very helpful. How many people in camp have golden hair… to my knowledge, nobody.

Lucas heard his heart thumping against his chest, *thump thump*, and felt ready to scream out loud, but Henry's voice calmed him.

"There is no need to frighten Lucas, my son," said Henry, softly. "It was only a vision and we know of the danger now so we can proceed with preventing it from transpiring?"

He sounds doubtful, like he doesn't really believe that it can be prevented.

"Let's put aside this matter for another time," Henry said, to his son's dissatisfaction. "Now then, Lucas, we have heard that you discovered a new ability recently."

It wasn't a question, nor was it a comment; it was a direct fact.

Who could have told Henry about my new abilities? I only told Josh and Ashley, unless one of them spilled the beans as they say. Who says?

Nonetheless, Lucas nodded and began to explain how he discovered it. He also mentioned the ability to feel the emotions of others, and likened it to his mind-reading which connected him to other's thoughts. When he concluded, the Camp Director and his son looked at each other as if they already knew the answer before he had said it.

Is there nothing Henry doesn't already know?

"When you discovered your ability, whose mind did you read first?" Henry finally asked after a long pause.

"Josh, but Ashley told me that I had this ability before I came here to camp. She called it a 'latent ability'. What does that mean?"

"It means you are beginning to unlock your potential, Lucas. It is vital that you begin training at once."

After a moment, Lucas's stomach began to twist in a knot, either from anxiousness or the indigestion from the other day.

It could be both.

"When you read Josh's mind, how did his voice sound?" Daniel asked Lucas. "Can you tell the difference between what you hear from others and what you hear from yourself?"

Lucas thought about this, reluctantly nodded.

"Not always, but sometimes yes." *Vague answer, good.* "In Josh's case, I've heard his voice but in his mind it was different. At first it wasn't sounds, more like what I thought he was thinking. I had to unlock the real sound like turning a locker lock."

Daniel gave his father an uncertain look, making the Camp Director nod.

"He has only just discovered his ability and already he has a level of self-awareness that most telepaths don't develop so early on. Even Jacob couldn't distinguish between a person's rational thoughts over what they really meant to say."

The Camp Director's son sighed and shook his head.

"I don't know if I can train him the way you want, father," Daniel admitted, to Lucas's shock. "How do I know his ability won't lose control and take over him? It's not just about his safety but the safety of everyone else in camp."

Uh, hello, I'm right here, the young telepath really wanted to say. Biting his tongue, he watched the two bicker amongst each other.

"Lucas is still young. He has much to learn and time enough for all that will come," Henry noted. "You would do well to remember your place in this camp, Daniel."

His son looked really hurt by this, as if he had heard this before.

He has; I can feel it.

Breaking the tension, Lucas had a question come to him. Something he felt no one else had asked or thought about in a short while.

"I was in the hospital ward and I didn't see Sasha there," Lucas noted. "What happened to her? Is she okay? What about the orb wielder from Orange team?"

Daniel looked plagued by thoughts that Lucas wasn't privy too. After a moment, the Camp Director was the one to respond.

"Sasha, as well as the Orange team orb wielder, were sent away from camp for the remainder of the summer. The game for Relic takes a toll on the orb wielders and some of the children are unable to recover from it. Though we do our best here, if a remedy cannot be found, they're sent back to their loved ones with immediacy."

So what he means to say is, 'you get hurt here, we can't help you, sorry you'll miss out on the rest of the summer'. He left that part out in the brochure to this place.

Before Lucas could ask further, Henry interrupted him.

"You must be tired. Get some rest, Lucas. You begin training after this weekend. In the meantime, enjoy the remainder of your free time. Spend these hours with your friends, and appreciate their presence while it lasts."

The last words the Camp Director spoke hung over Lucas's mind like an echo after he nodded and let himself out of the house.

I don't understand. I have a power no one else here has and all anyone wants to remind me of is how the last person like me ended up. I'm not being given a chance to succeed on my own.

He had gone inside the house in the hopes of talking to Henry, hoping that the Camp Director might understand his desire to return home. Lucas's mind replayed the last words he heard as if listening to a recording being played back just for him.

'Appreciate their presence while you can.' Why would Henry say that? It's probably nothing. I worry too much anyways. Still, no one wants to talk about Sasha or the other orb wielder. Why is that?

Lucas walked back to his cabin and spent the rest of the day indoors with Bill, who was the only occupant in that moment. While doing pushups, Bill started talking to break the silence between himself and his cabin mate.

"Camp Supernatural is more of a home then my actual home," Bill confessed to Lucas as he panted and struggled to keep from falling flat on his face.

"You don't like the outside world?" the young telepath asked like a child asking their parent if they like their job.

Why am I asking? I can read minds, so everyone is an open book to me now.

Bill shook his head, proving Lucas half-right.

"Well, the thing is, my folks don't exactly know about my intentions to stay on as a Camp Counselor. Vanessa still has a few years left and I plan to finish high school at least. Then I can dedicate my time to being here and helping others with their abilities," Bill decided almost with a conceited tone. "Plus all my friends are here and that includes you, Luke."

The way he makes it sound so casual and easy, like it's a choice anyone can make. I know my parents aren't looking forward to the day when Shelly leaves. With her gone, they'll be stuck with me and I'll have no one to comfort me when the bad days happen. Also, he called me his friend and he wasn't joking.

Lucas retired early to his bunk after that and slept through the morning. He got up to eat lunch the next day and made sure to go after his friends had already eaten.

Just once, I'd like to eat lunch alone, Lucas thought as he ate fried steak with mashed potatoes and corn.

Taking his medicine in a small dosages, Lucas felt his head hit the pillow of his bed and sleep overtake him until the following night.

Past midnight, Lucas awoke and could not go back to sleep. He thought about taking more medicine, but knew the risks of consuming too much at once.

Forget the warnings on the label; these things kept me from using my ability to the fullest. It still wouldn't be a good idea to take too many because knowing me, I'll sleep through the rest of the time we have off before training.

He tried to pace back and forth, hoping that the adrenaline would be enough to knock him out. When that didn't work, Lucas decided to exit the cabin and look at the stars, something he hadn't thought about doing until now.

I've secretly always wanted to look at a nighttime sky away from city buildings and street lights. At home the stars always felt more distant and faded like erasing words from a paper.

As the young telepath struggled to climb the sturdy wooden parts of the cabin, it didn't take long for the Camp Guardian to spot him. His dour eyes narrowed in Lucas's direction as if he were preparing to charge at him like Alexia had during the Relic game.

If he did, I wouldn't be able to react fast enough.

The monster stood over Lucas like a tall mountain, as he fruitlessly held onto the side of his cabin.

"Where do you think you're going? It's near midnight, camper," the Camp Guardian rasped in an irritable tone.

Lucas could tell that the Camp Guardian felt tired at this point in the day and did not relish the thought of someone making his job harder than it already was.

I almost feel bad for him, and I say almost because he could easily flatten me like pizza dough.

"I wanted to see the stars. I'm having trouble sleeping right now, so I was hoping that seeing the night sky would help put me to sleep."

Lucas tried to sound as innocent as possible, but the monster did not look convinced.

"You should be asleep. Camp Director James will be furious if you're not in your bunk like the rest of the campers."

The Camp Guardian's glare never left him.

He takes his job too seriously.

"If Henry finds out, I'll take the fall for it. It was my idea anyways," Lucas promised, sincerely.

This was something the monster did not expect.

Hesitating, the Camp Guardian finally relented as Lucas reached the top of the cabin.

"You can stay for five minutes. After that, back inside."

Lucas agreed, lay his back against the roof of the cabin, and began to gaze at the stars. The surface of the cabin felt cold and a little wet from the humidity of the night. Otherwise, it didn't bother him much.

He only wore his camp blue t-shirt with his cabins word's embroiled in the front and long grey warm ups with no socks on.

Big mistake. The cold always seems worse on my feet.

In silence, the Camp Guardian stood below Lucas and watched the stars with him as solemnly as he watched the camp during the day. The stars appeared like thousands of dots around the sky and the young telepath wanted to connect them all.

"Do you ever sleep?" Lucas asked the monster after a moment.

The Camp Guardian shook his head stiffly.

"I don't need to sleep. That's why I'm able to be out here night and day. I also don't need to eat," the Camp Guardian said in a calmer tone. "I still eat because it makes the children in this camp uneasy when I don't."

I'm not picking up any bad vibes from him. Just a lot of sadness. Almost like Henry's but there's something more. Like a longing for a life forgotten.

Lucas silently continued to watch the stars. He looked for constellations, but couldn't find any. Having no foreknowledge to draw from, and without Wi-Fi, he had no way of looking up pictures.

I know the big dipper, that's about it.

Becoming slightly bored, Lucas decided to read the Camp Guardian's mind.

Nothing worth mentioning.

Two minutes passed before the monster spoke up.

"Henry means well. I understand you want to go home, but he can't let you."

Lucas lifted himself from the waist up and looked at the dour-faced monster.

"Why won't he let me go home?"

"It's a camp rule and a necessary part of your training. Henry believes that outside interference will halt your progress and distract you. This rule applies for every camper here."

The young telepath felt disappointed by the answer, but knew he would not have received a better answer from Henry himself.

Henry wants me around for some reason. Why is he so concerned with my progress? Why does he care what I do with my abilities?

"What was your life like before Camp Supernatural?"

The monster glanced at him with an impatient face and beckoned for him to get down.

"Your five minutes are up, now back inside," he commanded sharply.

When did those five minutes pass? Lucas wondered. *Let me see if he can give me at least another minute or two.*

"Can I please have another minute or two?" Lucas asked with a yawn. "I'm really having trouble sleeping right now."

The monster shook his head stubbornly.

"No. Get down, now. I'll knock you out and drag you back inside if I have to," the monster threatened.

Lucas finally relented and groaned loudly to voice his irritation.

"Fine, you don't have to be so grumpy," Lucas murmured to himself.

When Lucas jumped down from the roof to the ground, he saw through the moonlit night the sad haggard face of the Camp Guardian. Without intending to, the young telepath heard the voice of the monster inside his mind.

It's true; I am grumpy. This job means everything to me because I have nowhere else to go, and Henry is the only real friend I have. But many of the kids here have never liked me, the Camp Guardian thought, sadly. *I don't mean to be this way, just as I didn't ask to come back as I am. To walk the earth alone, with nary a soul who can relate to me.*

Lucas felt a sudden surge of guilt at what he said and could feel the pain the monster was feeling as if it were his own.

I can kind of relate to how he feels. I was also probably viewed as unfriendly and moody back home.

Sometimes I feel so lonely that it makes those thoughts I have so much stronger. At least here, I'm among people who are outcasts like me. People who won't judge me because they've been judged themselves. Some of them, others not so much. Alexia definitely comes to mind. Regardless, we're all here for the same reason and that's what matters.

"That's not true. Guarding this place is a hard job. You're underappreciated, like janitors in schools or the workers who build roads and stuff. You deserve more recognition and Henry is right to give you that," Lucas asserted encouragingly. "You keep us safe and because of you we don't have monster invasions if those are a thing."

The Camp Guardian looked at him, both warily and doubtfully.

He doesn't trust me. I probably shouldn't hold it against him.

The monster paused for a moment, before finally bowing stiffly.

"Thank you, young camper. It is hard sometimes keeping the camp in check and bringing supplies for the activities. I don't protect the camp from monster invasions, but I keep out anyone who doesn't belong here," the Camp Guardian acknowledged, humbly. "Camp Director James has given me a home and purpose. For that I will always owe him my life."

Lucas nodded with a smile and quietly yawned once more.

I better try to get some sleep so he doesn't get in trouble.

"I better go back inside. I don't want to get you in trouble."

The Camp Guardian nodded, but stopped Lucas before he reentered his cabin.

"It has been a long time since anyone has shown me such kindness. In many ways, you remind me of Henry. You both have... a calmness to you. It's something I don't see in a person often. Daniel has no such warmth. Don't get me wrong, he's a good man like his father. The only thing is he needs to learn to be more patient with himself and others."

The Camp Guardian's tone sounded remorseful at the last description. Suddenly a question nagged at Lucas like a whisper in his ear.

I almost died during the Relic game. Daniel said Henry stopped the Camp Guardian from helping me. I have to know why.

"I know Henry didn't let you help me in the Relic game, and I know the orb wielders who were in the game are not in camp anymore," Lucas revealed to the Camp Guardian. "What I want to know is why Henry didn't let you step in like he said you would? Are the kids who are not in camp anymore protected just like we all are? Is Henry really doing everything he can for us?"

Lucas tried not to sound so harsh, knowing full well the monster's loyalty to Henry. However, these questions demanded answers even if they weren't satisfactory.

"Camp Director James believed you could handle it and he was right. As for the kids who are no longer in camp, I wish I could tell you more but I know nothing else. Henry has sacrificed much to get to this point and it has been for the benefit of others. Never once himself."

These answers weren't enough for Lucas, with the second being suspiciously doubtful. He decided to read the monster's mind to see for himself.

Henry stopped me from interfering because he believed Lucas needed to experience a near-death experience to unlock his abilities. I would have stopped the game the moment that happened. He promised me no one would get hurt this time.

The young telepath suddenly felt uneasy thinking he was pushed purposefully to use his ability when there was a chance it might not have worked out in his favor.

Ashley mentioned that idea earlier. It's crazy to think she was actually onto something. I can't believe Henry would do that to me. He basically guessed what my ability might be and even if he was right, it doesn't mean it was the only way. What if he had been wrong? What if I had died? One things for sure; Henry needs me and for what I don't know.

As Lucas entered his cabin, the Camp Guardian appeared to be calmer now.

"Get some sleep, Lucas. If you're struggling to sleep, close your eyes and picture a peaceful moment. I haven't known sleep in years, but I recall the dreams come easiest when imagining them."

The young telepath nodded and noted the words the Camp Guardian used.

That's not a bad idea. I think he's onto something.

"I'll give it a try, thank you and goodnight, Camp Guardian."

"Please, call me Boris."

Chapter 7

Control

Lucas spent the rest of his time before training mostly in his bunk, only leaving for lunch and dinner. On both occasions, he spent the time with Josh, Bill, Ashley, and Hailey. Vanessa ate with her cabin mates, so he hardly had a chance to talk to her alone.

"What do you think training will be like?" Josh asked. He turned his head in the direction of mostly Lucas and Ashley, as if he hoped one or both of them would answer.

"I don't know, but I'm excited to see what Daniel teaches us," Ashley said, as she ate her salad. "You were with Daniel one summer weren't you, Bill?"

Bill nodded with a small grin. After taking a sip from his soda, he answered Ashley.

"Indeed I was. Every counselor has their way of teaching, from how harsh Alexander and Richardson are, to being calm and collected the way Daniel is. I've mostly been with Marcus. He's not the most engaging counselor but I know it's because he prefers to promote independent learning. Daniel, on the other hand, is more hands on and encourages campers under him to work in units. It's why campers under him tend to discover at least more than one ability by the end of the summer."

Despite being the one who asked, Josh's attention seemed more focused on his chicken tenders than noticing what Bill was saying.

"Henry wanted to know whose mind I read first," Lucas heard himself say, to the attention of all except Josh on the table.

Bill looked oddly concerned, which made the young telepath feel the same way.

It does make sense when you think about it, Lucas heard Bill think. *I mean here's this kid, with a dangerous ability, and all of a sudden he's discovering more abilities than anyone does during their first year in camp.*

Lucas felt uneasy about it, which is why he tried to read the minds of Ashley. He hoped her thoughts weren't as conflicted.

I'm sure Henry had a good reason for asking, he heard Ashley think. *Daniel warned me that Lucas would hurt me.*

The young telepath couldn't keep that information to himself.

"Ashley, what did Daniel tell you about me?" Lucas said, to Ashley's shock and displeasure.

"We'll catch up with you guys later today," Ashley said abruptly. "Lucas and I need to go check on something."

Before Bill, Hailey, or even Josh could question what was happening, Ashley grabbed Lucas by the wrist and led him out of the cafeteria.

I wasn't finished eating, Lucas was tempted to say. But he stopped himself short when, after finding both himself and Ashley outside of the cafeteria and away from the ears of everyone else, he saw her very upset face.

"What in the Milo's Hatchet was that in there?!" Ashley said, in a voice so sharp and loud that Lucas swore everyone in the cafeteria would hear them even though they were no longer within the cafeteria.

"I read your mind, okay," Lucas truthfully said. "I wasn't trying to, but I did. When I read Bill's mind, he was feeling negative, so I tried reading yours thinking it would be different."

This got Ashley's attention.

"You can voluntarily switch between the minds you read?"

Lucas nodded.

"That is very unusual, Lucas. It's one thing how you're discovering your abilities but another that they're manifesting this way. I think the reason is because of how empathetic you are. Still, you can't just say what's on a person's mind out loud for others to hear without any consideration for how the person feels about that."

Lucas shrugged, emphasizing again that he didn't mean to do it.

"Why did Daniel warn you that I would hurt you? Why is he even saying stuff like that about me to you?"

"Forget about it," Ashley said, firmly. She sighed and began to try and calm down. "Alright look, I understand that you cannot fully control your ability and because your ability is mind based, the training process will be even more difficult for you. In the meantime, just try to filter what you hear, and keep it to yourself. Our thoughts are meant to be our own, even when they reflect our best selves."

Lucas felt embarrassed by that, but was forced to agree.

"Alright, I'll try to do that for you."

"Not just for me. I doubt Josh will appreciate you poking inside his mind and hearing all of his private thoughts."

Yeah, but he wouldn't know unless I told him, the young telepath thought to himself.

Lucas nodded and went back to his cabin while Ashley went to hers. Against his better judgment, he decided to read her mind once more.

Just a peek...

I know Daniel means well, but he's wrong about Lucas, Ashley thought. *I've never felt this way about anyone before, and I don't believe I'm wrong about him.*

Her last thought made Lucas feel slightly better and he went back into his cabin. That evening, the campers gathered around for a night of social mingling. He stuck mostly with his familiar crowd, but spotted Alexia with a group of her friends. The young telepath made sure to be within his social circle for the rest of the night when he felt Alexia's eyes on him.

As long as Boris is nearby I should be fine. Unless Henry decides to pull another fast one like in the game.

Speaking of Boris, the Camp Guardian was overseeing the evening and made sure that when it was over, all the campers would return to their cabins. He waved at Lucas, which caught Bill and Ashley's attention.

"Since when did you become friends with the Camp Guardian?" Bill asked with a surprised look on his face.

"Since last night when I snuck up to the cabin's roof and looked at the stars. They're nicer to look at than that television screen you're always glued too," Lucas found himself saying, boldly.

Ashley and Hailey giggled while Bill gave his young cabin mate a mocking expression.

"What did you two talk about?" Ashley asked out of curiosity.

"Just a few things here and there," Lucas said, vaguely. "He wasn't super pushy about me having to go back inside the cabin."

"You're lucky he wasn't in a clobbering mood," Bill quipped.

Boris isn't like that. I actually feel more comfortable saying his name than Camp Guardian.

The friends drank sodas and exchanged stories from home. Lucas found out that Hailey is the youngest in a family of four brothers, all of whom are in jobs that are physical in nature.

"My eldest brother is in the army" she revealed to Lucas and the group. "My second brother used to run marathons until he injured one of his knees. He still found a way to help others through dieting and exercising healthily. My third brother swims and has won several trophies for it since he was in high school and early college. Lastly, my fourth brother wants to join the army like my eldest brother, but his boyfriend is against it."

This surprised Lucas, with Bill asking the question he thought about.

"How do your parents feel about that?"

"They're trying to support him, but I know they don't understand him. He's finishes high school next year, then after that he wants to move out. His boyfriend is wonderful and supports him so much emotionally."

Shelly will also be graduating next year, Lucas thought to himself. *I'm glad Hailey shared all of this with us. I'm sure all her brothers are as great and friendly as she is.*

As the night ended, Lucas, Josh and Bill wished Ashley and Hailey a good night. They entered their respective bunks and slept peacefully that night. It wasn't until lunchtime the next day when the young telepath awoke. He used his Sunday to walk around the camp and view each cabin. He noted how Atlas's Agony appeared so ordinary on the outside, but when one camper went inside, he thought he saw a giant statute inside like the kind found in a museum.

Either that or maybe that's what I thought I saw.

Lucas decided to check out Vanessa's cabin, The Kruel Kingdom. The only prominent color on the cabin was a dark shade of green. The young telepath swore he saw what looked torch lanterns on either sides of the cabin.

I feel like some of the names in the cabins are too much on the nose for being the first letter of each alphabet. I wonder where Henry got the names from anyways.

The next cabin that caught his eye was the Underrated Unicorn. The outside was rainbow-colored and the giant unicorn was nothing more than a worn out stuffed doll that looked as old as the camp itself.

I'm guessing with all the rain this place gets, that unicorn used to have a brighter horn. They should really try getting a new doll up there.

As Lucas was walking by, he heard little girl campers giggling. One of the girls peeked out the cabin to see him. She was covered in glitter and glue on one side of her hair. Her cabin mates seemed to be looking similarly.

They exchanged a brief look, while Lucas decided to wave at them. The little girl with glitter scurried into her cabin like a squirrel on a tree.

Was it something I said?

The last cabin in the row, the Ziggy Zion, looked about as out of place as any cabin in the camp. Lucas noted how the cabin was painted pitch black like the night sky, with tiny dots around it to represent stars and what looked like a poorly manned spaceship attached to the top of the cabin. The roof was also prominent and resembled a Victorian church.

More like something someone forgot to finish halfway through.

Lucas was afraid it would fall down and crush him if he got too close to it so he steered clear from the cabin.

A lot of these kids seem to spend more time inside than outside. It's any wonder that I got the kind of cabin where I can just imagine whatever I want.

With the clock nearing lunchtime, Lucas decided to go to the tents scattered around the back-section of the camp where the training was to take place. They had the structure of small cottages, but were large enough to occupy the Camp Counselor and a small group of campers. Here he saw ten tents that were positioned like an upside down 'V'. From the very left was Richardson's tent. Next to him was Alexander. After that was Daniel's tent, while the two other tents near him appeared empty. The tents next to the empty ones belonged to the other counselors, with Marcus's tent being next to one of the empty ones.

Lucas wondered whose tents those belonged to. When he walked up to them, he saw the names that were embroiled on the tents entrances.

Zane and Naomi, Lucas read. The tent for Zane looked too nice to not be in use, while Naomi's was very plain and ordinary.

To his surprise, Marcus was in his tent and greeted the young telepath.

"Hello there," the adult counselor said, with Lucas feeling out of place. "It's alright, you don't have to be worried about wandering around here. Our tents are open to anyone; counselors and campers alike."

Lucas nodded and noted Marcus's morning attire. He appeared dressed for bed, with his pajamas robe on and a light beard that covered the lower half of his face. He held in his hand a cup that the young telepath assumed was filled with morning coffee.

"You'll be training with Daniel, right?"

Lucas nodded while Marcus took a sip from his drink and smacked his lips.

"Word to the wise; he doesn't like campers who show-off their abilities. He'll ask you to show him what you can do, but don't try to make yours seem better than everyone else's. Even if it is."

Lucas nodded and was tempted to ask him a question he couldn't ask anyone else.

"What is Daniel like outside of camp?"

Marcus looked confused about the question until the young telepath clarified.

"From the way you two talked before during the nature walk activity, it seemed like you have history together. Are you two friends?"

Marcus shook his head to Lucas's surprise.

"We're coworkers, which isn't always the same as friends. We both care about the same person and that's where it gets complicated."

The young telepath wanted to press for more, but he decided to leave any further questions for someone else.

"Well, I better go get some lunch."

"Before you leave," Marcus said, as Lucas was walking away, "you should know something about your abilities. Something no one else in camp will tell you."

The young telepath turned towards Marcus and waited for him to continue after he took a careful sip of his coffee.

"Jacob did more than terrorize people with scary images and unpleasant thoughts; he almost destroyed this camp. Most everyone from back than wrote it off as being his fault entirely, but I think there's more to the story. In any case, take your training seriously so you don't end up like he did."

Lucas nodded, as he headed out to find Henry, Marcus's words still ringing in his ears and mind.

Jacob almost destroyed this camp. Why hasn't anyone else mentioned that?

He was so immersed in his thoughts that he didn't see Daniel in front of him. The young telepath bumped into the Camp Director's son.

"I'm so sorry, sir," Lucas heard himself say, as he picked himself up and tried to help Daniel from the ground. He brushed off the young telepath's support, but thanked him for the effort.

"That was quite the fall we both took," Daniel said in a way that Lucas felt was both humorous and annoyed. "Be careful where you're standing because you might not see what's in front of you. What's the hurry? Are you looking for my father?"

"No. Is he at his house?"

"I believe he has some business outside of camp that he is attending to. Not that he'd ever tell me or anyone else for that matter," Daniel said this last part as if it was meant to be an inside thought.

He really doesn't hide whatever is going on between him and Henry.

Lucas nodded and prepared to walk off until Daniel called out to him.

"I feel like we got off on the wrong foot, Lucas," Daniel said, appearing apologetic. "Since I'll be training you this summer, I want us to get along. My father has an interest in you and while I do not understand it, I know you didn't ask for it. So tell me a bit about yourself. What do you like to do for fun?"

The young telepath suddenly felt like Daniel was more bipolar than he is. One second, he could be scary and intimidating, the next, friendly and easy going.

Why did he tell Ashley I would disappoint her?

"I don't know. I just like to relax, play video games, and take my mind off stuff that bothers me."

"Are you close with your parents?" Daniel asked with interest.

Lucas shook his head.

"I'm close to my sister, Shelly."

"Yes, my father mentioned to me that she's the main reason you want to go home?"

Lucas nodded.

"Why aren't you and Henry close?" Lucas heard himself ask.

The question looked like it offended Daniel, but he did his best to appear civil as if he were being watched at the moment.

"With all due respect, Lucas, that's none of your business. Whatever you think you know, I guarantee you know nothing."

What was that? Lucas thought in dread. *I thought we were past this.*

"Alright then, fine. You don't want to talk about how things are with Henry, but somehow it involves me," Lucas heard himself saying aloud. He feared Daniel's reaction, but instead the Camp Director's son looked at him intently. "If you don't want to tell me, that's your business. Your right about that. I just want to understand what's going on so that it doesn't feel like I'm getting in the way or something. That's not what I want."

What Lucas wanted was to leave the conversation. Before he could, Daniel decided to come clean.

"He left me and my mom when I was very young," Daniel revealed, in a low tone. "Before coming to camp, my mom told me that my father died in the war. It turns out she was lying to protect me because Henry was here all along taking care of other people's kids. Even when I was here for four years, it wasn't until I became a Camp Counselor when he finally told me the truth; that he was my father and had purposefully abandoned both me and my mom. It wasn't what he said that upset me; it was how he said it. He was so… emotionless about it. Like he didn't care whether I knew or not. I try to find time to spend with him, but he's always so busy with what he feels is more important. Something is always more important. Every year during Father's Day weekend, I've asked if we can spend the day together, just the two of us. The answer is always the same."

Daniel's tone in the end became his regular steadied voice. Even without reading his mind, Lucas could tell he was enraged on the inside.

Some of what he's feeling I can relate to. He feels misunderstood, lonely, and anger. Right now, the last one is the strongest feeling.

The young telepath wanted to say something. He wasn't sure if anything he said would make the counselor feel better, or make him think less of him.

I'm sure Henry had his reasons for leaving, was one response Lucas thought about saying. *If it's so important, maybe he'll tell you one day. Then again, if it were me, I don't know if any answer would ever be good enough.*

"I'm sorry, Daniel," Lucas said aloud, meaning every word of it. The Camp Counselor turned his demeanor from bitter to a calm one with a shrug.

"It is what it is. Anyways, I'll see you tomorrow. Don't be late for your first day of training," Daniel said, walking towards his tent.

As he walked away, the Camp Directors son still carried a conflicted aura with him. Lucas hoped that his words could have helped quench that fire, but instead Daniel kept what he really wanted to say to himself.

The young telepath walked back to his cabin and pondered the conversation he had with Daniel. It was one that had both unexpected results and started to help him understand his point of view.

I understand why Daniel feels like Henry acts distant towards him. All he wants to know is why his father left in the first place. I guess it would drive anyone nuts after a while. That's weird that he was in camp all this time and didn't know Henry was his father. Why did he wait so long to tell him?

One thing about the exchange felt off to Lucas.

He knows more about Henry's interest in me than he lets on. Maybe that's why he feels jealous of how much attention his father is showing me and not him.

After Lucas finished pondering and collecting his thoughts, he joined Josh and Bill for a movie night. To his surprise, Hailey and Ashley joined them as well.

"Won't you get in trouble for not being in your cabins?" Lucas asked Ashley.

"Only if we're not back by a certain time," she clarified. "How are you feeling?"

"I'm good, just trying to make the most of the time before we start training tomorrow," Lucas assured her, but when he read her mind she wasn't so sure.

He doesn't seem good. Why do boys have to be so secretive?

"So training tomorrow. That sounds exciting, training tomorrow," Lucas heard himself say aloud, to Bill's confusion.

"You said the same thing twice. Since when are you that excited about training?" Bill said as he prepared the movie.

"Since just now. Anyways, I'm all good, so let's watch this movie and end the night on a high note."

Josh brought everyone a soda and popcorn, while the movie began.

Something called Chronicle, Lucas observed. *It's one of those weird shaky cam movies.*

All throughout the films runtime, Lucas found his mind dwindling back to Daniel and the emotions he felt from him. *I'm thinking about this way too much. Daniel has some serious father issues that have never been properly dealt with. All of this is just making me feeling... ugh!*

Lucas became triggered at one point when one of the lead characters in the movie was the victim of bullying. He tried to hide this discomfort with Ashley being the only person among the group who noticed.

Not only did he hear her thoughts and concerns, he also heard the thoughts of everyone else in the cabin all at once.

I don't know this movie. The actors are not always on camera when they talk. Thank goodness for subtitles though.

This movie is very much a cautionary tale on the dangers that having powers can have. Daniel definitely has good movie tastes.

I like how Josh did his hair today. It looks different for some reason. Maybe he's trying a new hairstyle?

I can tell something is bothering him. I want to ask, but I don't want him to feel signaled out either.

Because of all these thoughts, the young telepath had a hard time following the film and went through it with the train of thoughts and his own voice drowning out all outside noises.

My head was occupied enough before I started hearing everyone else's thoughts! Now can't... hear... myself... right... I...

It took a hand on the shoulder for Lucas to come back to himself.

"Are you okay, Lucas?" Ashley asked him. She was sitting beside the young telepath as Hailey waited for her outside of the Imaginarium Illusion. Bill and Josh looked concerned over their cabin mate's mental state.

"I'm okay, that movie was a lot, but really good," Lucas pretended to note. He wiped his forehead clean of sweat.

"You can talk to me, Lucas. I just want you to be okay," Ashley affirmed.

I care about you, Ashley thought. *Maybe you don't feel you can share things with me. I wish I could just tell you.*

Lucas shook his head and felt himself become sad again at the memory of the bullying themes from the movie.

"I'll be fine in the morning, Ashley. Thank you for caring," Lucas said, trying to make the last part sound sincere. To his discomfort, it came off as condescending.

The young telepath made his way into his bunk without talking to anyone else and decided to give his thoughts one last glimpse.

I wonder what my life would have been like if I didn't have Shelly in it. She was always there for me and even when I was bullied for how I am, she accepted me. Maybe it was just because she's family. That still doesn't change my love for her. Even now, I miss the comfort she brought me, and the safety I felt when she was around. I've never felt so alone in my life.

Lucas woke up bright and early just as his mind finally became quiet. The fateful day of training was about to begin.

At exactly seven in the morning, he took part in a last minute meeting between the campers who would be part of Daniel's training group.

So far, it's just me and Josh here with Bill. We're still missing Vanessa, Hailey, and Ashley. Also, Gary and Mike are missing from our cabin. They've been gone a lot lately.

As he thought about them, the two young boys arrived. Mike wore a yellow camp shirt with a red flannel over it, while Gary had a purple camp shirt with a green cap that went with it.

I saw one of those at the gift shop. I like the red one I have better. Red and yellow are my favorite colors.

In the short time Lucas knew the both of them, he concluded that Mike is the quiet one and Gary is the loud one.

"Sorry we're late," Gary announced. "I thought we'd have some time before training started. I didn't know there would be a meeting here before that."

Bill looked displeased by this until Mike interjected.

"It's true. We weren't aware of this meeting. It was my idea to come and check just in case we needed anything before training."

Gary looked at Mike as if he had said something offensive. Despite this, he kept quiet about it.

"Don't worry about it guys. Just don't be late for Daniel's training session and you'll be fine," Bill instructed. Both Gary and Mike nodded.

When Ashley and Hailey arrived, Gary turned his attention to them and walked over to the pair.

"Oh wow, I knew this camp had pretty girls, but I didn't know I'd see one so soon in our group," Gary said. His flirtatious comment was met with an annoyed look from Ashley. "How about after this, we grab some lunch and you can tell me all about your powers?"

Hailey got in the middle of the two and towered over Gary like a tall building.

"Choose your next words wisely, little man," Hailey cautioned Gary. He simply shook his head and sighed.

"I was trying to talk to the pretty one, not the ugly one."

Hailey seemed hurt by this and wanted to do something when it was Bill's turn to intervene.

"Alright, that's enough you two. Vanessa will be here with the last of your group members, so try not to kill each other before that."

That didn't take long to happen, the young telepath observed.

Not long after, Vanessa entered with two other girls behind her. He recognized one from the Relic game and the other was someone he saw in Josh's mind.

That girl is the one he was thinking about a lot, and the other girl was terrified during the game, the young telepath recalled both instances. The scared girl had blonde hair like Ashley's, but instead of flowing down her back, her hair was tied in braids to each side. She wore an orange camp shirt which read, 'Would You Kindly', and overalls that covered some of the words. The other girl wore a similar shirt, only hers was black and her shorts were short.

Short shorts that are very short.

Josh and Gary were staring at the second girl with much interest. It wasn't long when both boys looked at each other and there was an invisible beam in-between their eyes.

Before another conflict could arise, Bill got everyone together and began to explain Daniel's training expectations.

"Alright, enough chit-chat. Eyes on me people. You two, Josh and Gary, knock it off. In about three hours, you all begin training for the first time," Bill began, as the two boys composed themselves. "Some things important to know are that Daniel is an awesome guy and a fair counselor, but he will probably be hard on you all since he will expect a lot. He doesn't like slackers and show-offs."

Everyone looked at each other and although there was a hint of nervousness in the room, Lucas could tell that everyone expected this.

I already knew about the part of Daniel hating campers to show-off, but not about disliking slackers. I guess it's like the same thing.

Bill then turned to Lucas.

251

"You've impressed Daniel out there during the game and in your participation in the camp activities, so he will be looking to you the most to see your progress. Are you feeling confident?"

Lucas nodded nervously and Bill grinned in satisfaction.

"Good. Do your best to learn as much as you can from Daniel and you'll be one closer to being a Camp Counselor. Another thing to keep in mind is you'll be paired with someone similar to your abilities. Most of you, from what I've gathered, are physical ability users. I think just Luke and Mike are mind based ones. Know your partner and be comfortable with the idea of working together. Any questions?"

When no one said anything, Bill nodded satisfactory.

"Then that's all. Take a shower, go eat breakfast, and relax everyone because this is meant to be fun, not challenging. Most of you know each other so that helps in getting to know your teammates. Learn to along Gary and Josh. You're cabin mates so act like it."

Gary looked displeased at being signaled out while Josh didn't know what his older cabin mate had said.

Gary doesn't seem like someone who will cause trouble around here. Maybe just the occasional stupid comment here and there. There's a reason he and Josh don't like each other beyond what's being said.

Ashley and Hailey walked back to their cabin to prepare with Vanessa going towards her own. Bill's sister didn't acknowledge or speak to Lucas during the time she spent with the group.

She must still be upset about the whole flower thing, Lucas thought in annoyance. *I didn't read her mind, but if she wanted to talk to me, she would have even with her brother around.*

Josh decided to stay and prepare with Lucas and Bill, while Gary and Mike let themselves out.

What does that say about Mike if he's supposed to be the nice one?

After a quick shower, Lucas departed from the cabin with Josh towards the cafeteria for some breakfast before training commenced. They were joined by Ashley, who sat next to the young telepath, and Hailey, who sat next to Josh.

I still can't believe he doesn't know how Hailey feels about him. Either Josh knows, or he doesn't care.

The breakfast special was blueberry pancakes with a side of eggs and bacon. As they ate their breakfast in silence, Lucas was looking around to see if the young lunch lady was in attendance today.

I wonder where she is. Maybe she doesn't have the morning shift today.

They sat there in silence, with none of them trying to make conversation in that moment. To fill his mind with noise besides his own, Lucas decided to read Ashley, Hailey, and Josh's minds altogether.

Food tastes better once it's eaten fresh.

Today is finally training day. I wonder if I'll be able to show off my new ability.

Daniel said he would take it easy on us. He mostly wants to see what Lucas can do with his abilities. The rest of us will just sit back and watch today.

Wait what? Lucas thought in a panic. *Daniel is going to put me at the front center of all this? Why me?*

After they finished eating their breakfasts, Lucas returned to his bunk and decided to take a short nap. He still felt tired from the previous night.

I wonder when I'll be able to talk to Henry, Lucas thought, hazily. *The longer I wait, the more anxious I become. Either that or I'm still feeling what I felt yesterday. I can't tell anymore. Did I take my medication yesterday or the day before that?*

Lucas closed his eyes and rested for what felt like only a few minutes.

Unfortunately, he did not anticipate sleeping past the time of training. His eyelids opened to Josh standing over him, shaking his shoulders erratically and bellowing, "Wake up, Luke. We are late!"

Josh's voice projected so loudly that his sound-wave ability shook the young telepath wide awake along with his bed.

That's a loud alarm clock, thought Lucas, catching his breath and steadying himself.

When he processed what Josh said, he immediately darted from the bed towards the front door.

I'm late!

Under Bill's previous advice, he wore a yellow camp T-shirt with the words of his cabin on it to make a good first impression on Daniel.

Maybe he'll forgive us for being late if I wear it now.

As he walked with Josh to the training session, he saw other campers going to their respective counselors. He spotted Marcus's group, which consisted of no more than ten campers, with kids he barely noticed during his time in camp.

I've spent so much time with the same people, I'm starting to realize how many other faces have become unfamiliar to me.

"I'm deaf, but I read lips. Talk already. I'm nervous and seeing people trying to talk to me helps calm me down," Josh signed and told Lucas, who was too busy looking around to acknowledge his friend's anxiety.

"Are you nervous about the first day?" Lucas asked his friend in genuine concern.

He didn't realize that Josh had already mentioned being nervous. When he understood what Lucas had said, he sighed in annoyance.

"And *I'm* supposed to be the one who's deaf. I already said I was nervous!" A soft rumble followed.

254

Lucas didn't bother with a response. They made the rest of the way in silence.

If Daniel says anything, I'll say Luke woke me up late, Josh was thinking, as the young telepath looked offended by this.

As much as I don't want to believe that's what I think he's projecting, it sounds too much like something he'd say.

They stopped in front of Daniel's tent and saw a student roster sheet on a board right next to the tent. It had the camper's names and their respective cabins:

1. Lucas Fargo- Cabin: The Imaginarium Illusion
2. Josh Tucker- Cabin: The Imaginarium Illusion
3. Ashley Bennett- Cabin: The Weeping Willow
4. Hailey Williams- Cabin: The Weeping Willow
5. Vanessa Cooper- Cabin: The Kruel Kingdom
6. Caroline Douglas- Cabin: The Kruel Kingdom
7. Mike Carpenter- Cabin: The Imaginarium Illusion
8. Gary Anderson- Cabin: The Imaginarium Illusion
9. Kendall Madison- Cabin: The Kruel Kingdom
10. ~~Sasha Bennings- Cabin: Cathedral Cove~~
    Bruce Hart- Cabin: Gloomy Gnomes

Lucas noticed that Sasha's name was crossed off and Bruce's name was put in in her place.

Sasha was going to be with us? That must have been before she was sent back home.

As the two cabin mates walked inside the tent, the interior proved to be like a living room rather than how condensed it appeared from the outside. The campers were seated on one side of the tent, with Daniel standing on the opposite end. He appeared displeased by their late appearance.

This place is incredible. It's like we just walked into a house or something. He's got furniture, a bed, a small kitchen, and a book shelf that has both books and some movies, Lucas thought in amazement.

The young telepath spotted Bruce seated near the far end of the group. He remembered him from the Relic game but hadn't seen him since. He was still semi-large and wore a red camp shirt. He gave the two late arrivals an indifferent look.

I don't think remembers us. He isn't thinking much either. Just about why Daniel is looking at me and Josh with disapproval.

"You're late, and on the first day," Daniel noted, looking at his wrist watch, then back at the two campers.

He waited for an excuse, while Lucas tried to think of one.

I overslept. I forgot that training is today. I still have indigestion, were some of the many excuses the young telepath was thinking of at that moment. Instead, Josh spoke up before he could use either of these excuses.

"I slept in late. Luke tried to wake me up, but I can't hear anything."

Lucas was both stunned and in disbelief.

He's taking the blame for me. Even after those thoughts from before.

Nonetheless, Lucas did not object to the story and nodded in agreement.

"Just don't make it a habit, boys. Take a seat with your fellow campers so we can get started," said Daniel, sharply.

There were only two empty spots next to Ashley and Hailey respectively. Lucas sat next to Ashley's side while Josh seated himself next to Hailey. Vanessa sat on the other side of the tent next to Caroline. Josh's crush was next to her. Mike sat next to both Caroline and Bruce.

I feel like we're in some secret meeting away from everyone else in camp, Lucas thought, and wanted to say that aloud so badly. *It would liven up the mood for sure.*

A few seconds later, Daniel began the training session.

"Hello everyone. My name is Daniel Harrison, but you will address me as Counselor Harrison during training sessions," instructed Counselor Harrison. "Now, I want you all to show me what you can do individually. Don't be shy. We're not here to judge. Just don't burn down this nice tent of mine."

The campers looked reserved and hesitant.

"If someone doesn't volunteer, I'll have to pick one of you at random."

I guess I may as well volunteer for being late.

When Lucas's hand went up, the counselor smiled and nodded.

"Lucas, very good, nice comeback after being late. Let's see what you can do."

I could use my mind control, but I rather show off my mind reading since it's the more recent ability.

He read Gary's mind and heard the boy's voice in his mind.

"Gary, you're thinking about: 'My nickname should be He-Art Man. I wonder if that hot lunch lady is in today. She's the one with more hair on her face than I have on mine,' end thought."

Gary flushed at this as the other campers began to laugh at him like a pack of hyenas. He shot Lucas a sinister look and turned to Daniel angrily.

"Wait a second, that's not what I thought at all!"

He thought about the hot lunch lady. The last part was improvisation.

Daniel seemed indifferent to this as he shrugged.

"I should hope not. Very good, Lucas."

"I can tell you more of what he's thinking. Give me a bit."

Before Lucas could do anything, Gary tried effortlessly to break his concentration.

"No more, stop reading my thoughts. You're all crazy!"

After that, Gary stormed out of the tent and marched outside while pounding the very earth with his sneakers. The others laughed behind his back, especially Josh, and clapped their hands in admiration. Despite this, the young telepath immediately felt guilty.

I know he can be a jerk, but I thought we were all supposed to be having fun here. If I can catch Gary in a good mood, I'll apologize and own up to this.

"I wonder, Lucas, if you can read my mind?" the Camp Director's son questioned.

Lucas tried to hear Daniel's voice in his head, but he suddenly heard a ringing noise. Like the end of a telephone line.

Argh!.......I   can't.......   hear...   anything! Must...think...like...this...

He felt a sharp stinging pain and winced backwards. As a result, Daniel sighed in disappointment.

"Let's make this a goal between now and the end of the summer. If you can read my mind by August, I'll consider you properly trained. That also includes the way you use your other abilities during training as well."

After saying this, Daniel shifted his attention to the rest in attendance.

"It's alright if you don't have a full grasp on your abilities yet. That is what we're here for, to help each other. I'm sure before coming here some of you were medicated or put through therapy to try and minimize what you could do. In Camp Supernatural, we encourage socializing and camaraderie. Before we continue, can someone please bring Gary back here?"

Hailey volunteered and dragged Gary back into the tent like a sack of flour. She shoved him easily inside the tent without breaking a sweat.

She handled him like a cat playing with a mouse. I would hate to be the mouse in that instance.

Daniel smirked in satisfaction as Hailey rejoined the group.

"Thank you, Hailey. Please show us what you can do, Gary."

He nodded, prickly, and took a deep breath as his heart began to beat against his chest hard. Then, Gary exited the tent, saying that his power would be dangerous in a tight space.

Maybe he'll explode, thought Lucas, humorously.

A few seconds later, Gary thrust a fist to the ground and caused a dent to the surface of the ground. The blow manifested itself across the camp and inside the boundaries of the tent. When he walked back inside he bowed his head as if to thank the silent audience for his performance.

"That was impressive. You activated your power based on your heart rate, correct?" Daniel inquired.

Gary nodded and brushed off dirt that had covered part of his shirt.

"I've seen an ability similar to yours before. It's dangerous though because of your heart condition," noted Counselor Harrison.

Gary shrugged it off and silently took back his spot amongst the others.

His heart condition makes it so that the faster his heart beats, the slower it becomes. He can't use that power too often, or else he risks permanent damage to himself. Speaking of which... I can actually feel his heart. It's like someone is punching my chest and I can't breathe unless I control my breathing. That must be what he does to keep himself from being suffocated by his ability and condition. No wonder he was on defense for the Relic game.

Daniel then turned to Josh, who looked as if he had no clue what was going on around him.

"Now Josh, what can you do?" asked Daniel, enthusiastically.

When he understood the question, Josh took a deep breath and let out a small concentrated sonic wave that burst a nearby glass cup. It shattered into millions of tiny pieces that scattered around the corner of the tent. Luckily, the wind took the shards and thrust them upwards away from the tent. Daniel laughed and clapped his hands together.

"Very good, Josh. I like how you can control the vibrations of the wave's frequency like any other muscle in your body. Thereby directing it towards your target as you control the velocity of the sound."

Josh nodded at every word and feigned a smile.

"No idea what you said, but thank you," Josh blurted out with a prideful grin.

Daniel nodded approvingly and looked at the other campers.

"Who's up next? How about you, Caroline. I know yours is especially good."

At first glance, Caroline was a meek looking girl. She had an almost babyish face despite being roughly a year younger than Lucas.

She looks like a farm girl with her hair like that and overalls, Lucas observed. *The way she's sitting is a little too formal, like that's how she sits back at home instead of amongst strangers.*

The Farm Girl made a nervous smile as the others fixed their attention on her. She pointed her right hand in the direction of Lucas's neck and without even touching

Shelly's necklace, yanked it off. It flew towards her hand faster than the speed of a bullet. She caught it with ease and held it in her small little palm. The others, including the young telepath, were astonished.

"Caroline has the power to control magnetic objects. A very useful ability, but it can also be highly unstable, much like your own ability, Lucas," Daniel explained as he nodded in approval. The Farm Girl began blushing and timidly returned the necklace to the young telepath before taking back her place.

How did she do that? I didn't even feel it come off.

Next, Mike stepped up.

"Anyone have something old that has preferably been washed at least once today?"

Lucas pulled out a quarter he had that said '1972' on it. Mike quickly rummaged through his pockets, but did not seem to find what he was looking for.

Where is it? Where is it? This isn't good. Fine, alright. I'll take it like that, Mike thought irritably.

He hesitantly took the quarter from Lucas's hand and held it carefully with two fingers.

Why is he being so fragile about it? It's just a coin. It won't break if he drops it.

After a minute, Mike said, "This quarter once belonged to one of the Presidents of the United States."

Lucas felt his jaw drop while Daniel suppressed a smile. The others, as well as the Camp Counselor, started laughing out loud like it was some kind of inside joke that the young telepath was not in on.

Too bad I couldn't read his mind before the punch line.

"I was just joking. I'm sorry, it's only a regular quarter."

Mike apologized and handed the quarter back to a stunned Lucas.

The young telepath felt like he had just been pantsed in front of everyone.

I don't know what's worse; the fact that I feel embarrassed, or the humiliation of being so gullible.

"My name is Mike," the young boy introduced himself to everyone. "I can find the origins of anything just by touching it. I can also build stuff but it's a fairly new ability I'm still working on. I made the sticky bomb Josh used during the Relic game. My lifelong dream is to build a hover board, maybe a flying car someday."

Lucas looked at Mike as he took his place amongst the others. The young telepath found it odd that the young boy kept his hands in his pockets firmly.

Maybe he doesn't like getting them dirty, thought Lucas, curiously. *His thoughts aren't easy to read. He thinks a lot about equations and acronyms. Right now he's thinking about the word 'Local'= Town, City, Village, District, Neighborhood.*

"For a moment there you had me excited. That's still a cool ability. Must come in handy when you're looking for spare change," Lucas said with intended humor in his tone.

Mike appreciated the joke and shifted his attention to the Camp Director's son. Daniel looked around the room with final approval.

"I think we got the general idea now. So, would anyone else like to volunteer, or shall we begin training?"

Lucas almost expected Ashley, Hailey, Kendall, Bruce, and Vanessa to show off, but they decided to keep quiet.

Ashley's thinking about how professional Daniel seems, Hailey's eyeing Gary more than Josh at the moment, Kendall is thinking about the new shampoo she wore today, Bruce hates how small the space is, and Vanessa keeps glaring at Ashley. Her thoughts keep going back to the fact that I didn't name the flower after her.

With no more demonstrations, Daniel nodded and rose from his place.

"Alright then, let's begin training. First off, you'll be paired with other campers who have similar abilities to each other. We categorize them here as physical abilities, and mental abilities. The first pairing will be Lucas and Mike. Then we have Hailey and Bruce. Followed by Josh and Vanessa. Ashley will be paired with Gary, and lastly, Kendall will be with Caroline."

Lucas didn't like the idea of being partnered with someone he barely knew, even if they were in the same cabin. Gary seemed more enthusiastic about being with Ashley than she did. Hailey and Bruce seemed perfect as training partners considering both had similar abilities. Josh was also excited to work with Vanessa, noting that being deaf meant he wouldn't be bothered by her ability.

That's probably why he was chosen to be with her, Lucas noted. *Kendall and Caroline are already cabin mates so they have more familiarity than the rest of us. I guess Daniel tried to keep it fair for all of us, even if it doesn't feel that way.*

Mike and Lucas began with mind reading. As part of the training, Mike began to think different thoughts that threw Lucas off.

Solve for X = Y. Round out to the fourth power. Atrocious. See what you can come up with this one, Lucas.

Lucas was startled by this test and the word. He prepared to do just that.

Angry, trash, revile, odor, conflicted, insane, out, under, and surprise.

The young telepath looked at Mike to see if he approved, but the young boy gave him a doubtful expression.

Try to match the letters words with the main word itself. Otherwise, you'll end up confusing yourself and me while we're at it.

Lucas nodded as they continued training. Meanwhile, Daniel was reading a book at the entrance of his tent as his campers trained. Josh and Vanessa were getting along well, with the sonic vibrations he emitted being able to counteract her bone crushing ability. Ashley helped Gary test his heart regulation, including how much it needed to beat for his power to activate. Bruce used his strength to see if he could break through Hailey's steel skin, but nothing he did worked. The last group, which consisted of Kendall and Caroline, saw the young farm girl using coins to stop her cabin mate from shifting past the obstacles in their way.

Shifting through? She is going through those trees like they're not even there.

After about two hours' worth of practice, Daniel called Lucas over to speak alone. The young telepath walked up, feeling queasy and nervous, both from his anxiety and all the thoughts that Mike projected into this mind.

I feel like I just got off a rollercoaster. Hopefully I don't vomit like the last time I was on one.

Without warning, Daniel placed his hand on top of Lucas's head and buried it underneath his hair firmly.

"I want you to mind control me to take my hand off your head, but do not use your mouth to tell me."

Lucas closed his eyes, trying hard to think. He said the words but didn't know if it had any effect on the Camp Counselor.

Get your hand off my head... Remove your hand from my head... Please?

The Camp Counselor's hand still nested on his head.

Let go of me, now. Please, take your hand off me.

Suddenly, he heard a concentrated sound wave through his ear drums like an emergency broadcast system. Lucas tried to suppress the pain the sound brought, but it must have been plain in his eyes. With a sigh, Daniel patted his head softly and withdrew his hand.

"We will get there, eventually," said the Camp Counselor in an encouraging tone. Not long after, he announced the end of training for the first day. "I want each of you to head back to your cabins and continue practicing individually, because tomorrow I'm thinking of trying something new. I hope you all like surprises," Daniel concluded.

After that, the campers proceeded to returning to their respective cabins. As they were walking, Lucas noticed Kendall's appearance even more than before.

She has shoulder length chestnut hair with a hair clip on the side. She's wearing a green cabin shirt and the short shorts. She's extremely pretty. Even more than Vanessa and Ashley. I better never say that out loud.

Just as Lucas was about to ask his cabin mate about her, Josh's eyes were fixated on the beautiful camper.

A girl like her would never be single for long in my school. I'm pretty sure she has a boyfriend either in camp or outside of camp.

Lucas immediately thought about Hailey and how crushed she would be if she saw Josh looking at another girl.

He wouldn't be so heartless as to break her heart like that, would he? Suddenly, the young telepath was afraid to read Josh's mind in that moment.

Before he could, Mike came over to talk to Lucas, but Josh ignored his greetings.

"Hey Lucas, that was a good first day of training. I'm sorry about the coin thing," Mike apologized again. "I'm glad of all the cabins I could have been put in for my first year, it was in yours. Even though he can talk a big game, Gary's not such a bad guy. Forgive me for saying so, but I wish you hadn't encouraged the situation."

Lucas agreed apologetically and admitted his guilt over it.

"I just did what I thought everyone else was expecting. That's no excuse though, I know I took it too far. I don't mean to be that way. So let's start fresh again."

He extended his hand for Mike to shake, but the young boy backed away slowly. Lucas looked at his hand in confusion.

"I'm sorry, is there a problem with my hand?" Lucas asked in a concerned tone.

I mean he handled the coin and seemed fine after… wait… Oh I see…

Mike shook his head bashfully.

"I have OCD. It's why you could hear all those thoughts at once. I'm sorry about that too," Mike admitted, shamefully.

Lucas suddenly felt uncomfortable, as the voice of Mike began to speak in his mind.

Where are those gloves? I had them this morning. I can't believe I actually touched that dirty filthy quarter without my gloves. I know I'm going to pay for it when I return to my bunk. Two plus two equals four. $E = mc^2$. Plato Bacon Necktie. No wait that's not right…

The rest of what Mike thought in his mind became obscured by a flood of words that Lucas had a hard time understanding.

This is even more unfiltered than during training. His anxiety must be getting too him more than he's letting

266

on. At least he can hide it on the outside better than I can.

Despite the discomfort Mike's thoughts brought him, Lucas did his best not to draw attention to it.

"Don't be sorry for being yourself," Lucas said, casually. "I have anxiety and bipolar which isn't good. Before coming here, I used to take medication for both and since being here I haven't needed it as much. I can actually talk to people here comfortably, for the most part at least."

Lucas tried to sound modest about it, but deep down felt the exact opposite.

His thoughts are louder than anyone else's I've heard so far from here. Now I see why Daniel paired us up together. If only he could stop thinking just for one…

"Wow. That has to be tough. But I'm glad to hear your managing yourself better. I look forward to more training with you. It's crazy to think we're among the few mental Alter Children in camp this summer. Anyways, I'll see you later today," Mike excused himself.

The young telepath sighed in relief as his thoughts became his own again. He then turned to Josh and suddenly heard his friend's voice in his mind.

Here we go again…

She's the hottest girl in this camp, in the whole world. She has such an amazing body figure and a has nice…

Lucas cut off the rest of the thought and suddenly felt unclean.

"What's wrong with you, Josh?" Lucas shouted impulsively.

Josh wasn't looking in his direction, so the young telepath got his attention and repeated the same thing again.

Once Josh understood, he was not at all happy about it and took it the wrong way.

"Did you read my mind? Stop doing that!"

"I wasn't trying to read your mind. It just happened," Lucas insisted defensively.

Josh glared at the young telepath and his eyes were enough to tell him that he didn't believe a word of it.

Why wouldn't he?

"If that's the case, what am I thinking now? Say it for all to hear!" Josh angrily signed and said aloud.

Lucas focused this time and heard Josh call him something vulgar.

How does he know that kind of word?!

"Hey, don't call me that. How do you know that kind of word?"

Lucas seethed at the word Josh had called him and felt grateful that he didn't blurt the word out impulsively.

"You heard that? Surprised even a Deaf Boy would know that kind of language," Josh gloated. "I watched adult cartoons, with subtitles of course."

As the pair walked back in silence towards the cabin, Josh's thoughts were constantly entering Lucas's mind. Even when he tried to ignore them, the words just seemed to be getting louder and more tenacious.

They won't stop! His voice is even more annoying when it's in my head! Its times like this I really wish I had my earphones.

When they entered the cabin, Bill greeted Josh, who proceeded to ignore him and walk past him. Josh only slammed the door shut to his bunk without saying a word to either of his cabin mates. Feeling concerned, Bill looked at Lucas.

"I've never seen Josh lose his cool like that. The last time he got angry was when I ate the last bits of his favorite cereal. But he didn't get as angry as he looks now," Bill admitted, as he turned his face towards the television.

When Lucas chuckled nervously, Bill turned back to him with a sharp look.

"Why are you laughing? Are you having fun with your new ability now?" Bill asked in annoyance.

Lucas looked stunned by this accusation.

"Fun? You think I have fun reading people's minds and hearing their thoughts along with my own?"

Bill shook his head and rose from the couch.

"It sure seems that way from here," Bill barked back in a sharp sarcastic tone. "You can't tell me it isn't convenient for you to know all about a person without having to talk to them. It sounds like you'd have a great time doing that considering you don't like to talk to people."

Lucas shrugged with his next response being a very poor and careless one.

"Yeah, right. How about this; you need to get your own thoughts in check. Like this one: you keep thinking about an actress named Kristen Bell and you're watching a movie right now just because she's in it. You don't even like the movie, but you like her."

Bill flushed both in embarrassment and anger at this. The young telepath expected his older cabin mate to continue being upset and argue against him. To his surprise, Bill slumped on the couch and appeared to have resigned to the truth.

"First off, that was a private thought, and secondly, most importantly, that was not cool of you," Bill admitted with disappointment. "Seriously, man, you really need to control that power of yours. I'll have you know that Kristen Bell is a beautiful actress and amazingly talented. There's nothing wrong with seeing a movie just because she's in it. Half the people who watch any movie see them because of whoever stars in leading roles."

Lucas knew the actress Bill was fond of because his sister used to watch one of her television shows.

It's not something I'd care to get into. Either way, it's weird to think that my sister and Bill are into the same actress and her roles.

After a few minutes of silence, Bill finally asked Lucas about Josh.

"So, what exactly did you do to upset a chill guy like Josh?"

Lucas explained to Bill about how he read a personal thought of Josh's (but left out the part about him admiring Kendall with suggestive thoughts) and that he got defensive and angry about it.

"I can't say I blame him. There's a reason why people's thoughts are private and why they should be treated as such by you especially."

Lucas did not like the turn the conversation took, but knew Bill wouldn't let this go either.

I better deal with it now or he might decide to bring this up in a more public setting.

"We are supposed to have a sense of security and safety within ourselves. You violated that right, even if you didn't mean to. In this camp, we are all trying to figure ourselves out as we go. I understand that you're going to have a harder time than most. All I ask is that you just try, Lucas. Try to leave your comfort zone without using your powers."

While Bill spoke, Lucas thought irritably, *I don't know what he's talking about. I mean, it's not my fault people think so many stupid thoughts at a time. My thoughts are messed up enough already without having to hear everyone else's problems too.*

A question suddenly came to him when he remembered something Marcus had brought up.

"Did Jacob try to destroy this camp when he was here?" the young telepath asked. Something about the question itself seemed to give Bill a different demeanor than what he had before. It was the same kind of behavior Lucas observed from his parents after they gave him the camp invitation.

"I don't know what you're talking about. Who told you that?"

Lucas shook his head, not wanting to give away Marcus's name and risk getting him in trouble.

"It was just something I heard. Is it true or not?"

"I don't know," Bill said, his body language suggesting he genuinely didn't know. "Look, it doesn't matter what Jacob tried to do. It only matters that he's gone and will never come back. Focus more on what is in front of you, like maintaining the friendships your making here. Josh will let this go, just don't make it a habit. You're not exactly winning popularity contests here to be picking and choosing your friends."

The young telepath nodded, considering the last words his older cabin mate told him.

When Lucas entered his imagery bunk, he fell flat on the floor, missing the bed by a few inches. Instead of crawling towards the bed, he sighed and made a feeble attempt to reach his bed. Before he could, he felt his chest hurt, his throat tighten, and his eyes beginning to swell in tears.

Everything looks so perfect here. It's like I never left home and camp is just a bad dream I haven't woken up from.

For a moment, he almost expected Shelly to burst through the door with one of her classic lectures on how he has no ambition in life or desire to excel at anything.

Between her lectures and Bill's, I'd choose Shelly's lectures any day of the week.

Lucas always envied how, regardless of his parent's harsh ways towards him and his sister, she always displayed more strength and courage than he did. Shelly knew what she wanted from life, right down to the man she would want to marry.

She said he didn't need to be handsome, but he did have to work a full-time job. He didn't need to be smart, but he couldn't be a pushover either. Other stuff too. I can't remember them right now.

In contrast, Lucas never considered the idea of marriage or dating for himself, despite the desire for both.

I don't see myself being with anyone who would be able to accept that I can hear their thoughts as if spoken aloud, Lucas pondered, miserably.

He thought about how easy it was to leave his home and to leave his sister. The feeling of regret hadn't sunken in until he had nothing else to think about.

I wish I had Mike's multiple thoughts to keep me busy. I can't stop thinking about everything now. When can I go home? What will Shelly and my parents expect from me? Can I tell them the truth or is that another lie I need to keep to myself?

Lucas tried to push back the thoughts he had that were making him sad. The thoughts felt louder in the company of his seclusion.

Why do I always do this to myself? Why can't I just be happy? I thought I was. But now, now I can't stop... no, I won't stop...

In the seclusion of his room, he became overwhelmed by his thoughts and began to weep softly...

Chapter 8

The Breaking Point

The next couple days of training were exhausting for Lucas, both physically and mentally. Daniel had the children working one part of themselves to improve their overall power. For instance, Lucas's ability manifested from his mind, so that meant he'd focus on his physical strength which, according to Daniel, would help keep his mind healthy as well. Mike created dummies out of salt, elastic, and grains from the cafeteria kitchen. They looked life-like, with one having the face of what the young telepath thought looked like a reptilian creature.

"I thought it would be cooler if they had an evil look to make it seem like you're fighting bad guys," Mike explained to Lucas, enthusiastically. "They look like Lizard People. You know, like that reptilian conspiracy theory."

Evil is not the word I would use to describe what they look like. What reptilian theory? That sounds like something from a movie Shell might like.

In addition, Mike constructed other work out equipment for Lucas such as dumbbells from bits of steel Caroline provided him, and a pull-up using the spare steel leftover. The young telepath used the dumbbells and tried the pull-up, only to give up after the second day.

At the end of each training day, his mind hurt twice as much after attempting to read and control Daniel's mind.

It's like I'm being attacked from both my physical body and my mental, well, mind.

The days began to fly by with the end of June fast approaching. Lucas began to feel hopeless and discouraged of ever succeeding in reading or controlling Daniel's mind. To his surprise, the Camp Counselor tried to encourage him by mentioning the Camp Director in his incentive.

"Like my father always says: 'True strength comes from the desire to change and improve upon the foundations already in place'. Don't try to force the progress on yourself. Try to find it within yourself and don't give up. My father and I don't like quitters."

Lucas nodded, but each attempt only produced more failures.

So much for finding my hidden strength. All I've found are hidden headaches and muscle aches.

That weekend, and for Father's Day, the young telepath decided to write a note home to his father. He wasn't sure when or if his father would ever get a chance to read it, He did it more for himself at that moment than in the hope that his father would read it:

Dear Dad, I am so sorry for the way I left, and I am sorry that I never listened to you and mom the way I should have. I miss you both and Shelly so much. Camp hasn't been perfect but it's had its moments. I've met some great people here and they're the first friends I've ever had. The Camp Director is a wonderful man. He's helped me through learning what I have and how to use it. I can't wait to tell you all about the camp and him after the summer ends. Until then, I hope you're okay, dad. Please don't hate me for how I left. I hope when you read this, it will make you smile. Love always, your son, Lucas Fargo.

The young telepath tucked the note away in his backpack, and patted the pocket he put it in. He wondered what his father's reaction would be when he read his letter.

I hope he appreciates it and my mom too. I wonder what Shelly is doing right now. Knowing her; taking summer classes and getting ready for the next school year.

During one of their off days from training, Lucas and Josh decided to go to the far side of the camp, past the cafeteria and Henry's home, and towards a small ridge where a lake nested. As Bill had predicted, Josh didn't seem to hold the mind reading incident against Lucas, but he wasn't completely comfortable being alone with him too much either.

Can't say I blame him. It'll take a while to earn back his trust.

There were two sources of water in the camp; the first being the camp lake, which many campers used as a swimming pool, while the other source of water was more like a stream-lined river. This was primarily used for the canoeing activity. The lake's clean water felt warm to Lucas, as he smelled the recent rain aroma.

It was mostly drizzle, but it just seems so… unnatural in a place that's isolated from the outside world.

During the daytime hours, the lake became lively with many children playing and splashing around. The younger children were supervised by Marcus and Betty while the older campers were allowed to roam in the deeper waters.

Lucas and Josh were joined by Hailey and Ashley. Hailey and Josh jumped into the lake enthusiastically, and proceeded to play the game 'Marco Polo'. He had to remind everyone, albeit humorously, that he is deaf and that, with a blindfold on, he wouldn't be able to know who was shouting the name. Instead, he proposed for them to splash water at him, while using his sonic waves on the water to feel the vibrations around him.

I'm beginning to think Josh just likes to cheat in everything, Lucas thought with a sigh.

Because Josh kept winning (through cheating), they decided to play 'Jaws Attack' with one kid literally cutting through the water as if he were an actual shark instead of human.

That kid was on the orange team. His teeth are cutting through the water like a knife on bread.

Meanwhile, Ashley and Lucas stayed on land and watched the others swim in the water. When the young telepath looked at his female friend, she smiled brightly at him. He quickly turned away and pretended that the sun had blinded him. She wore a purple cap over her tied back blonde hair. Underneath her cap, the sun's rays seemed to make her freckles appear sparkly. She was also dressed for the lake, with a white camp shirt that, despite not being wet, showed the outlines of her bra. Lucas noticed this and glanced down from her face to avoid eye contact with Ashley.

Of all the color shirts, why did she have to wear a white shirt, Lucas thought uncomfortably, as he tried his best to keep his eyes on her face. *I keep looking there and I don't know why. The sun makes her face look even prettier.*

"What are you staring at, Lucas?" Ashley asked him bashfully.

The young telepath shook his head and downplayed his eyes.

"I thought I saw some hair on your ear. Oh, wait, there it is." Lucas carefully brushed the bang of hair behind Ashley's ear, and both were suddenly blushing.

What did I just do? Why did I do that?

Suddenly, Lucas heard Ashley's thoughts in his head. *I didn't expect that, but it was nice. I wish he*

would have warned me a bit though. I didn't know if to say anything about it or not.

"Josh and Hailey would make such a nice couple. I hope they end up together," Ashley said abruptly, as the young telepath nodded in agreement. He suddenly remembered the girl his cabin mate was looking at with interest.

Maybe I should ask her about the other girl.

"Can you keep a secret?" Ashley asked Lucas as she leaned in towards him.

She was so close now that he swore if he moved a few inches closer, they'd be close enough to kiss.

She smells really good, like strawberries. Why am I thinking about her in this way? I like Vanessa.

"I know Josh is your friend, but please don't tell him I told you this."

Just as Lucas nodded, he heard the same words Ashley said in her mind come out of her mouth.

"Josh likes to flirt with a lot of girls. I don't know why he's like that and Hailey doesn't know about that. It would break her heart because she's kind of in love with him," Ashley confessed, sorrowfully.

Lucas wanted to laugh at the idea of love, since they were still teenagers.

What do teenagers know about love? We're barely figuring out our own stuff without figuring out each other, Lucas thought scornfully. *Last year, there was a girl two years older than me who I liked. She was nice, like Ashley. It turns out her friends put her up to talking to me but she didn't really want to. I wonder what she thought, if she felt bad about making me feel that way. I haven't liked anyone like that since. Not even Vanessa.*

"What makes you think Josh flirts with a lot of girls?" Lucas asked curiously.

What am I thinking? I saw him flirt with that young nurse and she kept giving him lovey-dovey eyes last time we were in the ward. I read her mind last time I saw her and yeah, she's definitely head over heels for him.

"Josh used to flirt with a lot of girls back in my old school, before the all-girls school one. He liked to hang around in the area whenever he could and occasionally I saw him talking to different girls. One of those girls was a friend of mine and she told me that he tried to ask her out on a date. When she said no, he immediately asked her friend. It didn't matter though because even when she said yes, the date never happened."

Lucas began to realize something that he hadn't understood before about Josh.

He doesn't understand what he's doing, Lucas told himself pitifully. *He thinks it's okay to flirt with multiple girls at a time. Dating might not be something he's actually interested in.*

Despite never flirting with girls much, Lucas was familiar with the concept through his sister, who taught him the basics.

'Flirting 101; Lesson one: be confident in what you say. Women like confidence and most times men, even handsome ones, lack it. Lesson two: compliments are key, even more so than direct intention. This leads to the third and final lesson, the most important one: Don't ever lie when you flirt. That includes if you don't find the person you're flirting with attractive. Flirting with lies will eventually leave someone hurt.' At least that's what Shell said.

He tried to think of his sister's words, and how they fit with Josh's behavior. It wasn't long before thoughts were beginning to focus on Shelly. Brushing them aside, he thought about the model girl and Josh's obvious crush on her.

"I'm sorry for asking about your sister before," Ashley mentioned to Lucas's surprise. "I was just curious about her because I don't have any siblings, so I like when people talk about theirs."

Lucas shook his head, still not wanting to talk about his sister. His hand went to his neck and touched the necklace Shelly gave him. Ashley noticed this and asked about it.

"That's a nice necklace. S in cursive."

The young telepath nodded and decided to let her hold it for a bit.

"I bought it for her on her twelfth birthday. She gave it to me before I left home."

Ashley handed it back to Lucas and playfully said, "That's really nice. If I didn't know it was your sisters, I would have thought it was from a girlfriend."

Lucas blushed at this.

"Nope, it's my sisters. I'm as single as a dollar bill."

Ashley chuckled at this and looked reassured.

Alright, I think I should mention the girl that Josh was thinking about. 'Do you know that girl with Vanesa and Caroline?'

"Speaking of, do you know that girl who is with Vanessa and Caroline? She looks like a model and very pretty for someone our age?" Lucas blurted out without thinking about the words he said.

That's always my problem; I always speak before I think about what I'm going to say. Even when I rehearse it in my head, something new comes up.

Ashley looked puzzled by this.

"Do you mean Kendall? I've only talked to her twice so far. She's really nice, a lot nicer than Vanessa. Our cabin ate with her and her other cabin mate Caroline a few days ago. She's a sweetheart too. As far as I know though she's not a model, just very pretty. You'll have to tell me later what you mean by 'prettier than our age'. For right now why are you asking about her?"

Lucas was ready to tell her when Josh came out of the water with his trunks soaking wet and shirtless.

His side of the story: he lost his shirt to the shark camper after being eaten in the game they were playing.

The young telepath looked at his deaf cabin mate's chest to see how physically fit he appeared. He was envious to see Josh's toned muscles and no sight of body fat.

He looks more ripped than most kids our age. Maybe he would make a good couple with Kendall; she's prettier than anyone our age and he's more fit than any other guy here. Except, well maybe Jeremy, the gift shop guy.

"Have a towel or something to dry up with?" Josh signed meekly.

Ashley rose from Lucas's side and prepared to sprint. "Hold on, I'll be right back."

Without a second passing, Ashley disappeared leaving behind a dust trail. Hailey then came out soaking wet and for the first time Lucas saw her in a different view.

She wore a plain grey t-shirt with swimming trunks that looked more like boxers. Her towering height could be clearly acknowledged and she appeared taller than any girl Lucas had ever seen. Her muscles were very noticeable without jeans or a long sleeve to cover them, including her pigmentations.

She's even more ripped than Jeremy and Alexia. Both her shoulders have what look like burnt spots, and her wrists also have them, though not as bad. Her hands and fingers are the same, Lucas observed.

He also saw how bright her brown eyes shone in the sunlight and thought they looked like dark chocolate.

She's not the prettiest girl in camp, but at least now she looks more feminine than usual. I wonder why Josh won't give her a chance.

Near a minute after she left, Ashley came back with two clean towels. The blonde-haired girl handed them to

Hailey and Josh, with both drying themselves out. After handing out the last towel, she nearly tripped on herself. Her left leg began to wobble and she tried to support herself until the young telepath grabbed her right hand to steady her.

"I'm okay, thank you, Lucas," Ashley said, as their hands still held each other. Quickly, both let go and pretended not to notice it. Ashley's breathe steadied.

"Hey, Josh, why don't we head back to the cabin already," Lucas asked his cabin mate. He gave him an uncertain look, until the young telepath's eyes glanced at Ashley then back to Josh.

"Yeah, sure," Josh signed, hesitantly. "We can do that."

Lucas nodded and led his cabin mate away.

I better go before Ashley brings up our previous conversation.

Before they could leave, Ashley followed and caught up to them.

Darn, I almost got away.

"I need to talk to Lucas real quick, Hailey. Can you please keep Josh busy?" Ashley asked her friend.

Hailey nodded with a smile while Josh did not understand what just happened.

When they were earshot away from the two, Ashley pressed for the previous conversation.

"Why did you ask about Kendall? Does this have to do with Josh?" Ashley demanded.

Wow, it's like she read my mind.

Lucas nodded hesitantly.

"I saw him looking at Kendall like she was the prettiest girl in camp. I mean she is, but that's beside the point." *Shut up, Lucas.* "Maybe he was looking in her direction, just not at her, you know? That's also possible." *About as possible as pigs flying.*

Lucas felt as unsure as he sounded.

At least she can't say I'm lying. Also, why did I have to bring up the prettier than anyone else here again, aloud of all things? Now she'll really think I'm like every guy in the world.

Ashley sighed and shook her head.

"Thank you for telling me, Lucas. You're right about what you saw. I know it's asking for a lot, but can you please talk to Josh about it?"

Ashley's tone suggested her concern directed itself more toward Hailey than Josh himself.

Why haven't you ever tried talking to him yourself? Lucas thought to ask. Before he could, she beat him too it.

"I've tried to talk to him before about Hailey, but he always brushes me off before I can say much."

She did it again. Either she's a mind reader like me or I'm just that obvious.

"So what makes you think I'll have any luck with Josh?"

Lucas was certain the only way Josh would listen is if he used his mind control ability on him.

Which is not allowed here, and anyways it's wrong to do. I know that and it isn't something I should do even if I can.

Ashley smiled shyly at him and said, "Because you're his best friend, silly. He respects your opinion. He's told me so since the Relic game. Why do you think he's always hanging out with you?"

Lucas did not expect this revelation at all.

Josh respects my opinion? Of all the people to respect, why me? Lucas thought dumbfounded. *I know Bill mentioned something similar to this, but I thought he meant just regular friends. Best friends has more of a title to it; more of an honor I feel. Regardless, that's not what I expected to hear.*

Without even realizing it, Lucas felt a smile appear on his face.

I admire Shelly more than anyone else. The only bad thing is I always felt envious towards her and how differently our parents treated her as opposed to me. It feels nice to know that someone respects me enough to think highly of what I think. Makes me feel... I don't know I guess... important?

Lucas wasn't sure how to feel about it, but Ashley's insistence didn't give him much time to ponder the thought.

"Just try talking to him, please. If he doesn't listen, that's okay. Don't force him to talk about it if he doesn't want to. I'll see you tomorrow," said Ashley as she walked back towards Hailey and Josh.

Lucas decided to go in the opposite direction and not wait on his cabin mate.

Maybe the pairing will happen on its own. Besides, Josh is apparently good at talking to girls. On his own, maybe he'll decide to look past whatever he's feeling and eventually give Hailey a chance.

The thought seemed comforting, but Lucas knew the odds of that happening were about as slim as reading Daniel's mind before the summer ended.

That can still happen. At the rate I'm going, it's not likely.

When Lucas reached his cabin, Vanessa burst through the front door and blocked his way.

"Hey Lucas, what's up?" Vanessa greeted him, almost too friendly. This was the first time they had spoken since the nature walk activity. The young telepath wasn't sure if she still thought about it.

I could just read her mind and find out, but I might see more than that if I do.

Lucas tried to look past her to see if her brother was inside the cabin.

"Is   Bill   inside?"

Vanessa shook her head.

"No, he's at one of those boring council meetings for cabin leaders. Do you have a minute?"

Lucas nodded and walked in after Vanessa. Her long hair seemed to flow down her back like a cape.

She looks even more beautiful with her hair loose... *Bill, wherever you are, hurry up and get here*, Lucas pleaded with himself. After a few seconds past, Vanessa's brother never showed up.

Thanks a lot.

"What's this about?" Lucas asked, warily.

Before Vanessa said anything, the young telepath heard her voice in his head and did not like the way it sounded.

No one should be here for a while, so let's see if we can make up for some lost time, Vanessa slyly thought.

Lucas decided to go to the kitchen and come up with some innocent excuse to stall her.

I shouldn't have come back alone.

"Want a soda? I think we have some cherry flavored ones here somewhere."

Cherry flavored? That's her favorite. Why did I say that out loud!

Vanessa grinned at him and walked towards the kitchen.

"And how do you know I want one that is cherry flavored?" Bill's sister asked him, suspiciously.

Lucas shrugged and berated himself for saying too much. He opened the refrigerator door and fumbled his hands through the drinks he began to imagine up.

Me and my big mouth strikes again. I really should use my inside voice instead of the one people hear most.

"Intuition. It's a new ability I recently discovered."

Unfortunately, he knew Vanessa didn't believe him.

She slammed the refrigerator door on Lucas and

looked at him as if she meant to charge at him.

"In that case, why don't you read my mind just to see what I am thinking about right now?"

Lucas gulped hard and said out loud her thoughts.

"You're thinking about me a lot and that you like me."

The last part couldn't be more obvious.

Maybe if I buy some more time, Josh, or Mike will come, Lucas tried to assure himself. *Vanessa wouldn't act this way if someone else were here. Much less her brother.*

She smiled so wide that Lucas could see her very white teeth. They looked so perfect and lined, not a gap or crooked tooth in sight.

"Since you read my mind, you know that I like you," Vanessa revealed, enthusiastically. "I'll admit I was annoyed when you named the flower after Ashley, but I'm willing to forget about it if you tell me a truth."

Lucas gulped again, with the thought of Bill using his heat vision to melt his face filling him with discomfort and fear.

If Bill knew this was happening, he'd probably burn me alive or color me green like spinach. My only crime would be that I like his sister back.

Vanessa tugged at Lucas's shirt collar playfully until he diverted his attention back towards her.

"What are you so afraid of?" she asked in a low whisper. "Have you ever had a girlfriend before? A nice handsome boy like you."

Lucas shook his head and attempted to move himself away from her by backing off.

"I don't know how to date and talk to girls. You make it easy by talking to me," Lucas heard himself admit.

He heard the words and contemplated them.

It's true; I would never talk to her otherwise. Even though I guess I did flirt with her during the Relic game.

I don't even know if she liked that because last time she didn't.

"What do you mean I make it easy to talk to you? Should I make it harder by playing hard to get with you?"

Vanessa seemed offended by this, but just as quickly as she brought it up, she went back to her flirtatious behavior.

"No, of course not. It's just that I don't know why you would like a guy like me. I overthink too much, I'm not handsome, I'm nothing," Lucas heard himself admit. To his discomfort, he saw how his words made Vanessa feel.

She seemed to consider what he said without providing a quick response.

More than anything, she's surprised by that. Not as much as I am for saying it all like that.

"Well, I like you because you're nice to me and when we talk your attention is always on me. Now, I want you to tell me the truth; do you like me back or are you just going along with what I feel? I'll know if you're lying and I won't forgive you."

Lucas didn't want to answer. He knew any answer would be like a double edged sword.

If I say I like her, which I do, she'll tell everyone that we're a together now. If I say I don't like her, and lie, she'll be even more upset than before.

Bill's sister waited for an answer. The longer the young telepath took to say anything, the less enthusiastic she became.

"I'm sorry, I don't know what to say right now," Lucas admitted.

I do like you and I'd love to date you. No I don't like you, I just see you as a friend and it's better that way. It isn't that I don't want to date you, it's just it would make things awkward with Bill.

286

All these lines played in his head like the scripts he concocted for himself in awkward situations. None saw the light of day.

"Alright, well before I leave, I want to give you your first kiss, but I want to play hard to get since that's what you seem prefer. So use your powers on me to make me kiss you."

The young telepath immediately shook his head. He knew it was wrong even if, deep down, he also knew it would make things easier.

I could even make her forget that we kissed if I had to. That doesn't feel right because I would be using my powers outside of training.

Vanessa was waiting for Lucas to use his powers on her.

When he didn't, she leaned in towards him and said, "Fine, I'll do it then."

Vanessa was so close to kissing Lucas that it wasn't until Josh burst in suddenly and saw them that their tension suddenly broke. The young telepath sighed heavily with deep relief.

Better late than never. Next time, sooner would be better, Lucas thought to himself.

After recognizing the situation, Josh crept inside slowly, as if afraid to step on a hidden trap.

"Don't mind me. Continue with kissing," Josh encouraged, awkwardly. "Remember, I'm still here even if I can't hear."

He walked calmly towards the couch and had his back turned to them. Vanessa stepped back from Lucas, still smiling.

"I better get back before Kendall and Caroline wonder where I'm at. You've given me a lot to think about, handsome."

She winked at him and walked away. As Vanessa exited the cabin, her older brother finally returned. Bill saw Lucas standing as still as a statue and greeted him with a friendly smile.

"Hey Lucas, how was training today?" asked Bill.

Vanessa grinned and walked over to her brother.

"He has quite the story to tell you, right, Lucas?"

The young telepath did not smile. He just walked towards Josh to sit as close to him as possible.

If I'm going down, I'm taking Josh with me, whether he knows it or not, Lucas thought, intensely.

When Vanessa left, Bill's had a perplexed expression.

"Did you two get together already?"

Lucas shook his head erratically, but after reading his older cabin mate's mind and sensing no danger, he calmed himself. Bill sighed and looked like something was bugging him.

"So did anything else happen, or was that it?"

Bill's voice sounded tense, which meant Lucas had to be very careful with the words he chose, or else his older cabin mate could get the wrong idea. The young telepath felt inclined to shake his head rapidly while trying not to seem nervous about it. It wasn't until Josh blurted out the truth that any plan he could have come up with fell apart.

"They looked like they were going to kiss. Then I walked in. Very awkward," Josh's voice was steady, as were his hand signs.

Bill looked like he was ready to kill both Josh and Lucas, but instead he burst into laughter. The young telepath did not understand why Bill laughed, until his older cabin mate patted his shoulder and walked into the kitchen.

"First it was the lip gloss mark and now this," Bill reflected, as he pulled a soda from the refrigerator. "I've seen her lose interest in guys quicker than the time it takes to breathe. To my surprise, she hasn't lost interest in you yet."

Bill gestured for Josh to change the channel.

"Find something loud with a lot of action and explosions."

He translated what he said into sign language as Josh understood it best.

He prefers lip reading though. He'll sign, but every time we've talked he doesn't ask for it, Lucas acknowledged.

While Bill and Josh watched their loud movie, Lucas silently retreated to his bunk. He tried to take his mind off of what happened by going through his phone. He knew he couldn't use it to make calls, text, or access the internet, but he hoped to still find something on it that was accessible.

At the very least, just something to take my mind off this place for a bit.

After a few minutes on his phone yielded nothing entertaining, Lucas groaned and threw his head on the edge of the bed. He began to recall a moment from his childhood when he overheard his parents arguing about financial troubles. The verbal confrontation turned into a physical one when his father slapped his mother across her face. Lucas had seen this briefly through peeking outside his room door.

It was so sudden that it could have been a motor reflex. I remember my dad gasped in shock and tried to apologize to my mom, but she wouldn't hear him out.

As he walked away before being noticed by his parents, he discovered his sister. She too had seen the slap.

When I asked her if mom and dad would be getting a divorce like other parents who fought, she only said, 'No Lucas, they won't get a divorce because it costs too much money.'

Later on, he asked Shelly if their parents loved each other, but she only replied in silence and he never asked her again.

I don't think they love each other anymore. They might love me and Shell, or just her. If I had mind powers back then, I could have known for sure. They just used to fight so much. The best thing I can say now is they don't anymore.

His thoughts were interrupted when Bill barged in abruptly.

"Hey Luke, Camp Director James wants to see you."

Lucas felt a smile across his face at the first good news in a while. He wanted to talk to Henry, hopefully alone this time, and discuss if he could return home sooner than the end of summer. He began to wonder how his friends coped with being absent from home for three months.

Most kids don't have someone waiting for them at home like I do and I wouldn't be here if it wasn't for everything that happened.

When Lucas walked out of the cabin, he spotted Daniel not too far from him. His good feeling began to melt away like ice left unattended.

I won't be able to do much talking with Daniel around, Lucas thought in concern. *Don't tell me, is he here to escort me to the Camp Director like I'm being led to the Principal's office or something?*

Daniel smiled amiably as Lucas exited the cabin.

"Hello, Lucas, my father wants to see you." The Camp Director's son said this with such authority that it didn't seem friendly. "I figured I may as well walk with you, since I happen to be going that way myself."

Lucas complied, but sensed that Daniel had a different agenda in mind.

Why does he keep wanting to talk to me every time no one else is around?

As they walked, both individuals were silent and would occasionally glance at the other for a second before resuming the walk forward. The distance between the cabins and Henry's house wasn't far, but it felt like a hundreds of miles away at the rate they went. When they got closer, Daniel broke the silence.

"It looks like you got what you wanted. My father want's a private audience with you. Why do you suppose that is though?" The Camp Counselor did not wait for an answer. "Want to know something else? He explicitly said for me not to stay this time. My father actually said that to me. But you can't go against the Camp Director's wishes. You did once say that he has his reasons for what he does."

Daniel's tone became unprofessional, as if he were venting to a friend rather than a student. Lucas shrugged and tried not to let the mixture of feelings he was getting from the Camp Counselor affect his answer.

"I know if he wanted you there, he would ask for you to stay," Lucas heard himself answer back.

I hope that isn't too much, but it's kind of the truth.

To Lucas's relief, Daniel nodded in agreement. He still looked dissatisfied with the idea.

"Forgive me for asking, but what is your relationship with your parents like," the Camp Counselor asked, as he stopped walking. "Because I feel that's the main reason you came to camp in the first place."

Lucas stopped walking as well and thought for a moment.

He wants to know about my parents? Why does he care? Is he going to tell Henry about it? It's none of his business. I'll just tell him 'You don't need to know' like how he got mad at me for asking why he isn't close with Henry.

"With all due respect sir," Lucas began, cautiously. "We're not as close as I'd like. My dad is a hard man to understand, and my mom is sadder than she admits. The best thing I can say about both is they love me and my sister. That's a fact. They kept putting up with me even with all that I did to make their lives harder. I wish I could say all that now to them."

Why did I have to tell him all that? That isn't what I thought at all! Where did those words come from?

Daniel's demeanor changed and the young telepath felt as if they were having an actual conversation now.

"I was in a lot of homes before I came to this one. Before I knew Henry was my father, he made me feel ignored and unwanted. My mother though, she was amazing. She was like your mother; sadder than she showed. She died when I was very young and I miss her, every day. Anyways, thank you for telling me this, Lucas. The person most important to me now is my girlfriend Keira. I have pictures of her. Would you like to see one?"

Before Lucas could say yes or no, Daniel took out his phone and showed the young telepath a picture of himself and a beautiful looking girl. Her hair was light brown, with light skin, bright green eyes, and a smile that reminded Lucas of Ashley.

She's really beautiful. Ashley wasn't kidding when she mentioned that, Lucas thought in admiration. The couple were hugging each other in the picture and Daniel looked similarly to now. The only difference was he had less facial hair, and longer unkempt hair.

"She's really pretty," Lucas heard himself say to Daniel. The Camp Counselor smiled approvingly.

"Thank you. We met in Camp Supernatural during my first year here and went to the same high school. Going back to what we were talking about before; my father is a hard man to understand, like yours. Even more difficult is getting to talk to him alone. I hope he tells you what you want to hear since he rarely does that for me. He always has an excuse ready for every occasion."

Lucas suddenly felt a surge of adrenaline run through him, as if he were about to have a stroke.

What's happening? Why do I suddenly feel... angry and... agitated?

"You know, the only thing I hate more than excuses is when someone feels their opinion is more important than someone else's," Daniel said, ignoring Lucas's distress. "I asked my father if we could do something for Father's Day and every year he has the same excuse: 'I am busy that day,' 'I have no desire to be free that day', 'I don't want to go anywhere that day'. I even tried asking him if he would like to meet Keira formally. You know what his response was? 'I don't have time for you or your girlfriend.' He never has time though, until now it seems."

Lucas grasped his chest as if he were suffocating, and was having a hard time breathing.

I feel so... angry... tight... hard... stiff... but this isn't me. It's him...

"Lucas, are you alright?" Daniel asked with concern. Suddenly, the young telepath began to calm.

"I need to speak to Henry alone now," Lucas said, in a voice that sounded sharper than he intended.

The Camp Director's son looked offended by this, but when he noticed Lucas's distressed look, he shook his head with a sigh.

"Alright then," Daniel said softly, as he turned to walk away, "I'll leave you to it. I apologize if what I said inconvenienced you in anyway or kept you from speaking to my father sooner. Now that I think about it, I see why he likes you so much. You both have more in common than I wanted to admit."

As Daniel began to walk away, Lucas again felt the slight discomfort in the back of his mind and chest.

Every step the Camp Counselor took, the young telepath felt. Every breath he huffed and puffed was felt too.

What's happening to me...? I feel so angry, like I want to hit something. Anything. Just so I can let out this pain. If only I had my... wait what?

The young telepath pushed the last thought out as he walked past the front door and straight down the hallway towards the Camp Director's office. Lucas found Henry writing something down in a small little notebook. He seemed so indulged in his work that he almost didn't acknowledge the young telepath's presence. When he finally noticed him, the Camp Director calmly slid the notebook into his drawer and smiled warmly.

"Hello, my child. Come in. Please shut the door behind you."

Lucas did so obediently and grabbed a seat before Henry could invite him to do so. The Camp Director just sat their impassively and calm. So calm that it helped soothe the young telepaths previous demeanor.

Something about how calm he acts is making me feel the same. I need to tell him about what just happened with Daniel. Its better he heard it from me than him.

The silence was so palpable now. So much so that Lucas swore Henry's face was like a portrait in that moment.

He looks like he's framed in time, Lucas acknowledged. *So peaceful, yet so far away.*

With a warm smile, the Camp Director spoke up.

"Would you care for a beverage? I have a variety of sugary drinks if you prefer."

Lucas shook his head and decided to wait for the Camp Director to speak again. Henry only continued to smile, and did not seem to be making any effort to speak first.

When the young telepath gulped nervously, he feared that Henry could hear him in the silent room.

Why am I here again? What did I need to talk to Henry about…? I can't think straight… so much… anger and calmness and… must… say…

"I understand you have concerns about returning home," said Henry, knowingly. "Is there a reason for your haste?"

The Camp Director's voice sounded faint, like a whisper, which brought Lucas back from his disgruntled thoughts.

Yes, that's it! That's what I wanted to talk about. Okay, here it goes.

"Yes, sir, that is exactly what I wanted to talk about," Lucas said, meekly. "But the thing is, I didn't come here because I wanted to. I didn't say this before when I should have, but I did something, some things, before I left home. I can't explain it, only the feeling. I was upset, sad, and confused. I felt this way about both things that happened. The first I can't remember at all, only what happened after. The second I can sort of recall, not much. Just that my dad was hurt because of me. That's all I know."

The young telepath feared what he was saying sounded too farfetched to be taken seriously, but the Camp Director gave him a reassured look.

"Explain further, my son?"

Lucas decided to reveal everything; how he flunked out of every school in his school district. The last school being the only one willing to give him a chance to redeem himself through summer classes. Since he couldn't explain the first instance further, he tried to do so for the second part that led him to coming to Camp Supernatural.

"My sister told me 'Don't leave here in anger,'" *Which I did.* "I tried to apologize to my parents. I didn't get to finish what I was saying." *Sorry isn't good enough.*

"I tried to stop myself. I felt my body tense up, and before I knew it, my father was on the floor unconscious. I think it was because of me." *I had to be the one.* "I didn't mean for that to happen. I don't mean for anything I do to happen." *Except when it does.*

The Camp Director looked troubled by this. Something else seemed to be bothering him and Lucas wasn't privy to this.

"Lucas, I want you to calm your mind," Henry instructed him. "Tell yourself these words to dispel the burning thoughts; 'It wasn't my fault' 'I didn't know' 'I couldn't know' 'I know now.' Say these words in your own voice."

The young telepath nodded and closed his eyes, thinking with his inside voice.

It wasn't my fault. My fault it wasn't. I didn't know. Know I didn't. I couldn't know. Couldn't I know? I know now. Now I know. Yes, I do know now!

"It wasn't your fault, my child. Please understand that. Much of this is uncharted territory. All that is known about telepaths is the distinction between reality and what is in your mind must be made known. Perhaps you thought you saw a version of yourself who hurt your father as you wanted to in that moment. Would you say that is correct?"

Lucas wanted to deny this. He felt it in his very core, and tried to say the words, but couldn't think them.

I did want to hurt my parents the way they hurt me. I hated them for making me choose something I didn't ask for. I just thought the feelings. What bad thing has ever happened because someone thought it? Unless the person actually does it, it's mostly harmless.

Lucas turned away and shook his head with tears forming in his eyes.

No, that can't be true. I know what I saw and I can't take it back.

296

"It was my fault, sir, even if I can't or don't want to admit it. I knew what I was doing. I had to have known what I was doing."

Lucas's voice quivered as he struggled to speak.

"I just want things to be the way they used to be. I know I wasn't always like this and I know what's real. What I feel for my sister is real. The friends I've made here, they're real for me."

Henry nodded and looked satisfied for the moment.

"That is wonderful to hear, my child. The progress you've made here has not gone unnoticed. The friends you've made think and speak very highly of you. Boris has even taken to asking about you on occasion. What is real for you can be real for others if you allow yourself to be that way. That is why I have such high hopes for you beyond just your abilities."

Lucas suddenly felt tension building up inside him, like a volcano about to erupt.

"Why don't you feel this way about Daniel? He's your son, a fact he makes sure everyone here knows. In fact, I just spoke to him before coming here. Now I feel like screaming and punching something and I don't know why!"

Lucas's tone rose as he spoke, but Henry never once showed emotion. He only gave the young telepath his benign and melancholy blue eyes, which seemed to calm him for the moment.

Every time I look into them, I feel like I see a reflection of myself. The part I don't want to admit is there.

"What you are experiencing is a combination of your mood swings, your telepathic abilities, and an emphatic link-based ability that is created between yourself along with those you form bonds with. Tell me, what made you decide not use your medication any longer? Have you experienced a culmination of emotions similar to these feelings before?"

When he calmed down, Lucas shook his head.

"No, I mean yes, maybe, sometimes. That doesn't mean I thought about acting on those feelings from others," Lucas insisted, defensively. "I just feel like everyone around me makes me sick. Like I'm drowning and even when I try to breathe, something keeps pushing me down again."

Henry looked even more troubled by this. Instead of pressing for more, he abruptly changed the subject.

"How much progress have you made in your training? Has Daniel taught you well?"

Lucas nodded, but began to feel uncomfortable thinking about the Camp Director's son.

He's the reason I'm still feeling like this right now!

"How much control would you say you have over your mind reading?" Henry asked in a tone as calm as a gentle breeze.

"Not as well as I'd like. I accidentally say things out loud that people think and I made Josh feel bad for that. During training, I'm paired up with Mike and his thoughts are like listening to five voices all at once," Lucas explained, his face involuntarily twitching.

Henry looked disappointed by this progress report.

"I see. This is truly an unforeseen melding between your mind abilities and the wide extension of empathy you are experiencing. Telepaths are difficult to train, not only because of the mind based ability, but what they feel is always more stronger. Mental illness of every kind takes different forms within various individuals. Some have a higher or lower range. Our goal is to assess your range and find a strong enough conduit for it."

The young telepath did not understand until the Camp Director continued.

"I would like for you to read my mind, if only to test a theory."

Lucas suddenly wondered if his powers would work on Henry.

Maybe I'll learn things about him that no one else knows.

Unfortunately, as he focused his mind on the Camp Director, he felt the same sharp pain he got from Daniel. Unlike that pain, however, this one felt like dozens of little birds pecking on his skull rapidly.

Argh! What just happened? Why couldn't I read his mind? I'm in pain, and yet I feel... nothing. Absolutely nothing.

Henry only looked at him calmly without any hint of disappointment or satisfaction.

"Perhaps now is not the time for this. Give yourself and your mind time to heal from all that you feel."

Despite feeling disappointed in his limited ability, Lucas was relieved that he no longer felt anxious or agitated. After recovering from the minor setback, he gazed at Henry's transfixed face. It suddenly made the young telepath feel insignificant to be in his presence. The Camp Director's aura felt both benevolent and welcoming, having no hint of hostility or discomfort in it.

I don't know if I'm calm, or just feel nothing right now. I only know that I want to feel this way all the time.

"Do you wish to ask me something else?" Henry inquired after a few minutes of silence.

Lucas shook off the nothingness and thought of a question.

The Relic game and why he stopped Boris from helping me. I can say 'Why didn't you help me during the Relic game when I didn't know my power. I could have died.'

"I've been wondering since the Relic game, you said that Boris would step in if things got bad. They were about to get really bad and he never came. Did you stop him from helping me?"

Lucas wasn't sure what kind of answer he would get, but the answer he heard both surprised and shocked him.

"Indeed, I did stop him," Henry said, nonchalantly. "I believed your abilities needed to be unlocked through a certain way. I've helped many children this way and many succeeded because of it."

The young telepath felt signaled out. It wasn't enough to know others had been through a similar process. In a way his answer was given, just not clearly.

But what if...?

"What if my abilities hadn't come out?" Lucas asked firmly. "What if Alexia brought down her war hammer on me and I was like a bug on a windshield? What then?"

The Camp Director gave Lucas a puzzled look and then sighed.

"What matters is the outcome, not the possibilities. You will lose your mind fixating on that which you cannot control and foresee clearly. Heed those words."

Hesitantly, Lucas nodded and accepted this as the final say on the matter.

For now.

"Before I go, can I ask how old are you, sir, and why is Daniel's last name is not James? Did he change it?"

Henry did not answer immediately. He seemed distracted by something at that moment.

After a few seconds, he responded.

"Which question would you like me to answer first?"

Lucas chose to ask for his age. Henry chuckled softly.

"I cannot give you an exact number. As you get older, birthdays become irrelevant. I am old though, and my son is a lot younger than me. That is to be expected," Henry explained, calmly.

That's not the answer I was hoping for.

"Okay, so how come his last name is different than yours?"

Henry looked at his clock, then back at the young telepath.

"You should return to your cabin. You have training bright and early tomorrow morning with my son. When you have free time, spend it with your friends. They are an important part of what is to come for you."

Lucas nodded calmly and left the Camp Director's home.

I should have asked him something related to camp. How he founded it or how he met Boris. There's so much I want to know. He gave me an answer without giving me a straight answer.

Lucas walked into the Camp Director's house hoping to find answers, but found that he left with even more questions than before.

I don't know why I feel this way. Suddenly, I'm okay with not asking anything anymore for now. The calmness in my mind makes me want to stay in camp more, even though I know I can't.

As he departed, Boris opened the door to enter. He gave Lucas a crooked smile and greeted him.

"Hello, Lucas, you were speaking with Camp Director James?"

Lucas nodded. Doubt must have been written all over the young telepath's face since Boris seemed to notice it.

"Is everything alright?" the Camp Guardian asked with a concerned tone.

"I'm fine. What are you going to talk to Henry about?"

"I'm going to discuss the Fourth of July dance arrangements with him," Boris replied.

Lucas had not heard of the Fourth of July dance until just this moment.

Where was I when this was announced?

When he asked Boris about it, the monster explained.

"It's just a dance with a lot of modern day music. One particular singer who is popular among the kids here is called The Lady of Gaga. Is that her real name or one of those names famous people make up?"

Lucas chuckled and explained the idea to the Camp Guardian.

"It's her stage name. Like Sting. He's a singer… my dad likes."

The monster shook his head stiffly.

"I'm not familiar with this singer. I do not seek out modern day music. In any case, you should go to the dance. Maybe that nice girl will ask you to go with her. I've seen you two talk on occasion."

Lucas wasn't sure who he meant so he mentioned the first name that came to mind.

"You mean Vanessa, Bill's sister?"

To his shock, the Camp Guardian shook his head and mentioned his second choice.

"Ashley, the one that is very fast."

Lucas pondered the idea for a moment before laughing to himself and shaking his head.

"No, she wouldn't ask me. We're just friends."

Boris did not look convinced.

That's not how she looks at him when they talk, Boris thought.

"Well regardless, I hope you go. It's really lots of fun and I'll be there making sure everyone behaves appropriately. If not, you and I will have a little talk afterwards," the Camp Guardian teased in a friendly way.

I don't think going to some dance is a requirement for my training, so I don't technically have to go, Lucas thought to himself.

Boris patted Lucas's shoulder softly and proceeded to enter Henry's home. Suddenly, the young telepath saw Ashley talking with Kendall as he walked to his cabin. They giggled and looked to be friendlier than she had previously let on.

When she spotted Lucas, Ashley put up her hand as if to ask a question. Lucas acknowledged her, but kept walking forward instead of joining them like she seemed to expect.

I don't have time for this. After finally calming my mind, I don't need any more added stress to go with it.

Ashley noticed Lucas being evasive and dismissed herself from Kendall.

"Did you talk to Josh about Hailey?" Ashley asked Lucas after she caught up to him at a steady pace.

She didn't even have to use her ability. I'm just that slow.

Lucas shook his head and said, "I didn't get the chance. Vanessa kind of made sure of that."

He realized he said the wrong thing when Ashley looked shocked from hearing her name.

"How did she stop you from talking to Josh?" she asked, perplexed.

Lucas shook his head and tried to walk away from Ashley, but she refused to let him go. In the blink of an eye, she was in front of him. Ashley had to steady herself in front of the cabin to keep from falling over.

"Please move, Ashley. I don't want to talk about it right now," Lucas said, irritably.

She crossed her arms and shook her head.

"Not until you tell me about what happened between you and Vanessa," Ashley demanded.

Lucas heard her voice in his head and felt her concern for him.

If it's nothing bad why won't he tell me? Lucas heard Ashley think. *I swear, Vanessa doesn't understand boundaries any more than she can appreciate Lucas for the person that he is.*

Despite hoping to avoid stress, Lucas also knew that she wouldn't budge this time.

She doesn't care about him. He's a good person, and I don't want him to get hurt when he doesn't have.

Finally, Lucas sighed.

"She wanted me to kiss her, there are you happy? She even tried to get me to use my ability on her, but I didn't. I swear I didn't even think to do it."

Ashley looked very troubled by this.

Her face and the feeling she is giving off makes me feel like I am guilty of something I didn't do.

"But you didn't do it, right? I mean, you didn't kiss her?"

She seems to be more concerned about the near make-out session than how Vanessa wanted me to use my ability on her, Lucas thought as he shook his head.

"I wouldn't be in one piece if I did," Lucas pointed out.

She nodded in agreement and smiled reassuringly.

"I guess you're right. But let's say you didn't have to worry about Bill. Would you want to kiss her?" Ashley asked, stubbornly.

Lucas began to feel uncomfortable about the subject.

Why does she care so much? It's not her job to look after me the way Shelly did. I don't need anyone to take care of me here. I'm not a helpless nutcase anymore. Now, I'm a powered-up nutcase.

"I don't know. Why is it such a big deal to you anyways? Is it because you think Vanessa is going to hurt me," Lucas angrily stated, the last part of which Ashley looked especially offended by.

"Really? You read my mind for that? Okay, so since that's out there, yes, Lucas, she's going to hurt you. I've known girls like her and let me tell you the truth about them; they don't know what they want any less than you do. She likes you now, but after a while, she'll meet another guy and forget about you. I just don't want to see you get hurt when you don't have to go through that. You deserve better than that and someone who will appreciate you for the person you are."

Lucas sensed the sincerity in her words and felt the warmness from her that wasn't like Henry's calmness. This was a form of affection he was unfamiliar with.

She can't. No way. We're just friends. I'll admit, I feel like I can tell her anything. Nothing I say will be judged by her and I've never felt that way about anyone.

Just as Lucas was deep in thought, Ashley brought back their previous discussion.

"Can I count on you to talk to Josh about Hailey? It would mean a lot to me."

Lucas nodded reluctantly.

"I will. I promise."

His words sounded more sincere than he really felt. Regardless, Ashley smiled and nodded, believing in his promise.

Just when it seemed like she was going to leave, Ashley gave Lucas a shy smile while blushing. Her face had fallen, with only her eyes looking upwards at him.

What is she doing? Why's she looking at me like that? I hope she's not going to ask me anymore stuff about Vanessa.

"One more thing... I don't know if you've heard about a dance on the Fourth of July. It's my first summer here and I would really like to go. Maybe if you wanted, I mean, if you feel the same... I think I'd be..."

Ashley began to stammer mildly. Her tongue seemed to be doing a sort of snake dance to try and get the words out she meant to say.

Regardless, it didn't take Lucas long to realize what she was asking.

She does like me, Lucas thought, dreadfully. *The only problem is that I would want to go with Vanessa. How do I tell her that without losing our friendship?*

Before he could think of what to say clearly, the words came pouring out of his mouth like a gust of wind.

"Sure yeah, let's go together," Lucas heard himself say before he could stop himself. *Wait what? I didn't say that? I did, but it wasn't me.*

To his discomfort, he saw Ashley's face glow with a bright smile.

That's not good. What have I done?

"Okay, it's a date. I'll see you," Ashley exclaimed swiftly. Just when he thought this couldn't get any worse, she added, "If it's alright with you, I'll tell Hailey in advance about Josh. We can go together as a group. Thank you in advance, Lucas, for everything. She'll be so happy."

The young telepath smiled nervously as he heard her voice inside his head playing like a recording. Even as she made her way to her cabin, he still heard her thoughts as if she were still next to him.

So it is true; he does like me. Bill was right, Ashley thought happily. *Daniel was wrong about Lucas. I know he's looking out for me, but he doesn't know everything about a person. I knew Lucas was different and I'm glad he feels the same way.*

Bill's getting back at me for what happened with Vanessa and Josh. The worst part is he's involving Ashley in this. I'm going to talk to him right now and give him a piece of my mind. I mean, mind tricks, whatever, Lucas thought, irritably.

Lucas went inside of his cabin and tried to calm himself down. He hovered over Bill, who was busy watching a movie. After about a minute, his older cabin mate finally noticed him.

"So what did Camp Director James want?" he asked, curiously.

Lucas looked at him with an accusing glare and waited until Bill's full attention was on him.

"Why did you encourage Ashley to go to the dance with me? She thinks I like her now," Lucas blurted angrily.

Bill smirked and turned his face back to switch the television off.

"She asked you to the dance? I'm glad to hear that," Bill admitted approvingly. "Yeah, I told her that somebody had a crush on her. A first year camper with shaggy hair, not too bright on social skills, and who can do mind tricks."

He did not just say what I was thinking!

Unintentionally, Josh emerged from the kitchen and looked at Lucas as if he didn't expect him back so soon.

"That was fast. What did the Camp Director want?" Josh asked the same question as Bill. Similarly, Lucas did not answer the question.

Calmly, Josh took a spot on the couch next to Bill and began to eat a bowl of cereal.

"Don't take this the wrong way, but how are you feeling, Lucas?" Bill asked with a different tone than before. *No nickname.* "You seemed a bit off when we saw the movie last time and Daniel was concerned about you after leaving you to talk to Henry. He asked me if you've talked about home and why you left to come here."

Lucas felt irritated by the mention of Daniel and even more so with the knowledge that he was talking about him to his cabin mates.

"And what did you tell the Camp Director's son about me?"

"Nothing bad," admitted Bill, casually. "Your fine. I promise. Daniel just thought the way you left him to speak to Henry was uncharacteristic of you. He said he felt bad about how he left things with you. When you have some free time, you should talk to him."

But why? Why is he telling me stuff that isn't true? Daniel feels bad about how we left things? If by things he means me getting sick of hearing him vent, yeah, it was annoying. I didn't have to sit there and listen to him like we're friends. We'll never be friends.

"What else did you two talk about? Does he want you and everyone in this cabin to spy on me now? Are you all afraid I'm going to go crazy the way Jacob did?" Lucas heard himself ask like a madman. "You're all just waiting to see how long it will take for me to go crazy, right? I haven't even had a chance to fail, so I'm being judged for that too!"

The tension in the room suddenly became obvious enough for Josh to notice. The mere mention of Jacob's name gave Bill an uncomfortable confirming look.

That's it, isn't it? They think I'm going to go crazy like Jacob did. No one seems to know why he did, so why does it matter?

"Lucas, I want you to calm down and listen to me very carefully; you are not Jacob. You are my new best friend and someone I have become quite fond of since you've been here. Josh likes you. Ashley likes you, and my sister too, if you can believe that." His older cabin mate tried to keep a friendly tone, but realized quickly that the young telepath was in no laughing mood. "Ask yourself this; if we were all here to spy on you, wouldn't you know since you can read minds? You can even do it now as I speak and see what I mean."

He's got a good point, Lucas thought in conflict. *Just to be sure.*

The young telepath concentrated and read Bill's mind.

He actually scared me a bit there, but I think he's fine now. Just have to avoid mentioning what else Daniel and I talked about.

"What else did you and Daniel talk about?" Lucas heard himself ask aloud. Bill looked upset by this question.

"You just read my mind, didn't you?" Bill asked, sharply. "I thought that to see if you'd actually do it and you did."

"You were testing me? I thought you trusted me," Lucas admitted, disappointingly.

"I do trust you. I just want you to be respectful of our thoughts and feelings, Lucas. Even if you have this ability, this power, whatever you want to call it, you have to use it responsibly. Just because you can do something doesn't mean you should."

Lucas rolled his eyes and scoffed.

"That sounds like something someone would say when they don't have a power like mine."

"We don't get to choose what we have. Do you think I chose to be color blind? To see what I think is color and struggle to tell the difference? All we can choose is how we use these abilities for the betterment of ourselves."

Lucas couldn't argue against that logic.

"That's fair, but I still won't tell you what Henry and I talked about. That's personal and I don't want you to know even if we are, as you say, best friends."

The last comment seemed to hurt Bill's feelings. Lucas suddenly regretted phrasing it that way, but offered no apology.

"Why did you tell Ashley that I like her? Is it because of what happened with Vanessa earlier? I told you that nothing happened between us. There is no us! Why did you have to tell Ashley that I like her?"

Bill was still mauling in his head what the young telepath had told him. After a moment, he decided to tell him the truth.

"Because she likes you, you idiot. You're just too stupid and blind to see that," Bill snapped back sharply. "For someone who can read minds, you don't have a clue, do you?"

Lucas scoffed in anger.

"Well, thanks to you, I'm in an awkward position now with her. I can't just tell her I changed my mind and go with someone else instead."

On the contrary, Lucas's tone suggested otherwise, and Bill recognize this.

Why am I acting like this? This isn't me.

"You would do that, wouldn't you? Break her heart like that just to be with my sister," Bill said in a disapproving manner. "Don't try to deny that. I don't need to read your mind to know you'd pick Vanessa over Ashley. I love my sister, but she is a lot of things. Understanding is not one of them. Besides, that'd be a new low, even for you, Lucas. I honestly expected better from you than that. If I were you, I'd stop talking before you say anything else that can't be taken back."

I guess we're both disappointed with each other then.

Lucas wanted to say more, to assert his point, but he knew saying more now would only cause more harm. Without another word, the young telepath walked back into his bunk and slammed the door shut.

It was in this moment when Lucas felt like everything had been turned upside down for him.

What am I going to do? If I tell Ashley that I don't want to go to the dance anymore, she will know that I want to go with Vanessa. But if I go with Vanessa, I'll hurt Ashley's feelings. What do I do? Do what I do. Why me? Me why?

He suddenly felt a yearning he had tried so hard to suppress the moment he entered camp.

I can't take it anymore. I thought I could stay here until the end of summer, but I can't. I know what I feel, and what is real now; I want to go home …

Chapter 9

The Fall

On the last week of June and the week before the Fourth of July dance, Lucas decided that morning to tell Josh about how Hailey feels.

Today is the day. Not tomorrow, not the day after; right now. I promised Ashley, so I'm going to do it.

Lucas hadn't slept well due to the events of the previous day. Although he felt troubled about having to choose between Ashley and Vanessa, he thought talking to Josh about Hailey would take his mind off the difficult situation.

If nothing else, it will get Ashley off my back and maybe get on her good side. At least until I tell her the truth about my feelings for Vanessa.

The young telepath walked with Josh to the cafeteria for breakfast where they were intercepted by Vanessa. Kendall, the model camper, accompanied her as well.

"Hi, Lucas. Hey, Josh. You remember Kendall."

Vanessa gestured a friendly hand towards the young beautiful girl. She smiled shyly at Josh, who blushed so red that his face looked like it had been sunburned.

She is pretty, too pretty to notice our existence, Lucas thought doubtfully. *She is way out of his league.*

"Hi, Kendall," is all Josh could say aloud before biting his tongue.

She didn't greet him back. Instead, she continued to smile in his direction.

She's thinking that Josh is cute and what to talk to him about. Wait what?

313

"Can I borrow you for a moment?" Vanessa urged Lucas. "Let's leave these two love birds alone."

Despite the prospect of talking to Vanessa, he did not like the idea of leaving Josh with Kendall.

What if Hailey sees them together? Lucas thought with concern.

After they were earshot away from each of their cabin mates, Vanessa turned to look at Lucas with big eyes.

"Have you heard about a dance coming up next week?" Bill's sister asked him.

Lucas had been so preoccupied with his own thoughts and desire to go home that he didn't realized that the first week of July was next week already.

Just my luck, he thought with a sigh. *This month flew about as fast as my thoughts always do.*

He shrugged and feigned being unaware of the dance.

"I haven't heard, why? Do you want to go with me?"

Vanessa blushed slightly and suddenly had the same look as Ashley did when she asked him.

"That is the plan, unless you have something else going on. Are you too cool for dancing all of a sudden?"

"What else would I have going on?" Lucas assured her, nervously. "Also no, I'm not cool at all."

"That's not true, Lucas. You're the coolest guy I've met in camp. Honestly, you can read my mind to know this but I rather tell you myself; I was just messing with you in the beginning to annoy my brother. Now, I really do like you and I know you like me too."

The young telepath felt both relieved and saddened to hear that since it confirmed what he thought in the very back of his mind.

The fact that she changed her mind says a lot about her. Maybe she's not as bad as everyone says.

"Since I was honest with you, I want you to be honest with me when I ask you this; has Ashley already asked you to go with her?" Bill's sister pressed with a tone that betrayed her previous intention.

She better not have, Vanessa thought. *It's not a contest or anything, but I liked him first. Plus I'm prettier than Ashley is.*

I don't know why anyone would think reading minds is cool. It feels very uncomfortable and invasive when someone is thinking about another person in a mean way.

Lucas prepared to lie about it, until he remembered the lecture he received from Bill.

I hate to admit it and I'll only admit it to myself, but he's right. Vanessa has shown a lot of growth and courage in telling me the truth about why she first showed an interest in me. I need to tell her the truth now or she'll never feel the same way about me again.

"Yes she did and I said yes," confessed Lucas, quickly regretting his phrasing and tone.

Vanessa's smile and face turned from happiness to shock and disappointment. Her face fell to the ground and away from him.

Why did I have to say it like that? Now she'll feel like a fool for confessing how she feels about me. This isn't how I wanted things to be.

Before he could say anything, she shook her head and spoke first.

"I understand," Vanessa said, calmly. "Ashley is pretty and nice, the things boys seem to like. You should go with her."

How could he do this to me? I thought he liked me back. He wanted to kiss me that day, I know he did...

Lucas shrugged and tried to give her a reassuring look, but she looked unconvinced.

"It's Bills fault," Lucas admitted. "He set me up with Ashley because he didn't want me going with you. I swear that there's nothing going on between us."

Vanessa nodded, looking only half-convinced by that.

No, more like she's not convinced at all. Now she thinks I'm too much of a coward and idiot to pursue how I feel about her.

"Yeah, I believe he would do this to me," Bill's sister said, sadly. Her eyes began to swell with tears. "It wouldn't be the first time he did this to me. My big brother just can't let me have this one thing in my life. I wish he would mind his own business about who I like."

I don't like being referred to as a 'thing' but I know that isn't what she means.

"Don't worry about Bill. He's becoming a counselor next year. I'm sure if he knew how serious you felt, he'd feel differently about this whole thing," said Lucas, with a lot of doubt in his mind.

This made Vanessa finally look at Lucas in the face with hope in her eyes.

"You think so?"

Lucas nodded, smiling, and decided to go with it.

"I know so. Anyways, it's just a dance and it doesn't mean anything. I'll go with Ashley, because we are friends. After that, we can talk about what comes next. If you still want to."

She seemed happy with this idea and he swore that she appeared radiant just now.

Knowing that helps a lot. So that's what we'll do; I'll go to the dance with Ashley and then, I'll tell her the truth about how I feel for Vanessa, Lucas decided. *I'm a good person.*

Just then, Josh came towards them. After noticing the looks between them, he became uncomfortable.

"Me and Kendall are going to get breakfast. Want to join us?" said Josh, awkwardly.

Lucas didn't realize that Vanessa held his hand. After regaining his senses, he abruptly wrenched his hand free and shook his head.

"Actually, I'm not hungry. Let's head back to our cabin."

Lucas gave Josh a look that suggested he had something important to tell him. His cabin mate understood and went ahead of him.

He left Vanessa, who gave him a reassuring smile, but the young telepath was feeling even more stressed than the day before.

What have I done? I've dug myself another deep hole. One was enough, now I have two! Or one giant hoe that would give sinkholes a run for their money.

Lucas entered the cabin after Josh and to his happiness, no one was around. He finally had the chance to talk to his cabin mate alone about Hailey.

"I got to know Kendall, sort of. She tried using sign language, but she didn't know how to say much beyond, 'How's my day' and 'If I'm hungry', which I am by the way. So let's do this quick," Josh both said and signed.

Lucas took a breath and prepared himself.

Here goes nothing.

"Josh, you know how Hailey feels about you, right?" Lucas asked his friend.

Unfortunately, his cabin mate immediately understood him, and refused to respond. After a few seconds he brushed it off.

Not him too. No, I don't want to talk about this, Josh thought irritably.

"I'm hungry. If that's all, we should go before they run out of food. Kendall's saving me a seat and you can be with Vanessa."

Before Josh could reach the door, Lucas slammed it shut and shook his head stubbornly. The tension he had tried to keep inside began to surface.

I'm not letting him leave. Not until he listens to what I have to say.

"I promised Ashley that we would talk. Now, you're going to shut up and listen to me."

Lucas's tone sounded stern and near exploding like his temper. Once Josh understood what he said, his face darkened.

"No way. I don't have to listen to you. Move out of my way before I make you move!"

Josh lurched himself forward and had nearly forced his way outside of the cabin when, without hesitation, Lucas said the word to trigger his ability.

STOP!

Josh's whole body became stiff, as if paralyzed. His face struggled and twisted when he tried to move.

"What are you doing to me, Luke?! Let me go right now!" Josh demanded angrily.

Lucas shook his head defiantly.

"Be quiet and listen to me!"

Lucas then used his mind control to close Josh's mouth, leaving him unable to speak or use his power on him.

I didn't want it to come to this, but it's the only way he will listen to me.

Lucas felt the tension that his cabin mate was feeling from being unable to move. The thoughts he heard and felt were erratic like what the zoo animals projected when he read their minds.

The young telepath did his best to speak using hand gestures he felt were sign language, but most of what he said was with his mouth instead.

"Look, Josh, Ashley is worried about Hailey. She just wants what's best for her and Hailey is in love with you. You are never going to find another girl like that. Not even Kendall could feel that way about you. I mean, let's face it, you shouldn't be picky at all. Be happy that someone feels that way about you, because Kendall is out of your league. If she likes you, it's because she's being nice."

It's a bit of tough love with some truth in it, Lucas justified to himself.

While Josh could not speak or use his power on him, he glared at Lucas with such loathing contempt. His thoughts were also on full-volume inside Lucas's mind.

The way a jar of bees is after shaking it; that's what I can expect from Josh after I release him from my mind control.

Lucas decided to keep what he said short enough to get the idea across.

"I didn't want it to be like this and this is the only way you would listen," Lucas admitted, breathlessly. "I know you like Kendall, but it's not love. Hailey loves you and I think, in time, you could love her back. I mean, you can try, which is more of a chance than you have with Kendall. That's all I wanted to say. I'm going to release you now and if you want to beat me senseless, go for it."

When he released Josh, he half hopped that his cabin mate's thoughts were in part because of his anger towards being mind-controlled.

I think I just made a huge mistake.

Too late, Lucas realized the error in his ill-conceived plan.

Instantly, Josh charged at him so fast that he barely blinked. Lucas closed his eyes fearfully and threw his arms up to defend himself. He didn't realize, until he could hear Josh angrily protesting, that his life was still intact. When his eyes fluttered open, Bill held him by both arms in a tight grip. He seethed with rage like a fire-breathing dragon and his arms flapped through the air as if trying to fly off. Lucas lay there on the floor with bruises on his face, pain in his stomach, and blood running down his nose.

After Bill released Josh, he breathlessly declared, "I vote to kick out this psycho mind freak. I don't ever want to see him again!" His sonic waves emitted themselves steadily.

Josh stormed out of the cabin, pounding his feet rhythmically against the ground. Bill looked at Lucas in shock and helped him up from the ground, only to shove him to the couch.

"What the hell was that? What did you do to him?" Bill demanded angrily.

Lucas grabbed a spare shirt he saw on the couch and decided to use it as a rag for his nose. He winced in pain, wiping his bloody nose clean and feeling each bruise on his body as if he were on fire.

"I just wanted to talk to him," Lucas said, defensively. "I promised Ashley that I would talk to him about Hailey."

Bill groaned and pinched the bridge of his nose hard.

"For crying out loud, you really have no clue do you, Luke. He is not interested in her. Can't you take the hint?" Bill, insisted. "Even I can tell that and I don't have the same abilities as you. At least I respect his opinion enough not to bother him with it."

Lucas shook his head stubbornly. His defiant attitude proved to be too much for Bill.

He hates me now, but I don't care. He wouldn't listen to me!

"Josh avoided the question. That doesn't mean he isn't open to the idea." Lucas heard himself justify his wrongful action in a voice he didn't recognize. "I could have made him tell me the whole reason. I should have. Maybe next time I could mind control him into telling me how he really feels, or read that part of his mind forcefully in order to make him—"

Lucas was cut off when Bill slapped him hard on his bruised cheek. His hand flew so swift and fast it sounded like a plane taking off. When the young telepath tried to rise from the couch, his older cabin mate pushed him back, putting his hand up as if to say, 'stop right there.'

"You really messed up, Lucas. You broke a very important rule in this camp: you are never, and I mean ever, supposed to use your ability on another camper outside of training," rasped Bill in a snarl. "It's not just a very big camp rule; it's a very big rule in general. Do you realize what kind of damage mind control can do to a person when left unchecked? That's not even the worst thing; did you just hear how crazy you sounded right now? This is really bad and here you were trying to make a case for yourself that you weren't like Jacob. After this, I'm not so sure."

Lucas just brushed off Bill carelessly and shook his head impassively.

"It's not like I actually did the things I said I would. I wouldn't do those things."

"You may as well have. Mind control can be a good and bad thing depending on how the person uses it. You can either form meaningful connections or leech off of those you control. Not to mention his mind is basically an open book to you now. That sort of back-door access doesn't go away ever. When you read Gary's mind that was harmless because Daniel supervised, but you did this on your own. If this is left unchecked, you won't be able tell the difference between how a person feels vs. how you make them feel."

Lucas had not considered this. Regardless, he surmised Josh would not feel any long term effects from this.

I was careful. All I did was make him stop talking and moving. That's it. Controlling someone to jump off a building is different than planting the idea, isn't it?

Before Bill departed the cabin, he turned towards Lucas and gave him the kind of look that spoke for itself more than the words he said next.

"This is your final warning, Lucas: you better get your act together. I may not have been here when it happened, but I didn't like the end result. This thing with you not knowing how to use your powers and letting it control your actions ends right now. You better decide what matters to you most because you may have just ruined a friendship right now. The thing about Josh is he's more loyal than anyone I've ever met. He'd keep your deepest most personal secret to himself and he'd always have your back no matter what. He even forgave you for reading his mind last time. This new thing will be a tall order though. The question you need to ask yourself is do you feel worthy of being his friend after this display? Because if you want my honest opinion, you're not worthy of his friendship or anyone else's in the state your in."

Lucas nodded and hoped that Bill would leave, but his older cabin mate had one last thing to add.

"In case you're worried, I won't tell Camp Director James or Daniel what you did here since it will mean expulsion from camp. I've liked having you around, even if you're a pain sometimes, and I know you would be missed from here. However, if you don't fix properly with Josh, you won't be welcomed in this cabin anymore and nowhere near my sister. It won't be easy, but please do this for yourself."

322

Lucas knew Bill's words rang true, including his warning.

He's actually much angrier than he's showing.

"I believe you're a good person based on how little I know of you," Bill admitted, in a voice Lucas was surprised to hear. "It isn't your power that draws people to you, Lucas; it's you. I don't know how hard you had it out there, but you have a chance here to be better. You have a lot of people here who care about you too and to throw all that away would be such a shame. I really hope that the next time we talk, you see the light."

After Bill left, Lucas suddenly felt enormous guilt. He slummed down the floor and sobbed silently. He hugged his legs and wrapped his arms around himself in a protective state. He didn't even bother shutting the door at that moment. He didn't care if anyone saw him crying. The shame of embarrassment did not cross his mind.

I hate it. I hate it all! This stupid camp, Bill, Josh, Ashley, Vanessa, Daniel, everything, and everyone, Lucas thought, furiously.

He wanted to scream his rage out, but the lump in his throat suffocated the words before they could manifest vocally. When Lucas could not cry anymore, he made up his mind on what to do next.

I can't do this anymore. This place isn't for me. I'm out of here.

Instead of following Bill's advice, Lucas decided to begin packing his few belongings. After cleaning his face from the blood, sweat, and tears, the young telepath couldn't recognize his reflection. He looked like he had aged a few years, with bags under his eyes and his shaggy hair becoming more unmanageable by the passing days.

I felt just fine not too long ago. When did this start to happen?

Lucas knew full well that leaving the camp meant he

could never return, but at that moment nothing else mattered

If what I did is punishable by expulsion anyway, I may as well leave already. I need to be with Shelly and my family. Henry hasn't helped me the way he said he would and this has become more trouble than it's worth.

He donned his red sweater and wore the hood despite the heat outside.

The last thing Lucas wanted to make sure he took with him was his medicinal pills. He searched his pants pockets, hoping to find the containers. He finally found them in his back pocket for his ripped jeans. To his dismay, he no longer had the pills.

No... how long have I been without these? I can't even remember the last time... This is not good.

Brushing the fearful thought aside, Lucas slung his backpack over one shoulder and walked out of the cabin cautiously. He wanted to turn back and give the cabin one last scan. It had served as his home for almost a month and now he felt as if it were a part of him. Inhaling, exhaling, he walked out the front door without any second thoughts about it.

I'm doing this. There's no turning back now.

He tried to avoid being seen by someone in the camp that knew him personally. The ones he specifically looked out for were Daniel, Boris and his friends. Lucas assured himself that most of the campers would still be at the cafeteria eating breakfast right now.

The Infinite Forest isn't too far from here. I just have to get there unseen and before anyone notices where I am, I'll be long gone.

Even this early in the morning, the campground ended up being lively and very humid. The misty aroma suggested rain could be coming at any moment. None of the campers seemed to pay Lucas any mind though as he walked past the cabins with as much speed as his legs would muster. He almost made it to the clearing until Mike spotted him. He waved at Lucas, but the young telepath continued to walk. This caused Mike follow after him when he noticed the backpack and sweater.

No, please don't come over here. Not now!

When Mike reached him, he put himself between Lucas and the Infinite Forest.

"Where are you going? The cafeteria's that way," Mike asked him, cautiously. He noticed the bruises on Lucas's face. "Whoa, what happened to your face?"

"It's nothing. I fell down when I woke up this morning. I couldn't imagine a pillow fast enough."

Mike didn't buy it, with his eyes never leaving Lucas's backpack.

He's trying to leave, Lucas heard Mike think. *But why? I thought he was happy here.*

"Where are you going?"

"I'm leaving this place," Lucas revealed, bitterly. "I can't stand it anymore, Mike. I need to get out of here. I need to go home."

I'll use my mind control on him like I did with Josh if I have to. I'm already leaving camp anyways, so what more can Henry do to me at this point?

Mike shook his head and stopped him when he tried to move.

"How do you plan on doing that? There are only two ways to leave; through the forest or the front entrance and the Camp Guardian is always there."

Mike gestured his head towards Boris, whose back was turned to them. After weighing his options, Lucas ultimately made a decision.

"To the forest it is then," he announced boldly.

However, Mike did not budge.

"Please don't do this, Lucas," the young camper pleaded. "You won't be able to come back. Think about what this means for you and your friends here. Plus, you should get checked at the hospital for those bruises. That floor really hit your nose with intent."

Even through Mike's pleas, Lucas only regarded him with irritation.

"Get out of my way, Mike. I don't want to have to use my powers on you."

Mike was taken aback by the threat.

"You would really do that to me? Just for trying to be your friend?"

I don't believe he would, Mike thought, to Lucas's anger. *Lucas is a good person who is just in a bad spot right now. I get where he's coming from more than he knows.*

"I don't need a friend. I need to leave and go back home to my sister. You don't know what it's like to miss someone so much that it eats you away from the inside! How dare you even think that you can understand what I feel?"

Suddenly, Mike's face fell down. Lucas was about to walk past him when his cabin mate spoke up.

"I have a little sister named Sapphire," Mike revealed, calmly. "She just turned nine this past April. You want to know the sad part? She's spent most of her life in hospitals. She's at one right now in New Jersey, which is where I'm from. When she was four, Sapphire collapsed for the first time. It wasn't until the second time when the doctors said she was developing the early signs of a condition called Shwachman-Diamond syndrome. She's small for her age and has never been able to do things like run around the way the kids here do. She has to be confined to a hospital bed and has to be treated constantly to make sure she is okay. Our parents died in a fire when she was three and I was six. After that, we moved to my aunt and uncles house and they took care of us, until Sapphire permanently moved to the hospital. That's when I started to visit her as often as possible. It wasn't until I started showing signs of OCD that I had to stop going because even the thought would have sent me into a panic attack frenzy. It wasn't funny, Luke. I couldn't walk out of my room without having all these thoughts about getting dirt on my feet or touching the door knob because it had a small smudge mark on it. To calm myself down, I learned to memorize certain things, like how many times a person often blinks in a minute, fourteen, when the lights flickered, how fast and how slow, and it worked. For a while at least. The thing about it is I need to find a new way of coping with it each time. It's like medicine; the more you use it, the less it helps. That's when I came up with the thoughts you heard during training, the anagrams and equations. One day, when I came home from school, I got an invitation to come to this place and here I am."

Mike paused, before resuming his tale.

"Camp Director James welcomed me here, asking nothing in return, and offered a place for me here despite the fact that I have legal guardians. In the short time that I've been here, I've learned to control my abilities as well as my condition. And yeah I still have times where I lock myself in my bunk and stay there until it's shinier than a padded room, but I have learned to deal with what I have. I miss Sapphire, more than you'll ever know. I will see her again at the end of the summer, because Henry promised to look after her and has even contributed in taking care of her financially. My aunt and uncle stopped paying my sister's hospital bills even though my parents left them money for us."

Lucas scoffed at what he thought of as a sob story.

That's the stupidest story I've ever heard. I'd be an idiot to believe a word he says.

Even after Lucas read Mike's mind and found the story to be sincere, he still had his doubts.

If he loved her so much, then why'd he leave?

"Why would you leave her then if your aunt and uncle aren't supporting you two anymore? What were you thinking when you left?" Lucas spat back sharply. "If I were you and she was my sister, I'd be by her side regardless of what I had."

"I was thinking about her, Lucas. Like I have all my life. You don't know how hard it was to make that decision for myself. Henry has the resources, the power to give her the best medical attention that money can buy. Believe me, I never saw myself in a place like this either, but since I'm here, I choose to make the best of it. There's good people here, you included, my friend. Yes, you are my friend even if you don't want to be."

At that moment, Lucas felt sympathetic towards Mike. Then he realized something when he read the boys mind.

Just a little bit longer. The Camp Guardian will see what's going on and he'll help him. I'm sorry, Lucas... but in this instance, I'm thinking about you too.

I don't believe it... he's stalling me!

The Camp Guardian's face turned in their direction when Lucas looked at Mike remorsefully.

"How could you?" was all Lucas said before he pushed Mike down and ran into the forest.

As he ran, the young telepath did not dare turn back and feared what he would see if he did.

I might actually change my mind if I see Mike on the floor, or Boris running after me.

As he ran, a soft drizzle began, matching Lucas's speed until the skies themselves began to sob. He found himself running through the forest with the water beating down on him like a hundred fists. Lucas hit a lot of branches and ran like his life depended on it. He thought he could hear his own name being called out by many voices. Some he recognized and some he didn't.

LUCAS! LUUUUUUCAS! LUUCAAAAAAAS!!

But when he turned back he didn't see anyone as the voices were drowned out through the pouring rain.

I made it. I'm out of camp, thought Lucas with relief. *I went further into the forest than when we played the Relic game.*

When he was sure that no one followed after him, Lucas stopped to catch his breath and put his hand against an old tree that had sap on it. He got some on his palm and wiped it back against the tree but still had traces of it remaining.

Yuck, this stuff looks like saliva mixed with mucus.

The rain washed hard against him and beat down on the still fresh bruises covering his face. Catching his breath, Lucas took a moment to study his surroundings.

The forest appeared gloomy, desolate, and bleak like a cemetery. The trees were taller than the Camp Guardian, and their heads of leaves caught most of the rainwater. The rest fell down into flakes that hit the young telepath.

This place looks new and old at the same time. Like no one has ever lived here, or did, but not for a long time.

Lucas cupped his hands to his mouth and howled to see if anyone had caught up to him.

"HEEEEEEEEEEEEEEEEEEEY!"

However, the only sound he heard was his own echo. He then remembered the name of the forest.

The Infinite Forest. Bill warned me about this place. It doesn't matter what he said. I need to keep moving forward and find a way home.

When howling failed, he decided to cup his hands together to shade his eyes, and looked to see if he could find any way out of the forest.

The trees look exactly the same as the next one. How will I know where to go or where I've been?

Lucas took out his phone and found to his dismay that it still had no signal and that the battery life was about to die.

Yeah, I figured that was going to be the case. I had to try.

The young telepath decided to re-trace his steps, but ended up right where he started. This happened a couple times before he became hungry and was drenched in rainwater. Each time he ran into the same sap tree, Lucas tried to come up with a joke to lighten up the mood for himself.

This tree is making a sap out of me. Ugh! Even my jokes suck right now. Why is this suddenly so hard?

In addition to his already hopeless dilemma, Lucas also had trouble seeing the sky behind the pitch grey curtain of clouds. It felt like less than forty degrees outside as he huddled around his sweater and shivered rapidly. His teeth were beating together like a drummer pounding the drums erratically. He almost bit his tongue, but avoided what would have been a painful experience. To keep any further rain from falling on him, he put up his hood and continued to walk around the forest.

After trying one more time to find his way out, Lucas saw the same tree with the sap all over it and sighed. He knew that he had just gone around in circles for what felt like a hundred times.

This is hopeless. If I can't get out of here, then how will anyone find me?

Just as he wanted to give up, a noise came from behind the tree. He twirled towards the direction of the sound while swiftly grabbing a nearby rock. Lucas kept a firm grip on it, hoping that it wouldn't slip and sink into the mud puddles that were forming beneath his feet.

It must be a monster or a wild animal of some kind.

However, both assumptions proved wrong, as the figure made itself visible.

An old man emerged seemingly rugged with very old, tattered clothing and long white-snow hair on his head and face. His skin appeared wrinkled down and his nails looked broken. His eyes were narrow looking. His beard obscured his lower face below his crooked nose and his teeth looked perfectly white when he opened his mouth to greet him.

"Easy there, child. I mean you no harm," the old man croaked.

He threw up his hand's defensively at the sight of the feeble weapon Lucas carried.

Henry? Lucas thought, fearfully.

Nonetheless, he did not lower the rock and instead stared at the old man cautiously.

"Henry, is that you?" Lucas asked shakily.

"Henry? My name is Alistair," the old man said. "I'm searching for a place called Camp Supernatural. Have you heard of it?"

Lucas nodded as the old man smiled and sighed with relief.

"Splendid. Perhaps you can lead me to this place. I would very much like to meet their Camp Director, Henry James. It's been a long time since we've been acquainted," Alistair revealed.

Lucas finally lowered the rock but did not drop it. He still wore the hood over his head and decided to keep it that way.

The less he knows of me the better.

"You know Henry?" he asked the stranger hesitantly.

Alistair nodded.

"Indeed I do. How about this: if you take me to this camp, I will tell you everything you want to know about Henry," the old man promised.

Lucas reluctantly nodded in agreement, but then raised the rock again as if to throw it.

He could have been sent here by Henry to take me back to camp.

"I don't want to go back. Once we find the way back, you're on your own."

Alistair nodded in approval and took a small step forward.

"Thank you very much. What should I call you?"

"Lucas. Now, tell me how you know Henry."

Alistair nodded plainly and smirked.

"Let's get out of this part of the forest first, shall we? Rain water doesn't mix well with my age."

Lucas reluctantly agreed and threw the rock aside.

I should read his mind so I can get the answers he won't tell me.

When the young telepath did this, he felt a sharp stinging pain waiting for him.

Argh! This is different than the pain from Henry and Daniel. This one feels... like I'm burning up.

Luckily, Alistair didn't notice, as Lucas followed behind him through the damp forest.

The young telepath learned quickly how observant Alistair appeared. How he saw everything and rarely blinked even with the rain pouring down on him.

He's like Josh in how he observes the world, but he has the advantage of hearing, and pretty well for his age. He isn't blinking. How often did Mike say people blink in a minute? Twelve times?

The old man then broke the uncomfortable silence.

"Are you alright, Lucas?" Alistair asked him. "You appear to have wounds on you. Were you involved in a scuffle of some kind? Perhaps with a creature from this forest?"

Lucas shook his head and didn't answer back. He was relieved when the silence returned. This was broken when the old man asked another uncomfortable question.

"Tell me, how did you end up here? If you came from camp, surely others would be searching for you by now," he asked, curiously.

Lucas didn't answer immediately, hoping to evade giving a full answer.

I don't know what's going on with me. I should be able to read his mind no problem. Fine, I'll just give him a short answer and leave it at that. 'I didn't know the way, so I ended up here.'

"No one's coming. I came through another route," Lucas explained, too impulsively.

Before he could stop himself, he had unknowingly said too much, as Alistair's interest became piqued.

Me and my big mouth never ceases to amaze me.

"Oh and what other way are you speaking of?"

I better change the subject.

"I've never heard the name Alistair. It seems like a strange name."

"My family was strange. It's supposed to mean 'Avenger' or 'Defender of Men'. I have been called many things in life. Avenger and defender of men? Not once," Alistair cackled.

Lucas coughed a bit and tried to play it off like his throat was dry.

I need to try and keep as much of myself as I can from him. Just stick to the basics, only say enough without saying a lot. Hopefully at some point I can read his mind.

"My understanding of Camp Supernatural is that everyone there has an ability related to their disability," the old man noted. "Tell me, what is your ability?"

The young telepath felt cautious towards this question in particular.

"Why not ask about my disability?" Lucas answered Alistair's question with a question of his own.

"Very well, tell me about your disability then?"

Lucas pondered what to say and how to say it.

If I tell him that I can read minds, he'll know I'm a telepath. On the other hand, if I am too specific about what I have as a disability, he might put two and two together.

"I have a lot of anxiety," the young telepath chose as his answer. "Mostly social anxiety. It's hard for me to talk to people, to connect with them, and to be asked questions like this."

Alistair chuckled and seemed satisfied enough with the answer.

I wish I knew that for sure. If I mentioned hearing voices that weren't my own in my head, that would have been suspicious right off the bat.

They continued onwards for a while longer until Lucas couldn't walk anymore. After sitting down, he began sweating and panting heavily from the humidity.

"When I left it was still the morning. What time do you think it is now?"

Alistair shrugged and tried to see anything past the rain that never seemed to die down.

"It's been many a fortnight since I've seen a sunrise," said Alistair, longingly. "Alas, it appears I have been out here for quite some time."

This did little to reassure Lucas, who wanted more than anything to leave and be done with this mess he was now in.

I can't wait to get out of here and back home to Shelly. I wonder what she'd think of all this: I learned that I'm an Alter Child with unique abilities related to my disabilities. I mind-controlled the camp bully and my ex-best friend. Now I face both expulsion and I'm lost with an old man in the Infinite Forest. Oh yeah, and for the first time in my life, girls like me. I even asked two out to the Fourth of July dance, which is not happening anymore for me.

To his own surprise, Lucas suddenly found himself thinking about the possibility of returning to camp and explaining what happened to Henry personally.

Maybe he'll take me back and forgive this whole thing if I tell him why. He has to understand that I can't help how I've been feeling. Everyone has just been pushing their issues on me and I already have enough to fill all the cabins in camp.

However, Lucas knew that going back to camp wouldn't be possible with both what he did and because he left voluntarily.

I used my power on Josh, which alone should guarantee that my summer in Camp Supernatural is over. Plus, Mike tried to stop me from leaving, but I still did. So even if I go back with the best of intentions, I could never undo what I've done. Now that I've had some time to think about it, running away isn't exactly helping me look better or appear sorry for my actions either.

Lucas also thought about Ashley and the thought of her did more to calm him than thinking about Vanessa.

I wonder what Ashley would have worn if I had gone with her to the dance. She reminds me of Rapunzel from that animated movie they did awhile back. I'll bet if she wore a pink dress like the character, she'd be the prettiest girl in camp. Even more so than Kendall.

He imagined her wearing Rapunzel's pink dress, her long golden blonde hair streaming behind her majestically and smiling at him playfully the way she often did. For a brief moment, the thought made him smile, but this feeling died when the old man interrupted his train of thought.

"Let's rest here for a little while, then we can continue onwards. Does that sound agreeable to you?" Alistair asked Lucas modestly.

The young telepath agreed and set his backpack down to the side. He kept it close just to make sure the old man didn't try and rob him.

He looks weak, but he could always be a runner.

The old man pulled from his own pack a small can of beans and decided to start a fire.

It won't do him any good. The rain will wash off the fire before it can even start.

Nevertheless, Lucas went along with the idea and went to fetch wood for the fire while Alistair used a pair of flints to start it. The old man lightly brushed the two flints together, not enough to cause a spark of any kind. Despite this, the woods caught the spark and a fire ignited. The young telepath realized immediately that something appeared off about what he thought he saw.

I learned how to start a fire in one of the survival activities we did. You actually have to touch the two flints together in a fast way in order to start the fire. He did touch them together, but not enough to cause a spark. Also, the flame is still burning despite the rain water hitting it. That's not normal.

He decided not to bring it up, as Alistair cooked the beans in a small pot that he conveniently had. He also pulled out a small carefully wrapped roll of breads.

"I've had these for a while, but they are still as fresh as the day I got them. Please help yourself to my storage of food," Alistair offered amiably with a warm smile.

Lucas nodded happily and savored every taste of the meal.

I don't usually eat beans or foods from strangers, but I am very hungry right now.

"How do you know Henry?" Lucas asked curiously.

Alistair wiped small crumbs of bread that fell to his beard and contemplated.

"Oh, it must have been years since we first met. It feels like it was just yesterday…"

The old man looked dazed out at that moment, as Lucas leaned in to make sure he was still breathing.

He looks like he's ready to kick the bucket.

Without warning, Alistair returned to normal and continued.

"How is my old friend? I hear he runs himself a camp now. That sounds very tedious and boring," said Alistair drearily.

Lucas nodded and hungrily gorged down more beans.

"This is my first year so I don't really know the Camp Director like you do, but I want to. You said you'd tell me more about how you know Henry," Lucas demanded the old man.

He sounded like a child asking for a bedtime story from a parent.

I wish I could just read his mind. Then I'd know everything I want to know about Henry.

There was so much about Henry that he wanted answers for and more. He knew the Camp Director would never share his past with him openly.

Maybe Henry doesn't think I'm mature enough to handle whatever he has to say. I can handle anything he tells me. I just want to know who he really is and why he spends his time managing a camp when he could be doing other things instead. Also what's the deal with him and Daniel? They need serious father-and-son therapy or something. Daniel has enough baggage to fill a dump truck with.

Lucas's thoughts were erratic, so much so that he lost his grasp of time for a moment. Soon after, he regained his bearings. Alistair set aside his food and wiped his hands clean against his already tattered shirt.

"What would you like to know?"

Lucas had an array of questions, ranging from Henry's hometown, to the year of his birth, to what profession he studied in school, and when he fathered Daniel.

There's no way he knows the answer to all those questions anyways. I'll just focus on what I want to know most.

"How old is Henry?" was the first question he could think of at the moment.

Alistair snickered and made what looked like a sly grin, but Lucas couldn't tell behind his snow-white beard.

"Well now, I would imagine he is very old. What is your best guess?"

Lucas thought for a moment and realized he had no idea.

Maybe sixty or seventy. He can't be older than that.

"Aren't you two the same age?" Lucas asked, impulsively.

This seemed to pain Alistair, as he grimaced and made a coughing sound.

"I take exception to that, young man. In that case, I can see why you mistook me for him."

It almost seemed like the old man feigned his senile behavior, but Lucas could not be sure.

He's either toying with me, or he's just old. Either way I need to ask him something he has to answer.

Then it came to him.

I have to ask him something straightforward, like about Henry's family and where he comes from. I don't want to mention Daniel because maybe he doesn't know about him. So that's what I'll ask then.

The rain began to let up somewhat with the remaining drizzle being light, but it didn't seem to bother the fire as it continued to burn brightly.

Lucas decided to ask another question in the hopes of getting a satisfactory answer.

"Does Henry have any siblings?"

Alistair thought for a moment before answering.

"I think I remember he mentioned a sister before, a brother perhaps. I cannot be certain."

"Are they still alive? Maybe he just lost contact with them."

The old man shrugged.

"Have you ever thought to ask him these questions yourself?"

Lucas shook his head sadly.

"I've tried, but he likes to avoid personal questions. He probably thinks I don't notice but I do," Lucas insisted firmly.

Alistair laughed at that, which made Lucas feel foolish. The young telepath felt himself cough again, this time from a dry throat.

"Do you have anything to drink?" Lucas asked after the coughing subsided.

I can taste acid coming from my mouth, like the feeling of heartburn. I used to get that a lot when I ate spicy foods or after taking my pills.

Alistair pulled out a small canteen of water and handed it to him. After measuring how much it contained, Lucas shook his head, realizing it had too little for the both of them.

"It doesn't have a lot. You should hold onto it."

The old man shook his head and insisted.

"I can live without drinking water. Go on and take it. Whatever remains of the rain, I can collect in the canteen, so do not fret."

Lucas thanked him and drank the water. He noticed it had a sugary taste.

"I always have a burning sensation inside my mouth and the sugar helps to calm it down significantly," Alistair mentioned with encouragement.

Lucas drank more of the sugar water and suddenly felt full. Despite Alistair's hospitality and seemingly friendly nature, the young telepath still felt cautious towards him.

How does this guy know so much about Henry and more importantly how did he find me here? He made the fire happen, even with all this rain and I still can't read his mind. Is he even who he says he is, or someone Henry wouldn't want to see?

Lucas swore that the rain should have put the fire out by now, but the flames still crackled and split the wood as if it had been ignited mere seconds ago. After they finished eating, the duo resumed trying to find a way out of the forest, with little success.

Then, the old man decided to try something new.

"Let's mark every tree with a specific symbol," the old man suggested. "It will be like navigating a labyrinth."

Lucas reluctantly agreed to the plan, not thinking too much of it.

I ran into the sap tree a couple of times, so what difference is a symbol going to make?

Alistair pulled out a small pocket knife and began marking each tree. He continued this as Lucas watched every different line and symbol he carved on each of the trees. The young telepath made a sort of map in his memory of each one for later use.

Wait a second... some of those look familiar, like the symbols used to identify the cabins in camp. Not identical, but near.

Lucas didn't know if he still had the pamphlet Bill had given him. However, he remembered enough of the symbols to vaguely know what they looked like. But between the rain and the mist that was beginning to surface, he had a hard time telling how the symbols looked from how he thought they looked.

I think I'm just tired. I hope Shell kept my room fresh and clean for me. I'm so looking forward to the real deal, not that imaginary one back in camp. There were times when, even though it looked like my room, it never felt like home. I'll be home soon, just like I promised.

After hours of walking, or what felt like hours, Lucas fell to his knees and sighed.

"Look, this isn't working. Can you find the way to camp on your own?"

The old man shook his head feebly.

"I have a terrible sense of direction. Please I need your help. Henry will surely want to see me."

Lucas groaned and felt tension building up inside.

I can't take it anymore!

"I can't take it anymore," Lucas repeated out loud. "Do you want to know why I left? Because everyone there is crazy! This guy who's deaf is a total douchebag. Then there's my older cabin mate who hates my guts and can easily melt my face off. As if that wasn't the worst of it, his sister keeps hitting on me. The crazy part is I actually like her back. Then, there's this other girl that I like only as a friend who wanted to go to some stupid dance with me. I didn't want to go with her though; I wanted to go with my cabin mate's sister. If that didn't make me hate camp enough, there's a camp bully who I beat in this stupid game and now she hates me. I hate it there. I hate everyone there!"

Lucas heard himself raise his voice with each word, as the anger in him swelled. He hadn't taken his medication in a while and began to think his irrational behavior attributed to that fact.

I feel like my insides are on fire and my anxiety isn't helping either, thought Lucas, grasping at his side as if he had a wound.

He shivered and sobbed underneath the pouring rain. Impulsively, Lucas removed his hood and allowed the rain to pour down his bruised face. The old man only stared at him with the same emotionless expression as the Camp Director.

That's really creepy how similar they both are.

All of a sudden, a tree branch broke, with both the young telepath and Alistair turning in the direction of the sound. What emerged was a shadowy figure that took the physical form of a child. The child's hair was ragged and looked like bits had fallen off. Their face was sunken in, with hollow eyes. Their clothes looked torn and their skin the same color as Henry and the old man in front of Lucas. What caught the young telepath's attention was the child's feet.

Those feet look hairy, and bare. Bare feet... bear feet!

Before Lucas could get a good look at the child, they lurched towards him, but was stopped by the old man. He grabbed one of the pieces of wood from the fire and held it up to the child. The young telepath was able to see in much better light the child's appearance and saw that it was indeed Sasha, the yellow team orb wielder.

Or someone who looks like her! No, it has to be her!

"Don't hurt her, Alistair. I know her," Lucas admitted to the old man. Sasha tried to speak, but all that came out was a soft moaning. "What are you doing here, Sasha? I thought you were sent home?"

The young telepath proceeded to try and read her mind, but all he could hear was static noise and an echo.

It doesn't hurt like when I try to read Henry's mind. There's just nothing; total silence.

Swiftly, the old man touched the child's shoulder and she vanished into thin air. Lucas gasped and looked around to see where she went.

"What did you do to her?! Where did she go?"

Alistair shook his head and tossed the flaming wood aside.

"She meant to cause us harm. I just sent her back to where she came from."

The young telepath darted back and forth erratically, his distance from the old man growing. He kept trying to find Sasha, but could not.

"What happened to her? Why was she like that? Was that real?"

Alistair shrugged.

"This forest can play tricks on you, Lucas. It is best not to give it too much thought."

Lucas couldn't stop himself from thinking about it. What he wanted to know is why she looked half-alive and why she still could not speak.

If I'm wrong, I'm definitely crazier than I feared. If I'm right, then something is seriously bad is going on in this camp.

"Shall we continue forward then? Unless you prefer to be on your own as previously stated," the old man said, bringing Lucas back into reality.

The young telepath protested, and nodded compliantly. He followed the old man through the humid and damp forest. Alistair leveled his pace with Lucas and seemed to snicker.

"Fear not, you'll be home before you know it and this will all seem like a bad dream," the old man said in a low voice.

Lucas nodded and tried to wipe his face clean even as the rainwater kept beating down on him. Instantly, noises like soft little whispers began to project through the dark misty forest.

Sssssssshhhhhhhhhhh.   Sssssssssssshhhhhhhh. Aaaaaaaaaaahm. Aaaaaaaaaaahm.

"What is that? Who's there," cried out Lucas, in horror. The voices he heard were like the many minds he read before, only these ones didn't speak a clear language.

343

More like multiple broken languages. I can't understand what any of them are saying.

Alistair looked around and instructed him to be silent.

"Quiet. Do not respond or listen. Those are the Shadow People," the old man warned him.

The shadow what?! What's he talking about? First, I see someone who looks like Sasha, and now there's Shadow People? Is this why no one was meant to come this far into the forest?

Lucas shivered at the sounds and walked behind the old man.

"What are the Shadow People?" Lucas whispered anxiously.

"The Shadow People have been around since before the creation of mortals. They're dark beings who reside themselves into the darkest parts of the world. If you listen to their whispers long enough, you'll die," the old man cautioned.

But wait, if that's true then why is he listening to them?

"Why aren't they doing anything to you then? You're listening to them," Lucas pointed out, suspiciously.

Alistair stopped walking, as he realized that Lucas noticed that small little detail.

He doesn't know I can read minds. Even if it doesn't do me any good right now, I can still control him. I haven't even tried that. Now that I think about it, if he tries anything, I will.

The old man kept his calm composure as the rain poured down on him.

When they walked further, the malevolent voices began to die down.

Alistair gave Lucas a quick stare that made his skin prickle.

This doesn't feel right. Something is very wrong with this man. I don't know what it is, but he's not who he says he is. He knew something about Sasha and he knows more about the Shadow People than he's letting on.

"Did you know the person who—"

"We've arrived," the old man suddenly proclaimed, ignoring Lucas's question entirely.

Deciding to get a closer look, Lucas took a peak through a bush that seemed to be a bridge between the fog and their salvation. He ran out ahead of the old man, through the trees and branches. The young telepath had to steady himself because the ground felt like skiing on ice.

Finally, we made it back. Now I can get rid of this guy and find my way home with Henry's help. Once I tell him about Sasha, I'm sure he'll want to know more about it. Maybe I'll get a free pass for leaving the way I did.

As Lucas continued sprinting, he realized the bushes led right to the cliff overlooking the training field.

Unfortunately, he ran so fast that he began to stumble and struggled to balance himself.

Oh no! I'm going to fall!

His heart pumped dangerously and his arms flapped helplessly until a helping hand grabbed the back of his hood and yanked him backwards. Lucas flew back and landed on the ground, which felt soggy and moist. When he looked up, Alistair stood in front of him.

He saved me again.

"Thank you for saving me again, Alistair" the young telepath told the old man.

"Just watch your step, Lucas."

After regaining himself, Lucas took a quick glance and saw the soaking wet training field with no one in sight. The camp itself seemed deserted, possibly due to the weather. It was also hard to see much because the mist was especially thick like it had been inside the forest.

I wonder if they're looking for me right now. How can we get down from here?

He glanced at the old man, who only peered down at the camp with his beard hiding the faint line of a smile.

It looks like a smile, or it could be a frown. I don't know and I don't care, Lucas thought as he began to feel more relieved than before.

"Alright, I got you here like you wanted," Lucas noted. "How are we going to get down?"

Behind him, Alistair began to walk backwards.

"I would say that should be the least of your worries at this point."

Lucas's vision began to blur, as he turned back towards the old man, who suddenly started shifting from his appearance.

What... Who...?

He had a hard time making out the transformation through his distorted vision. The young telepath only saw enough of the old man's appearance as it changed rapidly.

Alistair's wrinkled skin became pale and smooth, reminding Lucas of Henry's skin. His long shoulder length hair was now a brighter gold and appeared youthful. His eyes turned bright piercing green and revealed the sense of mischievousness that had seemed obscured before by his age. He no longer had the appearance of a humble old man. He now adopted a much younger and malevolent appearance.

How... How did he do that?! He looks young now. As young as Daniel.

His beard vanished as well, to reveal a sinister smile.

The young telepath prepared himself and tried to mind control Alistair. The old man saw this coming and quickly appeared in front of him.

"That's not going to work on me," Alistair revealed with a snarl. "You're like him. I could tell when you tried to read my mind. I noticed that right away."

Lucas was speechless and so petrified he couldn't move or say anything.

"I didn't think you'd come here this easily. It saves me the trouble of having to look for you in the camp itself. Now that you're here, I can't let you go. Henry won't do it himself, so it's up to me. One less thing for him to worry about. Just know that this is for him."

One less thing for Henry to worry about? For him? What are you talking about? Who...who are you! Lucas was about to shout until Alistair pushed him off the cliff without any hint of remorse in his face.

Instantly, Lucas found himself falling faster than he could process the event.

I'm falling! No! Am I going to die? I don't want to die. I don't want to die. I don't want to die... please someone save me. Henry, Ashley, Bill, Vanessa, Josh, Mom, Dad, Shelly, Shelly, SHELLY!

The young telepath clutched his sister's necklace as he fell, so tight that he felt its binds loosen. Everything suddenly turned black in his eyes. The life inside him began to subside, as he fell deeper into the hard ground that had crashed underneath his body...

Chapter 10

Denial

....

Where am I? What is this...? I can't feel anything...

Even as Lucas opened his eyes, he could not feel his physical body. The only feeling his mind was able to project was coldness and stillness.

Is this what death feels like? Lucas thought as he tried to move. *This doesn't look like Hell or Heaven. Am I somewhere in-between? If I'm not in either, I must still be alive. Right?*

When his eyes adjusted themselves, he felt a burning sensation due to the bright room with no color. As it turned out, he appeared to be the only figure in the room with color.

A white room, thought Lucas, as he turned to look around him.

The young telepath heard ambient sounds that were akin to a mixture of violin and piano, along with a distant rumbling that sounded like war happening in the background.

In his peripheral vision, he saw two distinct birds that seemed to appear out of nowhere.

A Crow and an Eagle. They look big for birds.

They were perched on either sides of the wall where they hovered on something that Lucas could not see.

Maybe it's colorless like the rest of the room.

The Crow had a coal-black appearance with piercing red eyes that made it look demonic, while the Eagle looked light brown with sharp silver eyes.

349

I think they're like opposites. One looks good and the other bad, thought Lucas, uncertainly.

When they saw him, the violin and gunshot sounds intensified. It got to the point where the young telepath could hear the sounds of his heart beating faster. The rhythm his heart made were like speakers on the highest volume setting. A loud squeak escaped the eagle's beak. It caught its breath and began to speak.

"Hello there, mortal. We haven't seen your kind in many of your limited years. It has been long indeed," the Eagle coughed out in a high-pitched tone that sounded like a wheeze.

The Crow looked at Lucas as if to study his body structure and bobbled his head to the side.

What the...? They're talking. Like actual people they're talking! Lucas thought fearfully.

"Is he dead brother? May I eat him now?" the Crow cawed, deviously.

The Eagle screeched at the Crow, with the sounds amplifying themselves around the room.

"The boy lives, but he does not know it yet!" The violin and piano continued to play, but became more subdued now.

Lucas felt his body swerve towards the two birds as if the floor guided him. After stopping in front of them, they appeared both benign and impassive at his presence.

"Don't act like you've never seen a talking Crow before, boy. Well? Have you?" the Crow rasped.

Both birds had voices that sounded rough and hoarse, like when a person tries to talk with their mouth full or after swallowing too fast.

There is definitely something off about this place and it's not just the talking birds.

Lucas shook his head and the Crow began to cackle maniacally. The laugh sounded like there was something stuck inside its throat.

"Forgive my counterpart," said the Eagle, modestly, "he is quite the chatterer, especially with an audience. We haven't seen many-a-faces in what feels like eons."

Before Lucas could say anything, the Eagle bobbled its head and screeched.

"What is your name, boy?"

Lucas responded, but his name came out in a faint whisper. The Eagle tilted his head towards the young telepath.

"What was that? Speak up, boy. I don't think you got my good ear."

This gesture infuriated Lucas, reminding him of Josh.

Of all people, why him!

"My name is Lucas Fargo, you big dumb bird!"

The Eagle let out a laugh similar to the Crows. It echoed around the room and bounced against the unseen walls. The war sounds continued to rumble in the background. These sounds matched in rhythm with his heartbeat.

"He's a funny one, yes he is, don't you think?" the Eagle asked the Crow eagerly.

The maniacal creature nodded in agreement and cawed.

"He's an improvement over the last one who came to our domain."

Last one?

"Who was the last person to come here? Wherever this is?"

"The question of where doesn't matter as much as do you know why you are here, boy?" asked the Eagle, sharply.

Lucas paused before asking his question.

"Am I dead?"

The Crow shook his head and smiled crookedly through its coal beak.

"No, boy. You still walk within your existence," the Eagle assured Lucas. "Your body is broken indeed, yes. Your spirit is still intact. Entirely, no. Your vessel, no. Like a ship with no sail, you remain in one place, at the mercy of the ravenous sea."

The Eagle's head shook but not out of pity, it was similar to a mocking gesture.

My body... as in my physical body is broken?

"If I'm not dead, then why am I here?"

Lucas's tone almost broke with fear as he touched his skin. It bounced off his finger to his hand. He could not feel his body or hurt it. The Crow studied him with big bloodshot eyes that looked like cracks on a wall.

"The boy doesn't know where he is brother, no. He is a fool perhaps, yes. His vessel is still broken, indeed."

The Crow cawed as if it were trying to regurgitate something.

I can't take this anymore. I need answers and I need them now. Whether they want to give them to me or not.

Lucas concentrated and tried to read the birds minds, but he heard nothing. The young telepath only heard the sound of his own thoughts. He then tried to mind control them. This did not work either. The two speaking birds seemed to notice his dilemma. The sounds around them became like the gurgling inside of someone's stomach.

"Your powers won't work here or on us, boy," said the Eagle.

"Indeed, as my other half says, we have no minds for you to read, or hear, or feel," the Crow said, as it began to laugh, maniacally.

Now, the young telepath was beginning to feel both desperation and anger.

"So then how do I get back to my body? There has to be way," Lucas asked them fearfully.

The Eagle and Crow cackled at him, while their faces twisted into scowls like a lenticular image.

"Only you can make the choice, just as you came here," the Crow rasped with a cough.

Choice? I didn't choose to come here? Did I?

"If I chose to come here, can I make it again to go back to my home? My real home outside of camp?"

"You may," the Eagle admitted, "but that is not the plan."

The plan? What plan?

"He is not meant to know yet, brother, fair warning," the Crow screeched. "When he returns, more will he know, less will he have."

The Eagle laughed and replied with a similar tone to its other half.

"Oh yes. What this one has seen, cannot be unseen. His return will bring about the other one. He will come, surely. What the other brings will be terrors beyond which this one is not prepared for."

More will I know, less will I have, Lucas mused on the birds words. *Terrors I'm not ready for? What does it all mean?*

The Eagle's tone seemed to shift suddenly into one that was less malevolent as before.

"This form you take now is temporary by its nature. Your potential can create ripples in the dark. Face yourself in the light, to see your worth. Mind yourself, because without it, you won't see what's coming."

Mind myself? Face myself in the light? Ripples in the dark? They're more confusing than a fortune cookie.

Before Lucas could ask what those words mean from the maniacal creatures, he heard the sound of a foghorn and felt himself becoming engulfed by the sudden burst of light in the room.

Lucas heard the Eagles voice say, "When you see us once more, then you'll know what for," as the inside of his eyes became dark.

In an instant, he awoke with his eyes flickering as they struggled to open.

At first his eyes wouldn't open completely. Instead, all Lucas could hear was background noises, which sounded like static. Both voices were familiar to the young telepath, but in that moment he could not discern one from the other.

They sound like they're arguing. Over what, I don't know.

After what felt like a few seconds for him, his eyes finally fully opened themselves. Lucas was lying on a hospital bed, with a large blanket covering the bruises and bandages around his body. He softly jerked his head to the left and found get-well cards with a vase of freshly watered flowers.

I wonder who those are from, thought Lucas, as he smiled thinly at them.

To his right, he saw a heart monitor and an IV attached to the back of his right hand.

This is the first time I've ever had one of those. Good thing I can't feel it.

Even though he couldn't feel anything underneath the bed sheets, the numb feeling he had in his dreams still lingered.

That's odd. I thought that after waking up the feeling would be gone.

To Lucas's surprise, on a small chair near his bed sat Camp Director James. He looked like he had been there for some time.

Henry? What's he doing here?

When his vision began to clear up, he realized that Henry had traces of water running down from all over his face. Most notably his eyes. In his fatigued state of mind, Lucas couldn't tell for sure and heard what sounded like rain against the walls of the ward.

Henry probably got wet and forgot to wipe his face clean before re-entering the room, Lucas assessed.

When Henry noticed Lucas was conscious, he wiped his face with a nearby towel and smiled happily.

"Lucas, you are awake….I'm so sorry for what has happened to you. But do not worry, because you are safe and back in camp."

Back in Camp Supernatural, the young telepath thought, trying to hide his discomfort from the Camp Director.

Lucas moved only his head and looked at Henry in confusion.

"What happened to me? Why am I back here when I should be—?"

"You're in great care now," Henry said, cutting Lucas off from finishing his sentence. "You had an unfortunate accident, my child. Do you recall what led to it?"

Lucas shook his head softly and bit his lip.

Henry glanced at the heart monitor, but nothing out of the ordinary occurred. He called in a nurse and she hurried in to examine Lucas. As the nurse checked him, the young telepath looked at the Camp Director to see his expression.

He looks so calm. If he's worried, he's very good at hiding it.

"What song was I listening to when you first arrived in Camp Supernatural? What was the name of the musical group?" Henry asked as the nurse checked his pupils and dilation.

The young telepath was confused by the question, until the Camp Director explained. "You may be suffering from amnesia due to the fall. I wish to know how far back your memory goes. What song and what band?"

Lucas thought for a moment.

I remember this one... he said it was his favorite band... I remember hearing it when...

"Top of the World by the Carpenters. They are your favorite band."

"And what year is it currently?"

"2013. July something."

Henry smiled happily, nodded, and sent the nurse away when she finished checking him.

"Very good, my son. You still retain your memories from before. Now then, can you recall how you ended up in the training field?"

Lucas tried to think, but his mind kept going back to the white room.

Training field? I only remember two birds talking to me like people. I don't remember anything before I... tried to leave camp.

As the thought came back, the young telepath wondered if the Camp Director already knew the circumstances leading to his hospitalization.

Henry must know. Mike saw me leave and so did Boris. Either way, he's going to have to send me home now.

"I found you in the training field below a cliff that leads into the Infinite Forest. You were barely alive."

When Lucas did not reply, Henry did not wait for a response.

"It appears to me that you might have fallen. Is that what happened or did something else transpire?"

The young telepath didn't know what to say or how to explain why he left in the first place.

Either Henry doesn't know much beyond the obvious, or he's waiting to see what I'll say, Lucas observed. *I should just tell him what I can remember for now.*

"I don't know, sir. Every time I try to remember, all I can think about is a Crow and an Eagle," Lucas confessed.

"A Crow and an Eagle? Tell me of these creatures. Where did you see them?"

Lucas explained the White Room with the Crow and the Eagle, the sounds that he heard, how the birds were able to talk like people, and spoke like lunatics from an insane asylum. Henry nodded when the young telepath finished explaining the strange nature of the place he was in.

"That is… peculiar. Did they give you something by which to call them by?"

Lucas shook his head softly as tears began to build up in his eyes.

"I can't think straight, sir. I'm starting to hear more voices than I know what to think."

He referred to the voices of the nurses and doctors in the small hospital who were walking around assisting other patients.

There are so many of them. I feel like my head is going to explode! This is worse than before. I can barely hear myself think…

Henry rose from his chair and calmed Lucas with a gentle hand.

"I must do something that is important. Please remain calm. I promise it will be over quick."

I don't know if it's my power, but it hurts to just think… Whatever he's going to do, it better be quick because I'm very close to screaming out loud right now!

As his mind continued to rage, he felt the soft smooth hands of the Camp Director bury themselves in his long hair. Lucas's breathing grew heavy as Henry began to see something through the darkness of his eyelids. The young telepath couldn't see it. However, he felt it.

357

I feel... sadness... a lot of it... and... something else... something I can't tell the shape of but it feels like...

Before he could place the feeling, Henry returned and Lucas panted hard, sweating all over as more tears began to fall from his eyes.

"Henry... what just happened...?"

Lucas's head shook, and his necked ached. He wanted to scream, to pound the bed...

... My arms...

"Just rest, my child. Do not try to move," Henry said as he brought out a wet cloth and dabbed it on Lucas's forehead.

Lucas did in fact try to move at that moment and realized he could not.

Why can't I move? Wha... what's wrong with my body?!

"Why can't I move my body, Henry? Why can't I move my..."

Lucas heard himself ask the same question twice, then another time, until a lump formed in his throat.

Why can't I move my body?

He could feel the anxiety building up, as Henry's facial expression confirmed his worst suspicions.

No.

"Your body did not survive the fall," said Henry, regretfully. "I am so sorry, my child."

No... no no no no no NO! NO! NO!

Lucas's face was drenched in tears and he felt the lump suffocating him as he tried to speak. In the struggle, his words came out like babble. He had better luck screaming in his mind. He could only feel from the neck up and the rest of his body felt like something heavy and immovable.

This can't be true! Please don't let it be true... oh please, don't let this be true! Please no, please! I can't live like this! I can't!

"No... please, Henry, no. I can't live like this. I can't. Please, I'm begging you. Please help me," Lucas pleaded and sobbed at the same time.

Henry gave him a sympathetic look, but remained impassive as he spoke.

"I can help you, my son and I will. Just give me time to make the necessary preparations."

Lucas nodded stiffly.

"What are you going to do to help me?"

"Be patient. Everything will be alright. All according to plan," Henry promised him.

"According to plan? What do you mean?" Lucas asked in a calmer tone.

The Camp Director only smiled as Ashley, Josh, and Bill entered the room. Hailey, Gary, and Mike followed behind. A tearful Ashley walked over to Lucas and threw herself on him in a warm embrace. She sobbed hard and heavy against his cheek while her arms tightened around his neck. Her wet blonde hair fell in waves across his face and shoulders.

I wish I could hug her back. This is enough for now though; the feeling of her hair on my face. Just stay like this for a few more seconds.

"I'm so happy you're awake," Ashley exclaimed, tearfully. "What happened to you? Where were you this whole time?"

This whole time?

Her tone sounded fragile and shaky. She tried to fight the tears as the rain beat hard against the ward. Hailey put her hands on Ashley's shoulders as she withdrew herself from Lucas. She was the first to realize something was off when she touched her hand on his palm with no reaction.

She knows, he realized after reading her mind.

When she poked at his arm gently, the others seemed to understand as well without having to be told. She didn't need to ask; the truth suddenly hit her and the others as if the room were about to be flooded by the rainwater outside. She sobbed even more, while Hailey looked distressed by this revelation. Mike walked up to the young telepath and stared at his friend sorrowfully.

"I'm so sorry this happened to you, Lucas," Mike said, as he began to tear up. He thought, *I should have done more to help you. This happened because of me. onay eednay otay entionmay atwhay actuallyyay appenedhay.*

No, Mike. This was all me. You were trying to be my friend and I let you down. I let everyone down...

"What happened to you, Lucas," Bill asked with concern. "How did you end up out there? If you were feeling this way, why didn't you talk to us? We're your friends."

Lucas shook his head and clenched his teeth hard, so hard that he thought they would shatter like glass if he wasn't careful.

"I don't want to talk about it. Not now, not ever," Lucas said, breathlessly.

His cabin mate wanted to press the issue, but after seeing the young telepath's exhausted expression, Bill simply nodded and let the matter be.

I appreciate that, Bill. Even after everything I said and did... Thank you for that.

It wasn't until Ashley brushed aside the hair from his eyes when Lucas noticed how long it had grown. It didn't seem very long but the front covered his eyes like a veil and nearly touched the tip of his nose. His hair on the back was a bit longer too.

To break the uncomfortable gloomy silence, Josh took it upon himself to lighten up the mood.

"I brought one of those cards here for you."

He plucked it from the table to show it to Lucas.

It read, 'To my dear idiotic friend, Luke. Get better'.

It was a very short letter, but Lucas appreciated it.

It's thoughtful and truthful, he decided with a frown.

Bill patted Lucas's shoulder and gave him a wistful smile.

"You'll get through this. We're here for you in any way you need, my best friend," the older camper promised, encouragingly.

Unfortunately, Lucas did not feel this way. He tried to hide it for the benefit of his friends though.

"I will leave him in your care, Bill. Please look after him," Henry instructed. Lucas's cabin mate complied as the Camp Director turned to leave.

"Where's Vanessa, Bill?" Lucas asked his older cabin mate.

Bill shook his head and didn't say anything after that.

He won't like the answer to that question, he thought, which made Lucas feel slightly anxious.

When the Camp Director reached for the door, Daniel appeared and showed surprise at seeing his father there.

Daniel has a bit more facial hair right now. If he grew a full beard, maybe he would look more like Henry.

When his son tried to greet his father, the Camp Director brushed past him as if he didn't notice his presence. Daniel looked puzzled by this and turned his attention towards Lucas. Behind him, others were coming to see the bedridden camper. The nurses and doctors had to start telling some of them to return at another time, only allowing the friends that were already in the room to remain.

"How are you feeling, Lucas?" Daniel asked in a concerned tone.

Lucas did not reply.

I'm tired of getting asked that and of people looking at me like I'm a broken thing. Which I am, whether I like it or not...

"You saw this happening didn't you? I remember you told me and I didn't listen at the time."

Daniel sighed and neither nodded nor shook his head.

"I don't always see a clear picture. Just glimpses of a possible future. I only knew it could happen, not that it actually would."

Lucas couldn't be sure that it was the whole truth, but in the moment he didn't care.

"I can't do this. I can't live like this. I wish the fall had killed me," Lucas began to say, inconsiderably.

The room fell in silence the moment he said those words. Daniel walked over to the side, gently pushing past Josh and Ashley.

"Don't say that, Lucas. We're all very grateful that you're alive. After all, you're my star pupil."

Lucas gave Daniel a dubious look, even as the Camp Counselor gave him a reassuring smile.

"Sure I am. You don't even like me. You hate how much attention Henry gives me instead of you. Just now, he ignored you on your way in, like you don't even——."

"That's enough, Lucas, please," he heard Ashley cry out. Daniel looked hurt by those words, but he didn't argue against them.

Just then, as Lucas was feeling worse than ever before in his life, he started to feel something else. It was a voice he knew and didn't think he'd hear in this context.

It's okay and your right, Lucas. My father sees something in you I wish he saw in me. I don't think less of you for that. You're a good person with more potential than you give yourself credit for. Right now your body is broken, but your mind is still intact. Believe in yourself, just like everyone in this room believes in you.

After a few seconds, Lucas calmed down, and proceeded to apologize to the Camp Director's son.

"I...I'm sorry. That was rude of me to say when you were just trying to reassure me. I appreciate it, sir."

Daniel's nodded and gave the young telepath a satisfied look.

"It's alright. I know you didn't mean it."

The Camp Counselor smirked and patted Lucas's shoulder.

"I guess this means you won't be attending my training sessions anymore."

Lucas looked at him with an expression that brought irony to his choice of words.

"Unless you can drag my bed to the training field, then I don't think so. I just have to believe in myself, like everyone in this room does."

This sounded like a sarcastic comment to his friends, but Daniel understood the intent. He lowered his head towards Lucas's ear and whispered, "Well done. You finally read my mind. I knew you could do it."

He winked at Lucas, who smiled back at him.

I'm proud of you, Lucas. Really, I am. You've come so far and in such a short time. I hope you're hearing this right now, because I want you to know this isn't goodbye. We're not giving up on you, so don't give up on yourself.

After this, Daniel yawned and clapped his hands together.

"I think it's time to let him rest for the day. In the meantime, you all get the day off tomorrow to spend some time with Lucas or to catch up on any sleep you might be missing out on. We only have a few more weeks of camp left and we need to make the most of it."

Just as Daniel turned to leave, Lucas started to read his mind again, only this time, something different happened:

"How did you not glimpse this, Daniel?" Lucas heard Henry's voice ask with more emotion than usual. *"You assured me of the visions validity. If I find out you withheld any information from me—"*

"I tried to tell you, father. I tried to tell you everything many times, but you thought it was fine. You said he would be fine. How could you think I would do something like that?"

"It wasn't supposed to happen this way. This causality has created innumerable variables to which even you won't be able to see what is possible. All that's left is to trust what has been set into motion and hope that somehow it course corrects itself. Do not make this mistake again."

"Yes, father..."

I couldn't see that far ahead, Lucas heard Daniel's voice say now. *If I knew, of course I would have done something about it. I only saw part of the instant, not the whole instant itself. My father isn't worried that Lucas will end up like Jacob, but I am. That's why I'll do all I can to help him and make sure he doesn't become that way. Or stop him if my father won't...*

The last thought upset Lucas, but not as much as he expected. His mind was more focused on the fact that his body was immobile.

I want to be alone right now, but I'm scared to be alone at the same time. I don't know what to say or how to say it.

A thought then occurred to him.

What day is it?

"What day is it?" Lucas repeated out loud. "How long was I in a coma?"

Bill looked at a nearby calendar and pointed to the

third week in July.

"It's July 15th. You were in a coma for two weeks."

Lucas felt even worse than before.

Two weeks? I must have been in the forest for a week then. It definitely did not feel that way to me. So that means I missed most of July, including the dance.

He looked at Ashley who had stopped crying and was now stroking his long hair gently.

"You'll need a haircut soon," Ashley said with a faint smile. "It didn't feel right to give you one while you were asleep."

"I'm sorry that I missed the dance. I promised that I would go with you."

She shook her head and planted a small gentle kiss on his forehead.

"We will dance some other time," she promised, but as she said this, her voice began to break with tears forming in her eyes again.

He did not enjoy making her cry unintentionally. Regretfully, he knew why she felt this way.

I'm never going to walk again... or swim in the camp lake... or dance with anyone. I'll never learn to drive either, which was something I was looking forward to doing.

When a nurse whispered something to Bill, he nodded and turned back to the others.

"We'll let you get some rest now. Be strong, Luke. I'll keep your bunk in check. Inspections are tomorrow so consider it a favor. You'll owe me two when you get out of here."

The last thing Bill said was more wishful thinking on his part.

We just have to keep hoping for the best. At this point, I feel the worst is definitely over.

Despite not believing this, Lucas nodded at the thought.

"Get well soon," was all Josh said as he prepared to leave along with the rest of Lucas's friends.

He was about to leave when a sound entered his mind. Josh felt a sensation in himself he had never experienced before and something he thought would never happen to him in his life.

I'm sorry, Josh.

Josh turned back and stared at Lucas in disbelief.

"How did you do that?" Josh blurted out surprisingly and signed feverously. Lucas looked genuinely confused.

"Do what?"

"You said, 'I'm sorry Josh'. I heard you in my mind... I heard you," Josh exclaimed, shockingly. "It was kind of a grinding sound. Like the feeling I get when I grind my teeth together. I knew the words because I pictured your lips moving with them. That's how I think I knew what you said."

"I did say that in my mind, but I didn't say it to you."

Josh looked both shocked and bewildered, but ultimately let it be.

"You are the strangest and most annoying person I've ever met. But, to be honest, you and Bill are all I've got in terms of best friends these days," Josh acknowledged with a small smile.

Lucas smiled at that.

"I'll see you later, Josh."

"Take care, Luke."

In his mind, Josh projected something that both surprised Lucas and told him everything he needed to know about his best friend's mindset towards him.

I haven't forgiven you for what you did to me, Luke. You knew it was wrong but you still used your power on me. If Bill hadn't been there to stop me, you would probably be in the hospital because of me instead of what happened to you. Regardless, I don't enjoy seeing you like this. I really hope something can be done to help you. I would hate to see you go after we became best friends. I want to try to forgive you soon. We'll start with an apology and go from there.

Lucas knew the feeling his cabin mate had was completely justified and that Josh had every right to be angry at him. He hated himself for having used his power at all in that way.

I wish I hadn't used my powers on Josh like that. He didn't deserve that. Maybe what happened to me happened because of what I did. Like karma. Then again, if I hadn't tried to run away from camp, none of this would have happened. I just wish I remembered what happened when I entered the forest. What did I see or who did I see?

When the young nurse came in and switched the TV on for Lucas, he realized that no one else remained in the room with him. Although he watched the screen whenever his eyes allowed him to, he sidetracked often. He kept thinking about when Henry would come and help him like he promised.

I wonder what Henry plans to do. Maybe it has something to do with his mysterious powers. As long as he can heal me back to my old self. Then again, I don't know how far I fell, but it's still strange to think I survived with only a broken body instead of dying.

After close to an hour, he called the young nurse back in and asked for his medication.

"I'm sorry, Lucas, but we don't want to risk mixing what you already have in your system with new medicines."

"You don't understand," Lucas said, agitatedly, "I need to calm my nerves. I know I can't move my body, but I still get fidgety like I used to before. I can't sleep because I can't stop thinking. I need medicine to help me sleep like before."

367

After the young nurse shook her head, Lucas recognized her.

She's the one Josh flirted with before. I just barely noticed because her hair is slightly shorter than it was before.

"Hey, aren't you the nurse that my friend talked to last time?" Lucas asked.

The young nurse nodded and blushed.

"Yeah, that's me and your friend never called me. I tried to say hi to him when he came by to see you, but he ignored me. He didn't even notice that my hair was shorter like the way he said he liked."

Lucas sighed and softly shook his head.

Josh, ever the womanizer that Ashley said he was. She does look prettier with shorter hair though.

"What's your name? I feel bad for thinking of you as just the young nurse."

"My name is Melanie," said the young nurse, softly. "I'm not really a nurse to be honest, but more of an intern. I'm still a camper and this is actually my second year here. Instead of training like the other Alter Children, I come and volunteer here. Eventually, I hope to become a full-time nurse in camp."

Lucas nodded and understood for the first time why she looked so young.

She's only a year older than me and Josh. I wonder what her ability is and why she doesn't master it with training.

"What's your ability, Melanie?"

"I can make things float by touching them. The thing is I can only do that for a short time because if I do it too long, I'll be like a deflated balloon with the air finding some way out."

"Why don't you train with the other Alter Children then? Your power sounds like it can be stronger later."

"I prefer to heal and help others than relying on a power that is simplistic in its nature," Melanie admitted.

She's definitely smarter than she looks. I can't tell if she chose this line of work voluntarily or was pushed into it.

"My mom works a hospital clinic in the city I live in," Lucas revealed to Melanie. Her interest looked piqued by this.

"What does your mother do specifically?"

"She helps the doctors during their operations, checking to make sure that patients have everything they need, stuff like that."

To be honest, I have no idea what my mom does at her job, he admitted to himself.

"That's wonderful, it sounds like your mom is a great person. Are you excited to see her and your dad after the summer ends?"

Lucas did not respond and instead came up with a thought for her abilities.

She said she can make things float.

"In that case, can you do me a favor and help me read the get-well cards? Just open them up and float them for me for a short time, please. I think that will help calm me down a lot."

Melanie agreed to the idea and opened them one at a time. They only floated for a few seconds, but it was enough that the young telepath was able to read and memorize them. They all had signatures in the bottom, with most consisting of nothing more than, 'Get well soon' and 'Keep your chin up.'

I feel like the last one is in poor taste all things considered.

"Who sent me the most letters?"

Melanie plucked a number of cards up, indicating that they were all from the same person: "Ashley, the young girl who came to see you earlier. In fact, she was here every day since you were brought in. When they cancelled the dance because of your disappearance, she was here all that night. I kept her company while she said so many nice things about you. Here, let me read you some of her letters."

Wait what? They cancelled the dance because of me? Great, now I feel even worse than I did before.

Lucas felt a lump form in his throat, as Melanie read the letter Ashley left for him in one card.

"'Dear Lucas, we have only just met, but I feel like you're the most interesting guy I've ever known. I hope you wake up soon and know that I'll be here when you do. With love, Ashley'."

He smiled as she continued to read to him the rest.

"'Dear Lucas, today would have been the Fourth of July dance. Henry announced a few minutes ago that it had been cancelled and we were going to have a movie night indoors instead. I didn't have anything nice to wear for the dance anyways. I just liked the idea of spending more time with you. I know you'll wake up soon and I hope when you're ready to talk about what happened to you, that you'll trust me with the truth. I wish you the best, and I'll see you soon. Your friend, Ashley'."

The last letter he heard was the most recent one before he awoke.

"'Dear Lucas, I'm sorry for all the letters. I feel like I sent you a bunch of texts or something. No, I won't write 'lol', except in this instance. Anyways, I can't wait for you to wake up and to see you again. Everyone has been so worried about you and camp hasn't felt the same since that day. Why did you try to leave? Did you think about any of us? About me? I know you missed home, but you have a place here until then. I hope you feel the same way when you read these words. If you ever need to talk about anything, anything at all, please know that you can and I will always listen. Sincerely yours, Ashley'."

Lucas was surprised when Melanie began to cry a little.

"I'm sorry." She stifled a few more tears. "Your friends are so wonderful. You're truly blessed to have them."

Lucas nodded and tried not to cry himself.

I am, yes, blessed and lucky to have friends like them.

When he asked about letters from Vanessa, Melanie only found two. Their contents were short and quick to the point.

She's probably still upset about the fact that I said yes to Ashley and not her for the dance, Lucas assumed.

"Do you need anything else, Lucas?" Melanie asked. "I still have an hour on my shift."

Lucas softly shook his head.

"No, thank you. I know it's not any of my business, but it's his loss, not yours. You deserve someone who will call you and say hi to you in front of his friends. Also, I think your hair looks great. You should keep it that way for yourself, not for Josh."

The young intern nurse blushed and nodded.

He's as sweet as Ashley said he was, Lucas heard Melanie think in her mind. *I can see why she likes him so much. I wish Josh noticed me that way or even any guy in this camp.*

After thanking him, Melanie put the cards back on the table and offered to read them again to him if he wanted. When she was gone, Lucas decided to sleep.

At that moment, he didn't know what would come next. All he knew, at least for now, was that he was safe and back home...

Chapter 11
Broken Things

Following the accident, Lucas got frequent visits from Ashley and did not see Vanessa. According to Ashley, Bill's sister could be found in the training field, but nowhere near the ward.

How can she still be mad after what happened to me? I can't believe I'm saying this, thinking this, but I miss her, Lucas thought, ruefully.

The last full week of July past fast for Lucas, even though all he did was stay in his hospital bed. As August approached, he knew the summer was coming to an end. Soon he would have to say goodbye to all the new friends he made during his time in camp.

As happy as I am that summer is almost over, I'm actually going to miss camp. It has... grown on me I think, thought Lucas, with a smile. *Maybe if Henry says yes, I can come back next year. I want to see if Shelly can come too even though I don't know if that's allowed because she's not an Alter Child. That I know of, she doesn't have any disabilities.*

The Camp Director only came once or twice just to greet Lucas and would leave as fast as he came by. He never stayed long enough for anyone else in the ward to notice.

I don't blame him. I'm sure he's busy preparing for the end of summer and making sure everyone else in camp is fine. It still means a lot that he actually makes the time to come and see me.

Daniel made visits as well, sometimes accompanying Ashley, while visitors like Josh and Bill only came twice and always together. Mike only came the day Lucas awoke, with the young telepath understanding why he didn't come after that.

It must have taken everything he had to come that one time, so I don't blame him for not wanting to return.

To keep himself busy, Lucas spent most of his time in the ward watching TV or sleeping. Occasionally, he would peer out at the window of the ward to see the rest of the campers either training or running around. The sight made him feel bitter when he moved his head to see his broken body.

They get to run, to walk, to dance, and me, all I get to do is lie down and wait until Henry comes up with a way to help me.

When Ashley visited, she assisted Melanie in moving Lucas to avoid bed sores. He ate very little and refused to drink a lot of water, mostly to avoid going to the bathroom. On one occasion, Henry had to calm Lucas's nerves as he was forced to use the facilities. He resisted against Melanie and another nurse who assisted her.

I never want to talk about this to anyone.

He felt so weak and malnourished. Lucas missed the body he once took for granted. The young telepath would cry often at night, until his eyes became red and itchy from the tears by the morning.

On some occasions, Melanie would stand by Lucas's side in case he needed food or water when he had no visitors. It was during this time when the young telepath started to get to know her better without just reading her mind.

"What made you want to be a nurse instead of training like the other campers?" Lucas asked on one occasion.

"My mother is comatose and bedridden. I wanted to learn medicine so I can help take care of her. My father is in jail for trying to kill my uncle. I have a little sister who is seven and stays with my grandparents. I'm hoping when she's older that she'll be able to come to Camp Supernatural with me."

"When summer is over, do you go back home to your grandparents or do you take care of your mom?"

"No, I stay here in camp until at least the winter," Melanie revealed. "Henry allows it because a lot of kids here don't have homes to go back to. During the spring, I get to see my sister, grandparents, and mother. In the meantime, they are all provided for by the Camp Director. He financially supports the nurses and staff while they are away from their homes."

As she spoke, Lucas listened intently and felt everything she thought of.

She feels determined and hopeful. Here in camp, she can do more than at home and she can be more of a person here... I get it... I do... I can see her home life... Once, for her sister's birthday, she spent all the money she had to take her to a pizza restaurant so she could have a small party... But she never had a birthday party of her own. That's really sad.

"I'm so sorry," Lucas heard himself say, to Melanie's confusion.

"For what?"

Lucas wanted to tell her that he read her mind, but he was afraid how she'd react. As the thought continued to play in her head, Melanie seemed to realize what the young telepath was apologizing for.

"It's okay, I know you can't control your ability right now," Melanie said. "Can you see anything else I am thinking about?"

Lucas took a short moment and felt Melanie thinking about a memory of Christmas. She got her sister a tambourine so she could learn a musical instrument, while she got a stethoscope from her sister that she still uses when treating patients at the ward.

"Wow... I feel can your memories," Lucas admitted. "It's like I'm there with you experiencing them. Your sister is lucky to have you."

This made Melanie smile and brush a small tear from her eye.

"Thank you for that, Lucas. I'll let you get some rest now."

He wanted Melanie to stay, if only to keep him company, but he understood that his abilities were invasive.

She's too nice to say it, but I know it's not something she's completely comfortable with. I don't blame her. I would feel the same way if someone read my mind and felt what I feel towards Shelly and my parents... Like Bill said, there's a reason minds are private and that privacy should be respected.

During his time in the camp's hospital ward, Lucas began to re-evaluate his own life and think differently about what he would do if he regained the use of his body.

I wouldn't take it for granted, that's for sure. I'd dance with Ashley and take both my education and training for my powers more seriously. I need a future that involves learning to drive and maybe going to college.

He did not dare think if Henry's plan would fail. It became all that he clung to for hope.

If he can't fix me, then I don't want to continue living. Not like this. But I know it won't come to that, because Henry promised to help me. I just wish I knew how he's going to do it.

One day, when Ashley came to visit him, he decided to begin making amends for his behavior before the accident.

I should start with someone who is more likely to forgive me.

"I'm sorry, Ashley," Lucas apologized softly.

Ashley looked at him in confusion as she fed peeled apple slices to him.

"For what? You have nothing to be sorry for, Lucas."

"Bill told you that I like you," he said in-between bites.

Ashley nodded with a shy smile.

"It made me so happy to hear that, even if deep down I know you feel something for Vanessa."

Lucas looked at her sadly and said nothing.

She's not stupid. Of course she knows. Girls always know this stuff.

He tried not to read her mind, but heard the words before she said them.

I guess I knew all along. I still wonder and I can't help thinking if...

"Do you think that you could ever like me as more than a friend? I mean, if you didn't already have a crush on Vanessa?"

Lucas nodded stiffly and said his next words with profound confidence.

"You're a wonderful person, beautiful, and kind. There is nothing about you that I wouldn't say no to."

Ashley blushed and smiled thinly. Despite this, her face fell as she set aside the remaining apple slices.

"I know I'm going to hate myself for this then. If you tell Vanessa that last part you just told me, she will without a doubt forgive you for saying yes to me first."

"But what about you? I care about you too, Ashley. It's just, different, I think," Lucas revealed the last part with sorrow.

Ashley turned away abruptly.

"You think? It's only different because that's how you feel, Lucas. It's okay, it really is. I'm just glad I know how you truly feel now."

How I truly feel? I wish it were that simple...

"We're still friends. You know that, right?"

Ashley nodded with her head still looking away from him.

"Right, just friends. I think we can make that work," she said, softly.

Lucas smiled and thanked her.

"I'm sorry about what happened between you and Josh," Ashley said regretfully. "I feel guilty about it because if you hadn't tried to talk to him, maybe things would have happened differently. I still don't understand what made you want to leave Camp Supernatural. Was it something someone did, or something you were feeling that overwhelmed you? You can tell me anything, Lucas. I know you can't remember all of it, but please try, for me."

The young telepath shook his head, trying very hard not to think about that day.

It's still too much for me. I can't, Ashley. Please...

"...don't make me talk about it, Ashley," Lucas said aloud. She understood and didn't say anything after that.

Ashley fed Lucas the remaining apple slices and after that got up to leave his room.

Unable to help himself, Lucas inadvertently read her mind and to his dismay he realized that he failed to make amends: *Just friends. Yeah, he said I'm beautiful and wonderful. That he wouldn't say no to anything about me. Yet he just did. So being beautiful and wonderful isn't enough for him.*

In that moment, the young telepath felt what she was feeling. He thought if he could move his body right now, he'd jump out of his bed and catch up to her before she could leave the ward.

I want to imagine it like in a movie. Against all odds, I'm healed through the power of love, as lame as that sounds. Then, I catch up to Ashley, make things right for real, and... that's it... because all that's left is to... but not with her.

His last visitor before the end of the day ended up being Josh. Lucas felt surprised, especially because this was the first time they were alone since the day he used his powers on his cabin mate.

A day I wish I could forget.

"Hey Luke. I just thought I drop by for a bit and see how you are," said Josh with a low voice and rapid hand movements.

Josh offered yogurt from the cafeteria and Lucas thanked him for it.

Even though I hate yogurt, I still appreciate the gesture.

"Listen about last time…"

Before Lucas could finish, Josh cut him off and pointed to himself.

"You don't have to say anything. I'm sorry," he admitted. "Sometimes I just don't know when to stop talking and it's not because I can't hear the sound of my own voice."

Lucas nodded stiffly and suddenly felt troubled by another thought that came into his mind.

How does he do it? How does he live life being carefree when he's deaf?

"Why are you always joking around about things?" Lucas asked in a stiff tone. "I mean, compared to me, your deaf. So how come you never care about it? Because I've heard people make fun of you behind your back. Instead of noticing, you make jokes at your own expense."

Josh understood every word Lucas said in that moment, as he kept his calm face and composure. He took a deep breath and leaned in towards Lucas's bedside before responding with the most serious face the young telepath ever saw him have.

"You want me to be angry, upset, cry for being deaf? Will that give me back my hearing? No. Being funny makes me happy. It's what I'm good at and I like it. If I don't have that, then I really am nothing," Josh confessed solemnly. "I have cried and been angry, but I am done feeling sorry for myself. It's time you do the same."

Josh's calm demeanor never once waned as he spoke.

He got me and he is absolutely right… This whole time, I've been feeling sorry for myself and hopeless because of my situation. It doesn't change the fact that I messed up and the only thing I can do now is just hope for the best and move forward... not literally, because I can't. I need to try though, metaphorically, just to be clear.

After he really thought about it, Lucas felt like the bad guy and realized how arrogant and selfish he had been throughout most of his life.

I had to fall before I could finally see. The more I know, the less I have. Is this what those birds meant? I know now what I'm missing and I have less because I cannot make it happen now. That can't be it. Why do I still remember them and not the fall itself?

Lucas decided to use his telepathic communication with Josh so that his friend could hear him through the vibrations of his thoughts and understand the sincerity in his words.

I think you're an awesome friend, Josh. I'm sorry if I don't say it often, if not at all, but any girl would be lucky to have you. Especially Kendall.

Josh looked at Lucas surprisingly and gave him a convincing grin.

"I need to get used to that new ability of yours. Right now it's hard to understand. I am open to trying. You're right, all the girls of the world would love a guy like me. Handsome and full of charms. Even Kendall."

Despite pausing after saying her name, Josh was quick to revert back to his normal self.

"I should go. Don't forget to eat that yogurt. It cost me 2 dollars. You can pay me back after you get out of here."

Before leaving, Josh called in Melanie to help feed Lucas the snack. She smiled timidly at him, but he didn't seem to recognize her when she greeted him.

"Hi Josh, how are you?" Melanie asked simply, her fingers playing with her now short hair.

"Good, did you do something with your hair? It looks nice that way," Josh said aloud and signed bits of it, which made the young nurse blush pinker than a cherry blossom.

That's the best compliment she's going to get out of him, Lucas noted with a small smile.

As Melanie prepared to feed Lucas the yogurt, Josh turned back and said one last thing aloud.

"You'll get through this. If anyone can survive a near-death experience, it's the camps very own Mind Freak."

Josh used sign language for the last part and sounded out the rest in his usual monotone voice. Lucas gave his friend one last nod as he departed the ward.

He wouldn't be Josh without that sense of humor and a voice like someone making an announcement. I have to admit to myself; I'm getting used to both his humor and personality.

Melanie began feeding Lucas the yogurt as he read her mind.

He said my hair looks nice like this. Josh is so handsome. I like his hair a lot. I should have told him that. I wonder if he kept my number. If I knew he was coming, I would have had my hair up like last time. Maybe next time he comes, I'll have it that way and...

After that, her thoughts became incoherent, as Lucas grimaced in slight pain. He felt the back of his neck ache like a bee-sting. When Melanie asked if he was alright, he lied.

"It's nothing. I just need help moving my neck a bit."

The young nurse assisted him and ended her shift shortly thereafter.

Finally, it was the beginning of August when Henry arrived to fulfill his promise to Lucas. As he woke up quietly, the Camp Director made his presence known.

"It is time, my child."

Henry's night attire consisted of a grey robe with long sleeves that seemed to hang over his palms. He also wore worn-out slippers, with his face appearing ghostly in the dim moonlight. All these odd things weren't nearly as strange as the one thing that seemed to surprise Lucas.

Is that what I think it is?

The Camp Director had with him a very healthy looking puppy that appeared to be a newborn.

A puppy?

"Is he for me?" Lucas asked with a raised eyebrow.

Henry shook his head. The puppy seemed smaller than the Camp Director's hand. As he stroked the puppy's head, it yawned and closed its small fragile eyes.

"No, my child. It will help you to move once more."

Lucas looked even more bewildered.

Okay, but, how is a puppy supposed to help me walk again? Unless it has magical powers that can somehow fix every part of my body. At this point, that shouldn't surprise me.

The Camp Director proceeded to lay the small puppy on top of Lucas's chest. The puppy began to make a bed out of the young telepaths chest.

"This may help as well."

Henry pulled out a small little necklace from his robe pocket and put it around Lucas's neck.

Shelly's necklace! I didn't even realize it was gone.

"Where did you find it?" Lucas asked, gratefully.

Henry explained that Shelly's necklace had broken when Lucas fell and that he had it on his right hand.

"Mike managed to fix the chain so you can wear it once more. He is quite the capable young man," Henry said, in acknowledgment. "I assume it means something special to you."

Lucas nodded.

"It's my sisters," he confirmed. "I promised to give it back to her at the end of summer. Thank you for finding it, sir."

.

Henry's face grimaced. In the dim moonlit room, Lucas couldn't be sure if the Camp Director was frowning or scowling.

He looks upset by something. I don't know what.

"Now Lucas, what I am about to do is something that you can never tell anyone about. Very few know about this and it must remain that way," Henry explained reluctantly. "The price for such a power is more of a danger than the ability itself, so promise me that you will tell no one, not even your sister, of this night."

Despite promising, Lucas continued pondering the possible price the Camp Director mentioned for his power.

A price? Like money? What is he going to do, and how does the puppy fit into this?

The promise seemed to be enough for Henry as he nodded.

"This will be painless, my child, and will only last a moment."

He buried one hand underneath Lucas's hair, while his other hand was on the puppy. Then, the Camp Director became as stiff as stone. While Henry stood there, motionless, the young telepaths eyes never left the puppy. He felt the necklace around his neck, but couldn't reach out to touch it.

Just like Shelly; she's out of my reach.

The small puppy fell sound asleep against the young telepaths chest and its breathing was like a hearts beat. Lucas suddenly felt a wave-like feeling course through his body like vibrations.

Whoa... What's happening to me? I feel... I feel... like I'm waking up from a dream.

After a few minutes passed, Henry removed his hand from Lucas's head and the wave-like feeling faded.

Quickly, Henry gently lifted the sleeping puppy from Lucas's chest and stroked its small head.

"Try moving your toes now," he instructed the young telepath.

It didn't happen immediately, but when the feeling came back, Lucas could feel his toes wiggling.

I can move… I can move!

He cried out in happiness the same words that were in his mind. He could now move his arms and pick himself up. Abruptly, he winced to a halt when he realized how strained his body felt.

When Lucas lifted the quilt that was wrapped around him, he saw that, while his body still looked fine, he had a few minor bed sores and a thinner physique than before.

At least I can move again. That's all that matters, thought Lucas, happily.

He looked at the Camp Director, who appeared indifferent to Lucas's newfound happiness.

"Your body will heal soon enough, I promise," Henry assured him.

The Camp Director turned to leave with the puppy in hand, but he was stopped when Lucas pressed for an answer.

"Wait, sir. What was the price for this?" he asked, cautiously. "You said there might be a price for the power you used on me."

Henry paused before responding.

"There is none for this one time. The summer is nearly over, so take this moment to decide what you will say for your recovery and enjoy the remainder of your time here."

He smiled reassuringly and Lucas smiled back.

"Thank you for everything, sir," the young telepath said, as he lay on his bed, touching his sister's necklace with happy tear drops lining his cheeks. Lucas brushed both his tear-stained cheeks with his hands as tenderly as painting a blank canvas.

The Camp Director nodded and walked out of the room silently.

Lucas thought about how he would surprise everyone tomorrow with his miraculous recovery. His thoughts were so vibrant and alive, he feared he wouldn't get any sleep that night.

Tomorrow will be a new day where I can walk again, surprise my friends, and be a better version of myself, he thought dreamingly...

...As the Camp Director exited the ward with the sleeping puppy in his hands, he spotted a golden-haired man standing near the Infinite Forest with his arms crossed. He wore linen trousers with a dark leather coat that blended with the night. His footwear were green suede loafer slip-ons which looked new and fashionable. The man's shoulder-length gold hair appeared as bright as the full moon and fell in ringlets on either side of his head. The smile he showed off was as sharp as a sword.

When the man caught sight of Henry, his sharp grin widened and his arms stretched outwards as if he meant to embrace the Camp Director.

"Hello my good friend, Henry. It has been many moons, and not enough suns since our last encounter," the blond-haired man said in a not-so-friendly tone.

Henry nodded and responded in a similar manner, walking towards him.

"Indeed, my old friend. What brings you here?"

The golden-haired man scoffed and became serious.

"As much as I would love to catch up, I am here on business unfortunately. You never were much for small talk anyway."

The Camp Director gave the spiteful man a careful stare.

"Aren't you going to ask me why I did it," the golden-haired man snarled, impatiently.

385

Henry shrugged impassively, but decided to oblige his old friend.

"Why did you try to kill the boy, Alistair?" Henry asked, dully.

"Once I figured out who he was and his abilities as a telepath, something had to be done. I knew you wouldn't do anything about it because you still have plans for him. Plans like the ones you had for a certain other telepath who ended up being too much for even you to handle. Remember how that turned out? I thought I'd save you the trouble of dealing with that heartache again, my good friend."

Alistair said the last part with condescension, as Henry shook his head. His mind remained blank.

"It seems time has done no favors for your virtues, Alistair," his old friend said drearily. "You still act on impulse, without the forethought to consider what is to be, and what can be. I had hoped our years apart would have given you enough time to reflect upon this reckless nature of yours."

The Camp Director sounded remorseful, but Alistair seemed to catch the contradictive nature of his tone.

"You're one to talk. You've done things that even I'm shocked by. It was a mistake to save that little brat. All you've done now is set in motion something that could have been easily avoided."

The Camp Director sighed tirelessly.

"Well, it's not too late. I can still finish what I started and avoid at least one possible contingency."

Alistair pulled out a small pocket knife from his back pocket.

"This time I'll make sure he doesn't come back."

Henry shook his head.

"He will live. I have now seen to it," said Henry, with a cold tone.

This surprised Alistair, who gave his old friend an incredulous look.

"Really? And how did you—"

Alistair noticed the sleeping puppy in Henry's hands and his face turned serious.

"You used your power on him. Of course you did, you old fool. Does the boy know the cost of using it?"

Henry shook his head.

"No and it will remain that way for now."

Alistair sighed and shook his head.

"I swear, you used to be such a boy scout, Henry," said Alistair as he put the pocket knife away. "Maybe this is why we're not meant to live past a certain age; we become the very thing we swore against. Remember that girl with the weird looking feet? Your telepath basket case caught a glimpse of her. You'll be lucky if the fall made him forget all about that, but how long do you think you can keep hiding the truth from everyone else? About the failures and rejects who don't make the final cut."

Henry only looked at the man with impassive eyes and stroked the soft head of the sleeping puppy.

"When the time comes, Lucas and everyone in this camp will fall into place. Do you doubt what I have foreseen?"

"It's not about that and you know it. I did what I thought needed to be done at the time, and you can't tell me that I'm wrong about him. I watched that boy's behavior in the forest. He's reckless, dangerous, and a liability to those around him. The only difference between him and Jacob is that one of them can still be reared. But which one will break first? Your mind freak, or mine?"

"Jacob was broken long before he stepped foot in my camp. I did my best to find a path suitable for him, even if it wasn't what he wanted. Lucas desires a place to belong, to understand himself. He has a moral compass, while Jacob only has immoral beliefs about the human race."

Alistair scoffed and glared at the Camp Director.

"I can't say I blame him. You and I have been around long enough to know how bad people can be and most are not worth saving. Speaking of that, how many do you still think are out here? Of the kids who actually learn to control their abilities vs. the ones who fail? You've had me on clean up duty for far too long and now that there's a new telepath in play, still living I want to add, Jacob will start to make waves once he finds out, and he <u>will</u> find out. The question will be: How many more will fail so the few can succeed?"

When Henry did not yield an answer or reaction over the golden-haired man's comment, Alistair continued.

"You know what I think? I think it's easier for you to manipulate these kids in broad daylight, unlike me who operates within the shadows. If the boot fits, am I right? Except you wear yours close to your chest. If I could feel pity, I don't know who I would feel it for more; that self-entitled son of yours, or your pet telepath who was better being put down like a rabid dog. What I did was an act of mercy compared to what you want for him."

Henry chose to ignore what his old friend said. He appeared dazed then, as if his age were finally catching up to him.

"He is young and his future is still boundless with possibilities unforeseen," said Henry, stiffly. "Every failure paves the way for a succession. That is my belief on how Jacob and Lucas will differ from each other. They are as we once were in that way and both must face each other for what is to come."

Alistair appeared uneasy now.

"Something is off about you. You're drained more than you're letting on. More than that power of yours should have taken had you used it like before. What's different? A couple years ago, you asked me to work here with you and to help bring in more children to be trained for their abilities. I never gave you an answer, but I must admit that I almost considered the idea. Only for you to eventually turn around and tell me I was better suited to keep Jacob busy while you herded these new brats with promises of grandeur. Why did you make me feel false hope after saying you wanted nothing to do with me?"

Henry sighed and pinched the bridge of his nose.

"You know all that is necessary at this point. Anything else would be irrelevant to you. It's as you say; I keep my boots close to my chest. It must be that way in order for everyone to know nothing and for everything to happen as it should."

Alistair was no longer in a sardonic mood. He understood the gravity of this situation better than he wanted to show.

"You are playing a very dangerous game, Henry. If your gamble is wrong, it won't be like last time. By allowing that kids mind to get strong enough to rival Jacobs, you will have two problems, or one solution. You can't have two solutions since it's too late for that now."

Henry neither agreed nor disagreed.

"Regardless of the outcome, I've done enough meddling for one night. We both have. Now, if you would kindly exit the premises. The sun will be up in a few hours and this little puppy deserves its rest amongst the others. If you wish to talk further, you may return with Boris's supervision."

As Henry walked off towards his home, Alistair sighed and stared out into the nighttime sky longingly. The Camp Director heard his old friend's last words.

"You stubborn old fool. For your sake alone, I hope your right about all this…"

Chapter 12

Lucky Luke

Lucas awoke early the next morning eager to surprise his friends and the whole camp with his amazing recovery.

They're going to be so surprised. They'll think I have a new power because of this, he thought with a smile. *Finally, things are going my way.* Lucas had three days left to enjoy before the end of summer camp and he planned to seize them.

The young telepath tried to climb out of the hospital bed, but found that he had difficulty due to being bedridden for nearly a month.

Argh! My body feels so sore and stiff. My arms and legs feel loose, like they are going to come off if I move them too much.

When the doctor of the ward insisted that he use crutches to walk, Lucas tried to leave without them. Unfortunately, he couldn't make it past the exit without falling over himself.

In my defense, the floor does feel slippery. They probably mopped it recently, so it's not my fault I fell...again.

Before leaving, Lucas said goodbye to Melanie and wished her well for the rest of her internship.

"I don't know how it happened, but I'm so happy for you, Lucas. Take care of yourself," the young intern nurse said, happily. When the morning sun's rays touched Melanie's face, the young telepath ended up blushing at the sight of her.

What is Josh thinking? If I wasn't already interested in Vanessa, or if Ashley didn't have a thing for me, Melanie could be a close third maybe?

Lucas felt sweat from the warm morning sun burning against him and his eyes hurt from having to readjust to the real deal.

The most sunlight I got was from when the curtains were drawn open in my room. That made me feel like a houseplant.

He wore his most comfortable clothing, with a new blue cabin shirt since his red sweater had been destroyed from the fall.

And it was my favorite sweater, Lucas thought with a frown.

He noticed the end result of the rain that had poured heavily in the camp during the last few days. Lucas avoided stepping on mud puddles or going near the younger campers who were playing in them. Some of the counselors in attendance, such as Betty and Marcus, tried to keep the kids from messing with the puddles too much. To his surprise, the young telepath saw fewer kids around the camp than the start of the summer.

I wonder why that is, Lucas pondered. *Maybe some are in their cabins or the cafeteria right now. I remember it was a lot livelier than this back in June.*

As he continued to walk, he was forced to steady himself every few seconds.

The doctor said this will help build my strength back up. If Henry could heal my body, I wonder why he didn't also give me back my physical strength. I guess it did seem too easy.

As he walked by the cabins, he spotted in-between the Kruel Kingdom and the Lost Lord cabins a young boy crying. He had his back turned so Lucas could not see who he was. He walked carefully towards the youth and it didn't take long for him to recognize the cabin mate he least liked.

Gary? And he's crying?

"Gary? And you're crying?" Lucas heard himself say aloud, impulsively. The young dark-skinned youth noticed him and quickly made himself look presentable as if he were looking into a mirror.

"I wasn't crying. I was wiping sand from my eyes," Gary insisted, as his eyes adjusted to the sight of Lucas. "Hey, wait a second, you're supposed to be in the hospital ward. And you're walking! How is that possible?"

I better come up with a good explanation and fast. Maybe something cool like, 'My new power is I can heal after a while' or 'I'm invincible'. No, even he's not stupid enough to believe that.

"I just needed time to heal and eventually my body did the rest. A real mind over matter deal here. Like our cabin words."

Lucas hoped that the explanation was convincing enough, but upon reading Gary's mind, he realized it wasn't.

I saw how badly injured he was the first time they found him. No one thought he would live, let alone get out of that bed. He's definitely hiding something.

"If that's true, then why are you using crutches to walk? Also, this might be premature, but I have a bone to pick with you."

The young telepath looked confused by this until Gary clarified.

"After you read my mind during training and said what I was thinking out loud, that friend of yours Josh went around and told anyone who would hear him what you said I thought. Eventually, Alexia and her goons heard about it and they started picking on me for the rest of the summer. He-Art Man would have been a cool superhero name by the way. Thanks for ruining that too."

Lucas felt remorseful and said with sincerity, "I'm really sorry, Gary. That wasn't my intention."

When Gary didn't look like he believed him, Lucas continued. "I shouldn't have used my powers on you like that. I felt bad after what happened, but it just seemed like it was what everyone wanted me to do at the time."

"Going by other people's opinions isn't the best way to judge someone," Gary pointed out, a fact Lucas couldn't deny. "Look, it's whatever, if you're sorry, then that's good enough for me. But I don't want to be in a place that is just as bad as the real world. In case you missed the part about my heart condition, it's not good for me to be stressed out and to be humiliated the way I was. If that's what I have to look forward to by being here, then I won't come back next year. Even if I don't exactly have it great back home either."

Just as Mike seemed to accept this idea, Lucas found a way to insert a new one in him.

"You don't have to leave," the young telepath insisted. "You can stay here and try to be a new person when you return next summer. People here, I feel, have a short memory when it comes to anything less than what I did during my time here. Of all the places I've been to in my life, this is the most accepting of everyone. Don't give up on being here, alright? If you had told me this before my accident, I would have been with you on the first non-skeletal taxi cab out of here. Now, as crazy as it sounds, I think of this place as a second home. I hope, in time, that you can see it that way too. Who knows? It could become your main home eventually."

Gary considered this and his thoughts confirmed that Lucas's words swayed him.

"Alright, I'll give this place another shot next year," Gary said. "Maybe we'll get more girls our age coming here and more chances for me to have that summer romance experience. I remember that girl who likes you. The blonde one you're always talking to. She was so excited to go to that dance with you. Then, when Henry cancelled it, she was really sad; not because of the dance, but because of what happened to you."

The young telepath wished he hadn't known that. It made him feel extremely guilty about the whole thing.

I didn't mean to hurt her or Vanessa. If I had gone to the dance, I never would have been put in the hospital, and Henry wouldn't have had to help me the way he did.

"Thank you for talking to me, Lucas," Gary said with a smile, as he extended his fist towards the young telepath. "I'm glad your back on your feet again and I hope going forward we can be real friends. I still don't like Josh though. For a guy who can't hear his own voice, he acts like someone who enjoys it too much."

Lucas laughed, *Sounds like someone else I know,* and bumped his fist with Gary's.

"Yeah, Josh can be a handful, but deep down he's a good guy. Hopefully one day you'll see that."

Gary seemed to appreciate the young telepaths complimenting words, as he gave him a soft pat on the back.

They say people can't change overnight, but maybe they can if they have the right reason.

After leaving Gary, Lucas walked past the cabins and ended up coming across the orange team. To his dismay, Alexia was among them. She looked similar to her appearance from earlier in the summer. She was notably more buffer, had her curly hair tied back, and wore her signature camp tank top shirt. The young telepath looked at the hand that had been injured during the Relic game, only to find that it looked normal again.

She probably had a lot of time to work out during the summer. No doubt from Richardson and Alexander's intense training. It's good to see that hand of hers has healed. So long as she doesn't try to swing that war hammer at me again.

He half-expected her to approach him with her goons and beat the life out of him. Instead, she came alone.

That's strange, does she think she can take me on alone looking like this? What kind of dumb thought is that? If I have to I can use my power to stop her like before or make her think she's lighter than air.

The orange team members looked at her expectantly, like they were waiting for her to kill him. When the camp bully reached him, she spoke in a low voice.

"I thought you couldn't move. Everyone said you'd never walk out of that hospital?" the camp bully asked skeptically.

"Turns out it wasn't as bad as everyone thought," Lucas heard himself lie.

That's less convincing than what I told Gary.

"Look, I have a reputation to maintain as the Camp Bully and you humiliated me during the Relic game. I don't believe in beating up people in crutches, so I'm going to yell your brains out and you're going to pretend to be a scrawny little coward. After that, we'll call it even."

Lucas nodded, but before that he had one request.

"Please stop picking on Gary. Reading his mind was me being stupid and I regret it very much. I was able to talk him into coming back here next year and I want him to feel good about the idea."

Alexia agreed and proceeded with the charade.

"So you think you're better than me, Twig? I will show you how wrong you are!"

To his surprise, she pushed him softly. Lucas staggered backwards and even fell down to add dramatic effect. The orange team members roared with laughter and cheered for Alexia. She walked back to the team, as he limped away and pretended to be embarrassed.

I don't mind. Besides, she needs it. I get the feeling it's more than just about her reputation.

As the orange team continued to chant Alexia's name like a chorus, Lucas saw, to his shock, someone he hadn't recalled until this moment.

Orange teams orb wielder!

The young boy appeared fine and quite lively in Lucas's view. It made him almost recall something vital that he had forgotten. Before he could, the Camp Guardian saw him, but did not believe what he was seeing. He ran towards Lucas and was excited enough to wrap him up in a huge tight hug.

"Lucas, you are walking. It's a miracle. You are walking on two feet!" the monster exclaimed in delight.

Technically it's more like four feet with these crutches.

Lucas smiled as the giant monster hugged him, but he had to remind Boris that he was still physically weak. In the excitement, he had dropped his crutches.

"Thank you, Boris," Lucas said. "I am so sorry for-"

Before he could finish what he said, the Camp Guardian stopped him short.

"The way I remember it, you got lost on your way back to camp. It was pouring hard that day so you ended up in the field and slipped badly enough to have that accident. No one else needs to know the rest," the Camp Guardian said, giving the young telepath a soft pat on the shoulder.

He knows the truth, Lucas realized as he read Boris's mind, *but he doesn't care to make me feel worse for it.*

"How is this possible? What miracle was performed to make this happen?"

Lucas wasn't sure if Boris knew about Henry's ability. After reading his mind, he decided on what was best to say.

"It just took some patience to happen and it was worth it," Lucas heard himself say, calmly.

As the Camp Guardian helped him walk, other campers gathered around to see Lucas on his feet again. They all had looks ranging from delight, to disbelief, to pure shock.

They can't believe what they're seeing either. I don't blame them. I'm the one who's healed and I still can't believe it worked without a price to pay, Lucas thought, happily.

Then he heard his name being projected by Josh as he emerged from the crowd with Ashley following behind him. They looked as perplexed as the rest of the kids. Instead of standing in awe, they ran to his side and embraced him.

"You're moving again, Luke. That's amazing. No, another word. Lucky. You're really lucky. We should call you Lucky Luke! It has a nice ring to it, don't you think," Josh quipped with a smirk.

Lucas heard some of the surrounding campers saying the new name amongst each other in a whisper before taking up the chant as if it was contagious.

"Lucky Luke, Lucky Luke, Lucky Luke, Lucky Luke, Lucky Luke!"

The young telepath blushed as Ashley, Josh, and even Daniel began chanting the name while smiling at him.

Lucky Luke? Just put an F before Luke and it will be Fluke. Lucky Fluke. That sounds more appropriate given the way I look right now.

Lucas kept this thought to himself, as the excitement died down. Ashley and Josh wanted to help him walk, but the young telepath insisted on making the trip to Henry's home alone. Despite his wishes, Daniel volunteered to help accompany him.

"I knew you'd get out of that ward eventually," the Camp Director's son said with a wink. "I don't know how you did it, but I am glad for it. Truly. You're going to see my father?"

I'm that obvious, Lucas thought, irritably.

"I just want to talk to him about going home soon," the young telepath said. "That's all I want right now."

Daniel nodded and caught Lucas as he was about to fall.

"You admire my father, don't you?"

Lucas did not know how to answer this question.

Yes, I do, Lucas thought of as one answer. *I hardly know anything about him. He's been kind to me since I've been here. He's the reason I'm not in a bed anymore.*

Instead, the young telepath shrugged and came up with a different response.

"He's a great man," Lucas decided. "He made a place to help people like us to control our abilities and help us be better for it."

Daniel considered this response before offering his own.

"You know, you're right. My father made this camp with the intention of helping others like us. I only wish he would have prioritized his duties to me and my mother when she was alive. He must mean well if everyone here thinks so highly of him. Sometimes there are two sides to every story and my side is I know him differently than the rest of you."

Lucas could feel the turmoil inside Daniel. The intensity of those emotions was enough to make him feel unbalanced like before.

These thoughts and feelings are not mine… not mine…

"I think I can make the rest of the way on my own, please," Lucas heard himself say, to Daniel's surprise. The Camp Counselor took a moment, looking even more taken aback by the comment. Ultimately, he relented.

"I understand you know. Just some friendly advice, Lucas, because I do like you and I don't want to see you get hurt any further. My father is better at making promises than keeping them. If you're not careful, he'll eventually disappoint you too. Also, I know what my father says about your accident isn't true. The only way you could have been out there is if you were somewhere you weren't supposed to be. I hope I'm wrong about that, because Ashley likes you a lot. Did you know that?"

Lucas nodded while Daniel shook his head.

"But you like Vanessa. So do me a favor and don't lie to Ashley. She's like a little sister to me and she deserves to be someone's first choice, not their second. I'm sure you'd feel the same way about your own sister."

Of course I would, Lucas thought. *That's still a weird comparison, but I rather not turn it into an argument.* Instead of pressing the issue, the young telepath just nodded and hoped a silent response would end the conversation sooner.

Without meaning to, Lucas ended up hearing Daniel's thoughts and they showed a different side of how he viewed him.

I don't understand him. Most of the kids here would love to talk to me and hang out with me. I worked hard to get to where I'm at. Despite being the Camp Director's son, I was never the center of attention like Lucas is. All he did to get people to like him was being here. If my father showed me this kind of attention when I was still a camper, things would have been so much different between us.

"I'll see you next year, Lucas," the Camp Counselor said with a sad expression. "I'm sorry we didn't get to spend more time together during training. Maybe next year I can ask my father to let me train you and your friends again."

Lucas nodded, but as the Camp Director's son walked away, he was seized by words he wanted to say aloud for him.

I'm sorry, the young telepath heard himself think. *I know you just want to be heard the way everyone deserves. It isn't right how Henry treats you and that you just want to be closer to him. I feel what you feel, and that's why it's hard for me to talk to you. I want us to be on better terms, I just don't know how to tell you. I wish I could say these words aloud, but I'm afraid of how you'd take it. So, I'll just keep it to myself.*

After Daniel was gone, Lucas made his way to the Camp Director's home. Despite being closer to his destination than he was before, the young telepath still found himself moving progressively slow and hated every moment of using the crutches.

It's a small price to pay for being able to leave that bed. I just hope by the time I go home, I can lose the crutches or else Shelly and my parents will definitely not let me come back here next summer.

He stared down at his body and legs, and even though it looked like the accident never happened, the pain inside reminded him that it was no dream. Every step he took was a new muscle awakening again for the first time in a while.

Henry told me my body would heal eventually and he hasn't been wrong yet.

When Lucas finally reached the door to the Camp Director's home, he had trouble reaching for the handle without falling again. Luckily, Boris was nearby and caught him.

Before he could enter, Lucas heard noises coming from the front door of Henry's office.

"Who's in there with him?" Lucas asked the Camp Guardian.

Boris had a solemn look with no a hint of a smile.

"A man named Alistair. He's an old acquaintance of Camp Director James. I do not like that man. Be wary of him."

Without even being aware of it, Lucas felt goosebumps prickling his skin at the very name.

Why am I scared of someone I don't even know? Something about that name is like the feeling I get when I'm anxious around too many people.

Boris did not notice Lucas's uneasy demeanor as the young telepath recovered and brushed the uncomfortable thought behind him.

"Why don't you trust Henry's friend?"

"He talks too much," the Camp Guardian said, to Lucas's curiosity. "People who talk too much tend to think their opinion matters more than the other person. He also called me the Hunchback of Notre Dame," Boris said the last part in annoyance.

This guy sounds like a piece of work, Lucas thought to himself. *I wonder what his relationship is with Henry. Maybe he knows more about him than anyone else.*

The young telepath decided to wait until he was sure the noise died down before attempting to enter. Rather than eavesdrop, he decided to talk to the Camp Guardian to pass the time.

"What do you like to do for fun?"

The Camp Guardian thought for a moment before answering.

"When I am not working, which is rarely, I have a library collection that Henry helped me assemble from works such as Edgar Allen Poe, Joseph Conrad, James Joyce, Oscar Wilde, and Virginia Woolf to name a few. You may have noticed it in his office. My favorite book is The Metamorphosis. It's the story of a man who awakens as a humanoid insect and is driven into despair over his family's financial desperation and their inability to accept his new form. It is a tale that gives me familiarity."

I feel like that's the plot of a movie I've heard of, but never seen, Lucas wanted to mention, but kept it to himself. *How does the guy turn into an insect? Is it literal or metaphorical? Either way, it sounds interesting. Sad though, that he wants to provide for a family that won't accept him. Like how Boris protects a camp that will never truly welcome him.*

Just as he was about to ask more about the story, Lucas heard the door open. He saw the man named Alistair exit the house. His golden hair glistened as brightly as the sun and his youthful appearance made him look like he was as old as Daniel.

His hair is long enough to be like what a girl would have. He looks like he just got back from attending a rock concert, Lucas mused.

Alistair stood at almost six feet tall. He had a narrowed nose with wide piercing green eyes that looked almost animalistic.

He doesn't look like a nice person. Like Boris said; a guy who talks too much usually thinks they are better than everyone else. I don't have to read his mind to know that.

The golden-haired man brushed past Lucas and towards the Camp Guardian, shooting the boy an ominous glance.

He looks familiar. I just can't figure out why or from where?

"Hey there, Monster Mash," Alistair said to the Camp Guardian, who shot him a deadly look. "Don't worry, I'll be out of your scalp in a moment, since hair isn't your strong suit. If you want, you can always try wearing a wig or getting hair implants. In case you don't know what that is, it's when they give you fake hair that sticks. So for you, I'm sure they'd last long enough to get someone's attention."

The Camp Guardian did not reply, as Alistair turned back to look at Lucas. Seeing the young telepath made his smile widen.

"You must be this camp's young telepath I've heard so much about and Henry's pet project. He says you show great promise, but from where I'm standing, you look like if you take another step further you'll fall right on your face."

As the golden-haired man spoke, Lucas started to shake, his hand's quivering and fingers trailing like a fish on dry land.

Why am I so afraid? Boris is here and so is Henry. Who is this guy?

Lucas tried futilely to calm himself with comforting assurances.

Henry and Boris will protect me if this guy tries anything. I'll be home in a few days.

Even though Alistair noticed his fear, he decided to ignore it.

"After your therapy session with Henry, I would like the chance to talk to you as well. I'm not certified in the art of pretending to be nice so don't expect that from me. It's in your best interest to hear what I have to say."

The Camp Director appeared suddenly and Alistair directed his attention towards him.

"I promise to be on my best behavior. If you still don't trust me, which I won't be offended by, you can always tell the Thing here to try and crush me. What exactly does he do all day? Just look at flowers and reminisce about the good o'l days when he threw kids into lakes?"

The Camp Guardian looked near the end of his patience. When he turned to Henry, the Camp Director cautioned him.

"Very well, Alistair. You may remain long enough to speak to Lucas once we finish discussing matters. In the future, please refrain from insulting Boris. He is a valued member of this camp and a dear friend."

The Camp Guardian was touched by this and Lucas could tell that Alistair was particularly bothered by the last part.

I'll bet he's thinking, "How dare he call that monster a 'dear friend'?"

Instead of making his thoughts known, Alistair scoffed in Boris's direction.

"Fine, thank you for indulging me. I know it can be tiring, but admit it; you've missed me as much as I've longed for you."

Henry did not give his old friend a response and turned his attention to the young telepath.

"Let us talk, Lucas."

He knows me so well at this point.

Lucas nodded and walked into the Camp Director's office.

The young telepath heard Alistair call out and say, "Don't take all day. I got places to be too."

Now I see why Boris hates the guy; he talks way too much.

In his anxious state, he began to hyper focus on how Henry did not call him 'child' or 'son' this time. It was a feeling he suddenly desired.

I wonder why? I mean, I know it's more of a polite formal thing, but I liked it.

Lucas steadied himself on the seat across from his desk and lay his crutches to the side. Before he could speak first, Henry interjected with a random question in an uncharacteristically concerned tone.

"Do you believe this to be a suitable welcoming gift for April?"

Henry was referring to a knitted pink sweater with the picture of a bunny embroiled in the middle. The fabric looked recently made, and professionally done.

I got to admit, that's nicer than something I'd find in a store.

"It looks nice, sir," Lucas admitted. "But who's April?"

"Mike's younger sister. She will be joining us for camp next year. Has he not told you?"

Lucas shook his head.

Wait a second. I thought her name was Sapphire?

"I thought Mike's sister is named Sapphire... sir?"

Henry seemed dazed then, as if he had just awoken from a bad dream. After a few seconds, he regained himself

"Yes... my mistake. Sapphire is what I must have said. You probably misheard the month of which she was born in. That being April."

Lucas supposed that was true.

Yeah, it must be. Why else would he call her by another name?

"How old is Sapphire?"

"I believe she is nine years old."

Nine years old, Lucas thought, perplexedly. *I don't know any nine year olds who would like a pink sweater with a bunny on it.*

Henry seemed to read Lucas's expression and smiled thinly.

"I understand you wanted to see me about something?"

Lucas nodded and sat down calmly.

"I just wanted to say I would really love the chance to come back again next year and take my training more seriously. But first, I need to go home and make things right there. I've already been away longer than I had hoped and my sister doesn't know anything that's happened to me. I haven't been able to text or call her all summer."

Henry nodded and folded his hands together. It perplexed Lucas to look at the Camp Director's fatigued expression. Having an animated appearance prior to Lucas's accident, Henry's expression now seemed pained and sadder.

There's something he's not telling me. I just can't figure it out, Lucas thought with concern. *Either he's overworked himself or something is bothering him.*

"Yes, we spoke of this before," the Camp Director recalled. "Are you really in such a hurry to leave all your new friends behind?"

Lucas shook his head, feeling as if he had offended the Camp Director, until the elderly man began to chuckle softly.

"How can I explain what happened to me? Should I lie and say it was part of the process of getting better?"

Suddenly, Lucas himself felt fatigued. His stomach growled like a wolf barring its teeth and his left eye-lid twitched.

I feel anxious. Like I want to jump up and down for no reason at all, he thought, irritably.

After a moment, Lucas breathed steadily and calmed himself.

"You will tell them what you must," said Henry, calmly. "I'm confident you will make the right choice, my child."

Lucas nodded and felt a sense of warmness return to him.

Now I know what I was missing.

"Do you think they can ever forgive me for how I left?"

The thought sounded far-fetched, even impossible.

My parents won't forgive me and Shelly may not either. If anything, she's probably just worried about why I haven't called or texted her back all summer.

He hoped that the Camp Director would have something positive to say about this.

To his disappointment, Henry only shrugged.

"I do not know, Lucas. They are your parents. You should know them better than that."

The young telepath's face fell as he realized the truth.

I honestly don't know if they'd forgive me. I still have the letter I wrote for my dad for Father's Day. Maybe if he sees that, he'll understand that I am doing better now.

"That's the thing, Henry...I don't know my parents better than that. I thought I did. They sent me here because I always caused trouble for them. I wasn't trying to be bad. I just didn't know how to be good. I don't know how to explain it..."

Henry smiled thinly and shook his head.

"I don't believe that, not for one second. You have shown no such trouble or bad intent in your time here and for that you have my admiration."

Lucas felt honored to be trusted by Henry, but still felt guilty.

I have to tell him the truth, even if I get kicked out for it. The whole truth.

"I can't lie to you, sir. I did more than just try to run away from camp. Before..."

Lucas inhaled, and sighed.

"Before the accident, I..."

"...Used your powers on Josh and ran away from camp after Mike tried to stop you," Henry finished for him in an almost complete translation from his mind.

Lucas nodded shamefully and was amazed that the Camp Director already knew.

How did he know? I thought Mike and Josh were going to keep that to themselves?

"Mike came to me the day after you were found and explained what transpired. You should know he felt tremendous guilt. It took seeing you awake the first time for him to finally be at ease. What I wish to understand, Lucas, is why you tried to leave when you could have simply come to me and everything would have been resolved?"

Lucas shrugged and drew himself backwards to rest his aching body.

"I was angry, sad, and scared because I didn't want you to be disappointed by me," Lucas confessed. "I was afraid that if you knew I broke the rules, you'd kick me out and I'd have nowhere else to go."

"We all make mistakes, Lucas. It's not about how many mistakes we make; it's about how many times we learn from each one to prevent the number of future misunderstandings. You are young, so do not be ashamed of your faults. What you must do is strive to be better for yourself. Do not allow one bad mistake to overcloud the good that you have accomplished in your time here," Henry instilled on Lucas.

"Bill told me that what I did could have done permanent damage to Josh. Is that true?"

The Camp Director shrugged.

"I don't know. Regardless, I do not believe that you meant to cause him harm, correct?"

Lucas agreed, but it didn't make him feel any better.

I still broke the rules, Lucas thought miserably. *He should be sending me packing and telling me never to return for what I've done.*

"I still broke the rules, sir. I'm not like Jacob, but I could be. That's what no one here wants to admit. I don't want everyone to look at me in that way; the way they're scared of talking about Jacob. I understand if I'm too much trouble to invite back to camp..."

"Speak no more of this nonsense, my child" Henry said to Lucas's surprise. "Having you here has been quite the experience. One I have not seen in a long time. After all, you made history. Winning for the yellow team, discovering the rare flower, and learning about your abilities at a faster rate than most of the campers here. That alone should convince you of your place here. You made an error in judgment, yes, but you have also made such wonderful progress as well. With all that said, I believe I can forgive you for making a hasty decision."

Lucas was still unsure of himself and decided to bring up something else that was bothering him.

"I was able to talk to Josh in my mind. Usually I can hear the thoughts of people just fine, but they can't hear me thinking. I was able to talk to Josh and he heard me through what he thought was sound. How is that possible?"

Henry thought for a moment and the young telepath feared he wouldn't get an answer, until he saw the Camp Director's expression change.

"When you controlled Josh's mind, you made it so that you two now have a telepathic bond," Henry revealed. "It's not uncommon for this to happen to a telepath such as yourself. In fact, every mind you read is a backdoor that is opened and closed each time you use it. When you control someone's mind, however, the backdoor remains open and is left vulnerable to another with abilities like yours."

That's what Bill meant when he said that, Lucas realized in dismay.

"The only other person I've mind-controlled in my time here was Alexia. Would I be able to talk to her in my mind?"

Henry shook his head.

"It depends on the individuals bond with the telepath. In this case, you and Josh are good friends, while you and Alexia are foes. Think of the emotional states you were in when confronting both friend and foe. With Josh, you were desperate for him to listen to you, while with Alexia you were fearful for your own survival. Your sense of control on Alexia was absolute, because of the immediacy of it. In contrast, for Josh it waned because of your apprehension."

Lucas pondered this information and realized there was a lot more to his abilities than he ever imagined.

I can see why it takes some of these kids' years to master one or two of their abilities. Mine sounds like it will be a lifelong process.

Brushing the thought aside, Lucas decided to try and seize the moment of silence by asking the Camp Director a personal question.

"Do you have any siblings? A brother, or a sister?"

Henry did not answer the question like Lucas had hoped. Instead, he looked at his clock before returning his eyes to him.

Too bad I can't read his mind, thought Lucas with a frown.

"You should go and spend the short time you have remaining with your friends. I expect you'll want to go home as soon as possible."

Lucas nodded, but felt slightly disappointed.

Why won't he tell me anything? Doesn't he trust me? What more do I have to do?

"You're never going to tell me anything about yourself are you, sir?" said Lucas, a scowl forming in his face.

Henry looked at him with a calm expression.

"Understand that everything I do is for the good of this camp, and for the safety of everyone in it, Lucas. Our past, mine included, are inconsequential for what is to come. Until then, enjoy your youth, your friends, and loved ones. Time spent on loved ones is never wasted."

Even though he wanted to object and did not understand why Henry was being so secretive, Lucas had no choice but to accept the way the Camp Director wanted things to be.

I wish he trusted me more. He trusted me enough to show me his power, but I think that's as much as I am going to get out of him for now.

As Lucas was about to leave, Henry raised a hand and stopped him.

"You and your team will be receiving ten beads during a special ceremony we will be having before everyone leaves for the summer. Even so, I would like to give you this particular one personally because of its relevance."

He pulled out a small olive-colored bead from his top drawer.

It looked to be the size of a marble and in the middle was carved the initials 'L.F.'.

L.F. Lucas Fargo, he realized, happily.

He smiled brightly as Henry got a piece of silk string to tie the bead on.

"I had it especially made for you, my son, to commemorate this momentous occasion."

He fastened the bracelet over his right wrist and when he finished the Camp Director returned to his desk.

"It has been a pleasure to have watched over you this summer and I hope to see you again next year," said Henry with a warm smile.

I hope so too. Besides returning home, I want to come back here again next year.

After thanking Henry for everything, Lucas got his crutches and moved towards the exit. Before leaving, he turned back to look at the room. It was in that moment when he realized where his second home was.

I want to come back not just to see Henry again and my friends, but for myself. This camp has become more of a home to me than I thought it would be. These abilities I have need to be controlled and to be mastered. Even if Shelly isn't an Alter Child, maybe Henry will let her come for a bit. First I have to make things right between my parents. After that, we'll see.

When Lucas exited the Camp Director's home, he saw, to his dismay that the golden-haired man was indeed waiting for him.

I better go see what's going on.

Alistair was talking with Boris, who was not talking back to him. The Camp Guardian looked rather irritated by the words the talkative man was saying.

Boris's thoughts are all about him wanting to beat the guy senseless. I'd really like to see that happen.

As Lucas got closer, he started to hear what the golden-haired man was saying. He was asking the Camp Guardian if he was ugly before or after he was reanimated.

If it weren't for the fact that Henry knows this guy, I'm sure he wouldn't be allowed to be here, let alone to talk to me. Still, there's something about him that's familiar somehow...

Alistair turned his attention in the young telepath's direction.

"Well, if it isn't Lucky Luke. You know, if you put an F before Luke it becomes fluke. I think that sounds better, don't you agree? Lucky Fluke."

That's exactly what I thought and somehow, he found a way to ruin that.

Lucas tried to avoid eye contact with Alistair and held tightly to his crutches to avoid falling in front of him and Boris.

"You know me?" Lucas asked in a whispered tone.

Alistair heard him though and shook his head.

"Not really. Truth be told, I don't care to know you. I heard you can read and control minds. It's not every day a telepath becomes known to our world. What's even more impressive is you haven't gone mad with your power yet."

While Lucas didn't know the man standing in-front of him, there was a part hidden deep within the young telepath that knew Alistair was dangerous and untrustworthy. His heart began to pump rapidly and his fists clenched against his crutches.

That does it. Let's see if I can read and control his mind.

When he tried though, Lucas felt a sharp pain surge through him as if his head were burning from within. Boris noticed his pained face and moved forward to aid him.

"Are you alright, Lucas? Perhaps I should take you back to your cabin?"

Lucas shook his head and regained himself.

"No, I'm alright. Let's get this over with; what did you want to ask me?"

He tried to say this calmly, but it came off as more harshly than he intended.

"Nothing of consequence. Just one question. One inconsequential question. Then I'll be out of your mess of a hair."

The young telepath waited for the question and looked at the Camp Guardian, then back to Alistair.

"How far along are you with this ability of yours? The way to judge a telepaths abilities is in how they use it, like any other ability you'll find in this camp. What I want to know is can you differentiate between what you see with what you know is real? It's an important distinction and one you must be able to make. Otherwise, your powers won't work for you."

Lucas was puzzled, as if he didn't understand the question and words being spoken.

"I know what's real and I know who I am," Lucas answered, plainly. "I won't lose myself to my abilities the way Jacob did if that's what you're worried about."

"I am worried about that, but not for your sake. Your life isn't the only one that's effected by the choices you make."

Lucas wasn't entirely sure what Alistair meant by this. Being unable to read his mind made him even more anxious than before.

Argh! I can't think straight. Where is this pain coming from?

When he didn't answer immediately, Alistair finally sighed and shook his head.

"Well if you believe in your own sanity and that's good enough for Henry, it will have to suffice for now. Riddle me this; suppose you run into Jacob at some point because you two are of like minds. How will you deal with him and keep him from harming those closest to you."

"You asked your question before and I answered," Lucas barked back. "You should go now or I'll show you what I can do."

If my powers won't work on him, what can I actually do?

Alistair gave him a snide grin and nodded.

"If it were up to me, you seem like more trouble than your worth," said Alistair, scornfully. "A kid like you, with what you have, you're the next Jacob just waiting to happen.

The difference between you two is that he'd make what you can do look like parlor tricks in comparison."

He talks about me like he knows who I am. How can that be?

Despite feeling tension building up inside him, Lucas kept his nerves in check for the moment. The Camp Guardian made his presence known and that Alistair's time was up.

"I'll make this as clear as day for you; it's not you I'm concerned with, it's Henry. If you do anything to derail him in anyway, you won't be able to think twice about it. That's not a threat, boy; it's a deadly promise."

In an instant, the golden-haired man disappeared faster than the time it took the young telepath to blink. He was engulfed in what looked like a purple mist.

That happened faster than how Ashley runs, Lucas pondered.

Once he was gone, Boris grumbled in irritation.

"I cannot understand why Henry deals with that man. I'd like to teach him a thing or two about shutting up for once," Boris remarked, irritably.

Lucas tried to laugh, but felt very queasy.

My hands. Ouch!

His palms had small nail-cuts from when he had clenched his fists while Alistair had spoken to him.

"I don't know who he is, but I hate him already," remarked Lucas, half-heartedly.

Boris nodded in agreement and patted the young telepath's shoulder.

"I'm happy to have met you, Lucas Fargo. It was... more fun with you here," Boris said with a thin smile. "Like Henry, you're a kind soul."

When they finished parting ways, the monster solemnly returned to his post as Lucas continued to limp even with the crutches helping him. He proceeded to the

415

cabins where he saw Vanessa outside of her respective one. She sat on one of the benches near the main pavilion alone.

She looks sad. I wonder why.

This was the first time he saw her since waking up from his coma. He thought about why she hadn't come to visit him while he was in the ward.

I get the feeling it's because of something I did and can't remember doing.

When Vanessa saw him, she looked at him sullenly.

"What do you want?" snarled Vanessa.

"Nothing. I just wanted to see if you were alright."

Bill's sister scoffed.

"Oh so now you're concerned about me?"

"What are you talking about? I haven't seen you since before I was in a coma. Aren't you surprised to see me walking now?"

"Not really. Josh told me and Bill about it. I'll bet you don't know this, but I went to go visit you when you were in the ward," Vanessa explained, bitterly. "I finally got you all to myself one evening. No one, not even Ashley was around. Even though you were still in a coma, you said one word that I will never forget, one name that came up in that whole time I was there: 'Ashley'. You kept asking 'where is Ashley?'"

After hearing her voice in his head, Lucas understood now why she was so upset.

She's jealous because of the attention Ashley gives me, Lucas realized. *She also thinks that because I agreed to go to the dance with Ashley first that I like her as more than a friend. I don't, don't I?*

Shaking off those thoughts, Lucas sat himself next to Vanessa. He wanted to be closer to her, but didn't want to upset her further.

"I don't know what I was thinking while I was out of it, but I like you, Vanessa. Ashley is just my friend and nothing more," he insisted.

Vanessa was not convinced.

"You spend a lot of time with her and I know she has feelings for you. Don't ever tell her I told you this, but the truth is I don't hate Ashley. I know I can be mean to her and it's because I think a part of me is jealous of her. Being nice comes so naturally to her and people like her for it. While everyone already expects me to be a certain way because of how I used to flirt a lot with other guys as Bill would say. It isn't true though. No one would even look at me until I got that back brace removed. I never liked anyone the way I like you, Lucas."

He felt everything Vanessa was feeling and something else that he hadn't thought she felt.

Insecurity. She feels insecure about herself as a person, and for the first time likes someone genuinely. But she doesn't know how to show it and how to be 'nice' with me the way Ashley is. They're both more alike than they realize.

The young telepath tried to think of something to say to convince Vanessa that his feelings for her are true.

What did I tell Ashley before? It was something she said Vanessa would appreciate as much as she had.

After a moment of thinking about it, he vividly remembered the advice Ashley had given him and decided to try it now.

"Vanessa, you're a wonderful person, beautiful, and kind. There is nothing about you that I wouldn't say no to."

In an instant, Vanessa looked as if a love spell had been cast on her. Her mood also improved from what Lucas could tell.

"Do you really mean that?"

Lucas nodded and the two embraced.

As they did this, Ashley watched from a distance with Hailey, but turned away to hide her disappointment at his final choice. Unfortunately, the young telepath heard her thoughts and felt as she did.

So that's it then. This is what Daniel said would happen and he was right. I'm happy for you, Lucas. I really am, Ashley thought, brushing the side of her cheek softly.

Lucas felt a small tear drop from his own eye, but when he touched his cheek, he felt no water...

Final Chapter (Chapter 13)

Familiar Face

It was official. Lucas asked Vanessa as a way to confirm it and she ended up clarifying it for him.

"Yes, babe, we are dating now," Vanessa said, planting a kiss on her boyfriend's cheek.

My first girlfriend... my first ever relationship... this is so unreal! Lucas thought, happily. *I thought things couldn't get better than this! I only wish this could have happened sooner than the end of summer.*

The next few days came in a flash and before long the last day of summer camp was upon them. Bright and early, Vanessa decided to tell Bill about them. However, Lucas was less sure of this.

I wonder which will change first; my face structure or the color of my hair, Lucas thought in fear.

To his surprise, Bill's reaction was simply a friendly smile and pat on the back.

And now here comes the face-melting...

It didn't happen.

"I approve of you dating my sister, Lucas," said Bill with a grin. "You have proven to be a trustworthy friend and I appreciate that you made things right with Josh. Just lighten up a bit by next year and learn not take things so seriously. You should work on your physique too. You're starting to look like one of the skeletal cab drivers."

Lucas chuckled and agreed.

I hope I see Francis again on my way home. It would be nice to hear him talking, even about his own death, which is something I never thought I would admit.

Bill began to pack his belongings while the young telepath gave him a puzzled look.

"Aren't you staying to be a Camp Counselor?"

Bill rolled his eyes and nodded.

"Duh, I'm packing because I'm going to visit my parents with Vanessa. By spring, I'll be back in time to prepare for the new recruits. That was why I couldn't visit you in the ward; I was off doing trainings to be a Camp Counselor and I did my last mission as a camper. When I go back to high school, I'll be a junior, and next summer, I'll be a Camp Counselor. I wish you could know how happy I feel right now, Luke."

I've got some idea since he won't stop thinking about it right now. I can also feel his excitement and it goes with my own anticipation for seeing Shelly along with my parents again.

His older cabin mate pulled out a dark red bead that looked like vermillion.

"I'm officially a Camp Counselor in training. Next year, you'll be calling me Counselor Cooper. It goes nicely with CC don't you think?"

Lucas nodded and extended his hand outwards for his cabin mate to shake.

"You take care of yourself, Bill. Thank you for everything and for being patient with me," said Lucas with a smile.

Bill looked like he was going to get teary eyed as he took his cabin mate's hand in gratitude.

"You too, man. Don't go breaking my sister's heart now. She may be a pain, but she means the world to me."

Bill was about to exit the cabin before turning back to Lucas.

"I'm glad you and Josh are talking again. He's the best friend you'll ever have in your life. Even though I'm great too, there's honestly no one else like him. Hopefully one day you'll appreciate that more."

Lucas felt the sincerity in his older cabin mate's words and understood it.

So much of my life has changed in so little time. I never thought I would have friends, let alone a girlfriend. I may have had a rough start, but it's turning out to be a strong finish.

As he left, Bill gave the cabin one last look.

"This was my cabin for four years straight. Now, I'll have my own tent like all the other counselors next year, so I hereby bequeath this cabin to you, my friend. Take care of it because it means a lot to me. During inspection time, I'll be coming to make sure it's in tip-top shape."

It means a lot to me too, Lucas thought, as he felt the same level of attachment as Bill did to the cabin.

After his former older cabin mate left, the young telepath decided to take a moment as well to appreciate the cabin that he called home for the duration of his stay in camp.

I used to think the name for this cabin was lame, but now I love it. I wonder who will replace Bill here next year. I believe I will be back, because things can only get better from here.

While he thought this, Josh entered and got his attention.

"Hey, Luke, everyone is gathering together for the closing ceremony," Josh said aloud.

There's no one else like him. Yeah, I do see that in a good way.

Lucas nodded and followed him outside with his crutches.

He saw Ashley with Hailey, both wearing backpacks. Despite not leaving yet, they already looked prepared to depart at any given moment.

"It was nice to meet you, Lucas. Hopefully we'll see more of each other next year," said Hailey with a friendly nod.

Lucas nodded back. He turned to look at Ashley, who was being evasive towards him.

I wish we could talk telepathically, Lucas thought with a sigh. *I can always think better what I want to say than saying it out loud.*

"I'll see you next summer, Lucas," Ashley finally said. Her tone was neither friendly nor wishful.

After Lucas nodded, he decided to read her mind and see why she was feeling upset.

Ugh, I should have known, thought Lucas with a sigh. *She's not happy about me and Vanessa being together now.*

"Are you going to be here next year, Luke?" Josh signed and asked aloud. "The cabin wouldn't be the same without you in it."

Lucas shrugged.

"Hopefully, if my parents let me. Maybe my sister can come too."

Lucas repeated himself when Josh failed to understand the first time. His deaf friend only caught the word 'sister'.

"I hope she can come. I'd love to meet her," said Josh, too enthusiastically.

I hope me and Ashley are the only ones who know what you mean by that, he thought as he looked at Hailey's cheerful expression.

"I'm not excited to return home. I have homeschooling and studies coming up," signed Josh with a groan. "I think this year my speech teacher is going to teach me how to say more words. As much as I like sign language, talking aloud is the only way people can hear my lovingly personality." Josh said the last part with his usual hint of sarcasm.

He means lovely.

The young telepath laughed and patted Josh's shoulder.

"Have a safe trip home, Josh."

"You too, Lucky Luke. You're my best friend and I want you to hear my voice say that."

Lucas smiled and ended up giving Josh a hug.

I'm not a hugger, but today I'll make an exception.

The next person Lucas hugged was Ashley. She hugged him back reluctantly.

"Be safe, Ashley," he said in a whisper.

Ashley shook a bit and Lucas felt her nod.

"You too, Lucas."

Before leaving, Josh decided to make a group chat with their contact info which included Ashley, Hailey, Vanessa, Bill, Mike, Gary, and Lucas. This comprised of their phone numbers and emails so they could stay in touch outside of camp.

Instead of joining his friends at the main pavilion where the closing ceremony was preparing to start, Lucas dismissed himself to find Mike and Gary.

I wonder where they're at.

The first place he though to check was inside his cabin despite having been there not too long ago. Lucas heard a muffling sound coming from one of the doors and knocked.

"Come in," a voice invited.

When he walked inside, Lucas found himself in Mike's room.

This was the first time he had been in another cabin mate's room. It looked like a plain hotel room with a bed, an AC, fan on the ceiling with all its blades, and no windows. On top of a drawer was hand sanitizer and little sticky notes decorating it like a collage.

He's a minimalist. I can respect that.

Lucas spotted Gary helping Mike with unpacking some of his belongings.

Unpacking? Why are they unpacking? Also it looks like Gary decided to give camp another chance after all, Lucas assumed happily.

When Gary saw Lucas, he greeted him enthusiastically.

"It's good to see you, Lucas," Gary said with a warm smile. "Are you heading to the ceremony already?"

Lucas nodded, as Mike noticed his presence.

"Sorry about the mess here. I meant to clean up but, well, something just came up," Mike revealed, hesitantly.

"What came up?"

"My sister is coming to camp," Mike said ecstatically. "I got a phone call from the hospital where Sapphire was staying at and the doctor told me that she made a miraculous recovery. He's never seen anything like it. One minute she was sick, the next, all better. She's still fragile, but not as much as needing to be bedridden like before. So now she's coming to camp and Henry is letting us both stay here as our new home. It turns out she's an Alter Child like us. "

It was good news like this that Lucas wished he heard more often.

Wow, this feeling that Mike is having... I can't wait to experience it again when I get home and see my family.

"That's awesome to hear, Mike," commented Lucas, gleefully. "I'm so happy for you both. Listen about what happened—"

Before Lucas could finish what he was saying, Mike cut him off with a soft smile.

"Don't think on it too much. I'm just glad everything worked out for you."

Lucas nodded as he heard Mike's voice in his head.

I mean it, Luke. I'm happy to have met you this summer. It's all good between us. No one else needs to know anything more.

"Take care of yourself, Mike, and I look forward to meeting your sister next year." Lucas patted Mikes shoulder with a stiff palm. "Sorry, I forgot you don't like to be touched." His young cabin mate shook his head and patted his hand gently.

"It's all good, Luke. I appreciate that you thought about it."

"I don't guarantee this, but maybe if my sister is able to come next year, she can be friends with your sister," the young telepath proposed.

The very notion made both boys laugh.

I think secretly Shelly's always wanted a little sister. I must have disappointed her by being born a boy.

Before leaving, Lucas clasped Gary's hand and the two wished each other well.

"I look forward to getting to know you more next year, Lucas," Gary said, as the young telepath wished him the same. "Thank you for what you said to me earlier. It helped a lot."

"You can call me Luke, Gary," the young telepath revealed. "We are friends after all."

Gary nodded and felt good about that.

"The only other friend I made this year in camp was Mike, so I'm glad to add you to the growing list."

Lucas wished his cabin mates the best and departed his cabin for the last time.

I'm really happy for Mike. His sister is coming and she can be in no better place in the world than Camp Supernatural to hone her abilities. It's crazy that she's an Alter Child too. What are the odds of Shelly...?

Suddenly, Lucas felt his pocket vibrating rapidly like popping popcorn.

My phone is vibrating!

Before he could look at it, Vanessa came calling out to him with a concerned look on her face.

"Lucas, someone is here to see you. She said you know her. Come quickly."

Vanessa sounded like she was out of breath as she beckoned for her boyfriend to follow her.

She took him to where Boris was standing next to someone. The expression on the monster's face looked grim. The person was drenched in dirt and their clothes were tattered. Lucas had a hard time recognizing this person beyond the mixture of rainwater and sweat.

Who is that? Someone I know? A familiar face?

When the person caught sight of him, they shouted his name out loud. Instantly, the name of the person came into Lucas's mind like a splash of hot water.

Shelly? Is that you? Shelly! My sister!

Lucas threw aside his crutches and limped towards her despite her mucky appearance. He threw his arms around her and held onto her firmly as he struggled to continue standing.

"The Camp Guardian found her in the entrance. Francis brought her here, but he's supposed to be taking campers home, not bringing them," Vanessa explained with breaths in-between a few words.

The scenario seemed almost too good to be true. Shelly was here, in person, but Lucas began to feel fearful. As his phone continued to vibrate, he lamented how he couldn't remove his arms from his sister's neck for fear of falling.

How did she get past the camp's fog, through Boris and the protection which only allows Alter Children inside the camp grounds? More importantly, why is she here right now?

Shelly looked very disturbed and frightened when Lucas looked her in the eyes.

Something's not right.

"Lucas, I need to tell you something. It's very important," she said in a frantic tone. The way she spoke seemed almost rehearsed. "I've been trying to call you and I've texted you a hundred times, but you never answered back!"

Lucas felt his heart race as he sensed something was wrong.

I'm too scared to read her mind. This is not like her to worry me like this.

Desperately, Lucas found his grip tightening on her as both struggled to keep themselves from letting go of the other. He clapped his hands together and was inches from his sister's face.

"What's wrong, Shelly? What happened? Where's mom and dad?"

His sister was silent, with her brother becoming increasingly worried. Her eyes went down and her lips began to quiver.

"Vanessa, can you reach into my pocket and get my phone for me, please," Lucas asked his girlfriend. She complied and pulled his phone out for him in an instant.

What is she not telling me? She's feeling so much sadness and... fear. A lot of fear.

He removed his hands from behind Shelly and grabbed her face while his feet pounded along the ground as if he were tap dancing. Vanessa looked at Lucas's phone, which continued to vibrate and go off like an alarm clock

"Shelly, please talk to me. What's wrong?!"

All Lucas could hear was the sound of his own heartbeat, pounding hard against his chest and Shelly's heavy breathing.

The wind began to pick up, as it blew a cold heavy breeze between the two siblings. The sky was also anticipating rain any second now.

"Oh no... Lucas...," he heard Vanessa mutter. Her hand covered her mouth, while his phone continued to vibrate.

I can't understand what she's thinking, the young telepath thought wildly. *Why can't anyone think straight right now?!*

It took a moment, but when Shelly finally spoke, her words were being drowned by the tears that began to fall from her eyes.

"Lucas...Mom and dad are...are..."

"Are what Shelly? Where are they? Why aren't you with them?"

When she didn't answer, Lucas turned to his girlfriend.

"What does my phone say, Vanessa? Why was it vibrating so much? Let me see it right now!"

Before she could show it to him, his sister turned his face back to hers and spoke, with each word sounding heavier than the last.

"They...are... dead...mom and dad are...dead..."

The words poured out like a river from her lips as she broke by the end. A thunderous clap of lightning hit the sky, and a soft drizzle began to cover the campgrounds. Lucas felt his whole world crash in front of him, as he tried to grasp what his sister had just revealed to him.

Mom...Dad...Dead.

He lost the strength to stand and collapsed to the floor, bringing his sister down with him.

No... this can't be true... please... don't let this be true!

The young telepath read his girlfriend's mind and confirmed what she saw on his phone.

There's a bunch of messages and voicemails on here... all the same; about his parents, what happened to them, wanting to know where he was, and asking when he was coming home...

Lucas was on his knees as the drizzle became a mild shower. The two siblings were on their knees as Shelly wrapped herself around her brother the way she used to. With his face buried on her shoulder, he began to weep uncontrollably. He could no longer fight the tears or sadness that had built up inside of him throughout the last three months. Now he realized the one thing he could never make right.

There is no home to go back to now... I'm sorry mom and dad...I'm so sorry...

Afterword

Camp Supernatural was conceived in the year 2012, during my time in college. I was always fascinated by the topic of mental illness, having autism and struggling with depression and anxiety for much of my young adult life. Many of the ideas that helped me write Camp Supernatural came from my own appreciation of summer camps, writing through a teenagers eyes, and growing as a person by empathizing with different people in the process of writing my story. The character of Lucas Fargo was named after two movies I enjoyed very much in my youth; Lucas starring Corey Haim, and Fargo by the Coen Brothers. Other names were chosen by random because as a writer, I enjoy what feels natural and comes to me in the moment.

The goal for Camp Supernatural is to make five books in the main series. My ultimate plan is to try and write a new book within the span of a year. The main series will feature many different POV's after this first book, which I wanted to use to introduce the characters, and allow audiences to connect with Lucas as a protagonist before handing the baton to others as well. Another big influence for my book is writers such as George R.R. Martin, Stephen King, Frank Herbert, and Rick Riordan. The target audience for this book is teenagers, but also young adults who are on the threshold of adulthood. I honestly feel that the characters are relatable and will grow just as the audience does.

Other influences I had in the making of this book include various television series, films, and books that I read in my youth. In recent time, I began to read again to better my writing, and I would always recommend reading above all else. My passions lie in both reading and writing various works. I hope my work reflects the person I am now vs. who I was before for both people who may know me personally and those who don't. I admit that I still have much to learn and being in my early thirties has given me a whole new perspective on life that I didn't have before. Having struggled with mental illness for much of my young adult life, I used to feel my dream of becoming a writer would be just that. Having this incredible opportunity to not only realize my passion, but to see it through with the possibility for more, has given me much in anticipation for future works.

An influential novel that has also given me much inspiration for my work is Dune by Frank Herbert, who revolutionized the hero archetype for an audience that was not prepared for such a radical change from the 'chosen one' trope. I appreciate ambiguity in both my own writing and the writings of others, which is a big part of how I choose to view various works. The title of *Mind Over Matter* came from Lucas's abilities as a telepath, but also the main theme of book one and the camps mantra which is to 'Control it, so it doesn't control you.' The words each camper must learn and live by through their lessons.

Ultimately, Camp Supernatural will reflect not only the direction I hope to go in as a writer, but also shows my own growth as a person. The interests I had more than ten years ago no longer reflect the person I am, and this novel can be published in that definitive vein. As a friend of mine affectionately dubbed it, this version that you have read is considered the 'Solis Cut' and will include everything I hoped to add in its very best form. I very much would love to write more and to obtain a loyal fanbase who will eagerly anticipate future entries. Thank you very much for taking the time out of your day or days to read this novel.

Jonathan Solis, 2025

Jonathan Solis lives in Rio Grande City, Texas, and began to pursue writing out of a love for storytelling and exploring the different aspects of the human psyche.

www.ingramcontent.com/pod-product-compliance
Lightning Source LLC
Chambersburg PA
CBHW020925020726
47495CB00002B/355